W9-ASY-008

Date: 1/6/14

LP FIC PERRY
Perry, Marta.
Lydia's hope : the lost sisters of
Pleasant Valley /

LYDIA'S HOPE

Center Point
Large Print

Also by Marta Perry and available from
Center Point Large Print:

Sarah's Gift
Katie's Way
Hannah's Joy
Naomi's Christmas

**This Large Print Book carries the
Seal of Approval of N.A.V.H.**

LYDIA'S HOPE

The Lost Sisters of Pleasant Valley
Book One

Marta Perry

CENTER POINT LARGE PRINT
THORNDIKE, MAINE

This Center Point Large Print edition is published in the year 2013 by arrangement with The Berkley Publishing Group, a member of Penguin Group (USA).

The text of this Large Print edition is unabridged.
In other aspects, this book may vary
from the original edition.
Printed in the United States of America
on permanent paper.
Set in 16-point Times New Roman type.

ISBN: 978-1-61173-818-6

Library of Congress Cataloging-in-Publication Data

Perry, Marta.
Lydia's hope : the lost sisters of Pleasant Valley / Marta Perry.
— Center Point Large Print edition.
pages ; cm.
ISBN 978-1-61173-818-6 (library binding : alk. paper)
1. Amish—Fiction. 2. Sisters—Fiction. 3. Family secrets—Fiction.
4. Large type books. I. Title.
PS3616.E7933L94 2013b
813'.6—dc23
                                                2013009790

This story is dedicated to the memory of my beloved sister, Patricia Perry Drotos.
And, as always, to Brian.

List of Characters

Lydia Weaver Beachy, wife of Adam Beachy; their sons: Daniel, eight, David, six

Diane Wentworth Weaver, Lydia's deceased mother; Eli Weaver, Lydia's father, also deceased

Joseph and Anna Weaver, Lydia's adoptive parents; their sons: Andrew, Joshua, and Matthew

Susanna Bitler, Lydia's birth sister, adopted by Jonah and Elizabeth Bitler

Chloe Wentworth, Lydia's birth sister, raised by their Englisch grandmother, Margaret Wentworth

Paula Schatz, Mennonite, runs Pleasant Valley's bakery

Bishop Mose, spiritual leader of the Pleasant Valley Amish

Kendra Phillips, Chloe's friend and colleague

Seth Miller, Englisch, son of Lydia's Amish neighbor

Emma Miller, Seth's mother

Jessie Miller, Seth's younger sister

Bradley Maitland, family friend of Chloe and her grandmother

Glossary of Pennsylvania Dutch Words and Phrases

ach. oh; used as an exclamation

agasinish. stubborn; self-willed

ain't so. A phrase commonly used at the end of a sentence to invite agreement.

alter. old man

anymore. Used as a substitute for "nowadays."

Ausbund. Amish hymnal. Used in the worship services, it contains traditional hymns, words only, to be sung without accompaniment. Many of the hymns date from the sixteenth century.

befuddled. mixed up

blabbermaul. talkative one

blaid. bashful

boppli. baby

bruder. brother

bu. boy

buwe. boys

daadi. daddy

Da Herr sei mit du. The Lord be with you.

denke. thanks (or *danki*)

Englischer. one who is not Plain

ferhoodled. upset; distracted

ferleicht. perhaps

frau. wife

fress. eat

gross. big

grossdaadi. grandfather

grossdaadi haus. An addition to the farmhouse, built for the grandparents to live in once they've "retired" from actively running the farm.

grossmutter. grandmother

gut. good

hatt. hard; difficult

haus. house

hinnersich. backward

ich. I

ja. yes

kapp. Prayer covering, worn in obedience to the Biblical injunction that women should pray with their heads covered. Kapps are made of Swiss organdy and are white. (In some Amish communities, unmarried girls thirteen and older wear black kapps during worship service.)

kinder. kids (or *kinner*)

komm. come

komm schnell. come quick

Leit. the people; the Amish

lippy. sassy

maidal. old maid; spinster

mamm. mother

middaagesse. lunch

mind. remember

onkel. uncle

Ordnung. The agreed-upon rules by which the Amish community lives. When new practices become an issue, they are discussed at length among the leadership. The decision for or against innovation is generally made on the basis of maintaining the home and family as separate from the world. For instance, a telephone might be necessary in a shop in order to conduct business but would be banned from the home because it would intrude on family time.

Pennsylvania Dutch. The language is actually German in origin and is primarily a spoken language. Most Amish write in English, which results in many variations in spelling when the dialect is put into writing! The language probably originated in the south of Germany but is common also among the Swiss Mennonite and French Huguenot immigrants to Pennsylvania. The language was brought to America prior to the Revolution and is still in use today. High German is used for Scripture and church documents, while English is the language of commerce.

rumspringa. Running-around time. The late teen years when Amish youth taste some aspects of the outside world before deciding to be baptized into the church.

schnickelfritz. mischievous child

ser gut. very good

tastes like more. delicious

Was ist letz? What's the matter?

Wie bist du heit. how are you; said in greeting
wilkom. welcome
Wo bist du? Where are you?

Chapter One

Lydia Beachy continued to tuck the log cabin quilt over her great-aunt, hands moving gently but automatically as she struggled to make sense of what the elderly woman had just said. Great-aunt Sara's mind must be wandering, for sure.

I still remember your mammi playing with you and your two little sisters in the apple orchard.

The apple orchard part made sense. The orchard was still there, still producing apples for Lydia and her husband and little boys. But she didn't have any sisters.

"You must be thinking of someone else, Aunt Sara." She patted her shoulder, just as she'd have patted Daniel or David when they lay down for a nap. "Rest now. A nap every afternoon, that's what the doctor said, ain't so?"

Aunt Sara flapped her hand as if to chase away the doctor's words. "I'll just close my eyes for a minute or two. You and your sisters, ja, and the apple trees with blossoms like clouds. Three sweet girls Diane had, that's certain-sure." She smiled, veined lids drooping over her china blue eyes, and in an instant her even breathing told Lydia that she was asleep.

Sharp as a tack, she is. Mamm's voice seemed to echo in Lydia's ears. She and Daad had brought

11

Great-aunt Sara to stay with them after she'd been hospitalized with pneumonia, even though she continued to insist that she'd be fine in her own little place.

Stubborn, that was the word for her great-aunt. She was always wanting to be the one who helped out, not the one who received help.

Great-aunt Sara had another role as well . . . that of family historian. She could tell the children family stories going back many generations and never miss a name or a date. But why would she say something so obviously wrong about Lydia's own family?

Lydia's forehead furrowed as she slipped quietly across the wide wooden floorboards of the house where she had grown up. Her great-aunt was confused, surely. Illness and age could do that to the sharpest mind.

But she'd said Diane. Lydia's birth mother was Diane, and she'd always known the name even though she didn't remember her. Diane had been married to Daad's brother, Eli, and Daad and Mamm had adopted Lydia when Diane and Eli had both died in an accident.

Those birth parents had always been misty figures in her mind, like a pair of Amish dolls with features she couldn't see. She saw them as young and happy one minute and gone the next in the accident Lydia didn't remember, even though she'd been involved as well and five at the time.

When she'd fretted at not remembering, Mamm had always soothed the worry away. *It is God's way of making it easier for you,* Mamm would say. *The accident was a terrible thing, and it's better for you not to remember.*

The memory kept Lydia company down the bare, narrow stairs of the old farmhouse where she'd grown up. Coming back here was like returning to her childhood, but home was where her husband and children were now. She turned left at the bottom as she always did, her steps taking her into the kitchen, the heart of any Amish home.

The square farmhouse kitchen was as spotless as it always was, the long wooden table maybe a bit empty-looking now that all of them were grown and mostly out of the house. April sunshine streamed through the window, laying a path across linoleum faded from so many scrubbings.

Mamm always had a calendar on the wall over the table for decoration as well as use, and this year's had pictures of frolicking kittens. A few violets had been tucked into a water glass on the windowsill, a reminder that spring had come to Pleasant Valley at last.

Mamm was bending over the oven door of the gas range, pulling out a cookie sheet. The aroma of snickerdoodles mixed with that of the beef pot roast that was stewing in the Dutch oven on top of the stove. Mamm looked up, her cheeks red from the warmth of the oven, and slid the tray onto a waiting cooling rack.

"Cookies for you to take to Daniel and David," she said, probably needlessly. The boys would be dumbfounded if Lydia came home from Grossmammi's house without some treat she'd made for them. It was a thing that never happened.

"Denke, Mamm. That will be their snack after they get home from school."

Lydia hesitated, wondering if she should speak. Her great-aunt's words kept going round and round in her mind. They made no sense. And yet, Aunt Sara had sounded perfectly rational.

Mamm glanced at her, face questioning, and closed the oven door. She dropped a crocheted pot holder on the counter.

"Was ist letz? Is something wrong with Aunt Sara?" She took a step toward the stairs, as if ready to fly up and deal with any emergency in her usual capable manner.

"No, no, she's fine," Lydia said quickly. "She's sleeping already."

"Ach, that's gut. Rest is what she needs most now, even though she doesn't want to admit it." Mamm reached for the coffeepot. "Do you have time for a cup before the boys get home from school?"

Lydia shook her head. The words seemed to press against her lips, demanding to be let out, even though she felt a reluctance that was surely

14

odd. She could talk to her mamm about anything.

"Aunt Sara said something I didn't understand."

"Ja? Was she fretting about the hospital bill again?"

Mamm's brown eyes, magnified by her glasses, showed concern. Hospital bills were nothing to take lightly when, like the Amish, a person didn't have insurance. Still, the church would provide what was needed when the family couldn't manage. That was the Amish way.

"It wasn't that." Lydia's throat was suddenly tight with apprehension, as if some unknown fear clutched her. *Just say it,* she scolded herself. She'd always been able to take any problem to Mamm, and Mamm always had an answer.

"Aunt Sara was talking about my mother. My birth mother, I mean. Diane."

"Ja?" The word sounded casual, but the lines around her mother's eyes seemed to deepen, and she set the coffeepot down with a clatter, not even noticing it was on the countertop and not the stove.

"She was . . . She must have been confused." The kitchen was quiet, so quiet it seemed to be waiting for something. "She said that Diane had three kinder. Three little girls. I thought certain-sure she . . ."

The words trickled off to silence. She couldn't say again that Aunt Sara was confused. Not when she could read the truth in Mamm's face.

"It's true?" The question came out in a whisper, because something that might have been grief or panic had a hard grip on her throat. "It is true."

Mamm's face seemed to crumple like a blossom torn from a branch. "Lydia, I'm sorry."

"But . . ." The familiar kitchen was suddenly as strange as if she'd never seen it before. She grasped the top of the closest ladder-back chair. "I had sisters? Two little sisters?"

Mamm nodded, her eyes shining with tears. "I'm sorry," she said again. "You didn't remember, and so we thought it best not to say anything. We didn't want you to be hurt any more than you already were."

Hurt. Lydia grasped the word. She'd been hurt in the accident that killed her parents. She knew that. She'd always known it. Her earliest memories were of the hospital . . . blurry images of Mamm and Daad always there, one on either side of the bed each time she woke up.

"Sisters." Having had three younger brothers, she'd always wished for a sister. "What were their names?"

Mamm moved around the table toward her, as cautious as if she were approaching a spooked buggy horse. "Susanna. She was not quite three at the time of the accident. And Chloe, the baby, just a year old."

Lydia pressed her palm against her chest. Her heart seemed to be beating very normally, in spite of the pummeling it had taken in the past few minutes. She had to hear the rest of it. "They died in the accident, too?"

Silence. She saw in her mother's face the longing to agree. Then Mamm shook her head. "I'm sorry," she said again, as if she couldn't find any other words. "They were injured, but they healed. Like you."

"But . . ." Lydia's mind kept tumbling, her thoughts rearranging themselves and breaking apart again. "I don't understand. What happened to them?"

Mamm pressed her fingers to her lips for a moment, as if to hold back the words. "They went with different families. I'm sorry. We didn't want to split you up, but . . ." Her voice broke, and it was a moment before she went on. "Since you didn't remember, it seemed best not to tell you."

"Best not to tell me?" Lydia's voice rose as she echoed the words. A wave of anger swept away the pain for a brief moment. "How could it be best for me not to know that I had two little sisters? Why were we split up? Why didn't you take all of us? Why?"

"Lydia, hush." Mamm tried to take her arm. "It's going to be all right."

Lydia pulled away. This was not something Mamm could make better with hugs and soft words.

"You have to understand how difficult it was."

Mamm's voice was pleading. "There were your parents dying out there in Ohio, and the three of you kinder in different hospitals, and the rest of the family frantic to get there—" Tears spilled over onto her cheeks, choking off her words.

Ohio, yes. That rang a bell in Lydia's mind. The accident had taken place when her family was in a van on the way to a wedding in Ohio. Mamm had told her that once, when Lydia was of an age to ask questions and wanted to know more about the accident.

"I *don't* understand. You should have told me."

"Just sit down and calm yourself. Your daad will be home soon. He can explain." Mamm reached for her, her face and voice pleading.

Lydia wanted to step into her mamm's loving arms. She wanted to feel the comfort that had always been there. She wanted to hear Daad's deep, soothing voice chasing her fears away, as he'd done when she was a child having nightmares.

Her breath seemed to catch in her throat. She had relied on them always, just as Daniel and David relied on her and Adam. Now it seemed she couldn't trust them at all.

The urge to flee nearly overwhelmed her. She had to get out of this house that had always been her sanctuary.

"I can't." Tears threatened to clog her voice, but she wouldn't let them flow, not yet. "The boys will be home from school soon. I must be there for them. We'll have to talk later."

Tears nearly blinded her, but her feet knew the way to the back door without the need to look. She was vaguely aware of Mamm's voice, protesting, urging her to stay, but she couldn't. She had to think this through. She had to talk to someone she knew she could trust.

She had to go home to Adam. He was her rock. He would know what to do.

Adam climbed out of the van at the end of the lane, raising a hand in acknowledgment as the driver pulled away. Strange to think that his time of riding in the van that carried Amish workers to the camping trailer factory in Fisherdale would soon end.

Usually the half-hour ride home from work was a time to exchange a few stories, air a complaint or two, chaff each other the way men did in their tight-knit community. Today the van had been as still as the farmhouse in the darkest hour of night. With good reason. They'd learned today that most of them would be unemployed come Friday.

Adam straightened his shoulders as he headed up the lane. No matter how shocked he felt, it wouldn't do to let Lydia and the boys see him looking down or uncertain. They relied on him to take care of them.

Maybe he should have seen this coming and been better prepared for the news. Times were rough for a lot of folks, and it seemed fewer of them were willing to spend the money on a new camping trailer. The factory in Fisherdale was a small one. It was certain-sure the owners couldn't afford to keep a full staff on when the orders weren't coming in.

Jobs were scarce all around, it seemed. It had been bad enough traveling to Fisherdale every day. If he had to go even farther to find work . . .

The farm seemed to unroll ahead of him as he walked, and the sight of it eased the knots of worry in his shoulders with its peaceful familiarity. The pastures on either side of the lane provided for the buggy horses and the two milk cows they kept, and the white frame farmhouse settled into the sheltering trees like a hen sitting on a nest, the outbuildings her chicks around her.

Beyond the house the orchard spread clear to the property line with the Miller place. As old as many of those apple trees were, they still produced fine fruit, bringing in extra money in the fall.

The farm was a productive place, with a good orchard. He should be counting his blessings that Lydia had inherited it from her birth parents, instead of fretting over the fact that it wasn't big enough to support a family of four with farming alone.

He spied the boys. Daniel and David were chasing each other among the apple trees, looking like twins from this distance in their black pants, blue shirts, and straw hats. Daniel was in front as always, with six-year-old David trying to keep up. He and Lydia joked that David might as well have been born saying, "Me, too, me, too."

Spotting his daad, Daniel veered from his course and raced toward Adam, David scurrying behind.

"Daadi, Daadi, you're home!" They always greeted him as lavishly as if he'd been gone a month.

Adam scooped them into a quick hug, feeling a pang as he realized all over again how tall the two of them were getting. The boys were not babies anymore, and no others had come along to fill the cradle. He wished for more children just as Lydia did, and he had to keep reminding himself that it would be as God willed.

Daniel took Adam's lunchbox, always proud to carry it to the house. David tugged at his sleeve, his face tilted up with a serious expression.

"Mammi's sad, Daadi. You have to do something."

"Sad?" Adam's heart seemed to turn over. He'd counted on telling Lydia the bad news himself, finding a way to break it gently so she wouldn't worry. How could she have found out from someone else so quickly?

"Her eyes looked funny when we came in from school," Daniel said, with the precision that always seemed to mark his words. "And she gave us an extra snickerdoodle and said to go play. So we think she's sad." Daniel's hazel eyes, so like his mother's, were fixed on Adam's face. "I told David you would make it better, ain't so?"

"I'll do my best," he promised, hoping he could find a way to make good on those words. "Suppose you two get moving on your chores. I'll go in and see your mammi, ja?"

"Ja, Daadi." Daniel nodded, handing him back the lunch pail. "Race you to the barn, David," he said, starting off slowly so that his little brother could catch up.

Daniel had a kind heart. And David had a gift for making people smile. Adam watched them for an instant before he headed to the back door. Good boys, both of them.

They were his responsibility, just as Lydia was, entrusted to him by God. He was the husband and father. He had to take care of them, and right now he wasn't sure how that would happen.

He went quickly up the two steps to the back porch and into the hall that served as a place to hang up coats and take off muddy boots. Lydia was always in the kitchen when he came in, with supper on the stove and a smile that reminded him how lucky he was every day of his life.

Supper was almost ready, all right. He could smell the chicken cooking and the biscuits baking when he moved through the doorway. But Lydia's gentle smile was missing, her peachy skin pale and her hazel eyes shadowed. When she saw him, her lips trembled, and tears filled her eyes.

"Adam." In an instant she was in his arms, clinging to him. "I'm sehr glad you're home."

He nestled her close against his chest, feeling the familiar warmth of her slender body, and his heart hurt that he was the cause of her tears. "Hush, now. It's all right. Don't cry."

"I'm sorry," she whispered, her voice soft with the tears. "I shouldn't be acting like a boppli, crying all over you. It was just such a shock."

He smoothed his palm down the long, sweet curve of her back. "It's not that bad, after all. We'll manage."

She shook her head, her hair silky against his cheek. Then she stepped back, wiping tears away with her hand the way David would.

He opened his mouth to say that he would find another job, that she could count on him like always. But she spoke first.

"Here I am carrying on, and you don't even know what it's all about." She tried to smile, but her lips trembled at the effort.

He didn't know . . . Maybe it was just as well

that Lydia didn't seem to expect him to say anything, because he was speechless. If this wasn't about him losing his job, what was it? Clearly the boys were all right.

"Your great-aunt?" he ventured, knowing she'd been going to her mamm and daad's place to visit with Aunt Sara that afternoon.

"She told me something . . . something I could scarcely understand or believe." Lydia's smooth, wide forehead furrowed. "She said she remembered seeing my mamm in the orchard, long ago, with her three little girls." Lydia's gaze met his. "*Three* little girls." Her voice emphasized the number. "She was talking about my birth mother."

Now his frown must match hers. "Your great-aunt must have been confusing Diane with someone else. Sara's been sick, and at her age it's easy to get mixed up, ja?"

"That's what I told myself." Lydia cupped her palm against her cheek in that way she had of comforting herself when things went wrong. "But when I repeated her words to Mamm, I could see in her face that what Aunt Sara said was true."

"True?" He struggled to get his mind around it. "But if you had sisters, for sure we'd know about it. How could we not have heard? I mean, your parents were living right here in this house when they died. Everybody would have known."

"They knew." Lydia's voice hardened in a way he'd never heard before, and he'd have said he

24

was familiar with every tone of it. "They knew, and they kept it a secret."

He realized what must have happened, and his heart hurt for her. "Your sisters died?" His voice filled with sympathy. "Is that it?"

He and Lydia had talked about the accident. Her parents had died, and people said Lydia was lucky to survive, and that losing her memory of everything that had gone before the accident was a small price to pay for having lived.

"No. They didn't die." Her voice was sharp with pain. "Maybe I could understand better if they had. But they survived the accident—two little sisters, and each of them was adopted by someone different. The family parceled us out to different people like . . . like leftovers." Her hands clenched into fists.

Somehow that gesture, so foreign to his gentle, loving Lydia, galvanized him. He crossed the small space between them, taking her hands in his. "There must be a reason for such an action. What did your mamm say?"

"She wanted me to wait until Daad came home. She kept saying he could explain it so I'd understand. But how can I ever understand something like this?" Her eyes filled with tears again, and Adam moved quickly to put his arms around her.

"It will be all right." The words sounded worse than useless, and he longed to have something better to offer her. "They must have meant it for the best. You'll see. We'll sit down and talk to your mamm and daad together, and they'll tell us everything. You'll see."

Even as he said the words, he wondered. Clearly there was more going on than any of their generation had been told. Something had happened . . . something so serious that not just the family but the whole church had decided to keep it a secret. He couldn't begin to imagine what it could be.

One thing was certain. He couldn't burden Lydia further at a time like this by telling her about losing his job. That news would have to wait.

He held her close, murmuring soothing nothings, just as she would do with the kinder when they'd suffered some hurt. How had their peaceful lives unraveled so suddenly and so completely? And how were they going to find the faith to accept all of this trouble as God's will?

Lydia wasn't surprised when she heard a carriage rolling up the lane not half an hour after she'd settled Daniel and David in bed. She'd known Mamm and Daad would come to talk to her again, and it would be after the kinder were asleep for a matter so painful.

She rose, brushing a slight dusting of flour from

her black apron, and exchanged glances with Adam. With two rambunctious boys around, they hadn't yet had much space for a quiet talk. Still, she hung on to the sensation of his arms around her as she headed for the door.

"That'll be Mamm and Daad."

"Ja." Adam followed her, maybe thinking she needed his support. "They'll be able to explain it all, so you can accept what happened as God's will."

She felt certain they'd explain, and now that she was calmer, maybe she'd understand. Or at least find the right questions to ask. But as for accepting . . . well, she wasn't sure acceptance would be easily found.

Adam supported her, just like always. But did he really understand that the very foundations of her world were shaken?

There was no time to talk about it now—Mamm and Daad were already at the door. Adam pulled it open.

"Joseph. Anna. It's gut you're here, so we can talk." Adam's voice had deepened with the gravity of the situation, his level brows lowered over his blue eyes, his strong face solemn above his short brown beard. He gestured her parents into the kitchen.

"Ja. We must talk." Daad's tone was heavy. As he and Mamm stepped farther into the light, a shock ricocheted through Lydia.

Daad's square, ruddy face seemed to have drawn tight against his bones. And her mother . . . Lydia's heart thudded against her chest. Mamm looked near as old as Great-aunt Sara, her eyes red-rimmed behind her glasses, the fine wrinkles of her skin turned into sharp valleys.

The urge to put her arms around her mother was almost too strong to resist, but somehow she managed. If she and Mamm started crying together, she'd never regain her calm, and somehow she had to stay focused enough to hear this story to the end.

"I'm sorry, daughter." Daad kissed her forehead gently. "Sorry that you had to find out this way."

Lydia pressed her lips together for an instant, feeling the flicker of anger again. *Are you sorry for telling me lies to begin with, Daad?*

"Let's sit down." Adam pulled out one of the chairs around the table. "Will you have coffee?"

"Not now, denke, Adam." Daad sank heavily into the chair at the head of the table, planting his elbows on the surface in the way he had when he was about to tell the family something they needed to hear. He'd looked that way when he'd gathered them to say that Grossdaadi had died, Lydia realized. In a way, maybe this was a death as well.

But if Daad looked square and solid and unmovable, Mamm seemed to shrink into her seat.

When Adam moved to take her jacket she shook her head, drawing it around her as if she were cold. She did remove her black bonnet, and the overhead lamp picked up the gray strands in her brown hair.

"Bishop Mose said from the start that we were wrong to keep the truth from you," Daad said. "It's the only time in my life I went against something the bishop said, and I feared we'd regret it one day."

So the bishop had known, too. Well, he'd have had to, wouldn't he? Every older person in the church district must have known, and they'd kept silent all this time.

Adam had seen that already, she realized with a separate little shock. That was why his gaze was so wary. He was afraid of what they were about to find out. She'd like to touch his hand for support, but he'd taken the chair across from her, the width of the table between them.

Lydia cleared her throat. She had to be strong, remember? "So I had two little sisters, and you never told me." If that sounded accusing, she couldn't seem to help it.

Daad nodded gravely. "Ja, but that's not where the story starts. If you are to understand, you must know first that your mother, Diane, was Englisch."

"Englisch!" The exclamation came from Adam. Lydia didn't think she could have spoken at all.

"Ja. Diane Wentworth, that was her name before they were married." Daad paused, shaking his head. "It's been so long since I heard it, I'd nearly forgotten the name."

"But I don't understand. My birth father was your own brother. Amish. How did he come to marry an Englischer? Was her family from around here?" Her mind scrambled for a connection with the name he'd said and came up empty.

"Not from around here, no. They met when Eli was working out west." Daad clasped his hands on the table and looked at them, but she didn't suppose he was seeing them. "My big brother always wanted to explore a bit of the world, so when he was in his twenties, he went off to work construction in Ohio. That's where he met Diane."

"She was lost." Mamm spoke unexpectedly, her voice soft.

"Lost?" Adam's face showed his lack of understanding.

"Not really lost, I guess," Mamm said. "But later, when we knew each other better, that's what she told me. She and her parents didn't get along at all. She'd left home, and she didn't have anyone else. She was lost. But when she met Eli, she said it was like she'd found her home."

Lydia struggled to swallow the lump in her throat. "So she became Amish for him."

That was a thing that almost never happened.

The other way around was more common, yes, when an Amish person jumped the fence, but it was so difficult for someone raised Englisch to adjust to Amish life.

"It wasn't easy," Daad said, echoing her thought. "But Eli and Diane were determined. They married, and they stayed in Ohio for a time, where they had friends who understood and helped Diane adjust. They moved back and took over this place when you were about two, I think, and by then Diane had been Amish long enough that most people didn't even think about her being raised Englisch. Susanna and Chloe were born here."

Adam looked around the house as if he was seeing it with fresh eyes. "They were happy here," he said, as if he knew it for a certainty, and his perception startled Lydia.

"Ja." A smile trembled on Mamm's lips. "Diane said she'd never known she could be so happy. She wanted to forget all about her life before, and we honored that wish."

Lydia stored up the words, knowing she'd want to bring those images of her parents out and relive them later, when she was alone. But now she had to know more about how their story had ended.

"The accident," she prompted. And the little girls, Susanna and Chloe. She said the names over and over in her mind, trying to draw up an image, but nothing came.

Daad sighed. "There were a couple of Amish families on their way to the wedding of a friend in Ohio, out in Holmes County. They'd hired a van and driver for the trip. The police said it looked like the van driver had fallen asleep at the wheel. He crashed into a tractor trailer and overturned, rolling down a hill."

Mamm made a small sound of grief or pain. Daad put his hand to his head, as if he were reliving it too clearly. It was a terrible picture, but it seemed so remote to Lydia, as if it had happened to someone else.

"We got word from the state police about the accident and hired someone to take us out to Ohio," he went on. "The van driver had died instantly. The rest of you weren't even in the same hospital. The kinder didn't have identification on them, of course, so no one knew who was where. We were frantic, trying to find all of you and make sure you were taken care of."

Lydia nodded, trying to picture the situation. The Amish community took care of its own, but it would have been difficult with the accident happening so far away.

"Bishop Mose had gone with us," Daad went on. "We were so thankful to have him there. He said each of you kinder must have someone with you to care for you and make decisions, so your mamm and I went with you."

"Why?" The word came out before she realized

she intended to speak, but it was the question of her heart. Why had Mamm and Daad been the ones to end up with her?

Daad looked confused at the question, but Mamm seemed to understand right away.

"We thought you felt the closest to us. We'd just gotten married ourselves a few weeks earlier, and you'd been so excited about the wedding. You'd wanted to help me, and I let you put some stitches in the hem of my dress, I remember." Her face softened with a smile. "It just seemed right."

"Ja," Daad said. "One of the Ohio Amish friends, a distant cousin, had been close with Diane when they lived there. She and her husband stayed with Susanna, your grossdaadi was sitting with your daadi, and your grossmammi with Diane, with Bishop Mose helping them. Another cousin and his wife went to the hospital where they'd taken baby Chloe, but when they got there, she was gone."

"Gone," Lydia echoed the word. "But Mamm said both of them lived."

"Ach, ja, she lived." Daad reached across to give her hand a squeeze. "I shouldn't have said it that way. I mean, she wasn't there. We learned that Diane's mother had come and taken Chloe from the hospital."

"The Englisch woman," she said.

Daad sighed and shook his head. "You have to

try and understand, Lydia. There we were in a strange city, trying to tend to everyone. At least we knew the baby would be safe with her grandmother, even if it was not what Diane might have wanted."

"No, she wouldn't have," Mamm said. "But what could we do? Your parents died, one after the other. You had to have surgery, and we nearly lost you, too. Susanna was injured and had to have surgery as well. For weeks all we could do was concentrate on you."

The gaze she turned on Lydia was pleading. *Please understand.* That's what it was saying.

Lydia nodded, her head seeming to jerk like a puppet's. Her throat was so dry and raw that if she tried to speak, she knew it would come out in a croak.

"After all was said and done, it seemed natural to say we would adopt you." Daad pressed her hand. "You felt like our daughter already. And we would have taken Susanna, as well, but Jonah and Elizabeth felt just as strongly about her. As for Chloe, she had disappeared into the Englisch world, and we didn't think an Englisch court would take her away from a wealthy Englisch grandmother to give her back to us."

Daad leaned back in his chair and blew out a long breath. "We should have told you before, I guess, but when you didn't remember, it seemed better not to give you more grief. But it's over now. I hope you can forgive us for keeping it from you."

Lydia sat for a moment, trying to digest the whole story. Then she realized that Mamm and Daad were waiting for something. She held out a hand to each of them.

"I forgive you." She said the words suspecting that this would be one of those times when forgiveness had to be repeated again and again before it truly took possession of her heart. "But how can you say it is over? It is just beginning. Now I have to find my sisters."

Chapter Two

Adam could see the shock he felt at Lydia's words reflected in her parents' faces, as well.

"No, Lydia, you can't mean such a thing." Lydia's daad echoed Adam's thoughts. "You are still trying to get used to the idea, ain't so? When you've reflected on this situation a bit, you'll see that you can't do anything about it after all this time."

"You don't understand what that news might do to them," her mother said.

Lydia pushed her chair back, as if she couldn't be still for another minute. She took a couple of steps to the counter and then turned, crossing her arms.

"I understand better than anyone, because it is happening to me." She pressed her lips together, maybe to keep them from trembling.

Her parents exchanged a swift glance, communicating without the need for speech. "We were wrong to let it go so long," Joseph said. "You could have handled knowing any time since you've been grown, just as your mamm and I could deal with it. But the situation is different for your sisters. For Susanna, at least."

"Why?" The word burst out of Lydia, and Adam could feel her frustration. "What makes hearing the truth easier or worse for Susanna? What do you know about her?"

"It's not just Susanna. It's her mother, as well." Joseph stared down at his clasped hands. "Telling you about her means breaking a promise we've kept for twenty-five years, but I don't see that we have a choice. Maybe it is a promise we never should have made, but we did." He glanced at his wife, as if hoping she would take over the story.

Anna sighed. "Jonah and Elizabeth Bitler had been close to your mamm and daad when they lived in Ohio. Elizabeth . . ." She hesitated, a little color coming up in her pale cheeks. "Well, Elizabeth had lost one babe before birth after another, grieving so after each miscarriage that the family feared for her health. The doctors said she must stop trying."

36

Adam tried to imagine what it must be like for a married couple to have no children in the Amish community, where big families were taken for granted. It was hard enough on him and Lydia, with just the two boys when they longed for more children. To have none at all . . .

"When she and Jonah were there at Susanna's bedside during those terrible days, it was as if Elizabeth poured herself into keeping that poor child alive," Anna said. "It seemed sometimes that Elizabeth's love kept little Susanna breathing."

Lydia blinked, and Adam could see that the image of her young sister fighting for life had broken through her absorption in the idea of finding them. "Susanna was badly hurt?"

"You both were," Joseph corrected. "You with a head injury so bad the doctors couldn't predict whether you would make a recovery, and little Susanna's leg was mangled so bad that they feared she'd lose it."

Lydia's fingers flew to her lips in an instinctive gesture of compassion. "Did she?"

"No, thank the gut Lord. But from what we heard, the leg was never quite right, either. Still, she survived, maybe because of Elizabeth's love and care. When Jonah and Elizabeth wanted to adopt her, who could say no? The one thing Elizabeth asked was that Susanna should never know she wasn't their child."

"But wouldn't she remember?" He could see in

Lydia's face the pain she felt that she didn't remember.

"Susanna was only three," Anna said. "At first she asked, ja, but soon she seemed to forget. When she first called Elizabeth 'Mammi,' I thought I'd never seen such love in a woman's face."

"Elizabeth asked for our promise, and we gave it." Joseph shook his head heavily. "If we could have seen this day coming—ach, there's no point in regretting the past."

Lydia moved, so slightly it was little more than a twitch, but Adam saw it, so closely was he watching her.

"You said they were from Ohio. Is that where Susanna lives still?"

Joseph hesitated, as if not wanting to answer that question. "No," he said finally. "They moved to Oyersburg a few years back. We haven't seen them," he said quickly, as if anticipating the next question Lydia would ask.

A natural one, since Oyersburg wasn't thirty miles away. Even Adam had been there, and he wasn't much of one for traveling.

"So close to me," Lydia murmured, tears sparkling in her eyes.

"It doesn't change anything," her father said. "Susanna has always believed Jonah and Elizabeth Bitler are her parents. Jonah died only a year ago, and from what we hear, Elizabeth is very

38

ill. We've tried to keep track of them, even though they didn't want to get together with us."

"The poor child," Anna murmured. "Cancer, her mamm has, and the doctors say there's little hope."

Joseph rose, hands braced on the table. "We understand your wanting to know your sister, Lydia. That's only natural. But it would be unkind to both Elizabeth and Susanna to tell them now, when Elizabeth is so sick, and I know that our Lydia is never unkind."

Adam saw those words had left Lydia with nothing to say. Whether she was convinced or not, he couldn't be sure.

Joseph nodded to Anna, and she got to her feet, clutching the table as if for support. "We will go now," Joseph said, his voice heavy. "If there is anything else you want to know, we'll talk again, ja?"

Lydia didn't speak, and Adam felt compelled to fill the gap. "Denke. This was hard for you, for sure."

He glanced at Lydia, willing her to make some loving gesture toward her parents.

Lydia nodded, understanding him without words. She went slowly to her parents. She stopped, and it seemed everyone in the room forgot to breathe. Then she put her arms around her mamm.

Gut. Some of the tension in Adam eased at the

sight. He couldn't blame Lydia for being upset at this discovery, but if she held on to resentment toward her mamm over it, she'd hurt herself as much as she hurt Anna.

"I'll walk out with you," he said, opening the back door and stepping out onto the porch with Joseph. Dusk gathered in, and the breeze that blew down the valley from the west was chilly.

Joseph nodded toward the orchard. "You'll have trees in blossom soon, ja?" He was making an effort to sound natural, Adam guessed. "Hope we don't get another hard frost."

"Hope not," Adam echoed, going to unfasten the horse from the hitching rail. "I'd like to get the garden in early this year."

He wanted to say something comforting to Joseph, but he felt pretty sure Joseph would be as embarrassed hearing it as he would be saying it.

The door creaked as the women started to come out, and Joseph leaned toward him. "You will help her understand, ja?" he said quietly.

Adam stiffened. He wouldn't ally himself against his Lydia, that was certain-sure; they were all caught in this difficult place because of the decisions Joseph and Anna had made. But there was one thing he could say from his heart.

"I'll try to keep her from getting hurt."

Joseph nodded, seeming satisfied. He helped Anna into the buggy, and in a moment they drove off down the lane. Adam stood watching until the buggy disappeared into the dusk. Now he must return to the house and try to help Lydia. He just wished he knew how. With a wordless prayer for wisdom, he mounted the porch steps.

Lydia was standing at the sink when he reached the kitchen. She wasn't doing anything, just staring at the faucet as if she'd forgotten what it was for. She turned at the sound of his footsteps, her features drawn tight.

"What were you and Daad talking about? Was he asking you to make me see sense?"

"Not exactly." Some questions were probably safer for a husband not to answer, he'd think. "I was just telling him that I'd do anything to keep you from being hurt."

His answer seemed to calm the waters. He could see the tension slip away from her expression.

"Denke, Adam. But I think the hurt is already done." Her voice was still tart, so they weren't out of the woods yet.

"I know you're angry with your parents," he said cautiously. "But whatever mistakes they made in the past, I think they're trying to do what's best now."

"I know what's best for me, and that's finding my sisters." Lydia threw the dishcloth she was holding into the sink. Then, apparently unable to leave it there, she rinsed it out and hung it on the rack.

He waited until she'd finished before speaking.

"Do you think that your telling them is best for your sisters, too?"

He saw the question hit home, saw uncertainty creep in. She hesitated for a long moment.

"I think so," she said, seeming to try for a sureness she might not feel. "I think they should have a chance to know me and each other. I'm the oldest. It's my job to do it."

Lydia was a nurturer—that was certain-sure. She cared for her plants and her orchard just as she cared for Daniel and David. Sometimes he almost thought there was no comforting left over for him, but that was foolish. He was a grown man, not a child.

And now she wanted to nurture these two unknown younger sisters.

"I know," he said, his tone careful. "But from what your mamm said, it might do more harm than good for Susanna just now, ain't so?"

He was still trying to get used to the idea of these unknown sisters. If things had been different, if Lydia's parents hadn't been killed, he might have known Susanna for most of her life and be thinking of her now as his own little sister.

Lydia's eyes clouded. "Maybe so, at least for now. But the little one . . ."

"Not so little now," he said quickly, hoping to veer her away from that direction. "Chloe would be a grown woman. An Englisch woman. You couldn't possibly find her." His heart shuddered at the thought of his Lydia going off into the Englisch world in search of an unknown person.

Lydia pressed her fingers to her forehead. "It's just so hard."

"I know." He did. He had experienced the loss of a much-loved younger brother and the sense of guilt that went with it. But he could see that Lydia wasn't thinking of his loss.

"You know what's worst of all?" The words burst out of her. "That I don't remember them. How could I forget my little sisters? It makes me feel so guilty."

Her voice broke on a sob. His heart breaking for her, Adam put his arms around her. Guilt, ja, that he knew.

"Hush, now, that's ferhoodled, it is, and even the bishop would tell you so. Your head was hurt in the accident, and you couldn't remember, no matter how much you might want to."

His poor sweetheart. He pressed his lips against the softness of her hair in a gentle kiss. He would do anything to take this pain from her. But he feared more pain was inevitable if she tried to piece her birth family back together again.

"Komm," he said, keeping his voice soothing. "You are exhausted, and it's no wonder. I'll make you a cup of your chamomile tea, and then you'll go to bed. Time enough to think it through in the morning, ja?"

She nodded, stifling a sob, and he had a sense

of relief. But it was short-lived. He knew his Lydia. Even if she slept tonight, she'd be back to worrying about her two little sisters again in the morning.

Later, much later, Adam woke suddenly in the double bed where he and Lydia had spent every night of their married life. Lydia's even breathing told him she was sleeping, and he turned cautiously on his side so he could see her.

A shaft of moonlight filtered through the window, turning her face to silver. Her expression was serene and remote in sleep, as if she had traveled far from home in her dreams. For an instant a shiver of fear went through him. He seemed to see his familiar Lydia drifting farther and farther away, lured by the thought of her two unknown sisters.

Ach, he was the ferhoodled one, thinking such a thing. Lydia was as close as ever, her face tilted slightly toward him on the pillow, the loose braids she put her hair in at night lying like soft ropes against her white nightgown.

Her forehead puckered. Her head moved ever so slightly in a negative gesture, and she made a soft, distressed sound.

"Hush," he whispered. "It's all right." A bad dream, that was all.

Her lips moved, and a word drifted out on a breath. "Lost," she said. "Lost."

Carefully, trying not to wake her, he put his arm

around her, drawing her closer so that she might feel his presence, even in her dream. Lydia gave a little sigh and seemed to relax, sliding deeper into sleep.

He lay awake, staring into the night. If Lydia persisted in this longing for her sisters, it would end in tears and heartache. It was bound to. She couldn't tell Susanna, and she couldn't find Chloe. And if she somehow did the impossible and found her, being rejected by the Englischer that Chloe had become might be harder for Lydia to deal with than never finding her at all.

He'd promised to love and protect and take care of Lydia all their lives. He certain-sure would never stop loving her. But with the loss of his job and the helplessness he felt at the news of her sisters, the protecting and caring for suddenly seemed in doubt.

Lydia spooned oatmeal into the boys' bowls the next morning, paying no heed to their pleas to have cold cereal instead. "It's not summer yet," she reminded them. "You need a breakfast that will stick to your ribs to last you until lunchtime."

David, having already given up the battle, was adding brown sugar and raisins to his oatmeal. After one last glance at her face, Daniel followed suit. Given the enthusiasm with which they were soon shoveling the food into their mouths, she suspected their objections had more to do with the brightly colored boxes of the store-bought cereal than any real dislike of oatmeal.

Lydia turned to the three lunch pails lined up on the counter. She was so used to the morning routine that it occupied only half her mind, leaving the rest free for the same subject that had filled it last night—finding her lost sisters.

Susanna, at least, surely wouldn't be that difficult to locate. Lydia had a name and a place, and Oyersburg wasn't a very large community. She'd been there herself a few times, when a group of women had hired a driver to take them on a shopping expedition to the big fabric store.

But how could she just drop in on someone, even another Amish woman, without any reason? What she needed now was more information. She had to find someone who'd known her birth family well enough to answer her questions without getting tangled up in trying to protect her. Surely, in all of Pleasant Valley, there was someone she could turn to.

The bishop? Well, Bishop Mose had apparently been there when her parents died, and he'd been aware of the decisions that were made, although Daad had said that he didn't approve of the secrecy. That might make him willing to talk to her.

Still, she couldn't seem to rid herself of a reluctance to confide in the bishop. What if he told her she was wrong to want to find her sisters? What would she do then?

A footstep sounded behind her, and she felt Adam's breath on the nape of her neck. For a moment he didn't speak, but she could sense his apprehension.

"Are you feeling better this morning?" he ventured.

She swung around, and the wary way he looked at her made her impatient. "I'm fine." The words came out too sharply, and three pairs of eyes fixed on her in surprise. "I didn't sleep well is all that troubles me. Are you boys about done with breakfast?"

"Ja, Mammi," Daniel said quickly.

Adam moved to the boys, talking to them in the soft cadences of Pennsylvania Dutch. Even though the kinder were learning English now that they were scholars, Pennsylvania Dutch was still the language of home, just as German was the language of worship.

A word from Adam sent the young ones scampering upstairs to brush their teeth before school. She handed him his lunch pail, forcing a smile. It was not right to take out her worries on the people she loved. She was ashamed of herself.

"I thought I might go into town today," she said.

"Ja, gut." Adam's expression lightened. "That will take your mind off things, you'll see."

She felt herself stiffen. "Nothing will take my

mind off my sisters," she said, with a quick glance to be sure the boys were still out of earshot. "I'm going into town because I need to find someone who can tell me more about my birth parents and my sisters."

Adam's expression seemed to close down, like a door slamming. "Lydia, can't you at least try to accept what happened as God's will? If you start digging into it, soon everyone in Pleasant Valley will be talking."

"Gut. That's what I want," she said with a surge of energy. "Maybe then I'll learn something useful. Don't you understand why I have to do this, Adam?"

"I understand that you could easily end up getting your heart broken." His shoulders were stiff, his strong jaw square beneath his chestnut brown beard. It was the way he always looked when he had to face something unpleasant. "Or you could be hurting someone else. How can I want either of those things for my wife?"

Lydia stared at him, her heart feeling as if a fist had closed over it. "I thought you would support me, Adam."

"I will always support you. But I can't encourage you to do something I think is wrong."

She couldn't speak. She could only watch as a chasm opened between them.

Adam glanced at the kitchen clock, a fine wooden piece he'd made with his own hands. "I must go. We will talk more when I get home, ja?"

The boys were clattering back into the kitchen, eager to be off. This was no time to embark on a difficult discussion.

Besides, what could she say? Adam had already made up his mind. She could count on the fingers of one hand the times they'd been in disagreement since their marriage, and this one was so big, so serious, she could only watch him go, feeling as if the ground had shifted under her feet.

Fortunately, Daniel and David distracted her with all their last-minute needs, or who knew how long she'd have stood there. As it was, she got them settled, books and lunch pails in hand, and walked them to the gravel lane that skirted the orchard and wound through the fields another half mile to the small frame Amish schoolhouse.

"Be gut today. Listen to Teacher Mary." She gave them the familiar words without much thought.

"Ja, Mammi, we will." Daniel paused to assure her, always the responsible older one. "I'll mind that David gets there on time." They both knew David had a tendency to stop in search of a handful of spring violets or to follow a wiggling snake, heedless of the time.

"I'll see you after school," she called as they trudged away.

Lydia waited until they'd both turned and waved, and then headed back to the house.

Usually, on a spring morning she lingered in the orchard, loving the hint of blossoms about to burst forth, carrying their promise of a bountiful harvest. But not today.

She would keep herself too busy to think about the disagreement with Adam. She'd clean up the kitchen and then be off to town.

Surely, if she could just think who to ask, there would be folks who'd know about her mamm and daad and wouldn't mind talking. One way or another, she had to know.

It took some time to get ready, of course. Unlike the Englisch, who seemed to jump into a car for the shortest trip, if you were Amish you walked, or took a push scooter, or drove the horse and buggy.

Normally, she would walk to town, since it was only a little more than a mile, but she felt too impatient for that today, so she harnessed the mare and set off in the buggy. Gray knew the way to town as well as Lydia did, so she could focus on her thoughts instead of her driving.

By the time she reached the village, Lydia had decided where she'd go first. Paula Schatz had been running her bakery in Pleasant Valley for as long as Lydia could remember. Even though Paula was Mennonite, she knew every Amish person in the valley. Surely she would have known Lydia's parents.

She drew up to the side of the bakery, fastening

the horse to the convenient hitching rail. Although most Amish and horse-and-buggy Mennonites did their own baking, folks still loved to stop at Paula's for a coffee and a sweet treat when they were in town.

Fortunately the morning rush was over by the time she went inside. Paula was wiping tables while Hannah, her niece and partner, piled loaves of bread into the wire baskets behind the counter.

"Lydia!" Paula's face creased in her welcoming smile. "It's nice to see you. What can I get for you?"

Her stomach was too tight to enjoy even one of Paula's sticky buns, but she had to order something. "Just coffee, Paula. And a little talk with you, if you have time."

"Ach, we always have plenty of both," Paula replied.

"At this time of day, anyway," Hannah added, reaching for the coffeepot. "Why don't you have a chat and relax a bit, Aunt Paula? I'll take care of what needs to be done in the kitchen."

"She fusses over me," Paula confided as Hannah vanished into the kitchen.

"It gives her pleasure to help you, ja?" Lydia followed Paula to one of the small round tables.

"Not as much pleasure as it gives me, having Hannah and her family here." The glance Paula sent toward the kitchen door was loving. "I didn't realize I was lonely until Hannah came home."

Lydia nodded, knowing what joy Paula had experienced when her niece came back to Pleasant Valley with her small son. Hannah was now wed to William Brand, and the family was whole at last. That was what she wanted—that sense of wholeness. It wasn't too much to ask, was it?

She toyed with her coffee mug, not sure how to begin now that she was here.

"Something is wrong, ain't so?" Paula's expression was kind, as always.

"A little." That was certainly putting it mildly. Lydia took a deep breath. She might as well plunge in. "Do you remember my birth parents?"

"Diane and Eli? Ja, for sure. I didn't know them well, you understand, but well enough to talk to."

Lydia thought she detected a certain reservation in Paula's voice, which told her that Paula might have guessed what was coming.

"You knew, didn't you?" she asked, directing a look at Paula's face. "About my two little sisters?"

Paula was silent for a long moment, staring down at her coffee. "Ja," she said finally. "I knew. And now, I guess from your question that you know, as well."

"Ja." At last, she knew. "I just found out about them, and I want . . . I need . . . to find my sisters."

"I understand." Paula's voice was soft, as if she were remembering something. "I lost my sister to the Englisch world, but at least I finally got Hannah back. I don't know how I can help you."

Lydia didn't either, but she had to try. "My mamm and daad told me about Susanna, but they don't seem to have any idea what happened to Chloe, the baby, after her grandmother took her away."

"That was a sad circumstance." Paula shook her head. "Still, I don't know that I can tell you anything that your parents can't." She hesitated. "I do know Diane wasn't on such gut terms with her mother."

Mamm and Daad had implied the same thing, but Lydia wanted to hear someone else's view of the situation, one that wasn't colored by the need to keep her safe. "Did Diane ever talk to you about it?"

Paula nodded slowly, her forehead wrinkling. "Once, I think, when I took a meal out after the last baby was born. I had picked up the mail from the box to carry it in with me, and I gave it to Diane. She picked one envelope out and tossed it on the table, and I saw that it was a letter she had written that had been returned unopened."

"From her mother?" Lydia had to say that this Englisch grandmother of hers wasn't sounding like such a nice person.

"Ja, that was so. Diane's eyes filled with tears." Paula's eyes were moist, as well. "She said that her own mamm wouldn't know about her baby daughter, because she wouldn't open letters from Diane. It made me feel so sad for Diane."

Lydia's throat was tight, and she had to take a sip of the hot coffee before she could speak. "Did you ever hear anything else about the woman?"

Paula shook her head. "I can't say I did. Your folks would know more than I would. Or your great-aunt Sara, maybe."

She was obviously wondering why Lydia had brought her questions to her.

"It hurts Mamm to talk about it," Lydia said, knowing she was being evasive. Still, that was true enough, wasn't it?

"Well, then, it's clear what you should do," Paula said as if she had no doubts. "Bishop Mose is the person to see, ain't so?"

So, in the end, Lydia went where the Amish of Pleasant Valley always did when in trouble—to the harness shop run by Bishop Mose. Over the years he had become more than a spiritual leader. He knew and cared for every member of his flock, and even the most rebellious teen usually responded with love and respect to his counsel.

The harness shop shouldn't be busy at this hour of the morning. Leaving Gray tied to the hitching rail beside the bakery, Lydia walked down Main Street toward the bishop's place of business.

The small village of Pleasant Valley stretched along either side of the main road. A mix of Englisch, Amish, horse-and-buggy Mennonites, and the more progressive black-bumper Mennonites, the town managed to thrive despite, or maybe because of, its varied population.

Lydia spotted Katie Brand sweeping the sidewalk in front of the quilt shop and waved. Much as she'd love a visit with Katie, Katie was too young to provide information, besides being a newcomer to Pleasant Valley.

When she reached the harness shop, Lydia hesitated with her hand on the door. Bishop Mose had put up a new cardboard sign, she saw. NO PHOTOGRAPHS, PLEASE. Sometimes tourists were either ignorant or disrespectful of the Amish ban against having photographs of themselves.

But enough dithering on the doorstep. Mustering her courage, she went inside, the tinny chime of the bell on the door announcing her arrival. The shop was empty save for the bishop himself, seated at the workbench in the rear. He glanced up, peering at her over the glasses he'd taken to wearing when he did close work on a harness.

"Ach, it is Lydia. I thought I might see you today." He put aside the leather he was working on and rose, wiping his hands on the heavy apron he wore in the shop.

"You did?" Lydia went toward him, passing rows of bridles and harnesses, the rich scents of leather and oil announcing where she was.

"Your daad stopped by for a talk." Bishop Mose gestured her into the work area and pulled out one of the stools. "Komm. Sit down. This has been a shock to you, ain't so?"

She nodded, accepting the seat. Maybe she should have guessed that Daad would have already consulted the bishop, but it hadn't occurred to her. Obviously, since Bishop Mose had been one of those who went to Ohio in the wake of the accident, he knew all about what had happened to her family.

The tiny flare of anger she felt at the thought was extinguished by his kind, knowing gaze. "I don't understand how everyone could keep it a secret from me all these years. I'd have said nobody could succeed in keeping a secret in Pleasant Valley."

"Ja, folks do talk a lot." His blue eyes twinkled. "Maybe that's why the Lord leads me so often to gossip for a sermon topic."

"How, then—"

He shrugged. "In this case, by the time you came home from the hospital, the immediate interest had died away. Folks were told only that the younger girls had been taken by other family members, and by the time you were old enough to understand a careless remark, most folks had half forgotten that you hadn't been born to Joseph and Anna."

Lydia turned his words over in her mind, realizing, now that the initial shock had worn off, she could more easily imagine how it had happened. "Maybe the fact of the accident taking place so far away made a difference, too." People had heard about it but they had not been able to jump into helping right away, as they normally would.

The bishop nodded. "Ja, that's so. It was like something they read about in the newspaper, not something they experienced up close."

"I understand that, I guess," she said, knowing her tone was a bit grudging. "But Mamm and Daadi still could have told me."

"Ja, maybe they should have. Your daad and mamm are upset now for sure. They're blaming themselves for the promises they made and fearing that things will never be the same between you."

If there was a question in that comment, it was one Lydia didn't feel able to answer yet. At the moment, she couldn't think of Mamm and Daad without remembering how they'd lied to her. Well, maybe not lied, but wasn't it the same thing, not telling her something she had a right to know?

Forgive, she reminded herself, knowing she would have to repeat that daily until she really felt it.

"Did you agree with keeping it secret at the time?" Once she'd asked the question, she feared it might be lacking in respect. She already guessed the answer, from what Daad had said, but she wanted to hear it from the bishop.

But Bishop Mose didn't seem offended. He stroked his chest-length beard, the way he did when he was considering something. "I understood the family's decision," he said finally. "I agreed to go along with it, though I feared one day it might explode in all our faces. As it has," he added wryly.

"Ja." An explosion was just what it felt like, shattering everything she'd thought she knew about herself. "Mamm and Daad seem to think I can forgive and forget and go on as if nothing has happened."

"Ach, Lydia, I'm sure they know that's not possible." He patted her hand, and his was as worn and wrinkled as a piece of the leather he worked. "A hurt like this will take time and healing."

She met his gaze. "Mamm and Daad, even Adam—they don't want me to get in touch with my sisters. But now that I know about them, how can I not try to see them? How can I not want to know about those years of my life that I can't remember?"

"Your parents and your husband love you," he said. "They want to take care of you." He paused for a moment. "You should understand that feeling. I'm certain-sure it's the way you feel right now about your little sisters."

His words hit her like a blow to the heart. He was right. That was exactly how she felt whenever she pictured those two little lost sisters.

Bishop Mose sighed. "Ach, Lydia, you were born to take care of others, I sometimes think. That is a good quality, but one which requires handling, because taking care of someone isn't always what's best for them."

She wrestled with that, almost wishing Bishop Mose didn't have such insight into the human heart. "It's not wrong, wanting to see them?"

"No, not wrong unless it leads to something that hurts them." Bishop Mose patted her hand again. "Think about how you feel right now, Lydia. Ask yourself if you want to make Susanna and Chloe feel that same way before you rush into telling them."

She didn't want to admit it, but he was right. She would have to be careful, very careful, not to do more harm than good.

Lydia could sense Bishop Mose's gaze on her, seeming to weigh her very thoughts.

"Your sister Susanna is Susanna Bitler," he said deliberately. "She lives in Oyersburg with her mother, who is very ill. She is partners in a craft and gift shop with an Amish woman named Dora Gaus. It would not be hard to find her if you decide to do so. Chloe's grandmother—well, your grandmother, too—is called Margaret Wentworth. All I know about her is that she came from somewhere near Philadelphia."

"Denke, Bishop Mose." He had put the information into her hands and showed he trusted her to use it wisely. She only hoped she could. She slid off the stool. "I'll remember everything you said. I will try to do the right thing."

"That's all any of us can do, ja? Just remember, too, that your parents thought they were doing the right thing, also."

She'd remember, Lydia told herself as she went out. But before she headed home, she'd find a telephone so she could make a call. She was going to arrange for a driver to take her to Oyersburg tomorrow.

As for what happened when she got there— well, maybe she couldn't see any farther than the next step. But she knew she had to take it.

Chapter Three

Adam bent over his workbench, hands steady as he slid the inside mechanism of the clock into position in the case he was making. He wasn't ready to place it permanently yet, but he wanted a look at it to be sure the proportion of the case was right.

One of the best things about clock-making was the way it focused his attention. He couldn't think of anything else while he worked.

Usually. This evening it seemed even the new

clock wasn't enough to keep his mind from straying.

He couldn't put it off any longer. He had to tell Lydia tonight about losing his job, before she heard rumors about the layoffs from someone else. It would be a difficult conversation to have at the best of times. With Lydia still so upset over learning the truth about her family, it seemed impossible, but it had to be done.

He frowned at the clock case, running his fingers along the curve of the wood. A maple mantel clock, it was destined to be a gift for Lydia's parents on their anniversary. Twenty-five years they'd been married, a reminder that they'd been newlyweds when they'd accepted the responsibility of raising Lydia as their own.

Lydia had been quiet since he got home, seeming preoccupied with her own thoughts. It didn't require much imagination to know what those were.

His fingers tightened on the tiny glue stick he was holding, snapping it in two, and he put it down in disgust. The truth was that for the first time in their marriage, he and Lydia were not in harmony.

Oh, they'd had their little disagreements over the past nine years, like any married couple would. Usually it was because he thought she was being a little too protective of the boys— coddling them, maybe because another boppli hadn't come along to seize her attention.

But now she seemed detached, not only from him, but also from Daniel and David. He'd actually had to remind her that it was past their bedtime, and such a thing had never happened.

She'd be down soon from tucking in Daniel and David. She'd come into the workshop, as she always did, and he would tell her about the cutbacks at the factory. He'd reassure her that he'd find something else. That he'd always take care of her and the kinder, just as he'd promised.

He heard her step, and his mouth went dry. How was he going to find the words?

"Adam?" Often she brought him a mug of coffee, but not tonight, it seemed. "Can we talk?"

"Ja, of course." He laid aside the tiny pair of pliers he used in working on the clocks. "There's something I have to tell you, in fact."

She didn't seem to hear him. "I went to see Bishop Mose today."

He was so startled that everything he'd been about to say went out of his head. "Why?"

Lydia stared down at the clock pieces on his worktable, but he didn't think she was actually seeing them. She moved slightly, her hands opening and closing, her face a little paler than usual in the light of the overhead gas fixture.

"I had to see him. I needed to talk to someone who knew about what happened with my sisters but wasn't so involved as Mamm and Daad."

Adam reminded himself to proceed carefully. "I think your mamm and daad told us everything they know."

"Maybe so. But what they said was colored by what they'd decided. They wanted me to understand and accept the decisions they'd made. Like you."

There was a slight emphasis to the last words. He didn't like it. It was as if Lydia was setting him apart, aligning him against her. But for the moment, he'd best concentrate on Lydia, not on his own feelings.

"Did it help, talking to Bishop Mose?" If anyone could bring Lydia comfort, surely it would be the bishop.

"A little." Her gaze flickered to the clock and away again. "He helped me to see better what it must have been like for them all these years. I still don't agree with the decision they made, but I understand why they did it."

"That's gut." A little voice in the back of his mind warned him not to make assumptions about how Lydia should feel. "Did you tell him about wanting to see your sisters?" Surely Bishop Mose would have shown her the danger of doing so.

"Ja, I did." Her chin lifted, and she looked right at him. "He told me what he knew about them."

Adam's stool scraped as he stood, unable to sit

still and look up at her any longer. "I'm certain-sure he didn't think you should go running off to see them."

"Well, then, you'd be wrong. He reminded me to be careful not to hurt them, but he understood why I need to see them. Which is more than my family does!" Her rare anger flared on the words.

"Your family wants what's best for you." His own temper slipped loose, and he fought to keep from saying something he'd regret. "I don't want you to be hurt, Lydia. Can't you understand how important that is to me?"

"I've told you. It's too late for me not to be hurt. Maybe *you* should try and understand that. Whether it is painful or not, I have to see them, at least." She took a breath, shoulders squaring as if for a fight. "That's why I hired Ben Miller to take me to Oyersburg tomorrow."

The elderly Englischer enjoyed driving the Amish to places they couldn't reach by horse and buggy. Adam suspected he'd probably never driven anyone on such a quest as this one. Still, Ben could be trusted to hold his tongue about anything he heard or guessed. That was the only good thing Adam could find to say about this proposed trip.

"Lydia, stop and think. What will you say to Susanna? You can't just walk in on a stranger."

"Bishop Mose says that Susanna has a shop with

64

another Amish woman. A shop is open to anyone. I don't need a reason to go in and look around and talk to her."

That was an unexpected setback. Adam hadn't realized Susanna would be so easily accessible. He fell back on the most compelling argument against this plan. "You can't give her news like this when her mamm is so ill."

"I have to see her." Lydia's tone was inflexible. "I'll be careful about what I say, but I have to see her." She turned and moved toward the door.

But he couldn't let her go. He hadn't told her his news yet. Annoyance rippled through him. Lydia seemed to think she was the only one with a problem right now.

"Wait, Lydia. There's something I have to tell you."

She turned, reluctantly he thought, and stood poised by the door as if to flee if he tried to talk her out of seeing Susanna. "What is it?"

"It's about work. My job at the plant." He sucked in a breath, hating that he had to say it out loud. "I'm being laid off on Friday."

She stared at him, eyes puzzled for a long moment, as if the sudden shift from one problem to another was too much for her to understand. "You've lost your job?"

"Not just me." He couldn't help sounding defensive. "They're laying off about half the workforce because orders are down so much."

It finally seemed to register. "Did you just find out about it?"

"Yesterday," he said. "I'd have told you then, but . . ." He let that die off. She ought to understand the reason for his delay.

"I'm sorry." Distress filled Lydia's eyes, and she took a quick step toward him. "I guess I didn't give you a chance to tell me." She reached out to him, and Adam clasped her hand.

He wouldn't have chosen this as a means to break through her obsession with her sisters, but it relieved him to see her focused on something else. On him.

"I don't want you to worry." He cradled her hand in his. "If new orders start to come in, they'll call us back, and if not, I'll just find something else."

"You're a fine worker," she said, her loyalty almost automatic. "Anyone would be lucky to have you."

They were the words he wanted to hear from her, but somehow he still sensed that she was torn. It was as if she had to force herself to focus on this new issue.

"You mustn't worry," he said again, tightening his grip on her hand as if that would call her back to him. "I promised to take care of you and the boys always, and I'll never let you down."

"Ach, Adam, I know you'll take care of us." She touched his cheek lightly. "I promise I won't fret about it."

He raised his hand, wanting to press hers against his skin, wanting to feel close to her.

But she was turning away before he could, and it seemed to him that her thoughts had already fled. They'd gone ahead of her to Oyersburg, he supposed, to the unknown sister she was so determined to see.

He'd told himself he didn't want her to be upset over his losing his job. That he didn't want her to worry about him. So why did he feel so disappointed at her reaction?

Lydia pulled her black sweater close around her against the morning chill as she peered down the lane. It wasn't quite time for Ben to arrive with his car, but sometimes he showed up early. She'd been ready since she'd seen the boys off to school an hour ago.

Well, ready in one sense. In another, she wasn't ready at all. What would she feel when she saw her sister? Was there any possibility Susanna would remember her? Apparently, she'd been not quite three at the time of the accident, so probably not. Certainly her adoptive mother wouldn't have encouraged her to remember.

A flicker of resentment toward the unknown woman flared in Lydia. If Elizabeth Bitler hadn't been so intent on having a child of her own, Lydia and Susanna might have grown up knowing each other, even if they'd been adopted by different families. They might have visited back and forth like cousins would, maybe, if not exactly like sisters.

A flash of white caught her eye from the other side of the orchard. Her neighbor, Emma Miller, was flipping a sheet out with a practiced hand before pegging it to the clothesline. Lydia waved, and Emma waved back, looking at this distance like one of the faceless Amish dolls every little Amish girl had.

Emma probably shouldn't be hanging out clothes, although she'd be offended if anyone tried to tell her so. But she'd had a slow recovery from a broken hip this past winter, and Lydia doubted if hanging sheets was part of her therapy.

Jessie ought to be helping her mother, but poor Jessie had problems of her own. The girl had always been a bit difficult, and a few months ago, she'd become something close to dangerous. Lydia hated thinking about the day she'd had to help Bishop Mose and Jessie's brother, Seth, get the girl into the psychiatric ward at the hospital. It still made her stomach quiver to remember the way Jessie had screamed and hit.

But Jessie was getting the treatment she needed at last, and the whole situation had seemed to bring Emma closer to her son. Even though Seth was as Englisch as could be after more than ten years away, he had at least finally accepted his responsibility in helping his mamm and his sister.

A horn beeped cheerfully, drawing Lydia's attention back to her own concerns, and Ben Miller pulled up. The retired Englischer seemed to get a lot of pleasure from serving as a taxi driver for the Amish community, and he'd proved himself a good friend to many over the years.

"Ready for your trip to Oyersburg?" He greeted Lydia with a smile when she slid into the front seat next to him.

"Ja, denke, Ben. I'm glad you were free today."

"I haven't been all that busy lately." He turned the car and started back down the lane to the road. "Those apple trees of yours are sure looking fine. They'll be in blossom before you know it."

Lydia nodded. Looking at the orchard brought to her mind the image Great-aunt Sara had drawn, of her mother and the three little girls playing under the trees.

She glanced at Ben. He'd lived in Pleasant Valley all his life, and he knew the Amish families better than most outsiders ever could.

"Do you remember when my parents lived in the house? My birth parents, I mean."

"Let me think, now." Ben adjusted the glasses that had a habit of sliding down his nose. "I knew they lived here. Knew about the accident, too, of course. Terrible thing, that was. But I can't say I knew them real well. That was before I retired, so I wasn't doing much driving then."

"Ja, I see."

"We probably bought our apples off them, same as we buy them from you now. My wife was fretting just the other day that she might run out of the applesauce she canned last fall and have to make more with store-bought apples. She always says nothing can beat your McIntosh apples for sauce."

Lydia nodded, smiling. It was the height of foolishness to be disappointed each time she spoke with someone and didn't learn something new about her family.

Ben glanced at her. "You know, you probably ought to talk to Emma Miller about your folks if you haven't already. She's lived in that same house for thirty or forty years, so she's bound to have known them, living right next door and being in the same church district and all."

"That's a gut idea, Ben. I will." It was something she should have thought of herself.

But Emma, as a close neighbor, would have known all along about Lydia's sisters, and had never said a word to Lydia in all these years. The thought unsettled her, reminding her again of how much had changed in such a short time.

The drive to Oyersburg usually took about half an hour or a little more, so Lydia settled back, staring out the window at the passing scene, although she didn't suppose she was really seeing much. Her thoughts were too preoccupied with what she was about to do.

Suppose she went against everyone's advice and told Susanna who she was? What would happen then?

Her thoughts wove a beautiful scene of her and her sister hugging each other, laughing and crying at the same time as they became a family again.

Lydia tried to cling to that image, but unfortunately her imagination, out of control, presented her with another picture, probably equally possible, in which Susanna was shocked and horrified and never wanted to see her again.

Lydia seesawed back and forth, and by the time they reached the outskirts of Oyersburg, she'd begun to wish she'd stayed home. What was she thinking, coming here against everyone's good advice?

"Here we are in Oyersburg," Ben said as houses and shops began appearing on either side of the road. "Where do you want to be dropped off?"

Lydia swallowed, her throat tight. "I'm not sure exactly. I want to go to a particular shop, but I've forgotten its name." That sounded thin, even to her. "It's a craft and gift store run by two Amish women. Do you know it?"

"I might," Ben said, eyeing her, curiosity written all over his weathered face. "It's probably Plain Gifts. I don't know the exact address, but it's along this end of Main Street someplace."

He slowed, peering out the window, and she leaned forward to do the same. Along one side of the road was a wide, shallow creek that meandered over flat rocks on its way toward the Susquehanna River. The shops and houses were on the other side of the road, facing the stream, and the shops seemed to be in the first floors of buildings that had once been houses, for the most part.

"There," Ben exclaimed. "That's it." He pulled to the curb in front of a two-story frame house with a wide front porch. Several rocking chairs were arranged on the porch, as if inviting you to sit and watch the world go by, and an assortment of decorated milk cans and birdhouses had dangling price tags.

Lydia slid out of the car and stood on the sidewalk. Ben leaned over to speak to her through the passenger-side window.

"If you have a lot of shopping to do, don't worry about me. I'll just go find a cup of coffee and read my newspaper."

"I should be ready to go in an hour." She started to ask him to pick her up here, but maybe that wasn't such a good idea, depending on how things went. She glanced around, looking for inspiration.

Main Street started a gentle upward slope beyond the shop, and about halfway up, there was what looked like a small park with benches.

"I'll plan to meet you at that little park in an hour," she said.

Ben gave her a look that was downright puzzled.

"You sure you don't need more time? I don't mind waiting."

"No, that's enough time." Either she'd have met her sister or not by then, have told her or not.

"If you say so." Ben raised his hand and pulled back out into traffic.

If her insides didn't stop shaking, Lydia figured she'd go in there looking half-sick, and that wasn't the impression she wanted to make. She probably wouldn't tell Susanna anything at all. She'd just enter the shop, look around, and then buy something so that she could engage Susanna in conversation. To her little sister, Lydia would be nothing but another customer.

Unless she decided to tell Susanna the truth, of course. Shutting her mind to that possibility, Lydia mounted the two steps and paused. From this angle, she could see across the backyards of the other buildings to where the river gleamed, wide and imposing. Susanna had picked a pretty place for her business, it seemed.

But she shouldn't stand here gawking. Lydia crossed the porch and entered the shop. She stopped just inside, still clutching the door. A small bell tinkled musically at the door's movement.

If she was going to look like a casual shopper, Lydia decided she probably should have checked out the items on the porch, but it was too late now. She closed the door and ventured into the shop.

The main section had probably been a parlor when the house had been a home. Now it was a display area for an array of crafts and artwork that Lydia found almost dizzying in their variety.

Clusters of dried flowers hung from hooks, emitting a faint aroma of summers past. A small oval table held a collection of pots and vases, no doubt handmade, in colors ranging from the palest milky white to a deep, rich burgundy.

She touched a burgundy pot that was nearly the color of the dress she wore. The glaze was smooth and cool under her fingers, and she could feel the slight ridges made by the potter's hands. The touch was oddly calming, and Lydia desperately needed calm before she looked into her sister's face for the first time. Or at least, the first time that she would remember.

Susanna or her partner would probably be in the back, where the cash register sat, but no one hurried forward to interrupt her browsing. Probably they were used to folks looking around. Birdhouses, napkin holders, and wooden boxes of all sizes marched across a shelf, while a large woven basket was piled high with quilted pillows.

A few steps carried her away from the scent of the dried flowers and into the stronger aromas of an arrangement of scented candles. Her gaze was caught by a wooden mantel clock similar to the one Adam was making, and the price tag on it took her breath away.

"May I help you find something?" The words were spoken in Englisch, but the speaker was undeniably Amish. She rose from a rocking chair in the corner, and Lydia's heart seemed to stop. This had to be her sister Susanna, didn't it?

"I . . . I thought I'd just look around for a bit." Obviously she wasn't very skilled at acting a part.

"Of course. Take your time. Just call me if you need any help. I'm Susanna."

"Denke." Lydia's voice came out a bit shaky, and she turned away quickly. Looking through a stack of quilted place mats gave her something to occupy her hands while she stole covert glances at her sister.

She was looking for similarities, she supposed, although plenty of sisters didn't look that much alike. Susanna had a heart-shaped face and a shy, sweet smile that showed a dimple in her cheek. Lydia put a hand to her face. She had a dimple in exactly the same place. Had their mother had one there, as well? For a moment she regretted the Amish ban on taking photographs, even though she understood the reason.

Susanna's hair was a darker brown than Lydia's, drawn back under her snowy kapp, and the deep blue of her dress matched the color of her eyes.

Lydia moved on to a display of hooked rugs, trying to concentrate on the color patterns woven through them. When she thought she could

75

trust her voice, she spoke. "Did you make these?"

Susanna, who'd been tactfully rearranging candles, turned at the question. "Not the rugs, no. We take many of our crafts on consignment from the makers."

Lydia nodded in understanding. Katie Brand did that in her quilt shop, too, giving some of the local quilters an outlet for selling their wares that they otherwise wouldn't have.

"Amish crafters, are they?"

"Most of them. A few things are made by Englisch, like the paintings." Acting on her interest, Susanna nodded to the pastoral scenes that covered one wall while she came around the counter. "You are not from Oyersburg, ain't so?"

Lydia shook her head. Obviously, Susanna would know all the members of her church district. "I'm in town to do some shopping. I live over in Pleasant Valley." She watched for any indication that the place meant something to Susanna, but Susanna's expression was one of polite interest. "My name is Lydia Beachy."

Susanna took a few steps toward her, and Lydia's heart twisted. Her sister walked with a definite limp. That must be her scar from the accident, just as Lydia's lack of memory was hers. Protective love surged through her, astonishing Lydia with its strength, and she fought to keep it under control.

"I especially like this painting of the stream and

76

the covered bridge. I know exactly where that was painted, just above where the creek flows into the river." Susanna smiled at the painting, as if imagining herself in the scene.

Did she ever imagine herself in the apple orchard? Or dream of it and wonder why?

"It is lovely. But not for me, ain't so?" Lydia managed a smile, knowing Susanna understood. The Amish didn't hang things on their walls unless they served a purpose besides being beautiful.

"Were you looking for something in particular?" Susanna's glance held curiosity. She probably didn't get many outside Amish coming in as customers, since it was far more common for them to make gifts rather than buy them. "Or do you have something you're interested in bringing in for the shop on consignment?"

The idea blossomed in Lydia's thoughts as soon as Susanna said the words—the perfect reason for her to visit the store not just today, but in the future.

"My husband makes clocks." She pointed toward the one she'd noticed. "Usually mantel or shelf clocks. I wondered if you might be interested."

"I'd be wonderful glad to find another clock-maker." Susanna's blue eyes lit with enthusiasm. Obviously her shop meant a great deal to her. "The man who made that one is retired, and he's not producing them any longer. Do you have any of your husband's clocks with you today?"

"No, but I could bring one the next time I come to Oyersburg." And there would be a next time, she could guarantee it.

"Gut. We'd be glad to have a look anytime. Do you often come here?" Susanna gestured, as if to take in the town.

"I will be coming more often in the future." Recklessness seemed to take possession of Lydia. Why not tell Susanna the truth? She seemed friendly, and once she knew, Lydia wouldn't have to make up excuses—

"Susanna?" A footstep sounded as the speaker came through a curtain that screened off a room at the rear. "Ach, I didn't realize you were busy with a customer. I wanted to remind you that it's nearly time to check on your mamm."

"It is?" Susanna glanced at the clock. "I was so distracted talking that I lost track." She turned to Lydia. "This is Dora Gaus, my partner in the shop. She can answer any questions you have. I must leave now, but do bring in a clock or two whenever you can." She started to the door, her limp more pronounced since she was hurrying. "It was so nice to meet you."

"Ja, for me, as well." Lydia doubted that Susanna had heard her, as intent as she was on her errand. She swept out the door, closing it behind her.

Lydia let out a breath, feeling herself sag. It was over, and she certainly couldn't find any excuse for hanging around until Susanna came back.

"Did Susanna say you might bring some clocks in?" Mrs. Gaus came out from behind the counter, wearing the black dress often worn by older Amish women, especially if they were widows. Round and sturdy, Mrs. Gaus had a pleasant smile that warmed her broad face.

"My husband enjoys making clocks," Lydia explained. "Susanna said you'd be interested in seeing them."

"Susanna is right, as always." Mrs. Gaus leaned on the nearest counter, seemingly prepared for a chat. "She has a gut eye for business, and the smartest thing I ever did was take her on as a partner."

"How long have you been in partnership?" She couldn't display too much curiosity about Susanna, but surely that question was natural.

"Goodness, it must be over five years, nearer six, now. Susanna and her mamm live just a block over, so it's convenient for her."

Lydia had to venture another question, even at the risk of making Mrs. Gaus suspicious of her. "I gather from what you said that her mother is ill?"

Mrs. Gaus's ruddy face seemed to draw down with sorrow. "Cancer, poor soul, and she isn't doing well, either. It's fortunate for her that she has Susanna. Only her daughter can comfort poor Elizabeth now. The doctor says she doesn't have more than a few months left." She shook her head.

Something seemed to shake inside Lydia, as well, at the close call she'd had. If she'd obeyed her impulse and told Susanna that Elizabeth wasn't really her mother, what damage might she have done to both of them? Bishop Mose had been right, as he usually was. She couldn't possibly disrupt Susanna's life and whatever time her adoptive mother had left by telling her the truth now.

Still, at least she'd seen Susanna for herself, and she'd made an initial approach. She'd have to be satisfied with that today.

If she were to reunite with either of her sisters in the near future, it would have to be Chloe. But how on earth could she locate a baby who'd disappeared into the Englisch world twenty-five years ago?

Chapter Four

Lydia couldn't seem to clear her mind for the rest of the day. Usually her duties stretched ahead of her in the peaceful routine of Amish life, but not now.

Finally, despairing of accomplishing anything in the house, she went outside. She'd walk through the orchard, the place that always restored her serenity no matter what troubled her. Not that she'd ever had a problem like this one before.

Shep, the shepherd mix who considered it his duty to guard the property, rose from the flagstone walk where he'd been dozing in the sun. He moved to meet her, his tail wagging lazily.

"You don't have thoughts that trouble you, do you, old boy?" She patted his head and ruffled his ears. "Will you walk with me?" She headed toward the orchard, Shep pacing patiently at her heels.

The boys would be home from school before long, and Adam from work. The farm would be suddenly busy and noisy, and there'd be no time for reflection. She normally loved all the hullabaloo, but just now, she needed to think through her encounter, brief as it had been, with her sister.

Her heart clutched painfully as she pictured Susanna limping across the shop. *God's will,* the Amish said whenever sudden change happened, bad or good. Susanna would have been younger than David was now when she was injured. She probably didn't remember a time when she could run and jump like a normal child.

Was that why Susanna was still unmarried at twenty-seven? Or maybe she was twenty-eight now, depending upon when her birthday was. The pain struck Lydia again. She didn't know her own sister's birthday. She took a breath, willing the pain to fade. There would be some way to find out—the births of each child would be recorded somewhere, surely.

Most Amish young folks started pairing off in their late teens and married in their early twenties. Susanna was lovely, probably with a disposition to match, judging by the sweetness of her expression. Surely there had been boys who'd have seen beyond the limp to the person.

Lydia stopped under the big tree in the center of the orchard. Its low, spreading limbs were tempting for the young ones, and she'd had to forbid Daniel and David from climbing it. Adam thought she was too protective, but she knew how daring her boys were, and David would undoubtedly follow Daniel right to the top, with neither of them ever stopping to think about whether the branches could support their weight.

Mamm had told her something about the tree once, when she'd asked a question about her birth mother. She'd said it was Diane's favorite place, and she'd given Lydia an image of Diane and a small Lydia sitting on a low branch, while Diane told stories to her child.

But that picture had been false, hadn't it? It had omitted the two younger girls, who no doubt had been there as well.

Leaning against the trunk, Lydia pressed her

palms on the rough bark and tilted her head to look up through the branches. If there were answers here, she couldn't see them. But just over her head, one of the apple blossoms had begun to open its white petals.

She touched it gently, and her pain seemed to ease. Her senses opened to the soft hum of insects, to the chatter of a robin as she chased a crow from her nest, to the gentle snuffling of Shep as he nosed his way through a purplish-blue clump of the bugle flowers that carpeted the orchard in early spring.

Maybe it was a coincidence that Adam had first kissed her under this tree, or maybe that had been part of God's plan for her. If she closed her eyes, she could see Adam standing there, his beardless face looking so young and serious. He had taken his hat off, and the sunlight, piercing through the branches, had brought a reddish sheen to his thick brown hair. She felt herself slip back to those moments in memory.

"You are going to marry me, aren't you, Lydia?" His blue eyes were solemn, reflecting the fact that choosing a mate was for life.

She felt as if her chest would burst from the pressure of her love for him. "Ja, Adam Beachy, I will marry you." She lifted her hand toward his face tentatively, longing to touch him and a bit nervous as well.

Adam smiled, as if he'd read her thoughts. He

clasped her hand in his and pressed it against his warm, smooth cheek. "I love you, Lydia," he whispered.

Her heart seemed to turn over. "I love you, too." Her voice sounded funny to her, maybe because her throat was so tight.

Adam kissed the fingers he held, and the pressure of his lips seemed to travel straight to her heart. Then he lowered his head, and his lips found hers. Her breath caught, and the world seemed to shrink until there was only her and Adam together. The Garden of Eden had surely been like this, and she never wanted it to end.

It hadn't ended, she assured herself, shaking her head a little as she came back to the present. She loved Adam in a way that the girl she'd been then hadn't even imagined. But the events of the past few days had driven a barrier between them, and she wasn't sure how to get past it.

How could he not understand her longing for her sisters? But she was at fault, as well. She should have been more attentive when he'd talked about the loss of his job. She'd make up for it when he got home, that's what she'd do. Adam deserved to know that she understood and cared about his feelings.

A flicker of movement caught her eye. A man was coming toward her across the orchard, but it wasn't Adam. It was Seth Miller, Emma Miller's son.

Shep deserted the flowers to trot over to Seth, sniffing him thoroughly before nosing his head into Seth's hand. Did Shep find it odd to see a man in jeans and a knit shirt, instead of black broadfall pants and suspenders?

"Seth, it is gut to see you. How is your mamm doing today?"

"Improving, I think." Seth grimaced, his smoothly shaven face expressing concern, and ran a hand back through the stylish cut of his wheat-colored hair. "She does too much, I know, but I can't seem to stop her."

"No one can," she assured him. "Emma is a strong woman, and she won't take kindly to being told to slow down."

Emma had had to be strong, bearing all the sorrows she'd had with the death of her husband and oldest daughter and the decision of her only son to leave the faith, compounded by all the worry over Jessie's mental health.

Seth nodded, but Lydia could see that he had something else on his mind.

"Mamm was telling me about your problems with this news about your family. She says to ask if she can do anything to help." He looked at her as if she were a kettle about to boil. "Are you okay?"

Okay? Not really, but she hesitated to say that to Seth. They had been close friends once, but the man who stood in front of her didn't bear much resemblance to the Amish boy she'd known so well long ago.

"I'm fine. I guess the news is all over the church by now, ain't so?" She shrugged. "People will be talking about it." She should have realized that word would spread through the Amish grapevine, traveling person-to-person until everyone knew.

"That's only natural, but they love you and your family. I'm sure they wish you well." He studied her face. "Would it help to talk to an outsider, like me?"

"Ja, maybe." But Seth wasn't really an outsider, despite the fact that he wasn't Amish now. He was still, at some level, the boy she'd grown up with, the boy who'd taken her home from her first singing. "It's just so hard to get used to the idea of having sisters." Suddenly the words that were on top of her thoughts spilled out. "I saw Susanna today."

Seth's eyebrows lifted. "That must have been difficult. How did she take the news?"

At least Seth assumed she had a right to share the news with her sisters. She shook her head. "I couldn't tell her. I wanted to, that's certain-sure. But her mamm is very ill, and it didn't seem right to hand her another burden just now."

He tilted his head, considering, making her wonder what he might have done in similar circumstances. "I can understand that, I guess. But at least maybe one day you'll be able to tell her."

"Ja, I hope so." Lydia nearly bit her tongue. That almost sounded as if she were looking forward to the death of Susanna's mother, and that wasn't what she'd meant at all, was it?

Luckily, Seth's thoughts didn't seem to be heading in that direction. "What about the other one? Have you talked to her yet?"

She shook her head. "Chloe was taken by her Englisch grandmother when she was just a baby. That means she was brought up Englisch, and she probably doesn't know anything about her real family, since she was so young." Her throat tightened with the impossibility of it. "I can't begin to think how I'd ever find her."

"Then this must be your lucky day." Seth grinned, the old, happy-go-lucky grin that had intrigued every girl who'd ever come in contact with him back in the old days. "Because you happen to have a friend who's Englisch as well, and has just the talents you need to locate your sister."

Lydia could only stare at him for a moment, untangling his meaning. "You can find Chloe?" Surely it couldn't be as easy as he made it seem.

"Unless she's gone into the Witness Protection Program, I can practically guarantee it." Seeing she didn't understand, he smiled again. "The Amish do a good job of living off the grid, but every Englisch person leaves a trail somewhere on the Internet. Just tell me what you know about her, and I'll start searching."

"I do know about the Internet," she said, her voice tart. "You don't need to sound as if I'm a dummy."

"Sorry," he said quickly. "You always were good at telling me off, Lydia. Maybe that's why I liked you so much."

She decided it was better not to respond to that comment. There had been a time when she'd thought she and Seth might end up together, but that had been long ago and very fleeting.

"I'd be wonderful glad if you can find anything out about Chloe. Her grandmother's name was Margaret Wentworth, and she came from some-place around Philadelphia."

He nodded, seeming to stow the name away in his memory. "How old would Chloe be now?"

She had to stop and figure. "About twenty-six, I'd say. And our mother's name was Diane, if that helps any."

"That's enough to start with, anyway." He glanced past her. "Looks as if your family is getting home, and I'm supposed to be running my mother and Jessie to the grocery store, so I'll be off. I'll let you know as soon as I find something."

He sounded very confident. She watched him stride briskly off toward the Miller house before turning away. But then, Seth had always been confident of what he wanted for himself, regardless of how much it hurt the people who loved him.

Adam's steps slowed as his glance swept the orchard and landed on Seth Miller, walking back toward his mamm's house while Lydia looked after him. As far as Adam was concerned, he already had enough weight resting on his shoulders today. He didn't want to contend with Seth, as well.

Seth's quick, confident stride carried him out of sight in another moment, but not, unfortunately, out of Adam's mind. There was not much of the Amish boy he'd been left in the Englischer Seth was now. But even when he'd worn broadfall trousers and had his hair cut in his mother's kitchen, Seth had managed to attract the attention of the girls and the envy of the other boys. Adam had never felt able to measure up.

Lydia was walking toward him now, raising her hand to wave. He waved back, trying to put a little energy into the movement. The last thing he wanted was to get Lydia worrying about him and his job at a time like this.

And it was just plain stupid to let his mind travel back to that first singing they'd gone to when they were barely sixteen. He'd sneaked glances at Lydia, sitting on the opposite side of the long table, and wondered if she would ever look his way. And when they'd taken a break for refreshments, he'd had to force his feet to move toward her, rehearsing in his mind the words he'd use when he asked if he could take her home.

But he'd taken so long getting up the courage that he'd reached Lydia just in time to hear Seth asking the same thing, and Lydia saying yes to Seth, not to him. The image of Seth helping her up into his buggy was one he'd never gotten out of his head.

"Adam, you're home early." Lydia reached him, smiling.

"Ja, the boss gave us our money and said there was no point starting something else." He jerked his head in the direction of the Miller place. "What was *he* doing here?"

Lydia's smile faded, replaced by a wary expression. "Seth? He came over with a message from his mother, asking if she can do anything." Fine lines marred Lydia's smooth forehead. "Everybody knows, I guess. They're all talking." Her lips trembled, and she pressed them together.

Adam ought to be ashamed, letting himself think of that old jealousy when Lydia was hurting. He touched her arm, wanting to ease the pain. "They mean it kindly, even when they do talk. And Emma Miller is a gut woman."

"Ja, ja, she is. I should go over and see her. I haven't been there in days."

That was his Lydia, always thinking of others. "Emma would like a visit from you, that's for sure." He pushed himself to bring up the subject he'd rather she forgot. "I guess she could talk to you about when you were little. Emma would have been your mamm's closest neighbor, ain't so?"

Lydia nodded. "That's true." She seemed to make an effort to smile. "Well, enough about me. How was your last day?"

Now it was his turn to make the effort to look pleasant, no matter how he felt. "Not bad. Mr. Owens was real sorry he had to let us go, and he came around and talked to each one. He said if the orders pick up again, he'll be wanting to call us back to work."

"That's gut news, ain't so?" Lydia linked her arm with his as they walked toward the house. "Maybe he'll be calling you back soon."

He smiled and nodded, because he didn't want Lydia to worry. But it seemed unlikely that Mr. Owens would get up to a full crew anytime in the foreseeable future. When money was tight, folks didn't buy vacation trailers. That only made sense.

There were fewer jobs all over, something he hadn't expected even a couple of years ago. He'd been asking around, and no one seemed to know of anyone who was hiring.

Lydia was staring at him, her eyes questioning.

"What is it, Adam? Are you worried about finding something else?"

"No, no, I'm not thinking that at all," he said hastily.

The trouble with hiding your feelings from Lydia was that she always seemed to sense them without your telling her. He'd need to divert her attention.

"You didn't tell me about your trip to Oyersburg. How was it? Did you see Susanna?" He probably should say *your sister* but the words still seemed odd to him.

"Ja, I saw her." Her face softened, and she seemed to be gazing someplace far away. "Ach, Adam, I knew the minute I saw her that she's my sister. She has such a sweet face and a gentle way about her." Lydia's expression clouded. "She limps, though, and I was afraid her leg was paining her. It's never been right since the accident. I wanted so much . . ."

She let that thought trail off, but he knew where it had been headed.

"You wanted to tell her." He clasped her arm firmly. "Lydia, you didn't, did you?"

Lydia shook her head, a tear spilling over onto her cheek. "I longed to. But she had to hurry off to check on her mother. When she'd gone, I talked with her partner in the shop. She told me how sick Susanna's mamm is, and how Susanna is her only comfort in her last days. I couldn't disrupt her life at a time like this, could I?"

"No, it's certain-sure you couldn't," he said, relieved. "You did the right thing in keeping silent." He put his arm around her, hugging her close to his side. "Maybe, someday, you'll be free to tell her."

"Ja." She rubbed her head against his shoulder. "Ja, I will, won't I?"

"That's right." At least this sister was Amish, and not living too far away. From the sounds of it, Susanna would be needing support in the future, and there was nothing Lydia liked better than helping someone. "You can look forward to that day, even if you'll never be able to see the youngest one."

Lydia pulled back, her eyes wide as she stared at him. "Why do you say that?"

"Ach, Lydia, you must think about it." Why couldn't she accept the truth? "If even the bishop doesn't know how to find the woman who took the little one, it's best to resign yourself to God's will."

"It's true I don't know how to look for her, but Seth says that he does." She clasped Adam's arm with both hands, her smile chasing away the sorrow. "He says it won't be hard at all to find her. He's going to start searching right away, using the Internet."

"Seth." Adam couldn't help it if he sounded disapproving. Why did Seth have to push his way in where he wasn't wanted? "I don't think it's a gut idea to involve an outsider in family matters."

That was not the reaction Lydia expected from him—he could see that in her face.

"Seth isn't an outsider. We've known him since we were kinder. We went to school together. Ja, he's Englisch now, but that's what makes him the ideal person to help me find Chloe. Don't you see? Maybe it's God's will that Seth finds her for me."

"I don't want—" Adam stopped, knowing the words he was about to say were unwise. Lydia was so excited at the idea of finding her sister that he didn't have the heart to throw cold water on the scheme, even though he hated the idea of having Seth involved with his family's trouble.

"Look, here are the boys." Lydia waved, her attention distracted by the sight of Daniel and David running toward them.

Adam made an effort to be sensible. He couldn't keep Lydia from an opportunity to find her baby sister just because he was jealous of Seth.

Besides, chances were it would come to nothing. Not even Seth could make bricks out of straw.

The boys came rushing into their arms, both of them talking a mile a minute. Adam stood with his arms around his family, smiling with the pure joy of it.

So what if Seth had driven Lydia home from her

first singing? In the end, she had turned to him, and the end was what counted.

Seth paused for a moment on Adam and Lydia's back porch that evening. Lydia, he was sure, would welcome the news he'd brought. As for Adam—well, it wasn't hard to read Adam's attitude. Adam hadn't exchanged more than a few sentences with Seth since his return to Pleasant Valley months ago, despite the fact that Seth's mother was Adam and Lydia's nearest neighbor and close friend.

Seth tapped lightly on the screen door. He hadn't expected to be greeted with open arms by his old community. Even though he wasn't under the bann, since he'd left before being baptized into the church, the *Leit*, the term the Amish used to refer to themselves, still looked warily at a former Amish who had achieved what they'd consider worldly success. As for what success actually meant—

The door swung open. Two small faces tilted up to him, expressions questioning. Seth couldn't help but smile. No matter how much they changed later, young Amish boys all seemed to look the same, with their fair hair, light eyes, black pants with suspenders crossing their shoulders, and usually, at this time of year, bare feet.

"You're Daniel and David, right?" His Pennsylvania Dutch dialect was a bit rusty, but it had improved rapidly now that he was hearing so much of it. "I'm Seth Miller. Are your mammi and daad here?"

Before the kids could respond, the door swung wider, and Adam seemed to fill the opening, almost as if he were on guard.

"Seth." He nodded in greeting and gave the boys a gentle push. "Time you boys were getting to your chores, ja?"

"Ja, Daadi." The older boy, Daniel, grabbed his brother's arm and tugged. The little one seemed to hang back for a moment, his gaze fixed on Seth, his blue eyes round. Then they both scurried across the porch and raced toward the barn.

"I hope I didn't interrupt your supper." Seth accepted the tacit invitation of the door Adam held open and walked into the kitchen.

"No, no, we're finished." Lydia came toward him, drying her hands on a dish towel. "Is it . . . you haven't found something already, have you?" Her expression was torn between hope and fear, while Adam just looked disapproving.

Seth decided he'd have to be a complete idiot not to sense the tension in the room. There was more going on here than he'd anticipated with his possibly rash offer. But it was too late to reconsider now.

"Actually, the search was even easier than I expected. So yes, I have news."

Lydia's face lit. "Ach, what am I thinking, to keep you standing here? Sit down, I'll get you coffee, and you can tell us all about it."

She sent a glance toward Adam that Seth couldn't quite interpret, except to know that they were not entirely in harmony, either about finding Lydia's sister or perhaps about accepting his help.

Too late now, he told himself again, and sat down at the long pine table. "Coffee sounds fine." It was a good thing he'd said yes, since Lydia was already setting mugs on the table and pouring.

"Not for me, denke," Adam said, positioning himself against the pine cabinets, hands braced behind him against the countertop.

Maybe he should have been able to predict it. Adam wasn't ready to sit at table with him.

Seth stirred sugar into his coffee. "As I told you, the Internet has made it fairly easy to find anyone. Well, anyone Englisch, at least. I assumed Chloe's grandmother would have given the child her last name, so I just had to search for a Chloe Wentworth in the greater Philadelphia area, and there she was. I double-checked the parents' names to be sure I had the right one, of course."

He opened the manila envelope he'd brought with him and pulled out the best of the photos he'd found online. "Your sister."

Lydia grabbed the picture and pulled it to her, earning a disapproving sound from her husband. She flashed him an annoyed look.

97

"Chloe was brought up Englisch," she pointed out. "Naturally there would be photographs of her."

He'd printed out a color photo that showed Chloe, head tilted slightly to one side, green eyes seeming to smile at the camera. She had the same warm, peachy complexion Lydia did, he realized, but her hair was a deeper brown. Reddish tones showed in the photo, and Chloe's hair was worn in a loose style that just brushed her slim shoulders. In the photo she looked poised, polished, and sophisticated, none of which were terms one applied to an Amish woman.

"She is beautiful," Lydia murmured, touching the pictured face with her fingertips.

Adam, curiosity apparently overcoming his reluctance, moved behind her. Lydia looked up at him, something pleading in her gaze.

"Ja," he said, his voice gruff. "She has a look of you about her, ain't so?" He touched Lydia's shoulder gently, and they seemed to communicate without words, making Seth feel like an outsider.

Which he was, he reminded himself. He pulled a printout from the envelope.

"Anyway, she apparently still lives with her grandmother in the family home. She attended school and college in Philadelphia."

"She's not married?" Lydia asked.

"No, and I couldn't find any engagement announcement, so I'm guessing she's not about to be." Chloe had attended exclusive private schools, he'd noticed, but he didn't bother saying, knowing that fact would mean little to Lydia and Adam. "She's currently working at a small museum in Philadelphia that specializes in Pennsylvania German Culture."

"A museum?" Lydia couldn't seem to take her gaze from the photo. "What does she do there?"

"According to the museum website, she's an assistant curator, working on folk art and furniture." He shrugged. "Maybe that's her Amish heritage coming out, even if she doesn't know about it."

Lydia looked stricken. "You think she doesn't know about her parents being Amish?"

He seemed to have put his foot in it, and Adam was giving him a warning glare.

"I don't really have any idea. But since she's never been in touch . . ."

He let that trail off, seeing the pitfall he'd ignored in his eagerness to do something for Lydia in return for her kindness to his mother. Lydia could end up getting hurt by this unknown sister. He sucked in a breath, trying to see a way out.

"I have her address," he said. "You could write to her, if you wanted."

"Write?" Lydia's voice rose. "I don't want to write to her. I want to see her. I must go to Philadelphia—"

"No." Adam's shocked voice cut across hers. "You cannot do such a thing. To go halfway across the state to a city you don't know . . . Lydia, this is impossible. It was one thing to go to Oyersburg, but you cannot go off to Philadelphia."

"I have to." Lydia stood, hands braced on the table, tears sparkling in her eyes. "If Chloe doesn't know about her parents and her sisters, I have to tell her. I have to see her."

Anger fairly sparked between Lydia and Adam, and Seth had an instinctive desire to flee what was rapidly turning into an emotional scene.

But he couldn't. He was responsible for this, so he had to find a solution.

"I'll go and see her." The words were out of his mouth before he had a chance to consider just how difficult such an encounter might be.

But he had to offer. The thought of Lydia setting off alone for the city made his blood run cold. For once, he and Adam were in agreement.

"You will go?" Lydia's face reflected both reluctance and hope. "I can't ask you to do that for us."

"It's the least I can do, after all you've done for Mamm and Jessie," he said, thinking of the debts he could never repay. "I have to go to Philadelphia anyway to handle some business, so I'll just move the trip up."

"Are you sure? Or are you just saying that to make me feel better?"

"I really do have to go," he assured her.

Her breath caught as if he'd just given her a gift. "When?"

Seth's thoughts ticked over the possibilities as he mentally rearranged his calendar. At the best of times it wasn't easy to balance the trips he had to make for the firm with the telecommuting he did the rest of the time while trying to care for his mother and sister. His boss had been surprisingly supportive of this unorthodox schedule.

"It might be best if I approach her at the museum, rather than trying to go to her house. So that means it can't be before Monday."

"What will you say to her?" Lydia clasped her hands together in a prayerlike gesture.

"It won't be that hard." He tried to sound more confident than he felt. "I'll just explain that I came for you, and who you are. I'll say you'd like to be in touch with her, and see how she responds."

She might well respond by calling security and having him thrown out, but he wasn't going to say that to Lydia.

"It's the best way," Adam said, putting his hands on Lydia's shoulders as if to keep her from flying away from him. "Denke, Seth."

The look he gave Seth was actually anything but thankful. Clearly he was blaming Seth for the disruption of his peaceful home life.

Well, Adam was deluding himself if he thought

Lydia's need to find her sister would have ended if not for Seth's offer. Lydia was gentle and dutiful, true, but she could be a tigress when it came to taking care of others.

No, his suggestion was the best of a number of possibilities, and Adam should realize that he and Seth had a lot in common. They both wanted to help Lydia and protect her from hurt.

As for the Englisch sister—well, she was an unknown quantity, and Seth had a healthy respect for the unknown, especially since he might be about to explode a bomb in Chloe Wentworth's life.

Chapter Five

Worship service was drawing to a close on Sunday morning, and only the faintest stirring of the Leit who sat on the backless benches in Amon Esch's barn betrayed the fact that they'd been here for nearly three hours already. Lydia found her attention was divided, as it so often was, between the minister's words and her family, seated on the opposite side of the space.

The boys were old enough now to sit with Adam on the men's side. A swift glance told her that Daniel was leaning against Adam's arm, his head tilted down. She couldn't see from here whether or not his eyes were closed. David sat erect, obviously modeling his behavior in worship on that of his father.

If she had a daughter, Lydia thought, she would have someone snuggling up against her in worship, but she didn't have that joy. At times like this, when the reminder was sharp, she found it necessary to repeat to herself that it was God's will, and that her children were God's gift.

Anna Fisher sat next to Lydia in the section occupied by young married women, with her three-year-old, Gracie, slipped in between her mother and Lydia. Anna's son slept in her lap, his head heavy in the crook of her arm.

Gracie slumped a little, her eyes drifting shut. Exchanging a sympathetic glance with Anna, Lydia eased her arm around the little girl so that she could slide down into Lydia's lap.

Lydia patted the child's back, wishing just for a moment that it was her own daughter dozing there. But it was God's will, she repeated.

She had gone to see Midwife Sarah, of course, concerned when there were no more pregnancies after David. Sarah, always cautious with her clients, had sent Lydia to the clinic that specialized in medicine among the Amish, but the doctors there hadn't found anything wrong. Nothing wrong, except that the years were slipping away without another baby to treasure.

Now even Sarah herself was pregnant, something the midwife had never expected. An Amish woman's dress disguised pregnancy fairly well, but Sarah wore a glow that seemed to light up the room. Lydia didn't begrudge her the happiness. She just longed to feel it herself.

The congregation slid to its knees for the final prayers. Lydia managed to get down from the bench without waking the sleeping child. The prayer was a formal one, recited from the prayer book by memory. Lydia couldn't seem to keep herself from inserting her own longings into the prayer—that there would be another baby to join their family, that God would pave the way for Seth tomorrow as he went to see Chloe.

And then worship was ended with the final blessing. The men stood up, stretched, and began sliding the backless benches into the brackets that turned them into tables for their noonday meal, while the women headed for the house to help with the food.

Lydia walked out into the spring sunshine with Anna, blinking at the bright light after the relative dimness of the barn. Gracie stirred in her arms, looked up at Lydia's face, and then wiggled to get down.

"Thank Lydia for letting you sleep on her lap," Anna prompted, touching her daughter's silky blond hair.

"Denke," Gracie whispered, and then hid her face in her mother's skirt.

A chuckle escaped Lydia, and Anna grinned.

"And denke from me, as well," Anna said. "Sometimes I think I don't have enough hands."

"I remember the feeling." Those early years when the children were so dependent passed very quickly, even though it didn't seem like it at the time. "How are Myra and the new boppli?"

Myra was Anna's sister-in-law, and the mother of a baby boy, come to join the two little girls in the family.

"Myra's doing very well, as is the fine healthy baby. As for my brother—you'd think no man ever had a son before to hear him tell it."

"Give them our best wishes. I would have taken supper over to them this week, but . . ." She let that trail off, thinking she shouldn't have let her own troubles make her forgetful of the needs of others.

"They've had enough food brought in to last a month," Anna declared. "Don't think a thing about it."

Anna's teenage niece, Elizabeth, came hurrying over just then, relieving Lydia of the need to respond. Probably just as well. No doubt Anna knew all about what had been going on with them, like the rest of the church.

"I'll take the kinder, Aunt Anna." Elizabeth took the baby in her arms and held out her hand to little Gracie. "Komm, let's go and play a bit, ja?" She led them off to join some other young ones on the sunny lawn.

Anna watched her, smiling a little. "Elizabeth has grown into such a sweet young woman. She'll have the boys flocking around her soon."

Lydia nodded, the comment making her think again of Chloe, who seemed never far from her thoughts. Seth had said she wasn't engaged or married, but surely, pretty as she was, there were men in her life, maybe even one special man.

She glanced at Anna, wondering just how much Anna had heard about her sisters. The whole story, she'd guess, since the Amish grapevine worked better than most anything at getting news around.

Anna had spent nearly three years in the Englisch world before coming home to Pleasant Valley. It could be that Anna might help her understand Chloe, if only she actually got a chance to meet her.

"Shall we go and see if there's any help needed in the kitchen?" Anna asked.

"I'll join you in just a minute," Lydia said. "First I'd better ask my mamm to keep an eye on the boys. Adam is still helping set up tables, and you know how the men are when they get to talking."

"Ja, for sure." Smiling, Anna headed for the kitchen, the spring breeze making her kapp strings and apron flutter.

Mamm was deep in conversation with a small group of older women, but the talk cut off quickly when Lydia approached, and Lydia could guess what they'd been talking about. Her cheeks flamed, but she managed to keep a smile pinned to her face.

"Mamm, will you watch David and Daniel for a few minutes? I'll go and see if I can be some help in the kitchen."

"Ja, of course." Mamm's smile eased the worry lines from her face, at least for a moment. "Go along."

It probably helped Mamm to talk with her friends about the subject on which she'd been silent for so long. Lydia ought to be happy it made things easier for her mother, instead of feeling even more betrayed. But she couldn't prevent a bit of resentment that at least the female half of the church was talking about her this morning.

She'd just stepped up on the porch when a voice rose from the group of men clustered just around the corner of the house.

"All I'm saying is that the Scripture says, 'Be not unequally yoked with an unbeliever.' "

The male voice was very decided, and Lydia suspected it was that of Isaac Brand, who seemed to have an opinion on everything.

"Eli Weaver went off and married an Englischer, and look at all the trouble it's caused, even after all these years. He should have known better."

Lydia froze, her hand on the railing, unable to move. So that's what some, at least, were saying —implying that her parents were at fault for loving each other.

"Scripture also reminds us to speak kindly of one another and to bear one another's burdens." Bishop Mose's voice was unmistakable. "That's a teaching we all might do well to heed, Isaac."

A little silence followed his words. Her heart eased, Lydia went quickly on into the kitchen before she could hear anything else.

Seth found the Pennsylvania German Cultural Museum in Philadelphia with only a few wrong turns that had him arguing with his GPS. It wasn't large compared to the city's art museum or the Franklin Institute, but it was an attractive brick building with a colonial air, surrounded by gardens. From the entry, wings branched out dedicated to the history of German-speaking immigration, traditional architecture, and a genealogical library that probably appealed to the current interest in tracing one's ancestors. The Amish generally didn't have need for that sort of help, since generations were preserved in the family's Bible.

He headed for the information desk and in a few minutes had talked his way through a maze of hallways into the office of Chloe Wentworth, only to find it empty. The young intern who'd shown him the way disappeared to locate her, leaving Seth alone.

Just as well, maybe. It gave him another moment's respite before plunging into a family situation that Ms. Chloe Wentworth would be justified in considering none of his business.

He glanced around, trying to get an impression of the woman from her office. The museum clearly put its money into the areas the public visited. Behind the scenes, the offices and storerooms were prosaic cement block.

Chloe Wentworth's cavelike space was equipped with a utilitarian desk and chair with a computer setup. The desk was totally surrounded by shelves filled with reference books, filing cabinets, and a worktable piled with books and papers. A scholar worked here, by the looks of the office, and Seth had trouble reconciling the setting with the sophisticated woman in the photo he'd found.

Seth circled the desk casually, looking for any clue to the personality of the woman he was about to meet. A small, silver-framed image of an older woman, elegant in silk and pearls, sat on the corner of the desk—the grandmother, no doubt. A small stuffed bear wearing a Phillies baseball cap leaned against the photo, drawing a grin. Somehow Grandmother Wentworth didn't look much like a Phillies fan, so presumably that was Chloe.

Footsteps echoed in the hall beyond the door, and by the time the door opened, he was several feet from the desk, staring at the titles of the reference books.

"Mr. Miller?" The female voice was crisp. "I'm Chloe Wentworth. How can I help you?"

He swung around to face the woman who was Lydia's little sister, still with no idea how he was going to broach the reason for his visit, and found himself tongue-tied.

Chloe was a surprise, tripping him up before he'd even begun. Instead of the glossy but classic beauty in the photo, the real thing definitely had a style of her own. The auburn hair was short and sleek, and huge black-rimmed glasses masked sea-green eyes. Her skirt was short enough to warrant a second look at her legs, and the scoop neck of her sweater revealed a tiny butterfly tattoo on her left shoulder. Chloe's appearance was about as far as could be from either Main Line debutante or Old Order Amish.

He caught hold of himself. He certainly wouldn't make the right impression by staring at her. "It's good of you to see me without an appointment, Ms. Wentworth." He moved a step to offer his hand, and she took it in a quick, cool grasp.

"No problem. Not many people seek me out at the museum, appointment or not." She nodded toward his business card. "I'm just a lowly assistant to the curator, and I don't deal with the museum's computer needs. If you'd like me to refer you to one of our tech people . . ."

"I'm not here on business for the software

design firm." He might as well admit that up front and get on with it. Either Chloe knew of the existence of her sisters and chose to ignore them, or she'd never been told. Either way, this was going to be a tricky conversation. "I had to be in Philadelphia on business, and I was asked to contact you on behalf of a friend of mine." He sucked in a calming breath. "Your sister, Lydia Weaver Beachy."

Chloe stared at him, forehead crinkling, and pulled off the glasses, tossing them on her desk. "Sister?" Those green eyes expressed nothing but confusion. "I'm afraid you have me mixed up with someone else, Mr. Miller. I don't have a sister."

A slight shadow crossed her face as she said the words. Was it regret?

So she'd never been told, then. He wasn't sure if that fact made this easier or harder. "Actually, you have two sisters, Lydia and Susanna, daughters of Eli Weaver and Diane Wentworth Weaver."

That was blunt, but he couldn't imagine any other way of telling the woman something so shocking. He took an instinctive step toward her, not sure how one offered comfort in a situation like this, but stopped dead when Chloe stiffened.

Seth eased himself back until he leaned against the worktable, trying to look as nonthreatening as possible. "I'm sorry to just come right out with it. I know that information must be a lot to absorb. But the truth is that Eli and Diane Weaver had three daughters, not one."

She glanced down at his card again, seeming to be a little reassured by the name of the firm. Then she shook her head.

"You're mistaken," she said, her tone flat. "Those are my parents' names, but your friend is not related to me. There must surely be more than one Eli Weaver in the world."

"Quite a few just in Pennsylvania," he admitted with a wry smile. "Weavers are common among the Pennsylvania Dutch, as are men named Eli. But I suspect only one of them married Diane Wentworth, daughter of John and Margaret Wentworth. And I doubt that any other couple with those names died as a result of an accident on an Ohio highway twenty-five years ago."

He could see he'd hit home with that string of facts. Chloe's eyes darkened. He'd better follow up while he could, so he slid the photocopies from the file he carried, letting them fall on her desk.

"Here's a copy of their marriage license and a copy of a newspaper article about the accident. I haven't been able to get birth certificates yet, but—"

"But you no doubt can produce something convincing, given enough time." Her voice snapped like a whip, yanking him around to face her.

"You think these are fakes?" Funny, but that

112

reaction had never occurred to him. "I can assure you—"

"I can assure you that this is not the first time someone has attempted to get to my grandmother's fortune through me." Chloe cut him off again. "Please leave." She reached for the phone, no doubt intending to call security.

"Look, I'm not a con man." He put his hand out and just as quickly withdrew it. He'd better not add assault to the list of complaints she was probably creating in her mind. "Lydia and her husband are neighbors of my mother out in central Pennsylvania. Lydia was injured in the accident that killed her—your—parents and only recently learned the truth."

Chloe lifted the phone and pressed a button. "Your story is even less likely than most I've heard. I'd suggest you leave unless you prefer to be escorted out. Security will be here in a moment."

Time was slipping away, and he hadn't accomplished a thing. "At least look at the documents. You were only a baby at the time, so you couldn't possibly remember."

"There's nothing to remember." Her chin lifted, and Seth saw the resemblance to the haughty grande dame in the photograph on her desk. Chloe might carry her parents' genes, but it seemed her grandmother had done a good job of transforming the rest of her.

"If you'll just look—" This time it was the door opening that cut him off. The museum guard was short, slight, and probably well past retirement age, but he carried the authority in this place, and Seth wasn't about to start a confrontation with the man.

"Mr. Miller is leaving, George." Chloe's voice was as cool as her eyes. "Please see that he gets off museum premises."

"Yes, ma'am." George's gaze swiveled from Chloe to Seth, and he gestured toward the hallway. "After you, sir."

It seemed Seth was out of choices. The woman wouldn't even hear him out. Her mind was closed. When he reached the doorway, he looked back, thoroughly annoyed.

"In the event you decide to step out of your secure little world and face the truth, you can reach me at the number on the card."

She didn't speak, and her face might as well have been carved from ice. Seth walked quickly back the way he'd come, hardly aware of the security guard trailing along behind him. Of all the superior, stubborn women he'd met, Chloe Wentworth ranked right up at the top of the list.

But by the time Seth reached the sidewalk outside the imposing museum building, his annoyance with Chloe had ebbed, to be replaced by sorrow and regret. He'd been so sure he could handle this for Lydia. Now he'd blown the only chance he'd get to bring her and her sister together.

Chloe tried to focus on the grant application that had occupied so many of her working hours lately, but her gaze kept straying to the papers Seth Miller had left on her desk. By the time she'd made her third careless error in the proposal for funds to expand the museum's educational programs, she shoved away from the keyboard, annoyed with herself.

Get rid of the papers he'd left behind, and she'd get rid of Seth Miller's intrusive presence. Leaning across the desk, she scooped up the documents and dropped them into the waste can.

There. Now she could concentrate. Her grandmother had been right in her often-repeated mantra. The world is filled with people who will try to take advantage of you because you're a Wentworth.

Seth Miller wasn't the first person to feign an interest in Chloe because of who she was. Not that Miller had seemed interested in her as a woman, aside from that one lingering look at her legs, but his story had been ridiculous, hadn't it? As for his supposed proof . . . anyone could fake something that looked like a photocopy of a marriage license. Given a computer and a few minutes' time, she could do it herself.

Frustrated, Chloe snatched the papers out of the

waste can and then dropped them back in. She shouldn't let herself be caught up in the man's story.

"Playing basketball with the trash?" Kendra Phillips stood in the doorway, looking at her with raised brows.

"Something like that," Chloe admitted, managing a smile for her friend. Kendra, a conservator who spent most of her days in the basement laboratory, wore a lab coat over a multicolored tunic and seemed to have forgotten the tiny paintbrush stuck behind her ear.

Chloe ought to be ignoring her previous visitor, but the urge to confide in Kendra was strong. Kendra, having battled her way from an inner-city school to one of the best grad-school programs in the country, had seen it all. They'd met when they were both pursuing their master's degrees. Kendra's fund of sometimes brash common sense could be relied upon to sort out the truth quickly, and she was a good antidote to the more hidebound members of the museum's staff.

"Well?" Kendra advanced into the office and perched on the edge of Chloe's desk, her long, beaded earrings brushing cheeks the color of milk chocolate as she leaned toward Chloe. "You going to tell me what's wrong, or should I start guessing?"

"Someone came into my office this morning." She gestured toward the business card that lay on her desk, and Kendra picked it up, scrutinizing it.

"He said he was here as a favor to a friend, a woman named Lydia Weaver something or other, I don't remember the last name. Anyway, he said that this woman is my sister."

"You called security, right?" Kendra's perfectly arched eyebrows lifted even higher. She'd never hesitate to have an annoyance kicked out. In fact, she'd probably do it herself, not bothering with the intermediary.

"Of course," Chloe said. "I don't have a sister, to begin with. But he insisted that my parents actually had two other children, both girls."

"I assume he provided some sort of proof? Like the papers you're tossing in and pulling out of the trash with such decisiveness?" Kendra grinned.

Chloe fished out the copy of the marriage certificate. "Look at it. Diane Wentworth and Eli Weaver. The dates and names are right, so that certificate is probably genuine, but the rest of his story was ridiculous. How could I have two sisters and not know about it?"

Taking the document from her, Kendra frowned at it. "Your parents died in an accident when you were still a baby, right?"

Chloe nodded. Maybe that sense of having no parents to rely upon had been what brought about her somewhat unlikely friendship with Kendra. But while Chloe had been taken in by her grandmother after her parents' deaths, Kendra had been bounced to a succession of foster homes.

"I was only about a year old when the accident occurred. My grandmother told me that she came to the hospital where I'd been taken. My parents died, so as soon as I could be released, she and my grandfather brought me home with them. If I'd had any siblings, she'd have told me, surely."

Wouldn't she? A faint flicker of doubt touched Chloe's certainty. Her grandmother seldom talked about Chloe's parents. Well, never, in fact, unless Chloe asked a direct question. It was as if their deaths had wiped them not just from this world but from ever having existed. Was that Gran's natural reserve at work, or something more?

"Did this guy offer any proof of your relationship to these so-called sisters?" Kendra, always practical, latched on to the most critical part of the story.

"No. He said something about not being able to get the birth records yet. Even if he had them, that wouldn't convince me. They could easily be fakes. My grandmother says—"

She stopped, having had a front-row seat several times to the antipathy between her grandmother and her friend. Kendra wasn't the sort of person Margaret Wentworth associated with, and Kendra had scant patience with what she saw as snobbery based on outmoded ideas of social class.

"Your grandmother assumes everyone's a con man after her money," Kendra said bluntly. "I doubt she's the best reference point in a situation like this." She tossed the business card to Chloe. "It would be easy enough to check up on this guy, anyway. You can see if he's who he says he is."

Chloe nodded reluctantly, not sure she wanted to pursue the matter even that far. She found herself picturing Seth Miller's face—the sharp line of his jaw, the determined set to his mouth, the cool way his gray-blue eyes had surveyed her.

"I have to admit he didn't look like a con man."

"Honey, no successful con man looks like one. That's his stock-in-trade." Kendra slid off the desk. "Get busy and do what you know you should have done from the minute the guy left. Check up on him, and check up on his story. You're a researcher, so treat it like any research problem."

"Pretend I'm searching out the provenance of an eighteenth-century dower chest?" Chloe managed a smile for the first time since she'd ordered Seth Miller out of her office.

"Exactly." Kendra headed for the door. "Do you want something from the cafeteria?"

"Chicken salad sandwich, please." They normally took turns picking up lunch at the museum lunchroom, sometimes carrying it out to a park bench near Independence Hall, where they could watch the tourists walk by.

"Get started on the research," Kendra ordered, and disappeared from view.

Kendra was right, of course. This was a research problem, pure and simple. And her grandmother need never know that Chloe had been digging into the story of her parents' deaths.

The logical place to start was with the man, Seth Miller. She picked up the business card, his final words echoing in her mind. *In the event you decide to step out of your secure little world and face the truth, you can reach me at the number on the card.*

She didn't like his snap judgment of her. She wouldn't be getting in touch with him, but he might be surprised at just how good she was at ferreting out the truth, starting with one Mr. Seth Miller, if that was really who he was.

Ten minutes later Chloe was staring at the photo of Seth Miller on the company website. There was no denying the identity of the face with the gray-blue eyes staring confidently at the camera. She flipped quickly through the site, searching for more information.

The software company was relatively well-known, so that lent an air of authenticity to the whole business. And apparently they thought highly of Mr. Seth Miller, designer. She ran the cursor down through a list of his achievements and awards.

So it appeared Seth Miller was genuine, in that he was who he had claimed to be. Still, a man could be good at his job and sleazy in his private life. His business reputation didn't mean he couldn't have some unsavory motive for contacting her.

Chloe frowned. She was starting to sound like her grandmother, who seemed to become more suspicious with each passing year. Still, granting that Seth Miller was the real thing, even granting that his motives were good, he was still mistaken.

His parting words slipped into Chloe's thoughts again, making her a bit uncomfortable. She prided herself on being independent. She didn't hide behind the Wentworth name.

She picked up the other paper, looking at the newspaper article. AMISH KILLED IN VAN ACCIDENT, the headline read. The piece was fairly brief, the dateline a town in Ohio she'd never heard of.

A van load of Amish people headed from Pennsylvania to a wedding in Ohio had crashed into a tractor trailer when the van's driver apparently fell asleep at the wheel. He had been pronounced dead at the scene; several adults and children had been taken to area hospitals.

Grandmother had told her about the accident when she'd been old enough to ask questions about her parents. Gran's voice hadn't wavered, but her skin had seemed to shrink against the bones of her face, frightening Chloe and making her hesitate to bring the subject up again.

She had, of course, as she'd grown older and understood more. Her grandmother had given her as little information as possible. Still, eventually the whole story had come out. Diane,

121

an only child, had been the stereotypical rebellious, troubled daughter, the way her grandmother told it. She had capped a series of problems by running away from the parents who'd loved her.

Gran said they'd learned, eventually, that she'd married an Amishman and joined his faith. Chloe could still see the distaste in her grandmother's face as she insisted her daughter had been sucked into something that was little more than a cult. According to Gran, Diane had died in an accident that never would have happened if she'd stayed in the world where she belonged.

That led, inevitably, to one of her grandmother's favorite maxims. *Stick with your own kind in life, and you won't get into trouble.*

So Diane's parents had been left to bring up Diane's baby daughter. Daughter, singular.

Well, obviously the next step was to find out if there was any truth to Seth's claim that she had siblings. It shouldn't be too difficult. Everyone left a paper trail.

Everyone left a paper trail except, it seemed, the Amish. A frustrating half hour later, Chloe had become thoroughly annoyed at what seemed the Amish gift for staying off the grid. It was almost as if they had something to hide.

Finally she found what she was looking for. Not even the Amish could elude the government's desire to register births. She was staring at the screen when Kendra came back in, carrying a plastic sandwich container.

Kendra put the sandwich container on the desk. "I was going to bring this in earlier, but you looked so absorbed I didn't want to interrupt. Did you find it?"

Chloe nodded slowly and turned the monitor so that Kendra could see it. "I wouldn't have believed it possible that my grandmother could lie to me about something so important, but there it is. Eli and Diane Weaver had two other children —Lydia, the person Seth Miller spoke of, who is four years older than me, and Susanna, two years older."

Chloe drove her fingers into her hair, as if in that way she could shake some order into her chaotic thoughts. How could her grandmother have done this to her? Surely she'd realized that Chloe would find out eventually. What right did she or anyone have to keep information like this from the person it most concerned?

Face grave, Kendra swung the screen back to her. "I'm not sure what I'd feel in your position. What are you going to do about this, now that you know?"

Chloe picked up the business card. "I guess I'll be getting in touch with Seth Miller again after all. But first . . ." She sucked in a breath, trying to still the quaking that had begun deep inside her. "First I have to find out why my grandmother lied to me."

Chapter Six

Lydia emerged from the orchard and headed across the yard toward Emma Miller's farmhouse. With the boys at school for a few more hours and Adam out making the rounds of people who might be able to offer him a job, she'd found she couldn't wait any longer to find out if Seth had called with a report yet. He'd promised her he'd leave a message on his mother's answering machine, and surely he would have seen Chloe by now.

Amish didn't ordinarily have phones in their homes, considering them a distraction from work and family. But with Emma's slow recovery from her broken hip and Jessie's bouts of emotional problems, Seth had insisted and the bishop had agreed.

But Emma had done some insisting of her own, which was like her. A strong woman, not to be defeated by a broken hip, she'd determined that the phone shanty would be at the end of the back porch, no closer.

Her lips quirking at the memory, Lydia paused at the phone shanty and peeked inside. The telephone sat silent, and the battery-powered answering machine showed no new messages.

"Lydia, I thought you would be here this afternoon. Looking to hear from my son, ja?"

Emma had opened the back door and was smiling at her through the screen.

"Seth hasn't called yet?" Lydia tried to conceal her disappointment but feared she wasn't doing a very good job.

"Not yet." Emma held the screen door open and motioned her in. "Komm. Have some coffee. Seth said he would call this afternoon whether he managed to talk to your little sister or not, and you can count on him."

Nodding, Lydia stepped inside. "I'm certain-sure he'll do as he said." One thing you could say about Seth—he did what he said he'd do. His trouble had been that what he said he'd do wasn't usually what the Ordnung decreed.

"You are still upset about what you learned about your family, ja?"

Emma's keen eyes scanned Lydia's face as she led the way to the table. Emma still limped a bit, and the lines on her face told of the pain she suffered, but she wasn't one to give in. Even now, the old-fashioned kitchen with its plank floors and simple wooden cabinets smelled of cinnamon and sugar.

"Just a little," Lydia admitted. "But I don't want to interrupt your baking—"

"Ach, it's nothing. Some snickerdoodles for the grandchildren is all. Naomi is bringing them over to visit later." She seized the coffeepot, ready on the stove, and began to pour.

"That's so nice. You'll be wonderful glad to see Joshua and Sadie." Lydia slid into a seat, knowing it gave Emma pleasure to have a guest to chat with.

"For sure. Naomi brings them every week. She's a gut mamm to them, that's certain, and a gut wife to Nathan." Emma's eyes held sorrow, and Lydia knew it was for her eldest daughter, Ada, the children's birth mother, who hadn't lived to see her offspring grow.

"Is Jessie here?" Lydia couldn't help a twinge of apprehension. She had been instrumental in the discovery that Emma's youngest daughter was so unstable she'd needed hospitalization, and Lydia didn't suppose Jessie had ever forgiven her for that act, although she never mentioned it.

"She had a doctor's appointment today." Emma set coffee mugs and a plate with thick slices of fruit-and-nut bread on the table and sat down. "Usually Seth takes her in his car, but this time he made arrangements with an Englisch driver."

Lydia accepted a slice of the molasses-rich bread when Emma shoved the plate toward her. "How is Jessie doing?"

"Improving, I think, since the doctor started her on some new medicine. I hope so, anyway. Sometimes it is hard to tell." Emma leaned toward her, her gaze intent. "But how are you? The truth, now, nothing else."

"I don't know." That was the truth, if anything was. "I can see Mamm and Daad think they did the right thing by not telling me about my sisters, even though they've said how sorry they are."

"All parents struggle with deciding what is best for their kinder." Emma seemed to look beyond Lydia, maybe into her own life, which had certainly had its share of trouble.

"Everyone agrees I shouldn't upset Susanna by revealing the truth when her adoptive mother is so ill. And Adam . . . well, he doesn't like the idea of trying to get in touch with my Englisch sister. We don't often disagree, but I just don't understand his attitude." She couldn't help the tiny edge that showed in her voice.

"Maybe he's afraid you're going to get hurt," Emma said gently. "He's protective of you. Your birth daad was that way with your mamm."

Lydia's breath caught at the unexpected tidbit of information. "You knew them well, ja?"

"As well as neighbors usually do," Emma said. She seemed to look back through the years. "I was a bit shy of them at first, I remember, knowing that Diane had been Englisch, but she soon made me feel comfortable. And she learned Pennsylvania Dutch so quick it was hard to believe she hadn't always spoken it."

The language was one of the biggest hurdles for someone wanting to become Amish, Lydia felt sure. If you weren't comfortable in the language people used with each other, it would be near-impossible to feel at home.

"It seems so odd to think that my mamm was raised Englisch," she admitted. "Did she ever talk about her family?"

Emma shook her head. "Not much. It was like she wanted to forget that part of her life ever existed. And she was so in love with your daad it warmed my heart just to look at them."

"That's nice to know." Lydia's heart seemed to warm, as well.

Emma gave a faint, faraway smile. "She was crazy about you girls, too. I mind seeing her under that big old tree in the middle of the orchard. Sometimes she'd bring out a blanket and put the baby on it. Sometimes she'd sit on that low limb with you and Susanna next to her, telling you stories."

Lydia stored the memory up, realizing that it was much the same as the image Mamm had given her. Obviously Diane had loved that spot in the orchard, just as she did.

"It seems strange to think of her living the way we do, with her having been raised in the city and all. She must have had a lot to learn, not just about living Amish but living on a farm, too."

"Ach, ja. Many's the laugh we had when I showed her how to make apple butter or can jelly. But she loved every minute of it."

"I'm glad to know that, even if I can't remember

it for myself." The loss of her early memories was like a splinter sticking into her, always there, always hurting just a little.

Emma reached across to pat Lydia's hand. "You must never think Diane had regrets about the life she chose with your daad, because she didn't. She seldom spoke of her parents, and as far as I know, they never got in touch with her."

"I'm glad she was happy." Lydia blinked quickly, not wanting to let a tear get away from her. "It seems so odd, though, that her parents didn't try to be part of her life."

And given that apparently bitter separation, it wondered her that Mrs. Wentworth had even wanted to take Chloe.

"I mind Diane saying something once about her mother," Emma said slowly. "She said that all her life she'd known she had to live up to what her mother expected, and if she couldn't, then she wasn't worth loving. It made Diane determined never to let any of you girls doubt her love for you. She was a fine mother to you girls, even though she had such a short time."

Lydia was glad to have that knowledge of her mother, but in a way it made her more apprehensive about her grandmother. That woman had had the raising of Chloe, and who could guess how such a person might have affected a child?

The telephone's ringing jerked her upright, and in an instant she was out of her chair. She hesitated, glancing at Emma, who smiled and waved her hand.

"Go on. It'll be Seth, calling for you, like as not. You might as well answer."

Lydia raced out to the phone shanty, fearful that he'd hang up before she got there, snatched the receiver, and said hello rather breathlessly.

"Lydia?" Seth sounded alarmed to hear her. "Is my mother all right?"

"Ja, ja, she's fine," Lydia assured him. Naturally he'd be surprised at her answering his mamm's phone. "We were visiting, and she knew you'd be calling to tell me what you'd found."

"Of course." His voice seemed to deepen. "You want to hear how my meeting with Chloe turned out."

"You saw her, then?" She tried in vain to control her excitement. "How did she look? What did she say when you told her?"

"She looked fine. Like her photo, only not so dressed up, since she was at work. As for her reactions . . . well, that wasn't so good, I'm afraid. She didn't believe me."

"Didn't believe you?" In all the imagining she'd done about Chloe, it seemed that response had never occurred to her. "But why wouldn't she believe it? Why would she think you'd lie to her?"

"At first she thought I had made a mistake," Seth said. "But when I insisted I hadn't, she thought I was trying to get something from her."

Lydia's mind must be working very slowly, because she couldn't seem to figure that out. "I don't understand. What could you get from her? You were trying to tell her the truth about her background."

"She didn't see it that way. I suppose when you have as much money as her grandmother does, you start expecting people to try to trick you out of it." His voice seemed to change, as if the answer had hurt him as much as it hurt her. "I'm sorry, Lydia. I really thought I could convince her."

"It's not your fault." She had to say the words, even though all she wanted was to let go and weep. "I know you tried your best."

"She may still change her mind. I left the documents with her, along with my card. She might look at them and decide to give me a call."

Lydia held the receiver tight against her ear for a long moment, trying to assess the emotion in his voice. "Tell me the truth, Seth. Do you think that's likely?"

Seth hesitated in his turn. "I don't want to hold out false hope, Lydia. She seemed pretty determined. I'm afraid we've reached a dead end. I'm sorry."

"It's all right." She had to struggle to swallow the lump in her throat. "I'd rather hear the truth, even when it hurts." So that was it, then. As Seth had said, it was a dead end.

• • •

As luck would have it, Chloe walked in the back door of the Wentworth house in Chestnut Hill, coming from the garage, just as she heard her grandmother entering the front door. Margaret Wentworth declined to drive herself in city traffic, instead calling a car service when she went out, and no doubt she had just returned from one of her many civic meetings.

Chloe had moved back into the family home when she finished grad school, partly because her grandmother had so clearly wanted it and partly because, until she decided that the position at the Pennsylvania German Cultural Museum was going to work out, she hated to invest in an apartment. Soon, she promised herself. Maybe the job wasn't perfect, but the Wentworth name had eased her into a better position than she'd have found elsewhere in her crowded chosen field.

She walked through the dining room and into the tiled entrance hall that was as cool and traditional as her grandmother. Gran turned at the sound of her footsteps.

"You're home early today, Chloe. I should have been as well, if not for the tendency of some library board members to argue over every issue." She frowned slightly, touching the elegant waves of her white hair. "We should have known better than to have invited so many newcomers to participate in board meetings." Gran made it sound as if the newcomers were the equivalent of a band of Viking marauders.

"I'm sure you straightened it out." Chloe had something more important than the travails of the library board on her mind.

"Of course." Her grandmother looked slightly surprised, as if the comment were unnecessary. Naturally she had straightened it out.

"I'd like to talk with you, Gran." And the sooner the better, before the wave of righteous indignation she was riding ebbed and she resorted to hiding her emotions, as she so often did when it came to a confrontation with her grandmother.

"Can it wait, dear?" Gran was already turning toward the stairs. "I have to dress for the Food for Africa dinner this evening, something you should be attending as well."

It had never seemed quite appropriate to Chloe to join a group of people who'd never gone hungry in their lives and dine on filet mignon while listening to stories of the malnourished, but she knew better than to say so if she wanted to get to the subject that was uppermost in her mind.

"Now, please. This is important, Gran."

That earned her a raised eyebrow. "More important than your charitable responsibilities? Really, Chloe, your priorities should—"

"I found out about my sisters today," Chloe said, her voice coming out breathless and weaker than she would have liked. "Why did you hide that information from me?"

Her grandmother didn't blink. She stiffened, that was all, as if taking a blow she hadn't seen coming.

"Really, Chloe." She repeated the two words she so often used when she considered her granddaughter to be unreasonable. No weakness showed in those syllables. Obviously her grandmother was made of tougher fiber than Chloe was. "Such dramatic language is not necessary. I didn't hide the information. I simply didn't feel it necessary to tell you."

"Not necessary?" A sudden spurt of anger strengthened her tone. Gran was acting as if this were as simple as not mentioning that the newspaper hadn't been delivered. "I had a right to know that I had two sisters."

"You were a baby when you came to us. You were hardly of an age to remember your sisters or anyone else from your earlier life." Gran put her leather handbag on the marble-topped stand in the hall, looking into the rococo mirror above it to check her appearance.

Chloe clenched her teeth. "I haven't been a baby in a long time, Gran. You should have told me."

"To what end?" Gran turned toward her, her face as cool and controlled as that of a marble carving. "I assumed that when you were old enough to understand, you'd try to find out. If you didn't, then perhaps it didn't mean enough to you."

It was a neat way of putting the blame on Chloe, but she wasn't accepting it. "Why would I try to find out when I didn't know anything about it? I thought I could trust what you told me about my past."

"You ought to trust me. I've taken care of you since you were a baby." Her grandmother's voice became tart as her detachment slipped ever so slightly. "There was nothing to be gained by involving you with those people. They certainly wouldn't welcome any overtures from you."

That cool certainty was annoying. "How do you know? My sisters might be looking for me."

One of them was, at least. Somehow Chloe wasn't sure she wanted to tell her grandmother about Seth Miller's visit. Maybe she was being overly cautious, but if her grandmother could keep a secret, so could she.

Her grandmother waved her hand, as if to dismiss the idea. "I doubt that very much. They're Amish, and the Amish don't mix with people like us, people who live in the normal world." She moved toward the stairs. "We'll talk about this another time, when you're calmer."

Ninety-nine times out of a hundred, Chloe would accept being put off, maybe because she'd been told so emphatically that her rebellious mother had broken her parents' hearts, and she hadn't wanted to do the same. She'd confined her rebellion to going out of state for grad school and dressing in a manner that clearly pained her grandmother. But she began to think Diane might have had some justification for her actions.

"You took me home from the hospital. Why didn't you take my sisters? Given everything you've said about the Amish luring my mother into their lifestyle, I should think you'd have wanted all three of us."

Gran stopped on the first step, hand resting on the intricately carved cherry newel post. She sighed, as if giving in to the unreasonable.

"When I received the news of the accident, I went at once to the hospital where you'd been taken. No one was there with you. The other girls were in different hospitals, and they were already surrounded by the Amish relatives. There was nothing I could do."

Chloe might buy that if not for the fact that she'd never known her grandmother to accept the idea that there was nothing she could do about any issue. "But if the Amish are all that you've said, how could you just leave them there? They were Diane's daughters, too."

Gran gripped the post, her eyes veiled. Then, as if giving in, she shrugged. "Very well, if you must have it. The reason I didn't attempt to gain custody of the other two is that they were older. They'd already been too influenced by their parents. After all your grandfather and I went through with your mother, I had no desire to repeat the experience." Her lips compressed on the words.

Chloe was speechless. Her grandmother had dismissed a five-year-old and a three-year-old from her life because of their parents' influence? She couldn't find the words to express her mixed feelings.

"But you . . ." Her grandmother's face softened. "You were a new opportunity. A chance for us to raise you properly and to counteract what Diane might have done. Can't you understand that we did it because we loved you the minute we saw you?"

She couldn't, but she also couldn't ignore the genuine feeling in her grandmother's face. It was there, slipping through the facade, and Margaret Wentworth didn't show emotion easily. Chloe's heart twisted.

"I know you love me, Gran." Her throat tightened. "And I love you."

"Good. I realize you're upset now, but believe me, you'll forget all this in a few days."

Chloe nearly agreed, just because she was so used to doing so and because she couldn't bear to be at odds with her only family. But this time she couldn't.

"I'm sorry, Gran, but I can't pretend this didn't happen. I can't."

Her grandmother stiffened. "You're determined

to find out about those people, I suppose. I can't stop you. But I can tell you this—it will end in heartache." She turned away in dismissal and went slowly up the stairs, her back straight, her head held high.

Chloe pressed her hand against her stomach, which seemed to be tying itself in knots over her temerity. Well, she'd stood up to her grandmother, but she wasn't sure what she was going to do next, except that it seemed certain she'd be seeing Seth Miller again.

Adam walked toward the strawberry patch in late afternoon, the two boys darting ahead and then running back to him like a couple of puppies. Most of the day had been wasted, it seemed, in going from one possible employer to the next, from one end of Pleasant Valley to the other.

The story was the same everywhere. Folks were sorry; they'd like to be taking on new workers, but business wasn't good enough. Maybe in another month they'd be able to hire.

Another month, and in the meantime, what was he to do? Plenty of work for him waited around the farm, for sure, but most of it wouldn't bring in money, at least not right away.

The Lord will provide. It's God's will.

The answers that should comfort him didn't seem to be having that effect. He should provide for his family.

Daniel grabbed his hand. "Is it time to uncover the strawberry plants yet, Daadi? It's been getting pretty warm, ain't so?"

"I want to do it," David said instantly. "Let me help, too."

"We'll have a look at them and see how they're doing." Adam put his hand on Daniel's shoulder for a moment. It was good that the boys took such an interest in the farm. "Even though it's been warm, we could still have a frost, you know," he cautioned.

Daniel nodded solemnly. "Can I uncover one plant? Just to see if it's growing?"

"Me, too," David said quickly, squatting down next to the straw-covered bed.

"You always say that." Daniel's expression turned a bit mulish. "I thought of it first."

Adam tapped him lightly on top of his straw hat. "Your little bruder wants to do what you do, ja? That's how it goes with brothers."

A memory slid into his mind, unbidden, of himself and Benjamin at about the same ages Daniel and David were now. He'd want to be doing something by himself with Daad, but Benjamin always pushed in. He'd been short with his brother more times than he could count, and the guilt that accompanied that thought was bitter.

He should have been more patient. He should have provided the understanding and guidance Benjamin needed. He'd take it all back in an instant if he could, but nobody got to live their lives over again.

"Daadi? Was ist letz?" Daniel was staring at him. He must have let his face show too much of his thoughts.

"Nothing's wrong." Adam squatted between the boys. Then, because he tried always to be honest with them, he added, "I was just remembering what it was like when my little bruder followed me around."

"Onkel Benjamin, you mean? The one who went away to be Englisch and never came back?"

"Ja." He put a reassuring hand on the boy's shoulder. He'd rather his sons didn't know about Benjamin, but maybe it was best that they saw how much it hurt the family when one person jumped the fence. And he'd certain-sure seen the results of keeping secrets in this trouble over Lydia's sisters.

Best to focus on the here and now. He bent over, pulling back some of the straw he'd put over the berry patch last fall.

"See, there is a plant, nice and green and ready to grow." He touched a tiny green leaf. "I think in a few days, if the weather is still warm, we'll pull the straw off so the plants can get some sun."

"But what if it frosts?" Daniel said. He was always a bit of a worrier.

"We'll leave the straw here, between the plants, so we can pull it back over like a blanket if the weather turns bad. If not, it will keep the weeds from coming up and choking the plants."

Daniel nodded solemnly. David, his attention waning, was already back on his feet.

"I see a blossom in the orchard!" he shouted. "I do, I see one!" He set off running, and Daniel followed, overtaking him easily.

Adam followed more slowly, his gaze on his sons, and worry crept out of hiding again. They were his responsibility, his and Lydia's. This was the life he wanted for them, living close to the land, living simply, obedient to God's teachings. If he could find work, even part-time, that would help to keep their lives the way they were.

Well, if not, they'd get along for a time. His family and Lydia's would help, though he hated to ask it of them. And this land and the orchard belonged to them free and clear, thanks to Lydia's birth parents.

He reached the boys, who stood staring up into the branches of the big tree in the center of the orchard. David was pointing.

"See, right there. That blossom is opening."

"I think you're right," Adam said. "It's the first one, but the others will soon start to follow."

"Mammi loves it when the trees are covered with blossoms," Daniel said. "That will make her happy again."

Adam turned to the boy, scanning his face. "Again? Is Mammi not happy today?" He'd not gone back to the house when he'd gotten back from his job hunt, because the boys had distracted him.

"Daniel made Mammi sad," David piped up.

"Did not." Daniel turned on his brother furiously. "You take that back." He gave David a shove before Adam could intervene.

Adam grabbed a boy in each hand, startled at how quickly the quarrel had blown up. The boys usually got along well, better than most brothers, he'd say.

"Stop now," he said. Lydia's sorrow probably had more to do with those sisters of hers than with anything the boys had done. "Quarreling doesn't make anything better. If Mammi is sad, it's our job to make her happy again, ain't so?"

"Ja, Daadi," they chorused, and Daniel hung his head.

"Gut." He pulled both boys against him in a quick hug as he spotted movement on the back porch. "Mammi is coming now, I think. What can you do to make her feel better?"

"I saw some violets back by the springhouse," Daniel said. "Komm, schnell. We'll pick some for her."

Their quarrel forgotten, the two of them raced off. He smiled a little. If only all their problems were solved as easily. He thought of Benjamin again, and his heart twisted inside him.

"Where did the boys run off to?" Lydia

reached him, and he saw the sadness behind her welcoming smile.

"They are getting something for you, so when they come back you must be surprised." He drew her against him, almost afraid to ask the question. "Has something happened?"

Lydia leaned her head against his shoulder. "I spoke to Seth earlier. He called the telephone at his mother's place while I was there."

It probably wasn't a coincidence that she'd been there to take the call, but Adam let that pass. "What did he say?"

"He talked to her . . . to my little sister. He went to the place where she works." Lydia paused, staring out across the valley as if she'd look beyond it to the distant city. "He said it didn't go well. She didn't want to believe what he told her. Or maybe she just doesn't care. He said that he left the papers with her, and maybe she'd get in touch with him, but I could tell he didn't think so."

A tear sparkled on Lydia's cheek, and Adam's heart twisted again with pain. He put his arms around her, holding her close, his cheek pressing against her hair.

"I'm sorry." He tried to find the words to comfort her, but he couldn't, and it made him feel helpless. And a bit angry at Seth, who'd given Lydia this hope and then snatched it away. "I hate to see you hurting over this. I wish your great-aunt had never spoken."

"Don't say that." Lydia pulled back a little. "I would rather know the truth, even if finding my sisters doesn't turn out the way I hoped. Wouldn't you?"

"Ja, I guess so." He'd best be a little cautious. It wouldn't do to let Lydia know that he actually felt a bit relieved.

She was hurting now, but it would get better. Maybe she wouldn't ever forget that she had a sister out there in the world someplace, but she'd get over her sadness and their lives would go on.

He leaned against the trunk of the apple tree, studying her face. "The boys spotted something that will cheer you up. Look, the first blossom is opening."

Lydia tilted her head back, staring up into the branches of the tree, amazement replacing the sadness in her face. "Ach, I should have known this tree would be the first."

"For sure. It's a special tree, ja?" He took her hands. "I kissed you for the first time under this tree, remember?" He wouldn't be forgetting. The Amish took smooching seriously, and a guy didn't go around kissing girls, not until he found the one he thought he'd spend his life with.

"I remember." She squeezed his hands, smiling so that her dimple showed. "You were so nervous I thought you'd miss my lips entirely."

"I hadn't had enough practice." He grinned, drawing her closer. "I do better now."

"Adam Beachy, you can't be kissing your wife right out here where anyone can see," she protested.

"There's no one around to see." He stole a quick kiss, and her lips were as sweet as they'd been that first time.

But when they drew apart, she glanced up into the tree again, and there was something in her gaze that seemed to put her far away.

"Emma told me something about my mamm, about how she loved this tree. She liked to sit on the low branch and tell stories to us girls."

"That's a happy thing to know, ain't so?" He wasn't sure what her expression was saying, and it troubled him.

Lydia's face tightened. "I wish I could remember it, not just hear about it from someone else. I would like to stand here someday with my sisters and tell them about it, and I'm afraid I never will."

He didn't know what to say. The storm wasn't over, and it seemed he could almost see her younger sisters, standing between him and his Lydia.

Chapter Seven

Chloe arrived at the coffee shop where she'd arranged to meet Seth Miller well ahead of the appointed time, selecting a booth against the far wall, away from both the door and the kitchen. She didn't want this conversation to be overheard, not that it was likely this late in the afternoon. The shop was nearly empty, with only one table occupied by a pair of older women who began gathering their shopping bags together even as Chloe sat down.

Good. She gave an order for tea to a bored-looking waitress and leaned back, trying to compose her thoughts. *Get a grip, Chloe.* She'd been feeling like a scull adrift on the river since that conversation with her grandmother. It was time to regain control, preferably before she encountered Seth Miller again.

Their previous meeting at the museum had degenerated into a blur of words and emotions. This time she would be calm, cool, and in charge. Despite the fact that the man's credentials had checked out, she had no intention of letting down her guard with him.

The server brought her tea, setting the mug down with a disgruntled clunk. Maybe she figured the amount of tip she'd receive for a single cup of tea was hardly worth the bother. Chloe sugared, stirred, and wrapped her hands around the mug, finding its warmth soothing. Despite the late afternoon sunshine radiating from the sidewalks, a chill had settled deep inside her, someplace where even the tea couldn't reach.

Seth had sounded surprised to hear her voice when she called. Natural enough, since she'd thrown him out of her office, something that was probably a first for the museum's staid premises. Maybe she should . . .

The thought drizzled away as she spotted him striding across the street toward her. He moved quickly—he'd be here in a moment, and she wanted a chance to see him before he saw her.

Light brown hair, stylishly cut, glinted gold where the sun hit it. He'd probably been blond as a child. He moved well, was lithe and athletic-looking, and his suit was the rising-young-executive type she saw every day on the street.

He loomed for a moment outside the glass door and then he was there, his gaze zeroing in on her across the room. His determined footsteps suggested a man headed straight for what he wanted, regardless of obstacles in his way, an impression strengthened by his square jaw and the intensity of his slate-colored eyes.

"Ms. Wentworth." He paused at the table, his look wary, reflecting the way they'd parted.

"Please, sit down." She was satisfied with the

coolness of her tone. He didn't need to know how off-balance she felt. "Thank you for meeting me."

"My pleasure." He slid into the booth opposite her.

The server approached, a little more quickly this time, and accepted Seth's order for coffee with a smile instead of a sigh. Amazing, the effect of a good-looking male.

"I take it you've done some investigating of your own," he said.

"What makes you say that?" she parried, not sure she wanted him knowing how thoroughly she'd checked into his bona fides.

"Why else would you get in touch with me?" His smile provided more warmth than the tea had.

Be careful, she reminded herself. A charming smile would be his best asset if he was trying to put something over on her.

"Yes, I did. You appear to be who you claim to be."

He lifted an eyebrow. "I suppose I should say thanks."

She made a gesture of dismissal. "You can hardly blame me for being cautious when someone turns up out of the blue and claims to know something about me I don't know myself."

"No." His eyes grew serious. "I don't blame you. It must have been quite a shock, hearing you have two sisters. I assume you confirmed that, as well?"

"I found their birth records." She hesitated, but he'd no doubt guessed what she'd do. "And I spoke to my grandmother. She told me it was true." If the words sounded as if they'd been chipped out of ice, she couldn't help it.

His coffee arrived, the server lingering until Chloe gave her a frosty look. Seth glanced at his cup, then hers.

"I see you like tea. Your sister Lydia always drinks tea in the afternoon. She says she can't have coffee keeping her awake when she has to get up early."

Chloe wasn't sure how she felt about being compared to this unknown sister. She eyed Seth cautiously. Apparently he knew Lydia well, by the sound of it.

"You're a friend of my . . . of Lydia's, I take it?"

If he noticed she'd changed that sentence in midstream, he didn't give any indication. "My mother lives right next door to her now. We're the same age, more or less, and we grew up in the same small community."

She had a sense of something left unsaid—something that perhaps she should probe. "But you don't live there now, do you? Your work must take you elsewhere."

Seth stared down at the black coffee as if it held a secret. "I left when I was eighteen. I hadn't been back much until the past few months, when . . ." His frown deepened. "Some family matters came up that needed my attention, so I've been in Pleasant Valley between business trips. I telecommute, except for a few days a month at the home office in Chicago."

"You make telecommuting sound so natural."

"It is, isn't it?" He raised an eyebrow, and she thought he relaxed a hair now that they were talking about business instead of his family.

"Not in my work. I can't authenticate a piece of eighteenth-century folk art unless I can see it." To say nothing of touch it and sometimes smell it as well. The genuine article had a quality that came through when she held it in her hands.

He nodded, as if accepting her words whether he understood what she did or not. "In that case, you'll have to see Lydia in person."

"What?" She hadn't expected that, and maybe she should have. "Why do you say that?"

"Isn't that how you authenticate things?" His lips quirked, and she realized he was laughing at her. Kendra looked at her that way, too, sometimes, just before she reminded Chloe that everything in life didn't have to be authenticated before you could enjoy it.

She couldn't help smiling in return, but . . .

"I don't think that's necessary. You can tell me about her. Is she married?"

The laughter still lurked in his gray-blue eyes, but he nodded. "To Adam Beachy. They've been sweethearts since they were teenagers. They have two little boys, Daniel and David, who must be about eight and six. Cute kids."

Her thoughts seemed to get stuck on those two little boys. Nephews. She had two young nephews. In an ordinary life she'd have known them since birth, have been buying them birthday presents and taking them to the zoo. She should have had that chance.

"Why did she wait so long to try and find me?"

"You didn't know . . . well, you wouldn't, I guess. Lydia was injured in the accident. Apparently all of you were, in fact. She had a serious head injury, and she was unconscious for a long time. When she did recover, she didn't remember anything of her life before the accident. The aunt and uncle who took her in told her about her parents, but I guess they figured that was enough for her to bear."

"I see." She did, in a way. Lydia would have been old enough to remember her parents, had the accident not wiped out her memories. How did a person cope with that knowledge? "When did she find out she had sisters?"

Seth's shoulders moved slightly, as if he was shrugging off something unpleasant. "Lydia just learned a few days ago, by accident. It's disrupted her life in all kinds of ways."

"Yes." She understood that, didn't she? "What about the other sister? Susanna?"

"She was taken in by another couple. I under-

151

stand, from what I've heard, that she was raised to believe they were her parents."

Chloe's hands tightened on the mug. So many secrets. Too many. "She should be told. If Lydia knows how to find her, why hasn't she told her?" Chloe needed to be angry with somebody . . . anybody. None of this was fair.

Seth looked faintly harassed. "Look, I don't have all the answers. I'm just the messenger. What you need to do is come to Pleasant Valley and talk to Lydia yourself."

A wave of something that might be revulsion went through her. "No. I can't . . . I don't want to go there." Her mother had become involved with those people, and as far as Gran was concerned, they were responsible for her death. Whatever her grandmother had done, Chloe couldn't seem to shake off her beliefs easily. "Why can't Lydia come here?"

"It's not as easy as that for an Amish person. She'd have to come by bus or arrange for a driver, and she's never been to a city." Seth's tone was that of someone explaining the ABCs to a child. "I doubt her husband would like it if she traveled that far, and there are the two little boys to think of. She wouldn't want to leave them."

"You could drive her." After all, he'd driven here today, hadn't he?

"Her husband would like that even less," he said, his voice dry.

"And I suppose she has to do what he says, as if she were living in the seventeenth century." Was that what life had been like for her mother, giving up her independence to become one of them? The anger that had been bubbling under the surface spurted through. "Maybe my grandmother is right about the Amish. She says they're little better than a cult."

Seth's face tightened, suddenly bleak and forbidding. "Your grandmother doesn't know what she's talking about, and it sounds as if you're no better. Are you always that intolerant of other people's religious beliefs?"

"I'm not intolerant. But my grandmother said—"

"Your grandmother's the one who told you a pack of lies about your family," he interrupted. "Are you sure she's a reliable source?"

Chloe experienced a strong desire to throw something at him—so strong it appalled her.

She took a deep breath. "I don't want to go to Pleasant Valley." Her mother had gone there, had gotten sucked into a life that wasn't her own. She had died.

Seth seemed to be making an effort of his own to regain control. He gave a short nod. "All right. You don't want to go there. What about meeting Lydia on a neutral site? There are a couple of nearby towns she could get to without much difficulty."

"I . . . I don't know." Meeting Lydia was the logical next step. Why was she so reluctant to take it?

He studied her, his gaze so intent she could almost feel it, as if he were touching her skin. Finally he nodded.

"Okay. Think about it. You have my card. If you decide you want me to arrange a meeting, let me know. I'll give Lydia your address. She'll probably want to write to you."

Chloe wasn't sure she wanted to receive a letter, but it would be ungracious to say so. Anyway, it was better than a phone call, or having Lydia show up on her doorstep.

"Isn't writing a letter a little archaic?"

His lips curved slightly, drawing her attention to that smile again. "It's an Amish thing. They write a lot of letters." He slid out of the booth, putting several bills on the table.

She picked up her bag. "You seem to know a lot about the Amish."

"I do." Again she had that sense that he was laughing at her. "Didn't you realize? I grew up Amish."

She was probably gaping at him, but he didn't seem to have anything else to say. She watched as he crossed quickly to the door and strode out of the café. And maybe out of her life.

She did still have his card. She could call him again. But doing so would mean involving herself with the sister she'd never imagined having, and she didn't know if she was ready to do so.

Chloe was torn, half of her longing to rush off and find her sister while the other half hung back, clinging to the security of the known. Despite her somewhat bitter words to her grandmother, she wasn't really sure she wanted to open herself up to something that would change her life, for good or ill, in ways she couldn't imagine.

Lydia pulled the tumbling blocks quilt over David, smiling when his busy little body responded to the familiar motion and relaxed under it. Adam was tucking the matching quilt over Daniel in the other twin bed. The boys were growing so quickly. Some days it seemed impossible that they could be eight and six already.

For an instant she felt the familiar ache in her heart for another baby to love, and she tried to chase it away. She and Adam were fortunate to have two strong, healthy boys. When and if another baby came to bless their family was up to God.

"Close your eyes." She smoothed the cornsilk-fine hair back from David's forehead. "Prayers are said, you've heard a story, now it's time for sweet dreams."

"Just one thing," he said, which was usually a prelude to asking for another story.

"One thing," she agreed.

David's face was serious. "Did the violets we picked for you make you happy again?"

The words startled her. "They made me very happy, that's certain-sure." She sent Adam a questioning glance, but his face gave nothing away. "Why would you think I was not happy?"

David's lower lip came out, the way it did when he didn't want to answer.

"Daniel? Did you think that, too?"

Daniel nodded, his face clouding. "You seemed sad today, so we wanted to make you smile. That's all right, isn't it?"

Lydia's throat tightened. She'd never dreamed she was giving away her emotions to the kinder. She should never let adult worries affect her family.

"Ja, of course it's all right. It was a very kind thought, and I love it when my boys are kind." She hesitated, not sure what or how much to tell them.

David tugged at her sleeve. "But why were you sad, Mammi? If it was 'cause I spilled the milk, I'll be really careful next time."

"Ach, no, for sure it wasn't." She bent to hug him, inhaling the sweet, just-bathed little-boy scent. "Everybody spills things sometimes. Spills are for cleaning up, not getting mad about, ja?"

"Ja." But he still looked a bit wary.

She had to tell them something. "It was nothing

about you. Last week I found out something that upset me, that's all."

It wasn't all, of course. They'd never be content with that explanation. She began to have an appreciation for how difficult it had been for Mamm and Daad to decide what to tell her about the accident.

"You see, a long time ago, when I was only five, I was in an accident." How could she tell this without frightening them or making them worry that it might happen to them? "We were on a trip, going to a wedding."

Daniel, propped up on his elbow, nodded. "We know. Grossdaadi told us you got hurt in a crash when your first daad and mamm died. He says that it made you not remember anything from when you were little."

She hadn't known Daad had told them anything, but it sounded as if he'd done a calm, matter-of-fact explanation.

"Well, that's gut that you understand. You see, I found out something from that time in my life I don't remember, and it upset me."

Daniel's face screwed up as he tried to follow the explanation. "It must seem funny, not to remember."

"Most folks don't remember a lot from when they were very little anyway," Adam said, his voice a reassuring bass rumble. "Mammi remembers the important things. Like you." He ruffled Daniel's hair, making him grin and duck away.

"But what made you upset?" Daniel, ever persistent, went quickly back to the point.

She exchanged looks with Adam. He seemed resigned.

"Best they hear it from us, ain't so?" he said.

She nodded. "I found out that I had two little sisters." She tried to keep her voice as calm as if she were talking about the weather. "After the accident we went to live with different families. I went with Grossdaadi and Grossmammi, and they went with other folks. So you see, I didn't remember them."

The boys digested that silently for a few moments, and she waited for the inevitable questions.

"I don't want that to happen to me." David hurled himself against her, and she hugged him tightly.

"You don't need to worry about that," she said firmly. "Something like that almost never happens, and we trust God to take care of us, ja?"

"Are you sad not to remember them, Mammi?" Daniel probably thought himself too big to require an immediate hug, but he leaned against Adam.

"Ja, that's so. And I'm also sad not to know them now."

"Why don't you just go to see them?" Daniel

said, as if surprised that answer hadn't occurred to her.

The truth of that was too complicated to explain, and again she looked at Adam.

"They live too far away," he said firmly. "Maybe someday we'll get to meet them, if it's God's will."

That, finally, seemed to settle it for the boys. It was probably best not to attempt any further explanations unless and until they asked again. She rose, settling the quilt around David again.

"Now, enough talking, I think. Time for dreams."

But Daniel was slipping out of bed.

"Daniel, what are you doing?" Usually he was so obedient.

He dropped to his knees on the hooked rug her mother had made. "I'll say another prayer, Mammi. I'll ask God to let you see your sisters."

She stooped to kiss him, blinking back the tears that filled her eyes. "That is a gut thought, Daniel. Denke."

Adam switched off the lamp, but moonlight washed through the room, touching the kneeling figure. She would not be able to hide the tears much longer, so she hurried out of the room.

Adam followed her, closing the door with a soft click. He turned to look at her. "Are you all right?"

"Ja." She wiped away a tear with her fingers

159

and then clasped his hand. They started down the stairs. "I'm glad you helped me explain. Do you think they are all right knowing that much?"

He nodded. "They are sensible boys. Don't worry about them."

"Ach, I can't help doing the worrying. It comes with being a mammi, I think."

They reached the bottom of the stairs. Lydia turned toward the kitchen and then turned back, realizing she had forgotten something.

"Adam, I never asked you about your day. How did it go, the job hunting?"

He shrugged, his expression not changing. "Nothing yet, but maybe soon. I'll find something. You don't need to worry about me, too."

"I'm not worried." Why would she be? Adam was the most reliable of men, and a gut worker. He'd find something. "I know you'll take care of us like you always do."

He nodded. "Think I'll do a bit in the workshop now."

"I'll finish up in the kitchen. Just tell me if you want some coffee."

The workshop he'd built onto the back of the house was definitely Adam's favorite place. Working with wood was common enough among the Amish, but not many men had his skill in building clocks. She glanced at the kitchen clock that had been a birthday present from him two years ago. He was making another one now, apparently destined for whoever in the family got married next.

Odd that neither of her sisters was married. Did Susanna feel that her limp prevented her from marriage? Maybe someday they'd be able to talk about that, like any two sisters surely would.

And Chloe, the unknown. The Englisch married later than the Amish, she knew that about them. Maybe Chloe had someone in her life. Seth had said she wasn't engaged or married, but she might be seeing someone. Did she feel the lack of a big sister to give her advice?

Trying to shake off the questions, Lydia concentrated on putting the dishes away. Maybe she could have used some advice herself, when she thought of how she'd let the children see her sadness. She longed to talk to Mamm about it, to listen to her wise counsel, but things had been so strained between them that she couldn't imagine bringing it up.

With a last glance around the tidy kitchen, she went into the living room and settled in her chair, picking up the mending basket. She surely didn't lack for mending to do, with two active boys.

Before Lydia had finished mending the rip in David's best pants, she was distracted by a light reflecting from the front windows. She laid aside the mending. Someone was driving a car up the lane.

Going quickly to the kitchen, she called back to the workshop. "Adam? Someone is coming."

The car had stopped by the back porch, and the interior lights came on for a moment, letting her see that it was Seth. Her stomach tightened. She'd just begun to adjust to the bad news he'd given her about Chloe, and now she'd have to relive it. Seth would be feeling sorry he hadn't made a success of the meeting with Chloe, and she'd have to reassure him.

By the time she'd opened the door and ushered Seth into the kitchen, Adam had come in from the workshop. He eyed Seth warily, it seemed to Lydia.

"I didn't expect to see you tonight, Seth." She set the coffeepot on the stove and got out the dried-apple pie she'd made earlier.

"I just got back, and I wanted to let you know what happened." Seth looked more cheerful than she'd expected after what he'd said on the telephone.

"Ja, you told me on the phone." Her little sister wasn't interested in her. Or she didn't believe in her, which came to the same thing.

"I know, but something happened after I called." He took the cup she handed him, nodding his thanks. "Chloe called me again later. She wanted to talk."

"She did?" Dropping the knife she'd held poised over the pie, Lydia clasped her hands together in

162

what was close to a prayer. "What did she say? Did she believe you?"

Adam moved past her, pouring coffee for himself and sitting down, his movements deliberate. He watched Seth, his expression giving no clue to his thoughts.

"Apparently she had followed through on the materials I left with her," Seth said. "She confronted her grandmother, and the grandmother admitted the story was true."

"What did she want from you, then?" Adam asked.

Seth's gaze flickered from Adam to her. "More information, basically. She wanted to know what I knew about her sisters. She didn't know, of course, about your loss of memory, and all she knew about your parents was what her grandmother had told her."

He hesitated, and Lydia found herself tensing as if she were preparing for a blow.

"What is it? Something bad?" Seth never had been very good at hiding his feelings from her.

"The grandmother apparently is very prejudiced about the Amish. She blames the faith for luring her daughter away."

"But . . . that's foolishness. Diane fell in love with my father, that's why she wanted to become Amish."

"I understand that, but as I say, Chloe only knows what her grandmother has told her. At least now she's questioning what her grandmother said about your parents. I told her what I knew about them, and also about you and Adam and the children."

Lydia nodded, trying to absorb everything. "Did you ask her about coming to visit me? What did she say?"

Seth shook his head, his lips pressing together. "I'm sorry, Lydia. She wasn't willing to come here, even though I told her that the answers she wants are here."

"But . . . you mean she just wants to forget?" She hadn't been able to tell Susanna, and that still grieved her. She'd thought that surely, once Chloe knew, it would be only a short step to their meeting.

Adam cleared his throat. "Maybe it's for the best. If the woman has bad feelings toward the Amish—"

"Don't call her 'the woman,' " Lydia snapped, her temper flaring. "She is my sister. Surely she only needs to meet us and she'll understand the truth."

"You heard Seth. She's not willing to, and there's nothing else you can do. You must let it go, Lydia."

"I can't." Why didn't he see that about her? She had always thought she and Adam understood each other so completely, but on this subject, Adam seemed to have a blind spot.

"There is one thing you could do." Seth had turned wary, but he slid a piece of paper across the table to her. "There is her address. You can write to her, at least."

She took up the slip of paper, not looking at Adam. "Denke, Seth. I appreciate all you've done."

He nodded. "I wish it could have been more." He pushed his chair back, rising. "I'll be on my way, then. Let me know if there's anything else I can do."

Lydia nodded, feeling the power of Adam's disapproval flowing right across the table at her. "I will. Denke."

She walked him to the door and stood there until he'd gotten into his car. Then she turned back to Adam. The width of the kitchen separated them, and something more, as well.

"I thought you understood how important this is to me." She threw the words at him.

His chair scraped the floor as he stood. "Ja, I know. But I think it is a mistake to get too close to the Englisch."

"Which Englisch? Seth? My sister? Or are you talking about my mother?" She'd never felt so distant from him. "My own mother was Englisch, remember?"

"I know. If she were not, we wouldn't be in this situation." He shook his head, looking stubborn and frustrated at the same time. Then he stalked back to the workshop and closed the door.

Chapter Eight

Chloe had expected that as the days passed, the revelation about her sisters would cease to shake the foundations of her life. Unfortunately, it had been nearly a week, and she still felt edgy and distracted. The letter she'd received from Lydia the previous day just confused her more.

Chloe should be concentrating on her proposal for expanding their educational outreach. Bringing in children and families could also bring new life to this staid old place. But the museum director was less than enthusiastic about the subject, so unless she could wow a sponsor, the project would die an early death.

But instead of focusing on the language that would sway a potential donor, her thoughts kept replaying her conversations with Seth Miller.

Conversation or confrontation? The man seemed to challenge her at every turn. He clearly thought he knew exactly what she should do. As did her grandmother, although their solutions were diametrically opposed.

It was her life. Her decision. Nobody seemed willing to grant that fact.

Giving in to the urge, she clicked out of the proposal folder and opened the one marked Ancestry. Anyone glancing through her files would assume from the title it was something connected with her work at the museum.

Not that anyone else should be accessing her computer, but a museum was just like any other institution, staffed by people who were short on funds and long on ambition, some of them. Infighting was a fact of life.

The folder held everything she now knew about her parents and siblings—what Seth had told her, what her grandmother had said, and the fruits of her own research. Even so, it was pitifully small.

Chloe frowned at the screen. Dozens of questions crowded her mind—questions she should have asked Seth Miller when she'd had the chance. Intent on persuading her to agree with his plans, he'd certainly have told her anything he knew. She'd let the opportunity slip away, partly because she was still in shock, partly because Seth himself kept distracting her from the matter at hand.

Chloe still hadn't wrapped her mind around the fact that Seth had been raised Amish. He looked so . . . normal. The fact explained how he'd come to know so much about her parents, but it raised another set of questions. Why had he left? How did that factor into his motivation in helping Lydia?

She could call Seth. She had his number. She almost reached for the phone, raising an image in her mind of his strong face, of the unexpected laughter in his eyes.

A rap on the office door deferred the decision, somewhat to her relief. "Come in."

The door swung open. Brad Maitland hesitated in the doorway, eyebrows lifting. "Am I interrupting something important?"

"Not at all. Come in." She managed a smile at the family friend, even while she wondered what had brought him here. "Just let me save my work and close it."

Not that she didn't enjoy seeing Brad or, to give him his full title, Bradley Jefferson Maitland, MD, PhD, and, goodness knows what other letters might come after his name. With his tall, lanky frame, his slightly thinning fair hair, narrow well-bred face and oversized glasses, he looked like what he was, a highly successful psychiatrist and member of Philadelphia's elite.

She'd known Brad all her life, and he'd filled the role of honorary uncle perfectly. If his advice always seemed to tally with her grandmother's wishes—well, that was only normal, she supposed. Her grandmother had probably enlisted him for the role, since Chloe had no other uncles.

Or did she? The thought startled her, bringing an image of a cluster of relatives she'd never imagined. She shook off the thought.

"It's nice to see you, Brad. What brings you to the museum, of all places?"

"I happened to be in the area, and I thought perhaps I could persuade you to have lunch with me."

She raised an eyebrow at that comment. Brad never just happened to be anywhere. His entire life ran on a precise schedule, and any deviation, no matter how necessary, was apt to bring a slightly pained expression to his face.

"I wish I could." She spared a moment's regret for the no doubt excellent lunch Brad would have provided. "But I'm tied up with work, so it will be a sandwich at my desk today, I'm afraid."

"That's a shame. Another time, then." He moved slightly as if to get a better look at her computer screen. "Museum work or personal?"

There was nothing judgmental in his tone, but Chloe found herself bristling anyway.

"I suppose my grandmother has been talking with you."

"Margaret and I often speak." He wore the look of patient waiting that so often caused her to tell him more than she wanted.

"About me." She made it a challenge.

"She worries about you. That's understandable, isn't it? You're her only family."

"Not quite true." Her temper slipped a bit, despite her determination not to quarrel with Brad. "If you've spoken with Gran, you know that she has two other granddaughters she's chosen to keep secret from me."

He leaned against the desk, his gaze on her face. "Why do you suppose that is?"

"Because—" Chloe nearly bit her tongue in an effort not to answer. She understood the technique Brad employed. He was attempting to get her to put herself in her grandmother's place. He'd done the same, she remembered, when she was eighteen and wanted to celebrate her high school graduation by going backpacking in Europe.

"Yes?" Brad prompted.

"I appreciate the effort, but I'm not interested in any counseling today, thanks. Gran and I will have to work this out ourselves."

That might be unfair to Brad, who would say he had her best interests at heart, but she didn't like the sense that he'd been conspiring with her grandmother behind her back.

"Of course." He nodded, as if accepting defeat. "It's natural to be upset after learning that you have siblings. I simply thought you might appreciate an unbiased eye on the matter."

"Thanks anyway." She glanced toward her computer, hoping he'd take the hint. Whatever Brad might tell himself, he wasn't truly unbiased, any more than Seth was. Brad stood firmly for the status quo, while Seth challenged her in uncomfortable ways.

"I'll see you on Friday evening, then." Brad headed for the door, leaving her frowning.

"Friday?"

170

"The charity dinner-dance, remember? I'm escorting you and your grandmother."

At Gran's instigation, no doubt. "I'm not sure I'll be going."

The glare she sent his way was intended to express her displeasure at having her social life arranged for her. Unfortunately, it didn't seem to faze Brad. He simply smiled.

"Of course. Whatever you decide. You know I always enjoy your company." He was calm, as if she were a rebellious teen instead of a grown woman who could make her own decisions and her own mistakes.

She sat staring at the door he closed behind him, wondering why Brad was willing to let himself be manipulated by her grandmother into interceding. That was a pattern they'd fallen into long ago, she supposed.

With a perfunctory knock, Kendra burst in. "I almost broke in on you and Dr. Dull a couple of minutes ago. I was afraid you were going to fall for that I'm-only-interested-in-your-welfare act he does so well."

"Listening at the door?" Chloe shook her head in mock despair. "What next?"

"You should be glad I'm nosy. Keeps you on your toes." Kendra handed her a cold bottle of iced tea and uncapped her own, plopping into the folding chair next to the desk. "I missed some of what was said. Dr. Dull was using

171

his soothing voice, darn him. What did he want?"

"I wish you wouldn't call him that." Chloe's protest was halfhearted. Face it, Brad *was* dull, if by that you meant predictable, steady, never changing. "He's a fine person and a family friend."

"You mean he's a good therapist. Just bear in mind he puts your grandmother's interests first."

"I suppose my grandmother did put Brad up to coming. She thought he'd convince me . . ."

"To convince you what?" Kendra prompted when she let that trail off.

Chloe held the cold bottle against her forehead for a moment, as if she could freeze out the tumble of thoughts and doubts. "My grandmother thinks I should accept the fact that my sisters are lost to me and move on. She claimed she wasn't able to gain custody of the other two."

Kendra tilted her head, considering. "I can't see your grandmother failing if that was what she really wanted to do. I mean, really—pitting the Wentworth money and influence against a couple of uneducated Amish farmers? It wouldn't even be a contest."

"No." That was what she'd been thinking, but Kendra had voiced it clearly. "If she'd wanted the other two, she'd have had them. She finally admitted as much. She claimed they were old enough to have already been too influenced by the Amish, but really, they were only five and three.

They'd have forgotten that life in months if she'd gained custody."

"She didn't want a whole family," Kendra said. "She just wanted to replace the daughter she'd lost. You were hardly more than a baby, so she could mold you into the person she wanted you to be. Or at least, she thought she could, discounting other external influences." Kendra grinned, clearly numbering herself among those influences.

Guilt stirred in Chloe. She shouldn't be talking this way about her grandmother. "Gran loves me. And it's true that she was terribly hurt when her daughter ran away."

Kendra shrugged. "There's a difference between running away and choosing your own life. Which was it?"

"I don't know." That numbered chief among the many things she didn't know, and Chloe could only be stunned at herself. "Why didn't I ask questions? Am I really that complacent?"

"Maybe." Kendra grimaced. "And maybe you shouldn't take my word for it. I was born a rebel, but then, I had to be. You still have a chance to find out, don't you?"

"I guess." Chloe reached into her bag and pulled out the letter she'd been carrying around for the past two days. "My sister Lydia wrote to me."

Kendra leaned forward. "What does she say?"

"Read it for yourself." She gave the envelope to Kendra. "I'd like to know what you think."

Kendra held it for a moment. "What did your grandmother say about it?"

"She doesn't know." Chloe threw up her hands. "All right, I'm a chicken. I just didn't want to get into another fight. We're both tiptoeing around each other, being excruciatingly polite."

"Cluck, cluck." Kendra laughed and unfolded the letter.

Chloe didn't need to have the letter in front of her to know what it said. She'd read it so many times she'd practically memorized it.

She'd had the sense that Lydia had written carefully, maybe judging the effect of every word. She was probably as apprehensive about this situation as Chloe was.

What had come through to Chloe on the pages was an image of a woman devoted to the two little boys she described, a woman shocked at the discovery of two sisters she'd never known she had, a woman longing to build a bridge between their lives. Nothing in the short letter seemed off-key or opportunistic.

Lydia had ended with an invitation to come to Pleasant Valley for a visit. *Your sister, Lydia.* Those final words were punctuated by a tiny bubble on the inexpensive tablet paper, as if Lydia had dropped a tear just there.

Kendra folded the letter, slid it into the envelope, and handed it back. "She sounds nice. Not well-educated or sophisticated, just nice. So

174

why are you carrying the letter around instead of answering it?"

Chloe knew what Kendra would have done in her place, but she wasn't Kendra. "I'm not sure it's a good idea to start a relationship with her. We're so completely different. I can't begin to understand why she wants to live the way she does, and I doubt she'd ever understand my life."

Kendra shrugged. "You might be underestimating her. Even the Amish can't be totally disconnected from the modern world, I'll bet. What's the harm in writing? Or even in going to visit?"

"None, I guess. But I can't forget that my mother probably wouldn't have died if she hadn't joined those people."

"Is that according to your grandmother?" Kendra inquired. "Listen, bad things happen to people every day. You could walk outside and get hit by a drunk driver. I admit, I don't get why your mother walked away from a life of privilege to ride in buggies and hang her clothes on a line to dry, but it was her decision. If you really want to understand it, you'll have to go there. You know that as well as I do. So what's holding you back?"

Chloe smiled ruefully. "Does the word *chicken* come to mind?"

"Even chickens can fly, so I've heard," Kendra said.

"Right." Chloe took a deep breath. "So I guess I'll be making a trip sometime soon."

Chloe's first impulse was to call Seth immediately, but she denied it. It would be far better to be prepared for the conversation, ready to suggest a day and a place to meet.

Resorting to the computer again, she looked up maps of the area. There were several larger towns in the vicinity of Pleasant Valley. Bearing in mind Seth's comments about the difficulties the Amish faced in traveling long distances, she narrowed the choices to Lewisburg, Oyersburg, and possibly Mifflinburg. She'd have to ask Seth which would work best.

She could drive to the area on Friday and book a motel room. That would get her out of the dinner-dance on Friday evening very neatly.

Tempting, but she knew Gran would be disappointed if she didn't go with her. Since she was going to be upsetting her grandmother in one rather large way, she may as well try to please her in this small one.

Chloe picked up the cell phone and punched in Seth's number. Would he be available? Surely the man must work sometimes.

Apparently not at the moment, because he answered almost immediately.

"Chloe." He sounded wary. "I didn't expect to hear from you so soon."

A woman's voice soared in the background. She sounded upset, although Chloe couldn't make out the words.

"If this isn't a good time to talk . . ." she began.

"It's fine." The words were clipped. "Just give me a moment."

Chloe heard his footsteps and the sound of a door closing. It cut off the woman's voice in mid-sentence.

Well. If she were his girlfriend, she wouldn't appreciate being walked out on. It could be his mother, she supposed, but the voice had sounded young.

"All right. I can hear you better now. Do you have more questions for me?"

Seth still didn't sound particularly delighted at her call. Well, why should he? He'd gone to considerable trouble to help out a friend, it seemed, and gained nothing but grief.

"I do have questions, but I'm not sure you're the best person to answer them." She took a breath, trying to quell the butterflies in her stomach. "I'd like to come and see Lydia."

There was a pause. "That's quite a turnaround. Her letter must have been very persuasive."

He seemed determined to nettle her.

"I appreciated her letter, but she didn't try to persuade me to do anything. I've decided it's the right thing to do. That's all."

177

With a little help from Kendra, she added silently.

"When were you thinking of coming? The apple orchard is in bloom right now, so it's quite a sight. Lydia will be—"

"Not to the house." She interrupted him, feeling a touch of panic at the thought of the house where her mother had lived. "I don't want . . . I thought we could meet for lunch someplace."

"A neutral meeting ground?" His tone was dry.

"Why not? I think you're the one who suggested that initially, aren't you?"

"I guess I did. Well, it's better than nothing. Why don't you want to come here?"

"Here? Are you at Lydia's now?" Had that been her sister's voice in the background?

"I'm at my mother's. Standing on her back porch, to be exact, looking past the orchard at Lydia and Adam's house. I should think you'd want to see it. Your parents lived there, after all. You were born there."

That hadn't occurred to her, but that only increased the sense of panic. She was learning too much, too quickly. "I'd rather meet some-where else, maybe for lunch in one of the nearby towns. What about Lewisburg or Oyersburg? Or is there an easier town for Lydia to reach?"

"You still didn't answer my question. Why don't you want to come here?"

178

It hadn't taken Seth Miller long to annoy her. She suspected it was intentional.

"Visiting someone's home involves a level of commitment I'm not ready to make." That was true as far as it went, and she hoped it would satisfy his curiosity. "And you didn't answer my question, either. Which town would be the best choice?"

Seth hesitated for a moment, making her wonder what he found difficult about deciding on a place. Then he spoke.

"There's a restaurant called the Plain and Fancy Diner in Oyersburg that's popular with both Amish and Englisch. When will you come?"

Chloe jotted down the name. "What about this Saturday? I'm in the middle of a project, so I'd hate to take time off on a weekday right now."

"I'm sure Saturday will be fine." He was brisk, probably not wanting to risk her changing her mind. "I'll confirm it with Lydia and get back to you."

"I'll plan to be there around noon, unless I hear otherwise from you." She studied the map she had open on the computer screen. "Oyersburg looks fairly easy to reach from the interstate. Can you give me directions to the restaurant?"

"When you come into town, you'll see a park right in front of you, bordering the river. Just pull into the parking lot. I'll meet you there and take you to the restaurant."

"That's not necessary. I don't need an escort." And she didn't think she wanted Seth's critical eyes on her when she met her sister for the first time.

"I'm not worried about you," he said. "I'm thinking of Lydia. It will make it easier for her if I'm there to introduce you."

That still didn't seem necessary to her, but if it smoothed the way, she could put up with Seth's disturbing presence for a short time.

"Fine. I'll look for you at the park."

"Think of me as your liaison with Amish life." The annoyance had washed from his voice, probably because she'd given in. Instead he sounded faintly amused, giving her a swift, vivid image of his strong face, lips quirking slightly, gray eyes filled with laughter.

"I'll see you Saturday," she said quickly.

"You won't back out, will you? I don't want Lydia to get her hopes up if you're going to bail on her."

"I've said I'm coming." Just as quickly she was annoyed with him again. "I do what I say I will." She clicked off. For better or worse, the decision was made.

Chapter Nine

Seth lingered on the back porch for a moment after disconnecting. So Chloe was willing to meet her sister. Unfortunately she was also wary and somewhat defensive, which wouldn't help this reunion.

What was behind this reluctance of hers to see the place where she was born? He could only think that she had some deep feelings about her birth family—feelings she wasn't yet ready to address.

He was a fine one to judge her on that score. He had his own set of complicated family feelings, and right now he'd better go inside and deal with the latest crisis.

But when Seth reached the kitchen, he found that harmony had been restored. He shot a questioning glance toward his mother, who stood at the stove, and she responded with a slight shake of her head.

Jessie emerged from the enclosed porch where Mamm stored some of the fruits and vegetables, an apple in her hand.

"Blackie deserves a treat for being so patient when we were at the store, ain't so, Mammi?"

Jessie was as pert and happy as if she were eight again instead of over twenty. Looking at her rosy cheeks and sparkling blue eyes, he found it hard to reconcile her with the virago who had been screeching like a crow only minutes before because Mamm had forgotten her favorite kind of pudding.

"Take it out to him," Mamm said. "But don't forget supper's nearly ready."

Seth tensed, waiting for a snappish response to Mamm's gentle words, but Jessie hurried out, her steps as light as if she were dancing.

He waited until she was out of earshot. "The new medicine isn't working as well as the last one, is it?" He put his hand gently on Mamm's shoulder.

"They said it might be some time before it would take effect, I think." Mamm's brow furrowed, as if she wasn't sure.

He should have gone along on that last doctor's visit. Mamm wasn't able to handle the repercussions of Jessie's bipolar disorder on her own.

"I'll come with you to the next appointment," he said, silently determined to confront the doctor on the subject of Jessie's medication. His mother had all she could do to deal with her own recovery from the broken hip.

He glanced at her, his heart taking a blow at the sight of her drawn face. He'd been gone too long, out in the Englisch world pursuing his own dreams and letting his mother carry the burdens alone. If he'd never jumped the fence—

Regrets were seldom useful, and he couldn't know if it would have made any difference if he'd stayed. He took down plates from the cabinet and began setting the table. It was Jessie's job, of course, but he was doing it for Mamm, not Jessie.

His mother checked the chicken potpie keeping warm on the back of the gas stove, her face intent. He'd suggested a few times that they have simpler meals or that he bring food in from town, but he'd seen how unhappy it made her. To Mamm, feeding people was her way of loving them, and he didn't want to take that away from her.

If he hadn't left, what would his life be now? It had been so long since he'd been Amish he found it hard even to imagine. He might have married a local girl, someone like Lydia, and have had a houseful of children. If so, Mamm and Jessie would probably live with them, and his imaginary wife would see to it that Mamm felt useful without overtaxing herself.

He shook his head, laughing at himself. A nice picture, but it wouldn't have been that way. He knew himself better. If he hadn't gone, he'd have ended up bitter and dissatisfied, probably making everyone around him unhappy as well.

Life was the way it was, and right now it was a delicate balancing act between doing the work he found so fulfilling and caring for his family. And that was difficult enough, without adding Chloe Wentworth to the mix.

"Seth? Your call—was it something wrong at work?" Mamm didn't usually ask about his job, preferring to ignore what she didn't understand, but apparently he was letting his expression show too much.

"Nothing like that. It's actually good news. That was Lydia's little sister, the one I went to see in Philadelphia. She wants to meet with Lydia."

"Ach, that is gut indeed." Mamm's tired face was transformed by her smile. She was as happy for Lydia as she would have been for herself. "Lydia will be so pleased. She has been grieving about it, I know. But you must go now and tell her." Mamm gestured with the dish towel in her hand, as if shooing the chickens. "We can wait supper for you."

"No, you can't," he said, escorting her firmly to her seat at the table. "You're going to sit right down, and I'll serve." He glanced at Jessie as she came in, cheeks rosy. "Mamm is looking tired, don't you think, Jessie? After supper maybe you and I can clean up while she has a little rest. I'll enjoy your company."

Jessie's response hung in the balance for a moment, but then she smiled. "You wash and I'll dry, ja?"

He nodded, lifting the steaming potpie with a towel. Lydia would be just as happy with the news whenever he delivered it, and first he was going to see Mamm off her feet and resting.

Lydia would be delighted to be meeting her sister, he knew. But he had a feeling Adam wouldn't consider this good news.

An hour later, Seth was discovering that doing the mundane chore of cleaning up the kitchen with his sister had an unexpected benefit. Jessie, away from Mamm's concerned presence, seemed to relax with him, chatting away as if they really did have a brother and sister relationship.

He didn't know her, he thought, his heart clutching as she laughed at something he'd said. Jessie was his own sister, and he didn't know her. The age difference between them was a barrier, of course, but he ought to admit the truth to himself, at least. He'd been so caught up in his own angst about Amish life in his teen years that he hadn't spared much thought or attention for his baby sister. Maybe that had been an excuse then, but it wasn't a very good one for his neglect of his family since then.

"You'll be going back to work after we finish the dishes, ja?" Jessie's hands seemed to slow on the pot she held.

"Not right away. I don't have anything that has to be finished tonight." He was a little behind on his current project, but nothing he couldn't make up in a few days' time. Working out of a motel wasn't the most comfortable situation, but he needed the amenities it provided. Maybe it would make more sense to give up his apartment in

Chicago and look for a small place to rent around here, but he'd been hesitant to take so final a step.

"You miss being in the city." Jessie made it sound like an accepted fact. "You're only staying around to help Mamm."

He was silent for a moment, trying to understand the intent behind her comment. "I want to help Mamm, yes. It worries me that she's still having so much trouble recovering from her surgery. But you know what? I kind of like it here. Gives me a chance to get to know my little sister." He smiled, flicking the dish towel at her, and was rewarded by her pleased flush.

"Do you miss it?" Her gesture seemed to take in the whole outside world.

"Some things," he admitted. "But not as much as I had expected. I like my work, and I can do it anyplace as long as I have a computer and the Internet." He paused, wondering how familiar Jessie was with the computerized world, but she nodded as if she understood.

"When you're here, people know what it's like to be a fence-jumper, ain't so? That makes it easier for you."

He hadn't expected that level of understanding from Jessie. "I guess that's about it. Out in the world, if I say I was Amish, some people look at me as if I was a freak. And even if they don't, they're still . . . curious."

That was the kindest word he could come up with for the often intrusive questions. People tended to assume he was relieved to have escaped, as they would see it. They didn't understand that there were plenty of things he still missed about this life, no matter how long he'd been Englisch.

Jessie seemed to turn inward. "It's hard," she said, her voice soft as a breeze through the apple trees. "To be different."

His heart twisted again. He'd often thought Jessie didn't even realize she had a problem. He'd been wrong.

"I have to go over to Lydia and Adam's to give them a message. Would you like to go with me?" He extended the invitation impulsively.

"You want me to come?" Her brows lifted in surprise.

"I have to tell Lydia something about her sister. Be sort of nice to have a woman along."

Jessie seemed to look at the comment from all angles, maybe to be sure he wasn't making fun of her. Then she nodded. "Ja, I would like to."

In a few minutes they were walking across the orchard, the breeze teasing strands of silky blond hair free of Jessie's kapp. She brushed them back with one hand.

"It's not bad news that you have for Lydia?" she asked when they'd gone about halfway.

"Not exactly. I think it will please her, but it's still an upheaval in their lives."

187

"Because she has an Englisch sister." Jessie nodded. "I know." She darted a sidelong glance at him. "Were you sweet on Lydia, before you left?"

"What makes you think so?" He parried the question, surprised at how accurate her intuition seemed to be.

"I just thought so." Her gaze slid away from his.

"Maybe a little bit," he said, remembering the night he'd taken Lydia home from the singing. He'd wanted to kiss her, but he hadn't quite dared. "It was a long time ago."

"They say people never forget their first loves." Jessie's voice was wistful. Was she thinking that was something she'd never know?

Lydia was already at the back door to welcome them when they arrived, no doubt having spotted them walking through the orchard. "Seth, Jessie. How nice." She gestured them into the house, her gaze perhaps a little cautious when it rested on Jessie.

Small wonder. Lydia had coped with Jessie at her worst. And here came Adam, hurrying from the barn, probably not too pleased to see Seth. Their lives were tangled together in ways that were impossible to ignore.

"Do you have news?" Lydia's eyes betrayed anxiety that she kept out of her voice. Adam, no doubt seeing it as well, moved closer to her.

"Good news, I think," Seth said quickly. "Chloe

called. She wants to meet you and Adam for lunch. We set it up for Saturday in Oyersburg."

"For sure?" Joy bloomed on Lydia's face, and she clasped her hands together. "That's wonderful-good news."

"What made her change her mind?" Adam's glance accused Seth.

"It doesn't matter. At least she's coming." Lydia's brows puckered. "But . . . why isn't she visiting us here, at home?"

"I'm not sure." Seth skirted the truth. "She seems to prefer a neutral site for your first meeting, and maybe that's best."

"I will finally see my sister." Lydia squeezed Adam's hand. "I'm so glad. Aren't you?"

In other circumstances, Seth might be tempted to laugh at Adam's expression. He was clearly torn between supporting his wife and his own inclinations.

"For sure he's glad," Jessie said, surprising Seth. "I have an Englisch brother, so I can tell you. Kin is kin, whether they are Englisch or Amish."

There was a little silence after her words. Probably no one had expected such a statement from Jessie, of all people.

"Jessie is right," Lydia said softly. "Chloe is my sister first, and Englisch second. We will be glad to welcome her, no matter where we meet."

Adam nodded, a bit reluctantly, Seth suspected. He smiled at Jessie. *Well done, little sister.*

• • •

Adam woke sometime in the night, struggling out of a suffocating dream. Lydia had been drifting away from him, her gaze on something he couldn't see, and as hard as he tried to reach her, her fingers slipped from his. He shuddered, knowing it was a dream but not able to rid himself of the fear, and reached out to Lydia's side of the bed to touch her.

Lydia wasn't there—the sheet was cool to his fingers as if she'd been gone for some time. He shot up in bed, startled and wide awake. Lydia . . .

He let out his breath in a swoosh of air. Lydia was sitting on the floor by the window, her elbows propped on the sill. She'd opened the window, and the chilly night air made Adam shiver as he slid out of bed.

Lydia didn't move. Didn't she hear him? She stared out at something in the night, and he couldn't see her face. An odd apprehension touched him. Seeing her this way was like seeing someone he didn't know at all, and that was a frightening thought.

Could she be walking in her sleep? "Lydia," he said softly, moving to her. "What are you doing?"

She turned to look up at him, her smile dissolving the fear that had gripped him. "I couldn't sleep," she said, her voice equally soft, although the boys slept so soundly it was likely nothing short of a siren would wake them. "Look how beautiful the orchard is in the moonlight."

He bent, his gaze following the direction of her gesture. Moonlight touched the white blossoms, turning them to silver. It was beautiful. It was also cold.

"Ja, pretty. Now come back to bed before you catch a chill."

Lydia shook her head, her unbound hair moving like water. "It's no use. I can't sleep. But you go back to bed. You need your rest."

He surveyed her for a moment and then turned back to the bed. Instead of getting in, he pulled off the double wedding ring quilt and carried it to the window.

Lydia looked up, startled. "What are you doing?"

He sat down next to her, draping the quilt around both of them. "If you are wakeful, then I am, too."

"Denke, Adam." She snuggled into the quilt.

He looked for signs of strain on her face. If she was unable to rest because he couldn't find a job . . .

"Are you worrying about something then?"

She shook her head, a tiny frown creasing her forehead. "I was dreaming about the orchard. I was a little girl, playing among the trees. My mamm was there, and she laughed and swung me around. Susanna chased us, and the baby lay on a quilt in the grass."

"Happy thoughts," he said gently, trying to understand.

"They're not memories. Only dreams." Her voice was choked. "I don't remember. It seems so wrong that I can't remember my mother's face. I'll never know what she looked like."

There was a world of sorrow in her voice, and he hadn't a notion of how to comfort her. "She was beautiful," he said finally. "I know, because you are."

"Ach, Adam, you always know what to say." She gave a sound that seemed caught between a laugh and a sob, and she leaned her head against his shoulder.

He wrapped his arms around her, wishing that were true. Instead, it seemed to him that he almost never knew what to say, especially lately. He was like that boy he'd been, so hesitant to speak that everyone else got there first.

Lydia stirred a little, turning her head to look into his face. "You didn't say much when Seth brought such good news."

"You and Seth did enough talking for all of us." He tried not to sound harsh, but as far as he was concerned, Seth's news hadn't been that good. And he didn't care for Seth's continuing presence in their lives. It seemed every day his Lydia was turning to Seth for answers instead of him.

"I guess I was excited. I wish Chloe would come

here, but meeting her in Oyersburg is better than not seeing her at all, ja? Aren't you happy for me, Adam?"

"If you're happy, that's gut." He felt as if he were walking on eggs, trying not to break them. But he couldn't tell Lydia less than the truth. "Having my family involved so much with an Englischer—well, I can't say I'm pleased, because I'm not."

And there they were, right back at the same argument again.

At least this time Lydia didn't fly into anger right away. Instead she leaned back against the windowsill, studying his face as if trying to understand.

"I know that your brother's jumping the fence hurt you, but that's no reason to turn against the Englisch. It was Benjamin's decision."

Pain had a stranglehold on his throat. But somehow he had to tell Lydia the thing he'd never told anyone.

"If I had been a better big bruder, maybe he wouldn't have gone." He shook his head, caught in the memories. "I was sorry, once it was too late. I tried to find him."

Her eyes widened. "I didn't know."

"No one knew. I didn't want Mamm and Daad to get their hopes up and then be disappointed. But I was sure that if only I could find Benj, talk to him, I could convince him to return."

Lydia was still. Waiting and listening, her gaze fastened on his face.

"One of his friends finally told me enough that I could locate Benj. He was in Harrisburg, so I went there. I took the bus."

"I didn't know you'd ever gone that far from home."

"I didn't want to. But I had to." He shook his head. "It seemed hopeless at first, but finally I found him." Pain choked him, and he had to force the words out. "He was living in an abandoned building. It was awful. Our pigs live in a palace compared to that place. And the people—ragged, dirty, on drugs or alcohol." He sucked in a breath. "And my brother was one of them."

Lydia gave a shocked, pained exclamation. "Adam, how awful for you. Why did you never tell me?"

He shook his head. "I couldn't tell anyone, not about seeing Benj like that. I tried to get him to come home with me, but he just laughed at me. Said he'd found the life he wanted, and I should leave him alone." He blinked, because tears were coming and he never wanted to cry in front of Lydia. "Two weeks later he was dead. A drug overdose, the police told me, though I never told Mamm and Daad that. They think he died from a fall."

Lydia touched his face and then drew him close against her, stroking his back and murmuring soothing words as if he were one of the boys. He held on, struggling to regain control.

"I'm sorry," she murmured. "I'm so sorry. But I don't see . . ." She let the sentence trail off, as if she didn't want to press on with it.

But he had to get all this said while he could. He clasped her shoulders, looking into her face. "You would say that your sister is not like those Englischers, and you are right. But don't you see why it troubles me? For our boys to grow up with an Englisch aunt, seeing that life, maybe thinking it is good—what will keep them from ending up the way Benj did? I should have kept him safe, and I failed. I have to protect our sons."

"I know, I know." She stroked his cheek. "You take such gut care of us, Adam. But it will be all right. Really, it will."

Her comforting touch soothed his sore heart, but it wasn't enough. Lydia was going to go through with this, and he couldn't stop her.

Lydia clucked to Gray, the buggy horse, and the mare started obediently up the lane to Mamm and Daad's farm. She hated feeling out of sorts with Mamm. Maybe today's visit would smooth things out between them.

Besides, she had to tell them about meeting with Chloe on Saturday. She couldn't let them hear it from someone else.

Mamm would be pleased about it, wouldn't

she? After all, the secret was out now, and there was no putting it back. And Chloe, no matter how different she was because of her Englisch upbringing, was Mamm and Daad's blood kin just as much as she was.

Adam . . . well, Adam didn't understand, and she ought not to blame him. His experience with his brother had been so terrible—she could hardly imagine what it must have cost Adam to see his little brother in that place. Just the fact that Adam had gone told her how much it had meant to him. Harrisburg was less than two hours by bus, but to Adam it had been a different world. Her heart ached for the pain he'd gone through— was still going through. He'd never be done grieving for his brother.

Why had he never told her about finding Benjamin? It hurt that he hadn't shared it with her at the time, but it must have been before they'd started seeing each other seriously. Poor Benjamin. And poor Adam, to carry such a burden for his little brother.

The lane, long and winding, finally drew up to the farmhouse and continued beyond it to the barn and the outbuildings, where it finally petered out. It looked as if Daad had taken advantage of the fine weather to disc the field already, and beyond the old well Mamm's rhubarb waved its fanlike leaves. Signs of spring, they were, when everything came to life.

Gray stepped automatically to the hitching rail and stopped, waiting while Lydia climbed down. She clipped a line to the harness, smiling a bit. She never used this hitching rail without remembering Andrew, her four-years-younger brother, running smack into it during a game of catch and knocking himself silly. She'd run to him, sure he'd killed himself, and been so thankful to find him still alive that she'd given him a good shake for scaring her that way.

What one of those boys didn't think of to do to himself, another one did. Joshua had fractured his arm falling out of the peach tree, and had broken a branch doing it, while Matthew, the baby, had a scar to this day from falling out of the pony cart while Joshua was driving it.

After patting Gray, she headed for the back door. Mamm was already opening it, her smile warm and maybe a bit relieved. She wouldn't have liked the strain between them any more than Lydia did.

"Komm, Lydia. I'm wonderful glad to see you." A warm hug accompanied the words. "Coffee is hot, and I made apple dumplings this morning."

"Sounds wonderful." She wasn't really hungry, but Mamm wouldn't be happy unless she ate. "Your rhubarb is coming along fast."

"Ja, and the strawberries are close to blossoming. We'll be eating fresh from the garden before you know it."

That was always a landmark in the seasons—

the first day Mamm could make a meal with something fresh from the garden. No matter how good something canned or store-bought tasted, it didn't compare to fresh.

"I was remembering the day Andrew ran headfirst into that hitching rail. Seems like most of the things I remember about the boys were them hurting themselves." Lydia shed her bonnet and sweater and took her usual seat at the kitchen table, where Mamm had already set a mug of coffee.

"Ja, they sure liked to have accidents." Mamm brought her own coffee and the dumplings, and sat down at the end of the table next to Lydia. "I hope your boys aren't quite as bad."

"Not so far." Lydia kept a pretty sharp eye on them, with her brothers' examples in her mind. She stirred sugar into her coffee. "All my memories of growing up are here."

Mamm gave her a questioning look. "Ja, well, here is where you grew up."

"I hardly remember asking or even wondering about my life before the hospital." She frowned down at the brew. "It seems funny now. You'd think I'd have been more curious."

"We talked about it, your daad and me. We asked the doctors, too. They all said just to answer any questions that you had but not to bring it up if you didn't." Mamm reached out to touch Lydia's hand. "You were such a busy, happy child. We were so relieved to see it after all that time in the hospital."

"I understand." Lydia closed her fingers around Mamm's hand, seeming to feel the love flowing between them. She tried to imagine what it would be like to see her child lying in the hospital for days on end, but her mind shied away from it. "I'm thinking maybe kinder just accept what they know as natural. And you're right. I was happy."

Mamm nodded, looking relieved. If she took that to mean Lydia accepted what they'd done, maybe that was for the best. No one could go back and undo the past.

Lydia glanced around the kitchen, searching for a change of subject. "Is Great-aunt Sara resting?"

"Ach, no, she's gone back to her own place." Mamm looked exasperated. "We wanted her to stay, but you know how she is, always so independent. I just hope she doesn't do too much and get down sick again."

"She does like to be on her own." Unusual for an Amish woman, who was usually surrounded by family. But her great-aunt hadn't had children, and maybe she'd gotten used to being by herself. "I'll stop by to see her in the next day or two. Maybe we can get her to come out and have supper with us, or I'll take supper to her."

Mamm nodded. "I was sure you would." She hesitated. "I think you came to talk about something other than your great-aunt's health or your daad's garden, ja?"

Mamm always seemed to know her heart, Lydia reminded herself.

"Ja. I wanted you to hear it from me, not from anyone else. I have found Chloe, my baby sister." She held her breath, waiting for the response she was praying for.

Chapter Ten

Mamm's eyes widened in surprise, but Lydia thought she read happiness there, as well. "Ach, I would not have dreamed it could happen so quick. Where is she? How did you find her?"

Mamm's interest soothed Lydia's heart. At least Mamm cared about finding Chloe.

"I talked to Seth Miller about it. He said it would be easy for him, and I guess it was, because he found her right away. She uses the name Chloe Wentworth, and she lives in Philadelphia."

"The grandmother who took her would have changed her name, ain't so?" Mamm's expression clouded. "Did you . . . Have you talked to her?"

Lydia shook her head. "Seth went to see her for me. She didn't know anything about her real family. He said she didn't believe him at first."

"Poor child." Mamm was immediately sympathetic. "She must have been shocked. Like you were."

There was no argument there. Mamm understood, having seen Lydia's reaction when she found out.

"Seth gave me her address, so I wrote to her. I said how much I'd like to see her. And I'm going to. She's coming to Oyersburg on Saturday, and we will meet there."

Mamm didn't speak. Her face seemed to freeze, and Lydia's heart sank. She'd thought, given the sympathy Mamm had shown for Chloe, that she'd be glad.

"You don't like it. You don't want me to meet my sister." Her throat went tight.

"Ach, Lydia, don't be so hasty." Mamm caught her hand, holding on when Lydia would have pulled away. "I'm just . . . cautious. I wouldn't want you to be hurt, or Chloe either, ain't so?"

"How could meeting each other hurt us? We've been separated for so long. I don't understand why no one is pleased." She sounded a bit like David when he didn't get his own way. Maybe that was the danger in being back in the family kitchen again—she reverted to being a child.

"Chloe has been raised Englisch," Mamm reminded her. "By Mrs. Wentworth. From the few things Diane said about her mother, I would guess that the woman can be . . . difficult. Very prideful, so Diane said once."

"That doesn't mean Chloe is like her."

"No. Maybe she is sweet and loving, like Diane was, like you are." Mamm patted her hand. "But does she know anything about Plain People? You know Englischers have funny ideas about us sometimes. It doesn't usually hurt us what they think, but it might hurt you, if it's your sister."

Lydia took a breath, searching for calm. There was something in what Mamm said, and she was saying it out of love.

"That could be true," Lydia admitted. "But I cannot show Chloe who we are unless I meet her."

"Ja." Mamm's eyes were still clouded with worry. "What does Adam say?"

Lydia had to make a conscious effort not to stiffen. Naturally Mamm would think of Adam's opinion.

"Adam is worried about our meeting. I think he would be happier if I could just forget about my sisters, but he knows that I can't." She looked down at the apple dumpling, still untouched. "He fears the effect of the Englisch on his family, because of his brother. You remember Benjamin."

Mamm sighed. "Ja, I remember. He was different from Adam as it's possible to be. I think he'd have gone his own way whether he had Englisch friends or not. Willful, he was."

"Adam thinks he should have been able to save his brother from what happened to him out among the Englisch." It seemed she could still hear the pain echoing in his voice.

"It's in Adam's character to take on the burden of responsibility for his brother," Mamm said. "Just as it was in Benj's character to jump the fence. You must be patient with Adam, ja?"

"I try to be. But I won't give up seeing my sister."

Mamm shook her head, and Lydia sensed she'd given the wrong answer. She tried to swallow the lump in her throat. She didn't want to be at odds with her family or with Adam, but whether anyone understood or not, she had to see Chloe.

Adam, watching from the kitchen window, saw Ben Miller's car turning into the lane late Saturday morning. His stomach lurched. This was it. It was nearly time to leave for the meeting with Lydia's sister. They could have ridden with Seth, he supposed, but Adam didn't like being beholden to him.

He took his hat from the hook by the door. Lydia's mamm had Daniel and David sitting at the kitchen table, snacking on milk and oatmeal cookies. They both looked at him, blue eyes wide, as if they sensed something out of the ordinary was going on.

Adam gave them a quick, reassuring smile. "Lydia? Ben Miller is coming. Are you ready?"

Lydia's light steps sounded on the stairs, and

she hurried into the kitchen. She had changed her dress twice, and now she wore the green one. She'd been so fussed this morning, as if it mattered to her sister what dress she had on.

"I'm ready." Lydia dropped a kiss on each boy's head. "You two listen to Grossmammi and don't get into any mischief. Daadi and I will be back in a few hours."

David nodded and returned to dunking his cookie in his milk, but Daniel looked up at her. "Will it be all right, Mammi?"

Lydia's smile trembled a bit. "Ja, it will." She moved quickly to the peg by the door and took down her bonnet. "I'm ready."

"Mind your grossmammi," Adam said. He exchanged glances with Lydia's mamm and then followed Lydia out the door. Ben was pulling up by the time they reached the lane.

Lydia paused, her hand on the car door. Adam couldn't see her expression because of the brim of her bonnet, but her back was stiff with tension.

"If you would rather stay at home, I can manage by myself," she said.

"I'm going," he said, and reached past her to open the back door.

Not that he wasn't tempted to stay home. But if Lydia insisted on pursuing this relationship with her Englisch sister, he was going to be with her.

He settled himself in the seat next to Lydia, exchanging good mornings with Ben. Ben seemed to glance at Lydia in the rearview mirror. Then his gaze met Adam's, and he started the car.

Ben was an old friend of the Amish, valued not only for the service he provided as a taxi driver but also for his friendship. He could be relied on whatever the need, and he wouldn't gossip. Whatever he saw, heard, or guessed today, Ben wouldn't spread it around.

Ben's discretion was one bright spot in this day. Adam glanced at Lydia, sitting very straight with her hands clasped in her lap, her expression closed to him.

Would she be happier if he hadn't come? He'd begun to wonder about that over the past couple of days. A month ago he'd have said he could read his Lydia's every thought and emotion, but no longer. It was as if the unseen cord that connected them had begun to fray.

Maybe their marriage had been too harmonious, too peaceful. Neither of them had been prepared for so big a problem appearing so suddenly.

He spared an annoyed thought for Lydia's daad. He hadn't spoken of this to Joseph Weaver, and he most likely wouldn't, but surely it would have been better if Joseph had confided in him about Lydia's family when Adam had asked to marry her.

Ben glanced in the rearview mirror again, probably taking in their expressions, and cleared his throat. Tactfully he began talking about the spring weather and its effect on the growing season, a gentle murmur of conversation that didn't require much in response.

Adam nodded, spoke from time to time, and tried to pretend that Lydia wasn't sitting there like a statue, staring out the window and most likely seeing nothing of the passing scenery.

An endless half hour later, the car turned onto the bridge over the river. "Almost there," Ben said with a hint of relief in his voice.

Lydia moved suddenly, reaching out to grab Adam's hand. Hers was like a chunk of ice, and he pressed it in his.

"What if I say the wrong thing?" Her eyes were wide and dark with fear. "What if she doesn't like me? What if she blames me for not finding her sooner? What—"

"Hush, Lydia, hush." He patted her hand, trying to sound strong and sure, the way she expected him to be. She was asking all the questions he had been thinking, but it was too late now to reconsider.

"But . . ." Her gaze focused on his face, pleading for reassurance that he wished he could give her.

"We won't know how Chloe reacts until we see her." He spoke in a low murmur of Pennsylvania Dutch, not sure whether Ben knew enough to follow his words or not. "You have done all you could. The rest of it is in God's hands, ain't so?"

Lydia nodded, her face relaxing just a little. "Ja," she said. "It is in God's hands."

Chloe arrived in Oyersburg early, pushed along by a powerful mix of apprehension and eagerness. Unfortunately the closer she got to the meeting, the more apprehension seemed to be winning.

Seth's directions had seemed too simple, so she'd taken the precaution of setting her GPS, but she actually drove into the park without incident. In comparison to the sprawling suburbs of the city, Oyersburg seemed isolated, enclosed by the ridges that ran along either side of the river valley.

The park lay along the river, probably a sensible use for land that might be subject to flooding. Trees were beginning to leaf out, and a cheerful row of daffodils danced in the breeze along the rail fence that surrounded the grass. Two teen-agers played what seemed to be an unpracticed game of tennis on the nearest court, and a pair of young mothers pushed strollers along a jogging trail, talking as they went.

Chloe slid out of the car. She was early, but it seemed Seth was even earlier. He was leaning against a late-model sedan, his face tilted toward the sun. At the sight of her he pushed away from the car and came toward her, light touching glints of gold in his hair.

"I see you made it." He gave her a questioning smile. "No problems? No last-minute jitters?"

"Certainly not," she said quickly.

Seth gave a questioning look, and despite herself she had to smile.

"All right, maybe a little. What if Lydia doesn't like me?" Chloe gestured to the slacks and soft shirt she'd put on with a short denim jacket after searching her entire wardrobe for something suitable. "I tried to dress conservatively, but nothing seemed right."

"You look fine." Seth's eyes seemed to warm as he looked at her. "I'll bet Lydia is wondering the same thing right about now."

Irrational as it was, his words and the smile in his eyes seemed to take the edge off her tension. She glanced around as if admiring the park, trying to get away from the gaze that seemed to read her too well.

"Nice park," she said. "Small, but nice."

"It's plenty big enough for a town of ten thousand, give or take a few. People here are very proud of it, so I wouldn't say anything derogatory in their hearing."

"I said it was nice. That's a compliment, isn't it?"

His smile flickered. "Nobody ever takes the word *small* as a compliment." He pointed across the river to the thickly wooded ridge that seemed to shoot upward abruptly on the far side. "The park prevents people from building too close to the river, among other things."

She nodded, understanding what he meant. The ridge would funnel any high water right toward the town. "Should we go? I don't want to be late."

"Sure thing. We may as well take my car." He touched her arm as they moved toward his sedan, and she felt his warmth through the sleeve of her jacket.

Focus, she ordered herself.

He held the door while she got into the passenger seat, and Chloe watched from the corner of her eye as he slid behind the steering wheel. Seth was a study in contradiction. Even here, on what was presumably his home ground, he exuded the essence of cool, urban professional. And yet he claimed to have grown up Amish.

He reached across to touch her hands, startling her. "Relax," he coaxed. "It's going to be fine."

She hadn't realized she'd been gripping her hands so tightly that her knuckles were white. She forced them to release. "Easy for you to say." She tried to keep her tone light. "You're not meeting your sister for the first time."

"No." An emotion she couldn't quite identify shadowed his eyes. "But my little sister grew up while I was away. It's been tough, trying to build some sort of relationship with her."

"I didn't realize." She tried to sort it out. "So if you were raised Amish, that means your sister is Amish."

"My whole family. I'm the only one who

jumped the fence." He darted a look at her, as if measuring her reaction. "That means I left. In my case, when I was eighteen."

"What happened?" The question was out before it occurred to her that he might not want to answer. But if she knew what made someone leave, it might help her understand why her mother had chosen to become Amish.

"Too long a story to get into now." His sudden coolness dismissed the subject. So he wasn't willing to get into his personal life with her, despite that occasional flare of something she felt sure was attraction. She couldn't blame him. They'd been thrown together by chance, knowing both too much and too little about each other.

Chloe turned to stare out the window. The tree-lined street that was perpendicular to the river ran past homes, a few small businesses, and a pair of neo-Gothic churches facing each other on opposite sides, followed shortly by a library and post office doing the same.

Seth stopped at a traffic signal where the street widened into a square with a fountain at its center. Along the curb, trucks and a few buggies were parked, and canvas canopies bloomed like flowers along the walks.

"Market day," Seth said, gesturing. "It's not too busy now, but once the growing season really gets going, it'll be crowded with farmers and customers three days a week."

Chloe spotted an Amish woman standing behind a folding table lined with jars of jam. Her stomach clenched. How could her mother, brought up with every advantage of wealth and education, have chosen to live like that woman did?

The light changed, Seth accelerated around the corner, and the woman disappeared.

"Here's the restaurant."

Even as he spoke she saw the sign—THE PLAIN AND FANCY DINER, it read, in a border of brightly colored hex symbols.

"We're a little early," he said, getting out of the car. "We're probably ahead of Lydia and Adam."

He moved as if to come and open her door, but she forestalled him by sliding out quickly. Together they walked to the entrance.

A bright-faced teenager, wearing a simple rose-colored dress and apron, her hair drawn back under a white kapp, welcomed them. "Two for lunch?" she asked.

Was she really Amish, or was that outfit a costume, as a seafood place's servers might be dressed in pirate costumes?

"I have a reservation," Seth said. "Miller."

The young woman consulted a chart and nodded. "Ja, Mr. Miller. You asked for a quiet spot, so we'll put you back in the alcove."

They followed her between mostly unoccupied tables. That had been thoughtful of Seth, to ask for a quiet spot. This meeting would be difficult enough without feeling that other people were eavesdropping on the conversation.

Their table was tucked away around a corner. Chloe sat down, some cowardly part of her mind suggesting that it wasn't too late to turn around and go home. Seth passed her a menu, decorated with more of the hex signs. She stared at them for a moment. She was familiar with them, of course. Since she specialized in Pennsylvania folk art, she could hardly help but be.

"Mesmerized by the distelfinks?" Seth asked.

She shook her head, managing a smile. "Amazing how examples of folk art hang on, isn't it?" She traced a hex sign with her fingertip. "I've never really understood why the Amish don't use hex signs on their barns."

"That would be doing something just 'for pretty,' and that's discouraged. To the Amish, any object they make should be useful."

"That seems rather harsh. Why would the church discourage artistic expression?"

They are nothing more than a cult. Her grandmother's voice echoed in her mind. *If your mother hadn't joined them, she'd be here today.*

"Objects can be both useful and beautiful," Seth said, his voice mild. "I take it you don't know much about Amish beliefs." He sounded disapproving, as if he'd expected her to do her homework before coming here to meet Lydia.

Now that she thought about it, researching

212

Amish customs should have been her first response. As it was, she had little more than an instinctive impression of an outdated patriarchal society that viewed women as subservient, and every independent bone in her body rebelled at the very idea. Why hadn't she reacted as any historian would and looked into it for herself? Maybe her grandmother's attitudes were ingrained in her more deeply than she'd realized.

A flicker of panic touched her. "I guess I should have prepared myself better. I don't want to offend Lydia."

"I doubt there's anything you could do that would offend her." Seth smiled, eyes crinkling. "She'd forgive her little sister anything."

Little sister. Chloe's breath caught. "I've never been a little sister before. I might not be good at it." Was she really asking Seth for reassurance? It certainly sounded that way.

He gave her hand a quick, comforting squeeze. "It'll be fine. You'll see."

And then he was standing, nodding to a couple coming toward them, a man in black pants, a blue shirt, and suspenders, with a crisp, curling beard. A woman in a green dress, apron to match, her head and face hidden by the brim of the black bonnet she wore.

Then the woman looked up, her gaze meeting Chloe's, and Chloe's heart gave an erratic thump. This was her sister.

Chapter Eleven

Lydia was vaguely aware of Seth standing behind a chair, but she only had eyes for the woman who was getting up next to him. Chloe. Even though she'd seen the photo, Lydia wasn't quite prepared for her appearance.

Her little sister—silky reddish-brown hair, worn shining and short around her face, wary-looking green eyes—had on a pair of tan-colored slacks with a fitted yellow cotton shirt and a short denim jacket. A pendant hanging from a gold chain was an intricate pattern of stained glass that looked handmade, and gold hoops swung from her earlobes. She looked more like some of the college students Lydia had seen in Lewisburg than the photo Seth had shown her.

Lydia was grateful for the firm clasp of Adam's hand on her arm as she faced the truth. Despite all she'd learned about Chloe, somewhere in her heart she'd been holding on to an image of the baby sister who needed her.

She took a strangled breath, her thoughts forming an incoherent prayer. Somehow, she had to rid herself of that false image of Chloe if she were to have a chance of finding a kinship with the woman Chloe was now.

The table, she saw, was tucked away in a little

alcove for privacy. She hesitated a step away, irresolute. She might long to embrace her sister, but Chloe's expression didn't give any hint that she would welcome that from a woman who was a stranger to her.

"Here we are." Seth's voice had a forced heartiness, as if he found the situation uncomfortable. "Chloe, this is Lydia Beachy. And her husband, Adam."

Chloe didn't move. Then, slowly, she held out her hand.

Lydia clasped it in both of hers, nearly overcome by the longing to draw her sister close. *Not yet. Be careful.*

"Chloe." Her voice trembled on the name.

"Lydia. Adam." Chloe nodded to each of them, reclaiming her hand. She didn't offer to shake hands with Adam, and a glance at Adam's expression told Lydia why. His face was a stern mask, with no hint of the warm person beneath.

"Come and sit down." Seth covered the awkward moment by pulling out chairs. "The server should be right with us. I imagine Chloe is hungry after her long drive."

In the bustle of getting seated, Lydia managed to regain whatever calm she had. This was her chance—maybe the only one she'd have—with her little sister. She couldn't let the opportunity slip away.

Chloe seemed to be eyeing her clothing, either

in surprise or disapproval. Surely she had seen folk in Amish dress before, but maybe not.

Lydia removed her bonnet, hung it on the back of the chair, and smoothed her hair with a quick gesture. There, now, Chloe would be able to see her better.

She cleared her throat. "How long did it take you to come today, Chloe?" That soft, hesitant voice surely wasn't hers.

"A little over three hours. I stopped once to have some coffee." She seemed to push herself to speak again. "What about you?"

"It is only about a half an hour by car from Pleasant Valley. We hired a taxi for the trip."

"Amish taxis," Seth put in lightly. "There are a number of people who enjoy driving the Amish when they have to make a trip that's too long for the horse and buggy."

"Do you come to Oyersburg often?" Chloe sounded like someone making polite conversation with a stranger, which was nearly the truth.

"Once in a while, for shopping," Lydia said, with a quick thought for her visit to Susanna's store. "We don't have much reason to leave Pleasant Valley." Chloe probably traveled at the drop of a hat, like many Englisch. She'd think them backward.

The server came just then, creating an interruption Lydia suspected they all welcomed. She glanced at the menu and picked the first item that caught her eye, a chicken sandwich she probably wouldn't eat. Adam asked for a hot roast beef sandwich, and his predictability almost made her smile. He would eat roast beef and gravy on the hottest day of the summer, if she fixed it.

Across the table, Seth was pointing to something on Chloe's menu, explaining the Pennsylvania Dutch name. The simple gesture made her breath catch. Her own sister had to have their food explained to her.

"Your grandmother doesn't make schnitz und knepp?" she asked.

Chloe blinked. "My grandmother doesn't cook. She has a housekeeper who takes care of the meals."

"Is your grandmother well?" Lydia couldn't think of Margaret Wentworth without remembering that she had taken Chloe away, but it would be rude not to inquire about her health. She must be getting up in years.

"She's fine." Chloe's tone was crisp. Was she out of sorts with her grandmother? Maybe the discovery of her sisters had caused a rift, just as it had for Lydia.

She sought for something else to say. There seemed to be too much that she wanted to say, but she didn't want to frighten Chloe away. "You have a job at a museum, Seth has told us. What do you do there?"

Chloe nodded. "The museum tells the story of

the Pennsylvania Germans—their history, art, and architecture. Right now I'm putting together a proposal for an educational program for schoolchildren. And we're also setting up a new display of hex signs and other arts and crafts." Her face seemed to brighten when she talked about her work, as if it gave her pleasure.

"Ja? There are lots of barns in the county that have hexerei painted on them. Amish don't use them, but other Pennsylvania Dutch do." Lydia shrugged. "And some Englisch, I guess, who just think they're pretty."

"Seth mentioned why the Amish don't put them on their barns." Her voice seemed to contain a challenge. "Painting a design on a barn seems a simple enough thing to me."

How to explain so that she would understand? Apparently Seth hadn't succeeded.

"We feel that things should be useful, not just pretty. That's why we are Plain German and the rest are Fancy, ja? Besides, some folks say the hex signs are a superstition." She tried to keep her tone light, not wanting to get into a disagreement with Chloe already.

The server moved away, leaving them in their secluded little corner. *Your only chance,* Lydia reminded herself.

"I have looked forward to seeing you every minute since I found out about you," she said, unable to keep her voice from getting husky. "I think you must have questions." Maybe talking about it would move them past this awkwardness.

"Seth told me that you found out by accident." Chloe darted a sidelong glance at Seth. "Your adoptive parents kept that information from you?"

"Ja." She didn't want to say anything that would put Mamm and Daad in a negative light. "I received a head injury in the accident, and I was a long time coming around. When I did, I didn't remember anything that happened before waking up in the hospital." She couldn't prevent a small quaver in her voice. "They had to explain to me about my parents. I think they felt that was enough grief for a five-year-old."

And you had been stolen away by your grandmother. But she couldn't say that to Chloe.

"How did you find out?" Chloe was showing more interest now, her expression not quite so stiff.

"My great-aunt mentioned it. She has been ill, and her mind was wandering a little. She remembered my mother—our mother—playing in the orchard with her three little girls. After that . . ." Lydia spread her hands. "Well, it all came out."

"The orchard," Chloe repeated. "So you live now where they lived then, Seth told me. How did you come to have that place?"

"A cousin and his wife moved in and took care of the farm after the accident. Then when Adam and I were getting married, they were ready to move out to Ohio to live with their married daughter, so we took it over." She hesitated, startled by a truth that should have been obvious to her from the start. "I guess the land really belongs to all three of us."

Chloe shook her head quickly. "I wouldn't know what to do with an orchard. Anyway, my life is in the city. You like living there?"

She smiled, wondering if Chloe could possibly understand. "I love it." She glanced at Adam. "We are very happy there. Our little boys play in the orchard, just like we did when we were small."

Chloe smiled, her face lightening as she seemed to relax, at least for a moment. "Since I was a baby, I probably didn't do much playing."

"Seth's mother told me that our mother liked to bring us all to the orchard. She would spread out a quilt for you to roll around on."

Chloe's smile seemed fixed, as if she'd forgotten it was on her face. Maybe she was more affected by the image than she wanted to let on. If only Chloe would let Lydia see the person she really was, instead of the facade she presented.

Their food arrived then, halting the conversation as the server put dishes in front of them and refilled water glasses.

Chloe had played it safe, it seemed, ordering chicken salad on a croissant instead of one of the Pennsylvania Dutch dishes. Adam bowed his head for the silent prayer, and Lydia did likewise. When she looked up again, Chloe was watching her, but she turned away quickly with a request for salt.

They ate in silence for a few minutes. Lydia had to choke down a bite of the chicken sandwich. They were talking on the surface, and she had no idea how Chloe really felt about suddenly discovering that she had Amish kin.

Chloe looked up, and their eyes met. For a moment Chloe seemed to lose her place, as if forgetting what she'd intended to say.

She took a sip of water. "You and Adam have children."

"Two boys, Daniel and David." Lydia hesitated, her glance inviting Adam to say more about the boys. But he was eating his roast beef stolidly, seeming oblivious to the conversation. "Daniel is eight, and David is six," she went on. "They are in third grade and first grade."

She'd have to make sure David was practicing his Englisch. He'd need it when Chloe came to visit. She would, wouldn't she?

"Do you have pictures of them?" Chloe was smiling again, seeming confident that Lydia would produce photographs.

"No, I . . ." She trailed off, looking at Seth for help.

"The Amish don't have photographs taken," he explained. "They believe it violates the Bible's injunction about creating graven images."

"No pictures of your children?" Chloe's voice lifted slightly in disbelief.

"That's their understanding of the Bible," Seth said, a bit of warning in his voice.

"If you come to visit, you'll see them for yourself," Lydia said quickly. "They would be so excited to meet their aunt."

From the corner of her eye, she saw Adam's hand tighten on his fork, and she could feel his tension through the few inches that separated them. If he said anything to keep Chloe away—

But he didn't speak, and after a moment the tension eased out of him. Lydia took a calming breath.

Chloe didn't seem to be paying attention to Adam, though. She studied the remains of her croissant for a moment, and then she met Lydia's glance. "Aren't you going to tell me about Susanna?"

Lydia could hardly miss the fact that Chloe had ignored the invitation to visit, but she tried to shake it off and concentrate on the question.

"Susanna was also hurt in the accident," she said. "Afterward, when the family was trying to decide what to do and we were all in different hospitals, an Amish couple who were good friends of our mamm and daad from an Ohio Amish community came to help. They stayed at the hospital with Susanna, and it was decided that they would adopt her."

"So she's in Ohio?" Chloe sounded impatient for her to get on with the story.

"No, actually, she and her adoptive mother moved back to Pennsylvania after her father died. Susanna was only three at the time of the accident, and they raised her to believe they were her parents. So as far as she's concerned, she is Susanna Bitler."

"You said she moved back to Pennsylvania." Chloe's voice was sharp, and she leaned toward Lydia as if to force an answer. "Where?"

She could not repeat other people's mistakes and fail to tell Chloe the truth. "She and her mother live here in Oyersburg."

"Here? Then why didn't you invite her to meet us? We could have all been together."

"Susanna doesn't know," she said, trying to sort out the best way of explaining. "I went to see her, to the shop she and another lady run. I hoped . . . well, it doesn't matter. The fact is that her mother is very ill. She has cancer, and it looks as if she won't recover. Susanna has such a lot to bear now. How could I make it worse by telling her that her mother is not really her mother?"

Chloe's chin looked determined. "She has a right to know the truth."

"Ja, she does. But I don't have the right to hurt a dying woman." She sent up a silent, fervent prayer that Chloe would understand. "And I don't think you do, either."

"Do you think they . . . your adoptive parents, my grandmother, this cousin . . . did wrong by hiding the truth from us all these years?" Chloe's eyes seemed to shoot sparks. So she had a temper, this baby sister.

"Ja, I think they were wrong, even though they were doing what they thought they must. But Susanna—" She leaned across the table, reaching for Chloe's hand. "I'm not saying to never tell Susanna. Just not right now. You understand, don't you?"

Their gazes clashed, but it was Chloe's that dropped first. "You may be right," she said, even though her voice said she doubted it.

I am losing her. Despair filled Lydia's mind. *I have only this one chance with Chloe, and I am losing her.*

Chloe found she was looking into Lydia's eyes, seeing something—a connection, maybe? Lydia touched her hand, and a wave of recognition went through Chloe, confusing her.

"Please understand." Lydia's voice was soft. "I don't want anyone to be hurt."

Chloe's indignation stilled, as if it could be muted by Lydia's gentleness. Chloe sat back, struggling with her response. It was all very well to accept that Lydia was her sister, but this was a visceral sense of kinship that startled her.

Her rational mind rejected the thought. She and Lydia might share DNA, but they had no memory of each other, they'd been raised in as opposite a way as could be imagined, and they had nothing in common except the accident of birth.

Seth was watching her, his gaze so intent that she could almost feel it on her skin. What more did he want from her? She was here, wasn't she? She was trying, at least.

Chloe toyed with her food, trying to think of something to talk about that wouldn't point out all the differences between them. "Tell me more about your boys. Do they look like you?"

Lydia's expression relaxed in a smile. "I think they look like their daadi." She glanced at Adam, and for the first time his aloof expression seemed to warm.

"Not so much," he said. "Daniel looks more like his mamm, but maybe he is like me in other ways."

Lydia nodded. "Ja, he is certain-sure like you. Serious and responsible, just like you. And David—well, he is a little schnickelfritz."

Before Chloe had time to look puzzled, Seth murmured in her ear. "Schnickelfritz is a mischievous child."

"You should know," Lydia said, smiling. "That was you, for sure." She turned back to Chloe. "David is doing well with learning his Englisch. He'll be able to talk with you when he meets you."

Chloe suspected that her confusion was written on her face. Once again, Seth stepped in.

225

"Old Order Amish speak Pennsylvania Dutch in the home. The children learn English when they go to school."

Chloe felt as if she'd stepped into an alien world. "But . . ." Too many thoughts were chasing around in her head, and she sorted out one. "How did our mother get along, then, if she didn't know the language?"

"From what my mother told me," Seth said, "I understand Diane mastered Pennsylvania Dutch quickly. Maybe she'd studied German in school. That would make it easier." He examined her face, maybe trying to decipher the mix of feelings written there. "Most Amish speak English fluently, as well as the Low German dialect. And the hymns and Scriptures are in High German. I'd guess not many other children learn three languages."

Chloe had a feeling he was warning her to be careful what she said about the children's language. Not that she would say anything derogatory, of course, no matter what she thought.

She glanced at Adam, sitting silent again after his mention of their sons. His face was stern and closed, and the beard gave him the disapproving air of some Old Testament figure. Lydia must see something in him that Chloe didn't, since the look they'd exchanged had been filled with affection.

Seth, maybe figuring they'd all sit there in silence and stare at each other if he didn't take a hand, began talking about the effect of the early spring weather on the fruit trees Lydia and Adam grew. Lydia responded, Adam sat mute, and Chloe put in a comment whenever she could think of something to say, which wasn't often. What did she know about horticulture?

She wasn't sure what she'd expected of this meeting. Probably it would be wrong to hope for too much. She and Lydia were strangers, after all.

Chloe glanced up, suddenly aware that they'd fallen quiet. All three of them were looking at her. She'd been so absorbed in her own thoughts she'd missed something.

"Lydia wondered if there were any questions you wanted to ask about your mother," Seth said, a hint of amusement showing in the quirk of his lips.

"Yes, sorry. I'm afraid my thoughts were straying." She met Lydia's gaze. "You look a bit like the pictures I've seen of our mother. Did you realize that?" Of course all the photos had been of an upper-crust Philadelphia girl, but the resemblance was there, in Lydia's eyes and the curve of her chin.

"No, I didn't know." Lydia's smile trembled, as if caught between joy and tears. "I have never seen a picture."

"My grandmother has some family albums. I could send you a photo of our mother. If that would be all right."

She added the last words, not sure what the Amish attitude would be. Still, maybe her grandmother wasn't all that different, even if her reasons were different. A person could search the whole house without finding a picture of Diane displayed. Chloe had only located the albums after a lengthy search.

Lydia nodded. "I think that will be all right." She darted a glance at Adam, who exuded disapproval like a fog. "Not to keep, just to see."

It would probably take her a lifetime of study to figure out all the ins and outs of Amish life, Chloe decided. But her mother had done it . . . not just figured it out, but chosen it above the way she'd been brought up.

"They must have loved each other very much." She realized she'd spoken the words aloud, even though she hadn't intended to.

But Lydia was nodding in agreement, understanding, her eyes misty. "Ja, they must have been quite a pair, to risk everyone's disapproval that way."

Funny. She'd been thinking about what Diane had given up for love. It hadn't even occurred to her that Eli had given something up, as well.

"It would have been a hard choice for both of them," Adam said unexpectedly. Then he glanced rather pointedly at their dishes. "Ben will be coming to pick us up soon."

"Ben said he would wait as long as we wanted,"

Lydia said quickly. "We do not want Chloe to rush away."

"That's all right." It had been a good idea not to commit herself to anything more than a lunch. This had been strained enough. "I do have a long drive."

Seth rose. "Adam and I will go and take care of the checks. Let you two have a moment alone."

Adam hesitated, but at a look from Lydia, he followed Seth across the room toward the counter. Lydia reached out to take Chloe's hand.

"This has been a gut start, ja?" Lydia blinked, as if tears were forming. "A month ago I could not have imagined finding a sister. Now, I don't want to lose you again."

"I'll call," Chloe said, and then shook her head. "I'm sorry. I forgot you don't have a phone. I'll write. And I'll send those pictures."

"You're sure your grandmother won't mind?"

Her grandmother wouldn't know they were missing. She had wiped Diane from the family tree with a firm hand.

"No, she won't mind." Chloe stood, coming around the table to Lydia. "I'll look forward to your next letter."

"Will you come to the farm for a visit? To see the boys, and the place where our parents lived?"

Chloe's stomach tightened, as if in protest at the idea. "I . . . I'll think about it. All right?"

"Ja." Lydia's voice was very soft. "That's gut."

Chloe stood, irresolute, torn between the longing to run back to the world she knew and the challenge to build a bridge to her sister's world. Then she stepped forward and put her arms around Lydia.

Lydia's hug was warm, and she murmured something softly in a language Chloe didn't know. But maybe she didn't have to know to understand love.

Nothing about this new family relationship was going to be easy, but it was too late to back away now. Now that she knew her sister, things could not be the same.

Chapter Twelve

Turning from the cash register, Seth glanced back at the alcove. Chloe and Lydia stood facing each other, and even as he watched, Chloe initiated a hug. So. It looked as if Chloe wasn't as impervious to her sister's affection as she might want people to believe. He realized Adam was watching, too, his jaw so tight that a muscle twitched.

"They're sisters," Seth said quietly. "That's a natural response."

"She's Englisch. I don't want Lydia to be hurt."

Seth censored his immediate reaction. It would do no good to confront Adam, who'd lost his brother to the Englisch world. That made him wary.

"Knowing Lydia, I don't think you can blame her for caring."

"No. I do not blame her." Adam's tone made it clear who he blamed.

Lydia and Chloe were approaching, so Seth couldn't respond. Just as well.

Seth hung back a step or two as they went outside, studying Chloe's body language. He couldn't quite make her out. She had moments of responding very naturally to Lydia, but then she'd put up her defensive barriers in an instant. Her grandmother had done a good job of inculcating her own prejudices in Chloe, it seemed to him. And yet Chloe showed her independence in the way she dressed—far more individual than the classic preppy style her grandmother would undoubtedly prefer.

Ben's car pulled up to the curb, final good-byes were said, and Chloe stood watching as they pulled away. Her face revealed nothing at all.

Then she turned to Seth. "You can just drop me at my car. Thanks so much."

He opened the passenger door for her. "Nice brush-off, but you may as well let me take you to Susanna's shop. I know where it is."

Chloe stopped, halfway in the car, glaring at him. "What makes you think I'm going to see Susanna?"

"Just a lucky guess."

She slid into the seat without comment, and he closed the door.

Once he'd pulled out into traffic, he glanced at her. "Well?"

"Yes, I intend to see Susanna. I'm not leaving until I've seen both of my sisters. You should understand. You're the one who suggested this town as the meeting place." Her lips closed in a tight line.

He recognized stubborn when he saw it. And she was right—he had suggested Oyersburg, convinced that Chloe would insist on seeing Susanna. But there was a lot more going on behind that polished exterior. He'd like to see who Chloe was when she put down those shields.

"You heard what Lydia said about Susanna and her mother's illness. You can't tell Susanna the truth about your relationship, not now."

A quick glance told him that she hadn't received his words well.

Her chin tilted upward. "Much as I appreciate all you've done, I really don't think it's up to you, Seth."

"It's not up to you, either," he said bluntly. "Lydia has been to see Susanna, and Lydia understands the situation far better than you could." He'd rather make Chloe angry with him than to let her stumble into making things worse for Susanna.

"I'm perfectly capable of understanding."

Chloe's tone would freeze boiling water. "Susanna's adoptive mother is ill. But it doesn't seem to have occurred to Lydia or you that Susanna might welcome the knowledge that she has sisters who could support her at a time like this."

"She might," he conceded. "Do you think Lydia hasn't considered that aspect? But you can't tell her without the information having an effect on how Susanna relates to the woman she thinks is her mother."

"Not necessarily—" Chloe began, but he didn't let her finish.

"It changed things for Lydia and her mamm, and Lydia already knew she was adopted. And can you honestly say it didn't put a strain on your relationship with your grandmother?"

Chloe was silent at his words, but he thought that shot had gone home. A good thing if it had, because they'd arrived at the shop and he was out of time.

He pulled to the curb and nodded. "That's it. I'll go in with you."

Chloe was already getting out of the car. She seemed to have gained control of her temper, because she didn't snap at him.

"So you think I need a chaperone?"

"No, but Susanna might."

He walked beside Chloe as she went up the couple of steps to the small porch that fronted

233

Main Street. Chloe paused, her gaze moving from the creek across the road to the row of two-story frame structures along the street.

"These look more like private homes than businesses."

"Most of them were, at one time. The only buildings originally built as businesses are in that three-block stretch of Main Street." He nodded to where the street rose up the hill and leveled off. "This area was once all residential, most of it built around the turn of the century. The last century," he added.

She nodded, opening the door. "It seems like a good location for a shop." She stepped inside and stopped again, looking around.

Seth, used to the small businesses that handled Amish-made items, tried to see the place through Chloe's eyes. Did she recognize the craftsmanship and artistry in the quilted place mats and carved wooden toys? Susanna's shop had the most extensive collection he'd seen in the area.

Chloe moved to a counter and picked up a maple napkin holder that bore a colorful hex design. "I thought the Amish didn't use hex symbols." Her tone was faintly challenging.

"Not for their own use," he explained. He ran his finger along the smooth finish of a cup holder. "But they'll make things for sale to the Englisch that they wouldn't make for themselves."

"Ja, that's true enough." A woman came out

from behind the counter at the rear, obviously having heard him. "I have one Amish lady who is making quilted covers for those tablet computers."

This must be Susanna. The age was right, and the woman had a certain resemblance to Lydia in the shape of her face and the tilt of her head. She came toward them, limping slightly, and Seth was sure. Lydia had said that Susanna had never fully recovered from her injury.

He glanced at Chloe. Her full lips trembled just a bit before she pressed them firmly together. She'd recognized Susanna, too.

"There's no reason not to provide what folks want to buy," he said, answering Susanna's comment and giving Chloe time to regain her composure. "You have a fine selection."

"Denke." Susanna tilted her head in acknowledgment.

"Is . . . Is everything handmade?" Chloe nearly had her voice under control.

"Just about." Susanna glanced around, as if seeking something that hadn't been. "Most of it is made by Amish or Old Order Mennonites from the area. We also have a few pieces from local artists."

Chloe had moved on to the quilted work. She touched a table runner, and Susanna quickly lifted it down and spread it out on the table.

"This is a design called Sunshine and Shadows. It's usually used for bigger items, like quilts, but one lady who quilts for us likes to adapt the design for smaller pieces. She says everyone who comes in might not want to spend the money for a full-size quilt."

"Do you handle traditional quilts?" Chloe's voice lifted with her interest.

Seth reminded himself that her museum had a collection of Pennsylvania folk art. She probably knew more about the contents of Susanna's shop than he did.

"Just a few. We don't really have room for a lot of them." Susanna sounded regretful. "But if you're interested in quilts, you might want to visit Katie's Quilt Shop over in Pleasant Valley. It's only about a half hour's drive, and she has a wonderful selection."

The mention of Pleasant Valley startled him, but it was natural that Susanna would know the other Amish shops in the area.

"Katie Brand," he said. "She does have beautiful quilts." In answer to Susanna's questioning look, he added, "I have relatives over that way, so I've seen it."

Susanna nodded, satisfied. She'd shown no reaction in mentioning Pleasant Valley. She couldn't know that it had once been her home.

"This is such an interesting building," Chloe said, gesturing toward the wide molding that surrounded the doors and windows. "Do you live upstairs?"

Susanna shook her head. "Some of the buildings along the street have apartments on the second floor, but we use it for storage. The basement can be damp, so we dare not put stock there." Then, as if feeling she hadn't fully answered the question, she added, "My mother and I live just up the street from here."

Sorrow darkened her eyes at the mention of her mother. Seth recognized it, hoping Chloe did as well. If she burst out with the information about Susanna's parentage, there was no way he could stop her, short of clapping his hand over her mouth and dragging her out.

An older Amish woman came in just then, the bell over the door jingling. She smiled and nodded to them and then spoke to Susanna in Pennsylvania Dutch.

"I can take over, if you're needed at home."

Susanna shook her head. "The hospice nurse is there with Mamm."

Seth kept his face blank, trying to disguise the fact that he understood them. Hospice—that didn't sound very hopeful for Susanna's mother.

Susanna's smile was strained when she turned back to them. "Is there anything else I can show you?"

"No, thanks."

Chloe's tone was muted, making Seth wonder if she'd pieced together the exchange between Susanna and her friend. Susanna had used the

English word *hospice,* dropping it into a rapid string of Pennsylvania Dutch as the Amish were prone to do when there wasn't a Pennsylvania Dutch equivalent for an English word.

"I'll take the cup holder." Chloe gestured with the one still in her hand. "And the Sunshine and Shadows table runner."

"Very gut." Smiling, Susanna took the items and led the way to the counter. "I'll wrap them up for you."

"And if you have a mailing list, I'd love to receive notices of any special events," Chloe said, opening her handbag and taking out a pen.

"Ja, of course." Susanna indicated a clipboard and pencil on the counter. "We will be happy to send you our flyers when they come out."

Seth watched as Chloe wrote her name and address on the list. Was this a way of staying in touch with her sister? Probably. But at least she hadn't blurted out anything that would upset the apple cart.

"There you are." Transaction completed, Susanna handed her the bag and glanced down at the list. "Chloe," she repeated. "A pretty name." A tiny frown formed between her brows, as if the name reminded her of something.

"I was named after a childhood friend of my mother's, I understand," Chloe said. "And your name?"

"Susanna. Susanna Bitler. I hope you'll visit us again."

"Thank you. I'm sure I will." Chloe was looking at Susanna so intently that Seth's nerves pricked.

"Ready?" he said, his voice louder than he intended in the quiet shop.

"Yes." Chloe didn't look at him, just at Susanna. "Good-bye, Susanna." She walked out of the shop without a backward glance, and he followed quickly, trying not to step on her heels in his haste to get her away.

Seth breathed a relieved sigh once they were clear of the shop and back in the car again. It had gone as well as it could, he supposed. But there was still something he should say.

"When Susanna and her partner were speaking in Pennsylvania Dutch, the partner asked if Susanna needed to leave to take care of her mother. Susanna answered that the hospice nurse was there."

"I thought that was the word she used." Chloe stared out at the creek across the street, probably without seeing its gentle movement. "It sounds as if her mother is in bad shape, doesn't it?"

He nodded, making the turn carefully by the curb market. The vendors were shutting down, and there was always a risk of someone backing into the street.

"I'm afraid so."

"You understand the language then."

"That's what I spoke when I was part of the Amish community," he said. "I didn't know much English until I started school, like Lydia's kids."

"Doesn't that hamper them, not knowing English as their first language?" Chloe sounded troubled, as if she were worried about the two nephews she hadn't met.

"Not if they stay Amish." That was the only honest answer he could give, and it applied to a lot of things about being Amish. "The kids learn English quickly because they hear it a lot, but Pennsylvania Dutch is the language of home." The language of the heart, he'd almost said.

He pulled up next to her car in the lot at the park. A group of kids were playing soccer on the grassy field, and their shouts drifted through the air.

Chloe hadn't moved, and he studied her face. She looked tired, her face drawn.

"Are you all right, Chloe?"

"Sure." She seemed to collect herself, picking up her bag and reaching for the door handle.

"You've had a stressful day. Maybe you shouldn't drive clear back. There are plenty of places to stay along the interstate."

"I'm fine." The sharpness in her voice denied the words. She shook her head, smiling ruefully, and her expression warmed. "Sorry. I guess I'm a little hypersensitive right now. I appreciate your concern. And everything you did to make this happen. I can always stop if I start getting too tired, but I'm ready to be back in my familiar surroundings."

"You're not sorry you came, are you?" He probed at the risk of making her annoyed with him, but he wanted to understand her reaction. He was responsible for bringing the sisters together, and if there was blame, it belonged on him.

She seemed to consider the question. "I . . . No, I'm not sorry. But it's much more complicated than I thought."

"I know. When I offered to help Lydia find you, it seemed so simple. But I guess nothing about families is simple."

Now it was her turn to study him. "That sounds like experience talking."

He shrugged. "I spent eighteen years being Amish and twelve years trying to be Englisch. For the past few months I've been walking a tight-rope between the two because of my family. So no, it's not simple."

"I guess it wouldn't be." For once, her barricades were down, the real Chloe showing in those clear eyes. "I felt as if I'd strayed into a foreign country today. I'm glad I had you here as translator."

"Anytime." He tried for a lightness he didn't feel.

She glanced at her watch. "I'd best get on the road. Thanks again." She reached for the handle.

241

Seth got out quickly. He walked with her to her car and closed the door once she was in. She started the engine and then pressed the button to lower the window.

"You never did tell me the story of why you left the Amish," she said.

"Next time."

Chloe raised her eyebrows. "Are you so sure there's going to be a next time?"

"Yes." He spoke firmly. "I'm sure. You'll come back."

But after she'd pulled away, he stood watching her car until it disappeared from view. He'd like to be confident she'd come back. For Lydia's sake, he told himself. Not his.

Adam glanced at Lydia as Ben's car approached their lane. She had been quiet during the ride home, too quiet. Something was bothering her, and it might be best to bring it into the open before they reached the house.

"Just drop us at the end of the lane, Ben. A little walk will feel gut after all the sitting."

"Sure thing." Ben drew up to the lane and stopped. "It's my pleasure to drive you folks any-time. Just give me a call."

"Denke, Ben. We are grateful." Adam handed over the money he had ready in his hand as he got out. Even so, Lydia had already slid out the other side before he could reach her.

"Denke, Ben," she murmured, and set off rapidly down the lane.

Adam repeated his thanks and hurried after her. Goodness only knew what Ben must be thinking about all these sudden trips to Oyersburg.

Adam caught up with Lydia in a few strides and fell into step with her. She was walking faster than she usually did, and he was reminded of a teakettle getting ready to steam.

"Was ist letz?"

"What's wrong?" She stopped and spun to face him, her eyes flashing. "I should be asking that question of you. What was wrong with you, that you sat all through lunch and didn't say a word?"

He took a firm hold on his temper, but a little slipped anyway. "Maybe I didn't have anything to say. It seemed to me that you and Seth were talking enough for all of us."

"That's the second time you've said that about him. Why are you so down on Seth? He was just trying to help me make Chloe feel wilkom."

"Well, then, you and he did a fine job." Adam didn't like the bitterness in his tone, but he couldn't seem to get rid of it.

"How could Chloe feel wilkom with you sitting there looking disapproving the whole time?" Angry tears sparkled in her eyes, making him feel guilty. He had never thought he'd make his Lydia cry.

"Ach, Lydia, don't be so upset. I wasn't trying to be disapproving, just cautious."

"I doubt that Chloe could tell the difference." Her voice was still tart, but the tears didn't spill over. "And what is there to be cautious about anyway?"

He paused. Lydia ought to know why he felt the way he did, after he'd told her the hard truth about his brother. But it seemed she'd forgotten in her excitement over this newly found sister.

"I think one of us should be wary," he said. "Chloe is a stranger, and Englisch besides."

"And she is my sister," Lydia added. "Just because your brother—"

She stopped abruptly, putting her fingers to her lips, her eyes wide with dismay.

He stiffened, feeling as if she'd struck him. Didn't she realize how much it had cost him to tell her about his brother? It seemed not.

"I have gut reason to be worried about Englisch influence on my family. I have already seen what it can do." His throat was so tight he knew he couldn't talk about this any longer. "I'm going to the barn," he said shortly, and stalked off away from her.

Well, she'd already moved away from him, hadn't she? He felt as if Lydia was on the far side of a swift-flowing stream, and he didn't have the slightest idea how to reach her.

As he neared the barn, he realized that his

father-in-law's wagon was drawn up by the door. He hurried his steps. Had Joseph come to pick up Anna already?

He stepped into the barn, empty and shadowed at this time of day with the horses and the milk cow turned out in the pasture. "Joseph?" His voice echoed.

"Ja, I'm up here." Joseph's voice sounded from above him.

Adam looked up to see his father-in-law in the loft. The boys popped up, one on either side of him.

"Look, Daadi, we're helping Grossdaadi with the hay," David said.

Adam smiled, his tension subsiding. "It looks like you've been rolling in it, as much as you have sticking to your clothes."

David looked down at his black pants and began vigorously brushing them off. "We were moving bales. Daniel and I moved one all by our own selves."

"Gut job." He looked an inquiry at Joseph.

"I brought a few more bales of hay over," his father-in-law explained. "I was chust making some space by the window. You want to climb in the wagon and toss them up to me?"

"Ja, denke." Joseph provided most of the hay they needed, since they didn't have much to cut themselves.

Adam hung his coat on a peg and went back

outside, clambering into the back of the wagon. Joseph was generous with the hay, refusing to accept money, of course, but they paid him back in fruit.

The hay window swung open, and Joseph shooed both of the boys away from the opening, being safe about the drop to the ground. Adam tossed the first bale up, Joseph caught it, and they were soon working in rhythm.

This was what he needed—a little physical labor to clear away the tension of the day. Maybe it would sweep all thoughts of Seth and Chloe from his mind.

Working together, he and Joseph soon had all the bales into the loft. Adam went inside and climbed the ladder to do the stacking.

Joseph glanced at his face and gave a satisfied nod. "You boys go outside now." He nudged Daniel and David toward the ladder. "There's not room up here for four."

David looked a bit mutinous, but Daniel nodded and shepherded his little brother down the ladder to the lower level and out of the barn.

Adam kept his face turned away from Joseph's curious gaze. It was certain-sure that Joseph had noticed something, but maybe he wouldn't speak.

"So, how did it go with little Chloe? She must have been happy to see her sister, ain't so?"

It was natural enough for Joseph to want to hear

about their visit. Chloe was his niece, too, his brother's child. "I think she was glad enough to meet Lydia," he answered carefully. "It seemed she doesn't know what to make of the Amish, though. She was a bit stiff in her manner, I thought."

"I can't say I'm surprised," Joseph said. He stacked bales easily. A powerful man in the prime of life, he'd reject any suggestion that Adam take care of this job alone.

"No?" He'd like to hear Joseph's view of the situation, Adam realized.

Joseph frowned, not stopping his work. "From the few things Diane said about her mother, it seemed the woman would never forgive her for marrying Eli. Diane sent her notes when the boppli were born, I heard, but she never responded."

"She knew enough about the family to grab Chloe after the accident." Adam swung the final bale into place. "I'm thinking she stuffed the girl's head full of nonsense about the Amish and how we live."

"Ach, now that Chloe has met our Lydia, she'll soon see how wrong that is, ja? Nobody could be kinder than Lydia."

Adam nodded, wondering if Joseph would say that if he'd seen Lydia's display of temper. But that was for him and Lydia to work out, nobody else.

"Getting the two of them together is a beginning, anyway," Joseph said. He turned and swung easily down the ladder.

Adam followed him. "Ja, it is." A beginning he'd be just as happy to see over and done with. "She said she would write to Lydia."

"Lydia will be running to the mailbox every day, then." Joseph's ruddy face split in a smile. "I'd like to see for myself how that sweet baby turned out. Maybe she'll come for a visit one day."

"Maybe." Adam kept his tone noncommittal.

"We ought to get on our way home, but I'd guess Anna and Lydia are still in there talking." Joseph hesitated. "I hope they are, for sure."

"Ja, I do, too." The gap between Lydia and her mother had been painful to watch.

Adam followed his father-in-law out of the barn, and they turned toward the house. Painful to watch, ja. And the one between Lydia and him was even more painful still, and he didn't know how to fix it.

Chapter Thirteen

Lydia hurried into the house after she left Adam, to be met by the aroma of baking. Her mother was pulling a cherry pie from the oven. She set it on the cooling rack beside the one she'd obviously just taken out, the dark red cherries bubbling up through the leaf-shaped vents she'd cut in the top crust.

"Ach, Mamm, you didn't need to bake, as well. You had your hands full watching the boys." Lydia gave her a quick hug, inhaling the comforting aroma.

"As if those two sweet boys take much watching," Mamm said. "You'll know I'm ready for pasture if I can't bake and watch kinder at the same time. Anyway, they are out at the barn with your daad."

"I hope at least you used our canned cherries instead of bringing your own." Lydia removed her bonnet and hung it on the peg near the door. If she kept the talk on simple things, maybe she could keep Mamm from seeing how upset she was, though Mamm always seemed to know what she didn't say.

Of course, she was the same way with Daniel and David. Maybe a mother never outgrew that sixth sense where her children were concerned.

"Ja, I did use yours," Mamm said, "but only because I forgot to bring mine. Your trees certain-sure produced plenty of cherries last year."

"I hope they'll do as well this year." She glanced through the window toward the orchard as she spoke, where the four cherry trees were clustered together at one end. "We talked about putting some more cherry trees in this spring, but we didn't get it done. Those trees are getting pretty old, ain't so?"

"Ja, I guess." Mamm poured coffee and carried it to the table without troubling to ask. "Seems to me they were put in after the apple trees were, but often cherry trees don't last as long." She pulled out two chairs. "Now sit, and tell me what has you troubled."

Lydia was surprised into a smile. "I should know I can't hide how I'm feeling from you."

"Was there trouble with Chloe? She came, didn't she?" The lines around Mamm's blue eyes deepened.

"She was there." Lydia sat down next to her mother and took a sip of coffee, its warmth seeming to ease the tightness in her throat. "You should see her, Mamm. So pretty, like a picture in a magazine." She hesitated. "So . . . Englisch."

"Ach, well, it's to be expected." Mamm was practical, as always. "Her grandmother had the raising of her, after all, and she didn't have much sympathy for Amish ways, from what I know."

"I should have been prepared. But when I saw her there with Seth, I felt as if I were looking at a stranger. Somehow I thought I'd know her in my heart." She put her palm against her chest and blinked away a tear.

"You do, really," her mother said. "It just maybe will take some getting used to."

She nodded. "I'm being silly, I guess. There

were gut moments. She was interested in the boys, and she asked questions about our birth mother. And then, just at the end, when I was thinking she was eager to leave, she hugged me." Another tear spilled over as she relived that moment.

"You see?" Mamm said. "It will be all right."

"That touched my heart. I did feel, then, as if we truly were sisters. But when I asked if she'd come here to visit, she didn't want to."

Mamm patted her shoulder. "I'm sorry if it wasn't all you hoped, but it seems to me things went fairly well from what you say, for a first visit."

"But why doesn't she want to come here? That's what I don't understand. Unless it's because Adam scared her off." Her annoyance with him dried her tears and flushed her cheeks.

"It is hard to imagine our Adam scaring anyone," Mamm said, her voice mild.

"Well, maybe it wasn't that bad, but he just sat there, hardly saying a word the whole time. It would be no wonder if Chloe felt he wouldn't welcome her to our home."

"She probably just thought he was shy," Mamm said. "I'm sure you and Seth kept the talk going, ain't so?"

It was hard to hold on to a grudge in the face of Mamm's common sense. "You always stand up for Adam," she said in mock complaint, a smile

251

escaping. "Anyone would think he was your child instead of me."

"I confess we've always been partial to Adam. Your daad and I were glad when you picked him. For a time we feared it would be Seth who won your heart."

She could only stare at her mother, dumbfounded. "Seth? Why would you think that?"

"All the girls were sweet on him, ja? Weren't you?" Mamm stirred her coffee absently, not looking at Lydia.

"He charmed all the girls, that's why. Oh, me, too, a little, but never seriously. You couldn't be serious about Seth. Anyway, I always knew he'd leave. Or be unhappy."

"You were wiser than we knew at that age." Mamm stroked her hand lovingly. "Adam is steady as a rock."

"And just as immovable," she said, her voice as tart as the pie cherries. "Even after meeting Chloe, he is still telling me to be cautious with her, not to care too much."

"Adam's a gut man, but he is a man, after all. They don't always understand a woman's heart. He should know that you aren't one who could care just a little."

"Ja, he should know that." She felt a bit justified to hear Mamm speak so.

"But you should know something about him, too." Mamm's voice grew serious. "You love him in part because he is so responsible, ja? And being responsible means he has to be cautious for those he loves."

"Ja, but just because his brother—" She stopped, swept by the sense that she was being disloyal. She could not betray what Adam had told her about his brother.

"Ja, you told me about his grief for Benjamin," Mamm said. "Poor Benj—a sweet boy, but always crazy to try something new. His family is grieving still, and Adam more than most, because he was the oldest and would feel responsible."

"He does." Her voice went husky as she relived Adam's pain over his brother.

"There are times in every marriage when the two are like harnessed horses pulling in different directions," Mamm pointed out. "You and Adam have been blessed with few troubles so far, but troubles are a test that can make a marriage stronger."

Lydia studied her mother's face, touched by the depth of feeling in her voice. "You and Daad . . ." she said, and then thought she shouldn't.

Mamm patted her hand. "Our first big trouble was the accident, and us only married for less than a month. We went from planning our wedding visits to rushing to the hospital to becoming parents." She smiled, but tears glistened in her eyes.

"I'm sorry . . ." Lydia had never thought of it from that perspective.

"We never regretted that part of it, that's certainsure. But when we were going through all of it, the burdens seemed too heavy to bear. Now I know that our marriage grew so much stronger because of what happened." Mamm paused, her gaze searching Lydia's face. "Just let God use finding your sisters to make you and Adam stronger together, ja?"

Her mother's words seemed to sink into Lydia's heart. "I'll try," she whispered.

Mamm and Daad stayed for supper, and Lydia managed to present a smiling face to the children. But once her folks had gone home and the two boys were settled for the night, she found she was reliving every minute of her visit with Chloe.

She ought to be dwelling on the positive, Lydia told herself. At least she and Chloe had spent some time together. She bent to pick up a block that had missed the toy box when the boys were cleaning up. And Chloe had said she'd write and send pictures. Those were promising steps.

Just because Chloe didn't feel ready to visit her here, on the farm where she'd been born, didn't mean she was shying away from their relationship. Maybe she thought it would be too emotional, being in the house where their mamm and daad had lived.

Lydia walked into the kitchen, running her hand along the wooden cabinets that had been installed long before the house came to her. Her father had built those cabinets, Daad had told her once. Eli had been a skilled craftsman.

She took comfort in being here, in being able to touch things her parents had touched, maybe even more so because she couldn't remember. If Chloe wasn't ready to face that, she must be patient. It would happen, in God's own time.

Please . . .

Lights reflected from the kitchen windows. Someone had just driven in the lane. Seth?

Lydia hurried to the back door. By the time she reached the porch, Seth had already jumped from the car. He stopped at the bottom of the steps, looking up at her.

"Is something wrong?" A tiny fear shimmered along her nerves. "Is Chloe all right?"

"Sure, fine, as far as I know." Seth shook his head. "Sorry. I didn't mean to alarm you by coming over so late. I won't stay, but I thought you should know that Chloe stopped to see Susanna after she left the restaurant."

"What? She didn't tell her, did she? Seth, you didn't let her."

"No, she didn't say anything." The corners of Seth's lips lifted slightly. "Although I don't think I could stop Chloe if she wanted to do something."

Lydia's heartbeat returned to normal. "Ach, you

scared me there for a moment. I suppose she wanted to see Susanna."

"I figured she wouldn't leave Oyersburg without having a look at both her sisters, so I made sure I went with her, just in case. It was all right. Susanna waited on her, and they talked a bit about the shop. Chloe bought a couple of things." He hesitated. "Maybe you didn't know this, but Susanna mentioned a hospice nurse when she was talking to Mrs. Gaus. I guess her mother must be nearing the end."

Lydia's hands clenched. "It breaks my heart to think she's losing her mamm without her sisters. But I fear it would break hers to learn the truth about her parents now."

"I'm sure you're right." Seth propped one foot on the step, and Lydia realized how tired he looked. Even Seth's light charm couldn't stand up to all he'd been through lately.

"Denke, Seth. You have been so kind during all of this upheaval. Especially when I know you have your own family to worry about."

"Well, maybe it gives me a break to worry about yours for a change." His attempt at a smile wasn't very successful. "You might feel a little disappointed about today, but I think you made a lot of progress. It's a big step for someone like Chloe, just coming to meet you. So don't give up hope, okay?"

"I won't. Not ever."

"Good night, Lydia." He went to the car.

Lydia watched while he turned and drove back down the lane. Seth was doing far more than she had any right to expect. Probably more than he'd ever thought possible a few months ago, when he'd been back in his busy city life. Pleasant Valley was having an effect on him.

She went back inside. Odd, that Adam hadn't come out. He was in the workshop, so he must have heard the car and known she was talking to Seth.

Lydia went to the workshop door, which stood ajar, and hesitated. She didn't want to get involved in another argument. But Mamm had been right —this business of her sisters was coming between her and Adam. If a marriage didn't grow stronger in time of trouble, what did it do? Did it break? She pushed the door open and went into the workshop.

Adam sat at his worktable, bending over the clock he was working on. He'd reached the point of sanding the wood, which meant it was nearly finished, but Adam would sand until the wood was smooth as butter. He was a perfectionist when it came to his clocks.

"Seth stopped over," she said. "I thought you'd come out when you heard him."

Adam didn't look up. "I don't suppose he came to see me."

She started to answer, when Mamm's words

slipped back into her mind. Mamm and Daad had thought she cared for Seth when they were all teenagers. Surely Adam didn't think so, too? That was ridiculous, wasn't it?

"He just dropped by to let me know that Chloe had visited Susanna's shop after we left. He thought I should know."

Adam did look up then.

"She didn't say anything to Susanna," she added.

"Gut." Adam turned back to the clock.

She lingered, not liking the distance she felt between them but not sure what to do about it. "It was kind of Seth to let me know. He's grown up since we were teenagers."

Adam made a noise that could only be called a grunt. "It took him long enough."

"Ja." She moved closer to the table, standing behind him and watching his broad, work-roughened hands moving over the wood with such delicacy. "I always knew he'd jump the fence one day. He couldn't be serious about anything for more than a minute, it seemed."

Adam's hands stilled. "The girls all thought he was something special, ain't so?"

"Not all the girls," she said. "Not me."

Was that relief in his face? She couldn't be sure, and she was afraid to say too much lest he feel she was thinking too much about Seth.

Adam put down the emery paper he was using

and tilted his head back to look at her. "You let him take you home from singing."

"Nobody else asked me." His face was intriguing, seen upside down. "I thought maybe you would, but you didn't."

His lips quirked, and she sensed that the storm was over—for the moment, at least.

"I was shy," he said.

"You were slow," she retorted, smiling. She bent to kiss him.

"You are upside down," he murmured against her lips. He turned, catching her around the waist, and pulled her down on his lap, to kiss her again. "That is better."

"Ja, it is." She put her arms around his neck and pressed her cheek against his. "I love you, Adam. I know I can rely on you."

He seemed to withdraw, pulling away from her even though he didn't actually move. "I should finish this work."

"Ja, all right." She got up, feeling suddenly chilled. Something was still wrong between them, and she didn't know what it was.

"Look, some of the strawberries are blossoming already." Mamm knelt in the berry patch, one hand cupping the tiny white blossoms with their yellow centers. "You'll have ripe berries in a month, for sure. Earlier than usual."

"If we don't have a hard frost." Lydia worked her

way down the row of plants, pulling out the weeds that had sprung up through the straw. "It has been a beautiful spring, ja?" She tilted her head back, letting the afternoon sun warm her face even as the breeze teased the hair from under her kapp.

Daad had come over to help Adam expand the run around the chicken coop, and Mamm had arrived as well, bringing a loaf of nut bread. She'd said she just wanted an outing, but Lydia suspected she really wanted to see how Lydia was doing now that she'd had a couple of days after the lunch with Chloe on Saturday. Yesterday had been the off Sunday when they didn't have worship, and she and Adam had gone to his family's for supper, so she hadn't talked to Mamm since Saturday.

She shielded her eyes with her hand. "I hope the boys aren't getting in the way of that chicken netting."

"You worry too much, Lydia," Mamm chided. "You know Adam and your daad won't let them get hurt."

"You're a gut one to talk. I seem to remember you doing quite a bit of worrying when my brothers were that age," she teased.

"More of the worrying when they were a little older," Mamm said, smiling. "Once they got to daring one another to do things, that was. You most likely talked them out of plenty of mischief we never heard about, ain't so?"

Lydia smiled, thinking of her rambunctious brothers. "I tried to head them off a time or two. But I think Daad was always one step ahead of them anyway."

She was relieved to be back to talking naturally with Mamm. She couldn't let Chloe be such a sensitive subject between them. She must speak naturally about her Englisch sister, too.

"I was thinking this morning that you were right about Chloe." She tucked straw under the leaves of one of the larger plants. "I shouldn't expect her to be close all at once. It will take time, and I have to be patient."

Mamm looked pleased. "I think that's the best way. You'll write to her. Tell her all about life here, so she sees that the Amish are just people, like any others."

"Do you remember Chloe from when she was small?"

"Ach, of course I do." Mamm, bending over to inspect the rhubarb that had sprung up, nodded briskly. "Such a pretty child, with those big eyes and soft hair. She had a head of hair when she was born, I remember, not bald like some babies."

"It would be nice if she came here, so you could talk to her." For an instant Lydia's voice faltered. Would that happen? She longed for it so much.

"When you write to her, you must tell her that I remember her." Mamm seemed to hesitate for a moment. "And since we're talking of remembering, I think you have forgotten about stopping to see your great-aunt."

Lydia sat back on her heels. "I did forget. I'm sorry. I'll go over tomorrow. I want to see what else she remembers about my sisters."

"Lydia Beachy." Mamm's voice had an edge that made her look up in a hurry. "Can you think of nothing else? You should be going to see your great-aunt as a kindness to her, and not for what you think you can get from it."

For an instant, Lydia could only stare. Her cheeks went hot. "Ach, Mamm, I'm sorry. You're right. That was thoughtless of me." She paused. "I guess I have been thinking of little else, but that's natural, isn't it?" She couldn't seem to help the slightly defensive note in her words.

"Ja, I'm sure it is natural. Still, you can't let your excitement about your sisters affect your duties to others." Mamm eyed her, as if checking to be sure her words were hitting home.

Lydia lowered her face. Mamm was right, of course. But she was right, as well. How could she stop thinking about Susanna and Chloe?

"I still have apple-currant jelly left from last year. I'll take a jar to Aunt Sara." Maybe that would make amends. "I know that's her favorite."

"Ja, gut." Mamm gave a short nod. "Why don't you send a couple of jars to Chloe, too? It would give her a taste of the orchard."

262

Lydia pictured the worldly-looking young woman who'd toyed with her food at the restaurant on Saturday. "I don't know. She's so . . . citified. I don't know that she'd have a taste for something so plain."

"You send them," Mamm said firmly. "A gift from the heart is always cherished."

Would it be? She'd hate to think of Chloe joking with her friends about the gift her Amish sister had sent. But Chloe surely was too kind for such an action.

"Here come the boys, running like they always do," Mamm said in the indulgent tone that was reserved for her grandchildren.

Daniel raced through the orchard with David a couple of steps behind, holding his straw hat so it wouldn't blow off. They were laughing, their faces alight with fun, and Lydia's heart clutched with love for them.

If only . . . But she wouldn't spoil her love for those two with regrets for the babes she hadn't been able to conceive.

"I wish I could send a picture of them to Chloe," she said, then bit her lip, wondering if Mamm would chide her again.

But her mother seemed to take the comment seriously. "I've heard Bishop Mose doesn't mind having pictures taken of kinder, so long as they're not for the parents to keep and be prideful about. What does Adam say about it?"

"It was just a thought. I haven't mentioned it to him." Mostly because she suspected she knew what he would say. Adam was a stickler for following the rules.

"Mammi, Daadi said we should come and ask you." Daniel, arriving first, panted out the words.

"Ask me what?"

"If we can have a snack," David said, grabbing her apron. "Please, Mammi? I'm awful hungry."

"Ach, when aren't you hungry?" She ruffled his hair, suspecting that this meant Adam wanted them out of the way for a bit. "Let's go in the kitchen. I think Grossmammi is ready for a cup of tea by now, ja?" She glanced at her mother.

"Ja, sounds gut." Mamm took a boy by each hand. "Walk nice with me instead of running just this once, ja?"

"Ja, Grossmammi." Daniel smiled up at her, and David swung her hand.

Lydia followed the three of them as they walked toward the house, smiling at the image they made.

Image. Picture. If she had a picture of the boys, Seth could send it to Chloe on his computer, she'd guess. In fact, he'd most likely be able to take it, as well.

What would Adam say if she asked him? On the other hand, did she really need to ask? It wasn't as if she wanted the picture for herself.

She considered the idea. It wasn't right to go behind Adam's back. But on the other hand, it would save them an argument, wouldn't it?

Chapter Fourteen

"That's gut and sturdy." Adam's father-in-law gave a shake to the new chicken wire they'd just stapled to the post. "Like those kinder of yours." Joseph's weathered face creased in a smile as he watched the boys run to Lydia.

"Those two are growing like weeds." Adam's gaze lingered on Lydia's face, glowing with love as she gave each of the boys a quick hug.

"It made no trouble, having them here with us while we worked," Joseph said, and Adam thought there was a question in the words.

"Ja, but I could tell from here that Lydia was worrying about them. She'd be sure Daniel would staple his finger or David would wind himself up in the wire."

Joseph chuckled. "That's our Lydia, for sure. Always worrying about the younger ones. She was like that with her brothers, too. Ach, you know what that is like as well as anyone. You are the oldest in your family."

Adam nodded, unrolling the chicken wire to the next post. What Joseph said was true enough, and it couldn't help but make him think of Benjamin. "You can't always protect your little sisters and brothers, no matter how hard you try."

Joseph's shrewd eyes studied his face. "Some folks find it hard to learn that lesson."

"Ja." Adam was struggling with it—that was certain-sure. And it didn't help that his daad saw things the same way—Adam was the oldest; Adam should have been able to keep Benj from making mistakes.

He looked at his boys, just going in the back door with Lydia and their grossmammi. "I pray I would never blame Daniel if something happened to David." He bit off the last word. He shouldn't have said that, though sometimes Joseph felt more like his father than his own daad did.

Joseph began setting in the last row of staples. "We all make mistakes with our kinder, sometimes because we're thinking too much of how it affects us." He paused, as if to let his words sink in. "We just have to do the best we can at the time, and ask God to keep making us better at it."

"That's not easy." Adam started gathering up their tools and the remnants of wire. Chickens weren't the brightest of God's creatures, and if they left anything they shouldn't, the silly birds would try to eat it.

"No." Joseph blew out a long breath. "Anna has been fretting about whether we did the wrong thing in not telling Lydia about her sisters to begin with. But we did what we thought best at the time."

"I'm sure of it." Adam led the way out of the chicken yard, fastening the door securely. Then he opened the hatch between the coop and the yard, letting the birds out again. They came squawking, unhappy at having been shut in during the day.

"At least things seem to be getting back to normal between Lydia and her mamm," Joseph said as they started walking toward the house.

"Ja, they are back to being close." Adam was glad of that, of course. He just wished he could say the same about him and Lydia. But they wouldn't be back in balance until he got another job, regardless of what was happening with Lydia's sisters.

Joseph paused at the edge of the apple orchard. "Which tree was it you wanted me to look at?"

"The big one in the center." Adam led the way. He'd been concerned about that old tree this spring, and he trusted Joseph's opinion on trees as on other things.

"You know, I happened to be in Caleb Brand's shop the other day." Joseph's tone was casual, almost too casual. "Katie was complaining that their wall clock was broken. Caleb wondered if you had time to take on the job of fixing it for them."

Adam had a feeling it wasn't Caleb who'd suggested that, and he stiffened. "I don't—"

"Ach, don't get all stiff-necked about it." Joseph slapped him good-naturedly on the shoulder. "So what if I mentioned you to Caleb? He needs a clock fixed and there's no harm in making a little money doing the work for him. You have a gift for clocks, ain't so?"

"Not sure it's a gift," he muttered, not quite ready to give up feeling embarrassed that his father-in-law was drumming up a job for him. "Daad always called it tinkering."

"Your daad's one of those who think farming's the only job for an Amishman," Joseph said. "Ja, the church needs farmers, but it also needs clockmakers. Look at Jesus' disciples—they didn't all do the same thing. Fishermen, tax collectors. And Paul, he was a tentmaker."

"Ja, that's so, but . . ." He let that trail off. There was a lot of sense in what Joseph said. True, he'd like it fine if he could farm full-time, but he couldn't.

Joseph wasn't one to beat a subject to death. He walked in silence until they reached the tree and then tilted his head back, studying it.

"You see what's wrong, ja?" Adam said finally, to break the silence.

"Ja." Joseph blew out a long breath, his forehead furrowed. "The tree is old. It had been bearing for some years even before my brother bought this place." He leaned closer, tracing a crack where one of the heavy branches was threatening to break away from the trunk. "You could prune it and hope for the best, but I'd say it was time the tree was felled. Otherwise there's no saying what it might take with it if it comes down in a storm."

"Ja, that's what is in my mind, too." Adam looked at the younger trees around it. He'd not like to lose any of those. "But Lydia has a special feeling for this tree."

"Because of her mamm," Joseph said, nodding. "Ja, I know. Diane loved this tree. She said it made her happy because it had weathered a lot of storms and still bore fruit." He smiled slightly. "She had an interesting way of thinking, Diane did. Seemed to me that was a fine description of how a Christian ought to live."

Adam had to admit there was a lot of truth in what Joseph said, but it didn't resolve the problem. "Lydia's not going to like hearing that the tree should come down."

"Lydia's a sensible woman," Joseph said. "She'll understand when you explain it to her."

Adam wouldn't like to contradict his father-in-law. But in this case, he had a feeling Joseph was wrong. He feared Lydia wouldn't understand at all.

The sun was sliding behind the ridge as Seth drove through the village on the way home from Jessie's doctor's appointment, sending long shadows reaching across the narrow street. He glanced in the rearview mirror to check on his sister.

Jessie leaned against the leather seat. The last time he'd looked, she'd been staring out the window. Now her eyes were closed, but it wasn't safe to assume she was asleep. Her appointments seemed to leave her drained, and it wasn't unusual for her to say little or nothing for the rest of the day.

It would be comforting to feel she was making progress, but he couldn't honestly say he thought she was. Still, the doctors had stressed that it could be a long process in Jessie's case, searching for the right medication and going through rounds of therapy sessions. Apparently there was nothing simple or straightforward about it.

His fingers tightened on the steering wheel. Stupid, to think there was a magic pill that would solve everything, but that's how normally healthy people tended to think, he supposed. His mother was more realistic than he was, or maybe just more accepting of what life threw at her.

He glanced at Mamm, sitting next to him. It seemed to him that she was making a conscious effort to sit up straight, and her face was drawn.

"Are you in pain?" he asked, keeping his voice low in case Jessie really was asleep.

"No, no." Her quick response only served to convince him that she was, but she'd never admit it.

"You should lie down for a bit when I get you home. I'll take care of supper."

"There's no need. I'm fine. Anyway . . ." She let the word trail off, and Seth had a sense of things left unsaid.

"What is it, Mamm?"

She moved slightly, maybe trying to get more comfortable. "I was chust thinking that you should probably be getting back to your job. It has been wonderful to have you close by, but I don't want you to lose your work. I know how important it is to you."

If she knew that, she knew more than he did. "It's not a problem. Remember, I told you about how much of my work is done on the computer? I can do that anywhere."

"But you can't be comfortable, living in a motel when you have a nice apartment in Chicago," Mamm protested. She seemed convinced that the perfectly nice upscale motel was a den of iniquity. "I can hire a driver to take us back and forth to appointments."

"I know, Mamm. But wouldn't you rather have me?" He gave her the teasing smile that had usually gotten him his way. She could, of course, hire a driver, and he'd be happy to pay. But his mother needed more than transportation right now. She needed support from family. From him.

"Ja, you know I would." She reached across the seat to pat his arm. "I just don't want to

271

take you away from your work. And your life."

"It's not a problem. My boss doesn't care where I am, as long as I'm working."

Peter Wilkins was a good friend as well as a good boss, and he never forgot the people like Seth who'd stayed with him through the struggles of getting his business off the ground. True, Pete might like having him close at hand, and there were issues that could be settled more quickly face-to-face.

But Pete understood that Seth's sense of responsibility to his family, even if it was belated, required that he stay here for the time being, at least.

He turned in the lane, relieved that his mother seemed to be giving up the subject. He didn't want her worrying needlessly. She leaned forward, peering out the window.

"Look, here is Lydia coming with the boys. It looks as if they are bringing some supper."

Lydia was carrying a large basket topped with a tea towel, a sure sign that it held food. Daniel was toting a smaller basket with an air of importance, while David darted ahead.

"She's always here." The snap in Jessie's voice was never a good sign.

Normally Mamm would correct any of her children who grumbled about a neighbor. Seth glanced at her. Mamm's lips pressed tightly together. She obviously wasn't saying anything for fear of provoking one of Jessie's outbursts.

"Lydia has been a good friend," he said mildly, unwilling to let it go without comment.

He could never forget just how good Lydia had been during that terrible time when Jessie had broken down entirely, flaring out at the bishop, even, and getting hysterical when confronted with wrongdoing. That had been the moment when he'd understood just how much his sister needed care.

Mamm had still been in rehab with her hip, so he'd been the one who had to sign Jessie into the hospital. He'd been so grateful for Lydia's calm helpfulness on that miserable day. That had been what finally woke him to a sense of what he owed his family.

He pulled up to the back porch just as Lydia and her boys arrived. Before he or Mamm could speak, Jessie brushed past and flew into the house. The two little boys stared after her.

"Don't mind our Jessie," Mamm said quickly. "She is chust tired after the long ride, ja?"

The boys nodded, their faces solemn. "I got sick one time when we rode in a van all the way to Lancaster for our cousin's wedding," Daniel said.

"That's probably it," Seth agreed. "Mamm, you promised you'd have a rest, too."

"Ach, I did no such thing. Lydia, it is so nice of you to come over." Mamm pressed Lydia's hand in silent apology for Jessie's behavior.

"We brought some pot roast for your supper." Lydia gestured with the basket she held. "And Daniel has a loaf of cinnamon bread."

"I could have carried it," David muttered.

"Mammi thought . . ." Daniel began what was probably going to be a comment about the bread ending up on the ground, but he stopped at a look from his mother.

"Did you know that our barn cat has kittens?" Seth said, hoping to divert their attention. "She's had them out already, so she'd probably let you look at them."

"Can we, Mammi?" In Daniel's excitement he nearly lost the bread, and Seth rescued it.

"Ja, but don't scare her," Lydia said. "And don't handle the kittens."

"We won't." Daniel was turning to run toward the barn as he spoke, with David right behind him.

"Let me carry the basket." Seth reached for Lydia's burden, but she went quickly up the steps with it.

"It's not heavy," she said. "I'll just put it on the counter. It's wrapped up, so it will stay warm awhile, or you can heat it up later."

"Denke, Lydia," Mamm said. She took off her bonnet and hung it up, her movements slow. "That is wonderful kind."

"You do look tired," Lydia said, her voice warm. "Why don't you do as Seth said and have a little rest before supper? I just need to ask him something, and then I must collect the boys and get home."

"You are all ganging up on me," Mamm said, but she was smiling as she went off toward the stairs.

Seth motioned to the door. "Let's go out on the porch to talk." She probably wanted to discuss something about her sisters, and no one else needed to overhear.

Outside, the breeze set Lydia's kapp strings dancing, and for a moment she looked like the young girl he'd taken home from her first singing.

"I'm sorry about Jessie," he said abruptly. "Sometimes she's fine, and other times . . ." He let that trail off, because Lydia knew as well as he did.

"It makes no trouble." Lydia's voice was tranquil. "Maybe I embarrass her because I saw her at her worst. That's natural enough."

"I suppose." It would be too much to hope that Lydia could wipe that day out of her mind. He certainly couldn't. "You wanted to talk to me about something?"

"Ja, I do." She hesitated, seeming at a loss for words for a moment. "Your cell phone—it is the kind that takes pictures, ja?"

He hadn't seen that coming, but now that she'd mentioned it, he understood immediately. "Yes, sure. You want me to take photos of the boys and send them to Chloe, right?"

"Right." She gave a decisive little nod. "After all, she is Englisch, so there's no reason for her not to look at pictures. And lots of Amish allow their kinder to be photographed."

He raised an eyebrow. "Does that group include Adam?"

"I . . . I hope he will understand." Her cheeks were pink.

In other words, she didn't intend to tell Adam until after it was done. Well, it wasn't his business to tell her how to handle her husband.

"I'll be glad to take a couple of photos of the boys," Seth said, pulling out his cell phone. "Why don't we do it now? I can send them right away." Before Lydia had a chance to worry about it or second-guess herself.

"Ja, gut." Lydia headed for the barn, and he had to hurry to keep up.

Funny thing. He wasn't thinking so much about the photos. Or about how Adam would react when he heard.

His mind was totally caught up in picturing how Chloe would look when she received them.

"What do you think—here or farther to the right?" Chloe held the illuminated fraktur design up to the wall, glancing over her shoulder at Kendra.

"If that's the largest one, it ought to go in the middle. What did you say it was called again?" Kendra was always good at making a quick

276

decision and she was an expert restorer, but she had a blind spot when it came to other areas of work.

"Fraktur," Chloe repeated. She and Kendra had a deal—they each supplemented the other's areas of weakness. "The combination of designs and words was only used on special documents, like marriage or birth certificates. This is the best one we have—it dates back to 1789." Her fingers hovered over the intricate designs whose colorful inks had barely faded over the years.

"It looks like something a monk would have done in copying the Bible back in the Middle Ages," Kendra said. She took a step back, eyeing the frame to be sure it was level as Chloe attached it to the mounting strip.

"It's probably a descendant of those manuscripts," Chloe explained. "The early immigrants brought the custom with them from Germany."

Lydia might well have a sample of fraktur hanging on the wall of the farmhouse she'd spoken of. The Amish and Mennonites had done some of the best fraktur to record the important events in the lives of their families.

"What comes next?" Kendra leaned against the table on which Chloe had put the items for the current display in the small section allotted to Pennsylvania Dutch folk art. "You want to work on the pottery?"

"In a minute." Chloe reached for the folder

she'd been carrying around with her. The room where they were setting up the folk art display was one of the smaller exhibit rooms, and they had it to themselves at the moment. "I want to show you something first. I received this last night."

Kendra pushed herself away from the table and came to look over Chloe's shoulder as she opened the folder. Two small, smiling faces looked up at Chloe, and her heart gave a surprising lurch.

"Adorable," Kendra said. "Who . . ." She stopped, obviously taking in the boys' solid blue shirts, suspenders, and straw hats. "They're your sister's boys, aren't they?"

Chloe nodded, touching the photo she'd printed. "Daniel is the older one, and David is the younger." Daniel's grin showed a missing front tooth. David's face was still round and babyish, and dimples indented his cheeks.

"So, you have two little nephews." Kendra's gaze was questioning. "To say nothing of two little great-grandsons for your grandmother. Did you show this to her?"

Chloe shook her head, wondering if she was being a coward. "Not yet. I'm not sure how she'll react."

"You won't know unless you tell her." Kendra was practical, as always. "But I thought the Amish didn't believe in taking pictures of themselves. How did you get this? Seth what's-his-name?"

"Seth Miller. I gave him my e-mail address, and he sent this to me last night. No message, just the photo. I suppose he took it on a cell phone camera. I just hope he had Lydia's permission."

"Look at those grins." Kendra smiled. "Who could resist those two? But why do you suppose Seth didn't say anything? You didn't have a fight with him, did you?"

"Not exactly." But they seemed to set off some kind of fireworks each time they were together.

Kendra twirled a strand of hair around her finger while she considered Chloe's face. "He ought to be happy with you. He got what he wanted. You met your sisters."

Chloe nodded. The trouble was that Seth expected a lot more than that from her. More, maybe, than she was willing or able to give.

"How did your grandmother react when you told her about meeting your sisters?" Kendra switched to the other thorn in her side.

"She didn't want to hear it, just like she didn't want me to go. She's maintaining a frigid silence over the whole matter, and believe me, nobody does frigid silence better than my grandmother."

Kendra gave a sympathetic nod. "Maybe she has more in common with the Amish than she'd like to admit. Banning you, in effect."

Chloe stared at her blankly.

"Come on, surely you've heard of banning. Even I have, and I'm totally not interested in the Amish." Kendra's face expressed disbelief.

"I . . . I'm sure I've heard something about it. That's when they throw out people who don't go along with all their rules, isn't it?" Her stomach twisted at the thought of her sister in that ugly black bonnet. What would happen to her if she just chucked it one day?

"I don't think it's quite as cut-and-dried as you make it sound," Kendra said. "Weren't you ever curious? I should think you'd have wanted to learn all you could about the Amish. I mean, even before you knew about your sisters, you knew that your mother had joined them. It seems unnatural not to be curious."

"I guess it does," Chloe said slowly. Seth had basically implied the same thing. "My grand-mother was so negative about the Amish that I suppose I didn't question it. Kids don't, for the most part. They accept their situation as normal, because it's what they know."

"I suppose," Kendra admitted grudgingly. "But I should think you'd have asked questions at some point."

"I did once." The memory came back, falling into her conscious mind as if it had tumbled out of a closet. "My grandfather was the kindest man on earth. So I asked him why my mother had gone away and become Amish."

"What did he say?" Kendra prompted her when Chloe didn't go on.

Chloe realized she was gripping a piece of redware pottery between her fingers. She set it down carefully. "He started to cry." Her voice became choked. "I'd never seen a man cry before. It scared me so much that I went running to my grandmother."

"Who promptly blamed you for upsetting your grandfather and scared you so much that you never asked again," Kendra said. "Don't worry, I can fill in the blanks. And your grandmother is very predictable."

"She's not as bad as I made it sound," Chloe protested. "I'm sure she means well."

"Means to have her own way," Kendra muttered, but she caught a look from Chloe and subsided.

"I suppose I ought to get over those feelings, but it isn't easy when something's so ingrained." Chloe wasn't sure when she'd started doubting her grandmother so much. "When I was a kid, I always wanted to be part of a big family. But this isn't what I had in mind."

"You haven't been talking to Dr. Dull about it, have you?"

Chloe couldn't control her smile, although she shouldn't encourage Kendra. "Don't call him that," she said, with no hope that Kendra would desist. "He's not dull, he's just . . ." She searched for a word.

"Boring," Kendra supplied. "Look, I have to get back to my own work. If I see one of those interns, I'll send him down to help you. Don't forget about the jazz festival tonight. And if you want to talk to someone about your family, call the guy who sent you the photo. You don't look like you're thinking of a father when you talk about him." She was gone before Chloe could retort.

That was ridiculous. She wasn't looking for a father figure. And as far as Seth was concerned . . .

Well, Seth wasn't anyone's idea of a father figure, not with the smile of a charmer and the depth of the seas in his eyes.

She picked up a piece of scherenschnitte, the complex, intricate, lacy patterns that were cut from paper and used to decorate Pennsylvania Dutch marriage and birth certificates—like a child's paper snowflake carried to its most elaborate extreme. She ought to get these hung, but first . . .

She set it down again. First, she was going to call Seth. Not because she was interested in him, she assured herself. Just because she hadn't thanked him yet for sending her the photograph of Daniel and David. He'd probably risked making Adam, at least, if not Lydia, angry with him, and she ought to let him know she appreciated it.

Seth answered his cell phone on the first ring, almost as if he'd been waiting for her call. "Hi, Chloe."

So he'd recognized her number or programmed her into his phone, as if he expected to be talking to her often.

"I hope I didn't interrupt you when you're working."

"Nothing I can't stop doing for the pleasure of talking to you." His voice was so warm it seemed the cell phone was sending off heat.

"I . . ." She cleared her throat and started again. Really, she couldn't let the man get to her. "I'm at work, so I can't talk long, but I wanted to thank you for sending the photo of the boys."

"Cute kids, aren't they?" There was a smile in his voice. "They were busy trying to convince the barn cat to let them pick up her kittens, so I retrieved them before someone ended up on the wrong side of her claws."

"Were they at your place?" Or had he been visiting Lydia? How close a friend was he, anyway?

"My mother's. Lydia and the boys had brought some supper over for my mother and sister, because they'd . . . we'd . . . been out all afternoon." Something about the way he said the words sounded as if it was serious.

"I hope nothing's wrong with your mother."

"No, we were . . ." Again he stopped, as if editing what he said to her. "She broke her hip a few months ago, and she's still on the mend. It was thoughtful of Lydia to bring supper so Mamm could have a rest."

His calling his mother Mamm the way the Amish did reminded her that he'd grown up Amish, and she still hadn't heard that story. Not that it was any of her business, of course.

"So, anyway, what are you doing at work today?" He changed the subject as if his family was out of bounds.

"I'm setting up a new display of Pennsylvania Dutch folk art. The museum owns more items than it can possibly display, so we keep rotating things in and out of storage."

"Sounds interesting. I'll have to stop by and see it the next time I'm in the city. Maybe you could give me a guided tour."

"That might be arranged." She wasn't flirting with him, was she? "As a thank-you for sending me the picture. I hope Lydia said it was all right," she added quickly.

"It was her suggestion. It surprised me, coming from her, but as she said, there's no reason why you shouldn't see a photo of the boys. It's not as if she wanted it for herself."

"Isn't that kind of silly? I mean, that whole prohibition against photos . . ." She stopped, reminding herself that Seth had been raised Amish and might not appreciate yet another negative comment.

"The Amish interpret the Bible in a fairly literal way, and they tend to equate photographs with the graven images that are forbidden. Although

I've heard the bishop say that the harm comes in the attitude—if you displayed a photograph it might be out of pride."

"It all sounds more complicated than I'd thought." She was reminded of Kendra's disbelief that she didn't know more about the Amish.

Seth's laugh sounded a bit rueful. "The Amish may be plain, but there's nothing simple about their beliefs. Anyway, Lydia wanted you to have the photo, so I was happy to take it and send it."

"And what about Adam?" The stern-faced man who'd said scarcely a word at lunch didn't look like someone who'd have a liberal interpretation of anything.

"Yet to be determined," Seth said, his voice light. "Lydia didn't say anything to him in advance. You know the saying, sometimes it's easier to ask for forgiveness than permission."

"She shouldn't have to do either." Chloe's voice was tart with disapproval. Women had every right that men did to make decisions.

"Well, Lydia doesn't see it that way, and we have to respect her beliefs."

"Even when those beliefs are hopelessly old-fashioned?"

"That's her choice," he said. "Just as it was your mother's."

Chloe's throat tightened at the thought of everything that had come from that decision. And everything that was still to come, most likely.

"Have you given any more thought to coming to Pleasant Valley for a visit?" Seth asked.

She might have known he would ask that question if given a chance. "I've been busy with the new display and all." That didn't sound like a very convincing excuse, and it annoyed her that she found it necessary to make any to him. "I said I'd consider it, and I will."

He was silent for a few seconds. "I hope so," he said finally. "Your sister would appreciate it. Thanks for calling, Chloe." He hung up before she could say anything else.

Not that she had anything left to say. She'd been rude. But he'd been pushy, so didn't he deserve it?

Chapter Fifteen

Lydia stood at the sink, swishing the dandelion greens she'd just cut in a pan of water. The trick with dandelion greens was to cut them early, while they were still small and tender. She'd fix a hot bacon dressing—

The back screen door rattled, and Adam came into the kitchen, wiping off his shoes on the mat.

"Look!" She held up a wet handful of greens. "A taste of spring for supper tonight."

His solemn expression vanished in a smile.

"Your favorite, ja? Dandelion greens with hot bacon dressing."

"Not just me, I think." She smiled up at him as he came to look over her shoulder, relieved that they were thinking in tandem again.

"There'll be some green onions from the garden in another couple of days, I'd say." Adam leaned against the counter, a sign he had time to talk. "You can fix some boiled potatoes with them."

"Ja, that will be gut. Maybe some ham to go with." It had been a favorite spring meal when she was growing up.

Adam nodded, glancing through the window over the sink. "Where are the boys?"

"They came home from school all excited because Teacher Mary gave them their parts for the end-of-school program. Daniel insisted they practice in the barn, so we'll be surprised."

"Hard to believe it's that close to the end of the school year." Adam was frowning slightly.

"Don't worry, we'll hear all about their parts," she said. "Can you imagine David keeping a secret for long?" Her smile invited him to join in her amusement, but he seemed suddenly far away.

A feather of concern touched her. He was worried about not having found a job yet, that was certain-sure, and she hated to see him so down.

"Daniel asked me what they should give Teacher Mary for her end-of-year gift." She went on talking, hoping she could bring back his smile. "David said he thought she'd like a base-ball, but I suspect that's really what he wants."

Adam focused on her. "A softball, maybe, for his birthday."

She nodded. "Anyway, I was thinking that maybe we could buy Teacher Mary a book. You know how she loves to read."

Adam's face tightened. "We can't buy every-thing you think of, Lydia. Baseballs and books . . ." He stopped, shaking his head, his lips pressed together.

Ach, she was foolish, talking so when Adam was worried about bringing money in. What had she been thinking?

"Teacher Mary would probably rather have a basket of my jams and jellies anyway," she said quickly. "And David can just as well use the ball we have already."

"I'm sorry," Adam muttered, making her heart twist. "I'll find something soon. I promise."

"Adam, you don't need to fret about it." She reached out to touch him, wanting to comfort him and not sure how. "We'll make out all right."

But he took a step away, as if her comforting wasn't what he wanted, and her heart hurt even worse.

"I had your daad look at the big old tree in the middle of the orchard while he was here." He seemed to push the words out, as if he didn't want to say them but he had to.

"Ja?" She looked at him, puzzled.

"The trunk is starting to split. It's an old tree, not producing like it used to. Your daad and I agreed that it's time for it to come down."

She could only stare at him, trying to process what he was saying. "Come down? You want to cut down my mamm's tree?"

"It's not what I want," Adam said. "It's what is the sensible thing to do. You know as well as I do that trees get old, just like anything else. We wouldn't want it to come down in a storm—"

"It's not going to come down in a storm." She seemed to have a band around her chest, constricting her heart, making it hard even to take a breath. "That tree has stood for years, and it will stand for more. You can't cut it down."

"Lydia, it's only a tree."

"It's not only a tree." Didn't he see what this meant to her? "It was my mamm's favorite place. It was where she told us stories and played with us. It's my connection to her." Tears blinded her eyes. "That's why you want to cut it down, isn't it? Because it reminds you of my Englisch mother!"

Unable to say another word without crying, she ran from the room.

Adam knew he'd made a mess of telling Lydia about the tree, just as he'd feared he would. But what was he supposed to do? Couldn't Lydia understand that he was only trying to do what was best? It was ridiculous to think he'd be taking his feelings out on a tree.

Not that he had feelings of any sort about Lydia's long-dead mother, Adam assured himself.

A rustle of movement made him turn. Daniel and David stood in the doorway. His heart seemed to skip a beat. How much had they heard? Too much, judging by their pale faces and big eyes.

"Daadi?" Daniel's voice squeaked. "Was ist letz? Why is Mammi crying?"

"Ach, it's nothing big." He tried to sound jovial and succeeded in sounding a bit ferhoodled. "I had to tell Mammi that the big old tree in the orchard is splitting, and that made her sad. She remembers sitting in the tree when she was a little girl, and she doesn't want to lose it."

David's lips trembled. "She sounded like she was mad at you."

Ach, Lydia, why aren't you here to cope with the boys? You would do it much better than I can.

He drew them closer, a hand on each shoulder. "You know, sometimes when we're upset about something we take it out on whoever or whatever is closest. Like when you threw your pencil when you couldn't get your arithmetic to come out right. Remember?"

They considered that explanation, and he thought they looked a little relieved.

"You can go out and play for a while before chores." He ruffled their corn-silk hair. "Go on now."

They went, but without the release of energy that usually sent them flying out the door for play. Maybe he should have said more, but he didn't know what else it could be. Dealing with hurt feelings was Lydia's job, not his.

He went to the bottom of the stairs and looked up, alert for any sound that would tell him what Lydia was doing. He couldn't hear a thing.

"Lydia?"

No answer.

"I'm going out to the barn. The kinder are outside playing." Settling his hat squarely on his head, he walked out, letting the back door bang a little louder than was really necessary.

Daniel and David were tossing a ball back and forth in the backyard. Adam went on past them to the barn. The latch on one of the stall doors was loose, and it had best be fixed before the buggy horse decided to take a stroll.

He checked the latch, discovered that the screw was stripped, and went back out to the toolshed to get a new one and the screwdriver. The game of catch seemed to be in recess at the moment. Daniel and David were standing eye to eye, most likely arguing over who should retrieve the ball. He could see it from here—a white shape gleaming under the rosebush by the porch.

Leaving the toolshed door open for light, he sorted through the box of screws to find one the right size. The routine chore was calming, smoothing away the rough edges of that exchange with Lydia. They would talk about the tree again, calmly. He'd show her the split that had him and Joseph concerned. Lydia would understand.

Taking the screw and screwdriver, he went back outside and froze. Daniel and David weren't glaring at each other. They were rolling on the ground, pummeling each other.

He ran toward them, shouting, "Daniel! David! Stop that at once!" He reached them, pulling them apart and holding them like a mother cat hauling her kittens by the scruff of the neck.

"What do you mean by this? Fighting is not how we settle disagreements in this family."

Even as he spoke he saw Lydia come flying out the door. "Are you hurt?" she said, looking from one to the other.

"They are not hurt. They are naughty." He gave them a shake. "Tell your mammi you are sorry. And tell each other, too."

"But Daadi, he was supposed to catch the ball. He missed, so he should go after it." Daniel seemed disposed to argue.

"You threw it over my head on purpose."

David's face scrunched up, and Adam suspected he was trying not to cry.

"I am ashamed of both of you." His tone was sharp. "If there are any more arguments, you will both get spankings. You understand?"

"Ja, Daadi," Daniel mumbled. "I'm sorry."

"Ja, Daadi," David echoed. He sniffled. "I'm sorry, too."

"Go in the house now, both of you." Lydia shooed them toward the kitchen door. Once they were out of earshot, she turned to Adam.

"You didn't need to take it out on them if you're angry with me," she snapped.

He blew out an exasperated breath. "That has nothing to do with it. I can't let them fight. They must be punished, so they'll remember that is not how we settle disagreements."

He spun and headed back to the safety of the barn. He would never understand women, and this woman in particular.

Chloe parked her car in the garage and walked through the garden to the back door of the massive Georgian house that had been home except for her years away at school. During her childhood, the lawn and gardens had been taken care of by an elderly man named Fred Parsons, who'd shown remarkable patience with a six-year-old who wanted to grow a tomato plant.

But times had changed, and Fred had eventually

been replaced by a lawn service, the vegetable patch turned into flower beds.

Enough maundering on about the past, she ordered herself. *You ought to be thinking about showing Gran the photograph of Lydia's boys, and insisting that for once she sit down and talk to you about your mother.*

Why had Diane become Amish? That was really the heart of the matter for Chloe. If she understood that central fact, she had a feeling everything else would fall into place.

The back door opened onto a hallway. She could hear the clatter of pans coming from the kitchen on her left. Nora, the housekeeper, was starting dinner preparations, which meant Gran was eating in. They could talk.

Her stomach twisted unhappily at the thought. She wasn't asking anything unreasonable, surely, in wanting to know about her own mother. That conviction battled the pressure she felt not to hurt her grandmother.

Chloe reached automatically for the mail that was always placed on the drop-leaf table beneath the mirror in the front hall. It wasn't there.

Nora appeared in the kitchen doorway, so on cue that she was like a jack-in-the-box, popping up at the appropriate point in the music.

"You're looking for the mail," she said. "Your grandmother has it." She jerked her head toward a closed door, not one of her iron-gray curls moving. "She's in the library."

Nora was apparently sending her a message, but what it was, Chloe couldn't guess. And she knew better than to ask. Nora operated on her own complicated version of household ethics, her sympathy often with Chloe but her loyalty to her employer.

The library was the room Chloe most associated with her grandfather. It was there that she'd gone every Saturday to receive her allowance, counted out in coins at first, then in larger bills as she grew. There, too, that she'd gone each evening to give her grandfather a good-night kiss, shepherded by Nora once she'd outgrown a nanny. Grandfather would be here, in his favorite wingback chair, smoking one of the after-dinner cigars that were forbidden in the rest of the house.

Shaking off the past again, she entered the library. She half expected to find Gran at the rolltop desk, but she sat in the wingback chair instead, her neatly shod feet resting on an upholstered ottoman.

"Hi, Gran." She bent to kiss one soft cheek. "How was your day?"

"As always." Gran clipped off the words. She gestured toward the desk. "You received a letter from Lydia Beachy."

So that was what was behind the strained atmosphere in the house. Chloe moved quickly toward the desk and picked up the envelope. It had been opened. For a moment she couldn't speak.

Then she found her voice, along with a flicker of anger. "You opened my mail."

Her grandmother's eyes didn't quite meet hers. "I felt it my duty."

"I'm twenty-six, Gran, not six." She held the envelope, trying to keep the anger from building. "When I moved back after grad school, you agreed to respect my privacy. This is unacceptable."

"Really, Chloe." Her grandmother sat up very straight. "It's not as if I intercepted a love letter. You have to admit that anything to do with your sister concerns me, as well."

Chloe was taken aback at that statement. "You've made it quite clear you don't want to hear about Lydia and Susanna. Have you changed your mind?"

"No." The word dripped ice. "The letter is nothing—just inconsequential babble about her life."

"Then why did you read it?" Her head was beginning to pound, a frequent result of trying to win an argument with her grandmother. "You must be a little interested."

Her grandmother shook her head. "I had to read it to be sure those people were not trying to sway you into their strange way of thinking, the way they did your mother."

"Why did Diane become Amish?" Chloe's pulse was suddenly pounding in her ears. "You act as if they stole her from her pram. She was a grown woman when she made her decision. I want to know why."

"She fell in love, of course." Gran's lips curled on the words, as if they didn't taste good. "I suppose she had some foolish ideas about giving up her privileged life and getting close to the land. She might as well have joined a commune. I'm sure she regretted it every day of her life, but she was too proud to admit it and come back."

That didn't mesh with the image Lydia had drawn of their mother's life. "What makes you so sure? Lydia seems happy to live that way."

Gran dismissed Lydia with a wave of her hand. "She's been brought up that way. It's too late for her. But I don't want you getting sucked into it, like your mother was." Gran's hands knotted into fists on the arms of her chair. "Diane broke her father's heart. She brought on his stroke and hurried him into an early grave."

And here Chloe thought she'd done that, with her questions about Diane. Maybe they were both tarred with that brush.

"I don't see how anyone can blame Diane for falling in love, but that happened months after she left Philadelphia. Why did she leave to begin with? What drove her away from this life?"

"Nothing." Gran surged to her feet. "How dare you imply—"

She stopped in midsentence, grasping the chair for support, her face losing its color.

"Gran!" Chloe rushed to her, the quarrel swallowed up by concern. "What is it? Let me help you."

She tried to take her grandmother's arm, but Gran pushed her away. "I don't want you. Call Nora."

Chloe rang the buzzer that connected with the kitchen and then eased her grandmother back into the chair in spite of her protests. Chloe might suspect that the fainting spell was a convenient way to win an argument, except that Gran's skin was alarmingly ashen.

Bile rose in Chloe's throat. Maybe she hadn't been responsible for Grandfather's problems, but her persistence had brought this on.

Nora bustled in barely a minute later. She bent over Gran with a glass of water and a pill bottle in her hand, her voice soothing. She caught Chloe's eye and jerked her head toward the door.

Chloe nodded, understanding. Gran would do better without her disturbing presence, obviously. "I'll wait out in the hall," she said softly. "Tell me if you want me to call the rescue squad or the doctor."

Nora gave a quick nod and turned her back on Chloe, all her concern for Gran.

Yes, all right, it was obvious that her presence wasn't helping matters. She went out quickly, her mind teeming with incoherent prayers.

It was a long ten minutes before Nora came out. She marched toward the kitchen. "I'll make her a cup of tea. That's all she needs."

"Are you sure I shouldn't call her doctor?" Chloe followed her with a guilty backward glance at the closed door.

"She's just upset herself." Nora switched on the electric kettle. "There's nothing wrong with her that a little peace and quiet won't cure."

"It was my fault. I shouldn't have . . ."

Chloe stopped, not sure she wanted to bring up the subject of her mother with Nora. Nora was devoted to Gran, and Chloe had never known her to voice the slightest hint of disagreement. But she must have had some feeling for Diane, who had grown up in this house just as Chloe had.

Nora stared at the kettle, as if willing it to boil. But then she sighed and shook her head, and Chloe realized she wasn't thinking about the water at all.

"There is no use talking to your grandmother about Diane," she said. "She can't do it, that's all."

"You could . . ." Chloe began, with no real hope.

"No." The kettle whistled. Chloe felt the urge to vent a little steam herself. Or a little frustration.

She turned away, realizing she still held Lydia's letter in her hand. Maybe she'd go out—

"You should talk to Dr. Maitland," Nora said abruptly. "That's what you should do."

Chloe blinked, surprised. "Why? Nora, if you think I need counseling over this disagreement with my grandmother, I can tell you right now it wouldn't change anything."

Nora gave an exasperated sigh. "I'm not talking about any of his fancy counseling. You should talk to him about your mother."

"Brad? Why would he know anything about Diane? I mean, I know he was my mother's generation, but he's never indicated they were close."

"Maybe he never talks about it, but he was crazy about her. She never looked at him that way, but she treated him like a younger brother. She talked to him."

Chloe's mind buzzed with a series of incoherent thoughts, and she tried to sort them out. Brad? He knew about her concerns over her mother. Surely, if he'd known something about why she left, he'd have told her.

Or would he? Like Nora, he seemed to feel he owed his loyalty to Gran, not her.

"You think he knows why Diane went away?" She zeroed in on Nora's face, but she was already shaking her head.

"I've said more than I should. I'm not saying

another word. And don't you tell him I sent you, either." Nora walked out, the china cup of tea held in her hands like an offering.

Chloe stood where she was, trying to wrap her mind around the revelation. Brad had had feelings for her mother? How was it she'd never known about it? She found the idea more than a little disturbing.

But if Brad knew what had motivated her mother, she intended to find out.

Chapter Sixteen

Lydia tried to push away the guilt she felt over having come to Oyersburg without telling Adam. But she hadn't wanted to confide her errand to anyone except her mother, who understood. She lifted the heavy box from the backseat of Ben's car, where she'd stowed it for the drive to Susanna's shop.

"Want me to carry that in for you?" Ben reached for the door handle.

"I have it. Denke, Ben." She managed to balance the box against her knee while she closed the car door.

"Okay. I'll be back for you in an hour." Ben waved and pulled out onto the street.

Lydia stood for a moment, composing herself. Across the street from Susanna's shop, the wide, shallow creek chuckled peacefully over flat rocks. Peace—ja, that was what seemed to be missing in her life just now. Susanna was fortunate to have such inspiring beauty practically on her doorstep.

Lydia hefted the box. She was doing the right thing, wasn't she? Susanna had expressed interest in Adam's clocks, so bringing one of them gave Lydia an excellent reason to visit the shop again.

That wasn't what troubled her. The difficulty was that she hadn't told Adam what she was doing.

Adam had picked up a couple of days' work helping Joseph Beiler in his machine shop, so he hadn't been there to see her take the clock from the workshop. Joseph's wife, Myra, had recently had a baby boy, and apparently work had been piling up for Joseph and his partner. He'd welcomed an extra pair of hands in the shop.

Lydia's lips trembled on a smile. Myra had a fine, healthy boy now in addition to the two girls. And since their last little one was a Down's syndrome baby, it was no doubt especially sweet to see the little boy unaffected.

Myra's longing for a son couldn't help but remind Lydia of her own desire for a daughter. Maybe it was human nature to yearn for what you didn't have.

Well, Adam was occupied today, and so was she. If Susanna thought the clock would sell, that was time enough to tell him. Things had been strained and silent between them for the past few days, but at least he hadn't brought up again the idea of cutting down her mother's tree. Maybe he'd given up on it. If she came home with hopeful news about the clock, maybe that would help ease them over this rough place.

Lydia opened the door and sidled in, trying not to let it bang after her.

"Here, let me help you. That must be heavy." Susanna came toward her, her limp more noticeable when she tried to hurry.

"I can manage," Lydia said, not wanting to burden Susanna. "I don't know if you remember me, but . . ."

"Ja, of course. You're Lydia Beachy, and you were going to bring one of your husband's clocks, ain't so?"

Lydia nodded, doubly relieved that Susanna was here rather than her partner and also that Susanna remembered. "Just tell me where I can put it down."

"Back here." Susanna led the way to the rear of the shop and around the corner. She pushed open a door. "We have a little workroom back here."

The workroom was simple enough, with a table in the middle holding packing supplies and shelves along one wall with boxes. But the room must be a spot for Susanna and her partner to take a break, as well, since it had a couple of comfortable-looking rockers, a small refrigerator, and a kettle that was steaming on a gas burner.

"Right here on the table," Susanna said, sweeping some foam packing material out of the way with one hand. "You know, I was hoping you would come back."

Lydia set the box down gently. She could have used some of the foam when she'd tried to figure out how to carry the clock without risking damage.

"I hope—"

The kettle began to shriek, interrupting her words, and they both laughed. Warmth touched Lydia's heart. She and her sister had laughed together.

"You will have a cup of tea?" Susanna lifted the kettle, and its scream turned to a soft puffing.

"Denke. That would be most wilkom." Lydia took the chair that Susanna indicated and sat rocking while Susanna brewed tea in a brown earthenware pot.

When Susanna picked up the tray, Lydia rose quickly. "Shall I take that for you?"

"Like you, I can manage." Susanna smiled. "I've had my limp for so long that I just automatically balance."

"I'm sorry. I didn't mean . . ." Lydia felt sure her cheeks were scarlet.

"Ach, don't be embarrassed." Susanna set the tray down on a small table between the chairs and settled herself before pouring the tea. "I just find it easiest to mention my disability first, so people don't have to tiptoe around the subject."

"You've had it a long time, you said?" *Since you were three, and you were in the crash that killed our parents. But you don't know that, do you?*

"Ja. It was an accident of some sort when I was very small. I don't remember it, so it's as if it never happened to me."

"I suppose that's gut, not to remember. If either of my boys were hurt . . ." Lydia stopped, seeing Daniel and David's faces in her mind.

"You have little boys?"

Susanna was probably just being polite. She couldn't really be interested in a stranger's children. She didn't know they were her nephews.

"Two boys," Lydia replied. "Daniel is eight, and David is six."

"That's so nice." A faint wistfulness crossed Susanna's face, as if she, too, were longing for something she couldn't have.

"They can be a handful sometimes. They're at school now, but they'll be off for the summer almost before I'm ready for it. My mamm keeps reminding me to cherish these years, because they go by so fast."

Again a fleeting expression crossed Susanna's face—sorrow, this time. For her own mamm, Lydia supposed. Like most Amish, Susanna would no doubt accept her mother's passing as God's will, but her feelings of loss would still run deep.

"Well, let us have a look at the clock." Susanna rose, setting her teacup on the tray. "I'll open it. You just finish your tea."

"The tea is delicious." Lydia sat, obeying, and sipped the aromatic brew while she watched Susanna open the box. "Mint, is it?"

"Ja, my own blend of spearmint and peppermint. I thought I might make it to sell in the shop, but I didn't really have enough plants for that, so we just enjoy it here with our special customers." Her sweet smile included Lydia in that group.

Lydia tried to keep her mind on the clock, surely one of Adam's best, but her thoughts persisted in straying to the subject close to her heart.

You are my sister, Susanna. She couldn't say the words, not now. Mamm had been right when she'd cautioned her. It would be unkind to upset Susanna's life at such a time.

But the longing was there, and one day, this longing would be fulfilled. One day it would be right to tell Susanna about their parents.

And then what? She had told Chloe, and that had certainly not gone as well as she'd hoped. She must be sensible about her dreams for her sisters. She could not expect instant love or an automatic relationship.

Susanna had the clock out on the table. Lydia drained her cup and went to stand next to her as she unwrapped it. *You are my sister, Susanna,* she said silently, watching her. *And one day you will know it.*

Susanna lifted out the clock, surveying it from all angles, studying it. Lydia held her breath.

When Susanna looked up, her face was transformed by her smile. "Lydia, this is wonderful-gut work. Your husband is a fine clock-maker for sure."

She could breathe again. "It's gut enough to sell in the shop?"

"I would be pleased to have it to sell, and as many more as you would like to bring in." There could be no doubting the genuineness of Susanna's enthusiasm. "I'm sure I can sell them. Maybe not right away, but once we start having tourists coming through town, sales will pick up."

"Adam will be wonderful glad to hear this." At least, she trusted he would be once she explained it to him.

"Then we can all look forward to a gut relationship, ain't so?" Susanna smiled.

"Ja, for sure." *More than you know, Susanna.*

When Lydia reached home, the house was suspiciously quiet. Her mother sat at the kitchen table, Lydia's mending basket in front of her, deftly fixing a torn seam.

"Denke, Mammi." Lydia knew better than to assume her mother would watch the boys without finding something that needed doing. "Where are the kinder?"

"Upstairs. They are having a little time thinking about how to behave."

"They misbehaved?" That was so unusual that Lydia had to force herself to believe Mamm was serious.

"Ach, don't look so upset." Mamm smiled, folding up the mended pants. "It would be a sad day when I couldn't handle two little boys fighting."

"I am so sorry they did that when you were here to watch them." Lydia sank down in the nearest chair. "They have been squabbling so much lately. I don't know what's gotten into them."

"They are chust being boys," Mamm said, her tone placid. "I mind when I was in the hospital after Matthew was born. You had your hands full with Andrew and Joshua fussing at each other all the time, ain't so?"

"Ja, that's so." Lydia felt her temples begin to throb. "They were upset because you were in the hospital, so they took it out on each other. But I'm not sick. Nor Adam."

"Ach, it doesn't matter what's wrong, Lydia. You should know that about kinder. They sense it when the grownups are upset, and that makes them fratch at each other."

Lydia sighed, rubbing her forehead where the

tension was building. "Ja, I guess we have been . . ." She stopped, shaking her head.

"Don't start telling yourself it's your fault, now." Mamm reached over to pat her hand. "You can't make everyone happy all the time. The boys will be all right."

Lydia shook her head. "I'm their mamm. I should have seen what was troubling them."

"They will be fine, and you will, too." Mamm crossed to the hall where she'd hung her bonnet. "And here is something else for you to think about. I brought something you should have."

She set a bag on the table, where it landed with a solid thud. Mamm's face grew solemn as she looked at it. "When we cleared up the house after your parents died, I kept some things of your mamm's. I thought maybe someday you would want them."

Headache forgotten, Lydia reached into the bag. The object inside was a wooden dower chest, the kind of small one that a loving father might make for a daughter to keep her treasures in. She touched it gently, imagining she could feel something warm in its smooth surface. "This was my mamm's?"

"No, the box was one your daadi made for you. I thought it was right to keep your mammi's things in it, so you'd have something of both of them."

Lydia gave her a questioning look. "But you never gave it to me."

"No." Mamm's face seemed to crumple, as if tears were not far away. "I realized that I couldn't give you her letters or her journal because . . ."

"That would have told me about my sisters." Lydia finished the sentence for her, her voice choked.

"Ja. I'm sorry." Mamm shook her head as if to clear it. "I could never read those things. It would be prying into Diane's secret thoughts. But you are her daughter, after all. Maybe this will answer some of your questions." She bent to kiss Lydia's cheek. "I must go now."

Lydia just sat where she was, her hands on the box, hearing Mamm go upstairs to the boys and their muted voices telling her they were sorry. In a moment they were down again, happily walking out to help their grossmammi harness her buggy horse.

The old house fell silent after the screen door banged behind them. Lydia caressed the box, her fingers tracing the fine workmanship, imagining her father making it for his small daughter. Love—there must surely be love in every inch of it.

She lifted the lid, aware of the wood scent that clung to it after all these years. A white handkerchief covered the contents, and she lifted it off with gentle fingers.

A handful of letters, tied together with a bit of ribbon—a study of the addresses and the postmarks told her they were letters exchanged between her parents before they were married. She laid them aside, not sure she ought to read them. How would she feel about Daniel, years from now, reading the letters she'd once written to Adam?

A fold of tissue paper, unwrapped, revealed a pressed violet. Fearing it would crumble at a touch, she lifted it to her nose, inhaling its faint perfume. It had been a memento of something, for sure, but no one left alive would know what. Still, she could guess. She had a pressed apple blossom tucked away, picked the night Adam first kissed her under the apple tree.

Beneath the pressed flower lay two books—nothing else. Vaguely disappointed, she took out the first one. It was an Englisch Bible, with her mother's maiden name imprinted in gold letters on the cover. Maybe Chloe would want to have the Bible.

The other book was fat and leather-covered, perhaps the book she'd used to press the violet. Lydia moved her fingers over the blank cover and opened it.

At first she didn't realize what she was looking at, and then she understood. The book was actually a journal. Not a diary, with a space for each day, but rather a blank book filled with handwriting.

She leafed through it. Her mother had written in

it sporadically, it seemed. Most of the entries were dated, with long stretches when maybe nothing had happened that Diane had felt was worth recording.

Lydia read a page: Diane talking about Aunt Sara—Lydia's great-aunt Sara, in other words—teaching her how to make strawberry rhubarb jam. Diane had had a gift for making the scene come to life. Lydia could almost see her standing there at the stove, stirring the jam so that it splattered, Great-aunt Sara clucking and laughing at the same time. It seemed for an instant that Lydia could hear women's voices and the sound of their laughter.

The children's shouts from outside recalled Lydia to the present. They would be running in the door soon. She'd best put these things away to look through more carefully later.

She leafed quickly through the book, curious to see how much of her mamm's life it covered. The earliest entry was, it seemed, the date of Diane's marriage. *Today I leave the old life with all its pain behind to start a new life with the man I love,* she'd written.

A lump in her throat, Lydia leafed through toward the back. The date of an entry caught her eye, and she stopped for a closer look. That must have been written sometime not long after Chloe was born, judging by the date.

Smiling, she bent over the book, prepared to

read about Diane's joy over her new baby daughter.

Maybe I've made a terrible mistake in coming here. The letters were jagged, as if they'd been written in a hurry. *What was I thinking? How could I imagine I was suited to this life? I should give up. Take the children and go back to Philadelphia. I don't belong here.*

A shudder of revulsion went through Lydia, as physical as if she'd reached into a flower bed and pulled out a snake. No. She slammed the book shut and thrust it back into the box.

But getting it out of sight didn't help. She could still see those words, imprinted on her brain. *I should give up. I don't belong here.*

Lydia pressed her fingers to her lips. How could this be? Everyone talked of how happy Diane was. Lydia had never even considered anything else. How could she accept the fact that her mother might have planned to leave?

"I am the snowy owl, hunting two little field mice that are out in the corn too late." Adam chased the boys into their room. He swooped David's nightgown-clad figure high in the air and plopped him into bed. "Now for the second mouse." In a few steps he'd captured a giggling Daniel and deposited him in bed, too.

He glanced at Lydia, who was tidying the room as she always did before the boys went to sleep.

Usually at this point she warned him not to get them too excited to sleep.

But she looked distracted, her gaze fixed on something off in the distance. She'd been that way since he got home, it seemed. Maybe the little dower chest her mamm had brought made her feel sadness for the father who'd made it for her.

"Now, then." He pulled the quilt up over Daniel. "Are you ready for prayers?"

Surprisingly, Daniel's lips trembled. He shot a glance toward his brother. "I . . . We . . . have to tell you something."

"Ja?" Adam sat down on the bed, wondering what mischief they'd been up to.

"We were naughty when Grossmammi was here." Daniel said the words so quickly that Adam felt sure he'd been practicing them. "We were fighting, and Grossmammi said we must remember that Amish don't turn to hitting to solve problems. And she made us sit in our room for an hour."

That made it sound as if Lydia's mamm had been here to babysit. He'd assumed she'd just stopped by to visit and drop off the dower chest. He sent an inquiring look toward Lydia, but she was turned away, her face hidden from him.

"Grossmammi was right. Violence toward another person is never the answer." He looked from Daniel to David and back again, hoping he was impressing the importance of this on each of them. "This is part of what being Amish means. We obey Christ's command to turn the other cheek. You know that, ain't so?"

"Ja, Daadi," Daniel whispered, a tear slipping down his cheek.

"Ja, Daadi," David echoed, maybe not quite so upset as his older brother.

"Did you tell Grossmammi you were sorry?"

They nodded. "She forgives us," Daniel added.

"Ja, I know she would forgive you, but that doesn't mean it's not serious, what you did." He could feel the frustration rising in him, and he fought to keep his voice even. "This fighting muscht stop."

"We won't fight anymore," Daniel whispered, and David nodded.

Adam could only wish he felt more reassured by their promises. His family life seemed to be spinning out of control, and he didn't know what to do about it.

Well, he knew one thing. When the boys were in bed, he and Lydia had to talk.

Adam waited until he felt sure Daniel and David were settled. He followed Lydia into the kitchen.

"Your mamm was babysitting the boys after school? Where were you?"

Lydia's gaze slid away from his. "I . . . I went to Oyersburg."

"You went to see Susanna? Why?" Had she

forgotten already that she'd agreed Susanna shouldn't be told?

"The last time I was there, I told her about your clocks. She was interested. She wanted to see one, saying maybe she could sell it in the shop."

"You took one of my clocks to her to sell?" He was repeating her, he realized, but he was having trouble wrapping his mind around the idea. Lydia had kept a secret from him. They didn't have secrets. At least, they hadn't used to. Several questions crowded his mind, and he picked the most important one. "Why didn't you tell me?"

"I didn't want you to be disappointed, in case Susanna said it wouldn't sell." She was looking at him now, the embarrassing part apparently over. "I just thought . . ."

"I don't want you deciding things for me." That came out harshly, but that was how he felt. "I'm not one of the kinder."

"But you might have said no, just because of Susanna being my sister. So I thought I'd ask her first." Her eyes sparkled suddenly. "And she loved the clock. She said the workmanship was very fine, and she wanted to put it in her shop. Adam, she put a price on it of five hundred dollars."

"Five hundred? That's foolishness. No one would pay that for a clock."

"Susanna says they would. Some of her Englisch customers would pay that and more. It might take a while, she said, but when the tourist

316

trade picks up, she's sure it will sell." Lydia put her hand on his arm coaxingly. "Don't be angry. I know you've been worried about the job and not having money coming in, and this could make that easier, ain't so?"

"Ja." He had to admit the money would be a help, if it really came to pass. If. "But no more secrets, ja?"

Except that he was as guilty as she was. He hadn't talked to her about how worried he was about his lack of a job, although she seemed to know it without his telling her. He'd wanted to protect her, he rationalized, knowing it was an excuse.

Lydia nodded, sobering. "No more secrets." She touched the miniature dower chest that still sat on the kitchen counter. "So I must tell you what I found in the box."

"You said it held some things of your mamm's. And that your daad made the box for you when you were little." He could understand that making her feel sorrow for the parents she didn't remember, but Lydia looked more upset than sad.

"Ja." Lydia pressed her palm against her cheek, something she only did when she was feeling distressed. "There were some letters inside, and an Englisch Bible. And a book. A journal that my mother wrote her thoughts in, sort of like a diary."

"Many people write in diaries. Amish, especially, maybe." Just like they wrote letters, which

317

nobody else seemed to do anymore. "Did you look at what she wrote?"

"I didn't intend to read it then. I just looked through it." Lydia seemed to be circling around and around the thing that troubled her.

"I know a journal is private, but your mamm has been gone a long time. She wouldn't mind if you looked at it."

"That's not what upset me." Lydia's eyes were shiny with unshed tears. "One page caught my eye. It must have been written when Chloe was very small." Her voice seemed to choke on the words. "Oh, Adam, she said that maybe her becoming Amish was a mistake. That she didn't belong. That she should take the kinder and go back to Philadelphia." The tears spilled over, and Lydia covered her face with her hands.

"Ach, Lydia, don't cry." He put his arms around her, trying to find the words that would comfort her.

But he couldn't. He'd known from the beginning that it was a mistake for Lydia to get in touch with the Englisch side of her family. It could only cause trouble.

And now this—learning that her mother might have regretted her decision and wanted to go back to the Englisch world.

Lydia was hurting. But all he could think was what if it made Lydia start thinking that she had made a mistake, too.

Chapter Seventeen

Seth reached for the cell phone on the corner of the motel room desk, automatically checking the incoming call before answering. It was Chloe. Two calls in a few days—he could almost think she liked to talk to him.

"Hi, Chloe. How are you?" He leaned back in the desk chair, staring at an uninspiring beige wall of the motel near Pleasant Valley that passed for home at the moment.

"Fine, thanks. I received a package from Lydia this morning." She sounded a little surprised. "Three jars of apple butter. It . . . It was lovely of her."

He couldn't help smiling at her tone. "But you're wondering what to do with all that apple butter."

"Not at all," she began stiffly, and then her voice relaxed into laughter. "I guess I was."

"Like most Amish women, Lydia gives food as a sign of affection. Put it on cottage cheese for a lunch salad."

"Apple butter on cottage cheese? You're kidding, right?"

"Not kidding. You call yourself Pennsylvania Dutch and you don't eat one of their favorite things?"

"Actually, it never occurred to me to call myself

Pennsylvania Dutch until quite recently." Her voice was warm in his ear, almost as if she were sitting next to him. "Anyway, I thought maybe you'd tell Lydia I received the package and how much I appreciate it."

"I'll be glad to, but you could actually write her a letter, you know."

"I did, but I guess I'm too used to instant communication. I didn't want to wait."

"You'd never make an Amish woman with that attitude," he teased.

"No computer, no phone, no electricity . . . nothing that makes a connection to the outside world? No, thanks." There was more laughter in her voice.

"It sounds to me as if you've been reading up on the Amish. You're better informed than you were the last time we spoke."

"Yes, I guess it was time I educated myself. A friend pointed out that as a researcher, I was being very inconsistent not to look into my parents' lifestyle."

So she had confided in someone about the situation. "Man friend or woman friend?" He couldn't seem to help asking.

"Woman friend. Kendra. We work together. There's not really anyone else I'd trust with something as sensitive as this is."

His feelings were mixed—glad she didn't have a boyfriend lurking in the background, sorry she didn't have more people she could rely on.

"Have you ever wondered why you avoided learning anything about the Amish?"

"I don't . . ." She stopped, seeming to change course in midsentence. "I guess it was just how I was raised."

She was holding something back—something she wasn't ready to tell him, he supposed.

"There's something I want to know," she said, and he could hear determination in her voice. "Why did my mother decide to become Amish?"

The question surprised him. He'd think she'd be more focused on her sisters. "I don't really know. I guess I assumed it was because she fell in love with Eli."

"There must have been more," she protested. "You can't change your whole life for love."

"Can't you?" It seemed to him that plenty of people did just that. Or tried to, anyway.

"If you don't want to help me . . ."

"I'll ask around," he said quickly. "See what I can find out. I'll call you back, all right?"

"That's great. Thanks, Seth. I . . . I appreciate it."

"Anytime," he said, and meant it.

After he'd disconnected, Seth got up, his mind churning with possibilities.

Lydia was the obvious place to start. He could drive over there now and catch her before the boys came home from school.

On country roads with little traffic, it took him less than twenty minutes from the motel by the highway to Lydia's place. He pulled into the lane and spotted Lydia almost immediately. She was in the backyard taking sheets off the clothesline.

He pulled up beside the house and got out to cross the lawn toward her.

"Seth, wilkom." Lydia's smile slipped into a more concerned expression. "Is something wrong?"

"No, nothing." At least, he didn't think so, although his initial desire to help Lydia had produced some unintended results. "I had a call from Chloe. She received the package of apple butter, and she wanted me to tell you how much she appreciated it."

"Ach, that was thoughtful of her." Lydia smiled, her hands continuing to fold the sheet she held. "I hope she enjoys it. I could send her more."

"Three jars is probably plenty for now," he said, mindful of Chloe's perplexed reaction. "She's only one person, after all."

"Ja, that's true." She put the sheet in the basket at her feet, her movements almost jerky. Her face, when she wasn't looking at him, seemed drawn and tired.

"Now it's my turn to ask," he said, keeping his voice casual. "Is something wrong?"

"Ach, no, I—" She stopped, the mask draining

away to show the worry underneath. "I learned something I didn't expect, is all."

"About what?" He caught the end of the sheet as she snapped it, straightening his end.

Lydia accepted his help without objection, bringing her ends to his, snapping and folding. It was as if they were engaged in an intricate dance.

"Mamm gave me some things that had belonged to my birth mother, Diane," she said finally. "Some letters. A journal."

He nodded, encouraging her to go on. At a guess, she'd learned something she didn't like from those items.

"I didn't read everything. I just happened to spot one page in her journal." Lydia stopped, holding the folded sheet against her breast. "She said that maybe she had made a mistake in choosing this life. That maybe she should take the kinder and go back to Philadelphia." She looked down, her mouth trembling.

Seth's heart ached for her. Poor Lydia. Every promising step forward seemed to end in disappointment of one kind or another.

"Did you read the entire journal? Maybe that was just a momentary whim. A reaction to a bad day."

"No, I didn't." She pressed her lips together. "I should, I know. I will. I have to find out if she intended to leave. I'm just afraid I'm going to learn that she didn't want to be Amish at all."

All he could think was how ironic it was. Chloe was desperate to learn why her mother had given up her life to become Amish, while Lydia was terrified she'd discover her mother wanted to be Englisch again.

"You boys go and play with your cousins, but remember that you're the biggest," Lydia cautioned the boys as they jumped down from the buggy at her brother's house the next afternoon.

"Daniel and David, you be wonderful gentle to the little ones," Adam added.

"We will," Daniel answered for both of them, and they raced across the lawn.

Lydia climbed down, and Adam handed her the basket containing the pies she'd brought. "I'll take care of the horse," he said.

"You mean you'll find my daad and brothers and avoid the woman-talk," she teased.

Adam nodded, smiling but looking a bit cautious. As nervy as she'd been lately, poor Adam probably didn't know what to expect next.

But she was feeling surprisingly better today. The talk with Seth seemed to have cleared her mind. It had been stupid to react so emotionally to those lines in her mother's journal. She needed to read the rest of the journal for any hints her mother had left, and then she needed to talk to Mamm about the whole thing. If Diane had intended to leave, surely someone would have guessed.

She started across the backyard of the farmhouse where she'd grown up. Her next younger brother, Andrew, worked the farm with Daad now, since Daad claimed he wasn't ready to retire to the grossdaadi haus yet. Andrew and his wife, Carol, lived in the frame house right across the lane from Mamm and Daad's, and they all seemed to get on fine that way. Well, it would surely be a poor daughter-in-law who couldn't get along with someone as kind as Mamm.

Lydia headed for the picnic table under the trees, where Mamm and Great-aunt Sara sat watching the kinder. Mamm held Andy and Carol's youngest, three-month-old Sara Jane, in her arms.

"Ach, look at that precious girl." Lydia bent over, hand on Mamm's shoulder, to peer into the tiny face. Sara Jane slept with the intensity only a boppli could manage, her little rosebud mouth working as if feeding. A pang touched Lydia's heart and was gone again. Someday, maybe. When God willed.

"She is a precious lamb, ain't so?" Aunt Sara beamed at the baby who shared her name.

"For sure." Lydia clasped Aunt Sara's hand. "You are feeling better every day, ain't so?"

"Ach, what else, the way everyone is spoiling me, like you with that pot of chicken soup Adam dropped off," Aunt Sara said.

Mamm reached up to pat Lydia's cheek. "And you—how are you?"

"I'm fine, Mamm. But I'd best get these pies to the kitchen, or Carol will think I'm avoiding work."

"Carol will think no such thing, and you know it," Mamm said. "But go along with you. Aunt Sara and I will keep an eye on the kinder."

Lydia nodded, carting the basket to the house. Today they were celebrating Andy's birthday, and no doubt Carol had made a cake, but she'd asked Lydia to bring her dried-apple pies, knowing they were Andy's favorites. A generous gesture, Lydia thought, to let someone else make your husband's favorite.

"It smells gut in here," she said, shoving the door open with the basket.

"Ach, Lydia, let me help you." Matthew, her youngest brother and the only one not yet married, came to relieve her of the pies.

"You're just hoping to snitch a piece of Lydia's pies early," Becky teased him. Becky was her brother Joshua's wife, just married in November and expecting their first already. Since she'd been a neighbor and playmate of the boys from the time they were toddlers, she had no hesitation in treating Matt like a brother.

"It's ser gut to see you." Lydia took off her bonnet and went to kiss each of her sisters-in-law: Becky, dark-haired and rosy-cheeked, already putting on a little weight with marriage and her pregnancy; and Carol, slim and tall, her abundant light-brown hair smoothed back under her kapp and her apron as clean as if she'd sat in the shade all day, which she obviously hadn't to judge by the array of food in various stages of preparation.

"Two roast chickens plus a pot roast?" Lydia gave Carol an extra squeeze. "It is just family, isn't it? Or did you invite the whole county?"

"I just want to be sure I have enough," Carol said, eyes crinkling with laughter. "You know how those brothers of yours eat."

"Ja," Matthew said. "Don't forget about the brothers part, chust because you have two new sisters now."

Carol and Becky combined in glaring at Matt, and he spread his hands, his freckled face bewildered. "What?"

"If somebody told Matt to be tactful, it was a forlorn hope," Lydia said, since it was obvious that was exactly what had happened. "Don't worry, Matty. You'll always be my favorite youngest brother." She gave him a hug and then a push. "Now get out of the kitchen and out of the way."

"Sorry," Carol said when he'd gone. "As scatterbrained as that boy is, it's a wonder he doesn't forget his head sometimes."

"Ach, I don't mind Matthew," Lydia said, setting the pies out on the table. "Your husband was just as bad at that age, and he grew out of it."

She was actually glad Matty had said something, because it had been a good reminder. She had been so focused on her new sisters lately that she had been in danger of ignoring the family she already had until Mamm had reminded her to visit Aunt Sara. She was ashamed, and she would do better.

The afternoon slipped by like a hundred other family celebrations. They ate until everyone was groaning, they gave Andy the small gifts they'd brought, the men talked about the growing season and the women about babies.

Finally Lydia had the opportunity she'd been watching for—a time with Mamm with only a cooing baby and a sleeping toddler for company.

"The family knows about Chloe and Susanna, ja?" Lydia said, wondering why she hadn't asked the question earlier.

"We had to tell them something," Mamm said, bouncing the baby on her knees. "But they don't know their names or where they live. Your daad thought it best for now. I'm sure they've guessed that the youngest one lives in the city, and I think they have the idea your middle sister is still out in Ohio." She caught Lydia's surprised look. "They just assumed, and I didn't correct them. Can you imagine Matty keeping a secret?"

"I guess not." She shook her head. "I don't think

I ever realized how hard it is to keep a secret. So many things to think of and remember."

"It was hard, at times," Mamm admitted. "But sometimes I just forgot all about it." She smiled gravely. "You were always my daughter, you see. From the day you came home from the hospital."

Lydia nodded, afraid to speak because of the lump in her throat.

Mamm stroked the baby's feather-light hair. "Have you had a chance to look at your mamm's things yet?"

"Ja. And I need to talk to you about something I found."

Mamm's eyes widened with apprehension at her tone. "What is it?"

"In one place in her journal, my mother wrote that she thought she had made a mistake. That maybe she should take us girls and leave, go back to Philadelphia."

Mamm pressed her free hand to her mouth, as if to hide the words. "Ach, no. That is a terrible thing for you to read." The baby, as if sensing her tension, began to fuss, and Mamm rocked her automatically. "I am so sorry. If I had known that, I would have burned them."

"I'm glad you gave them to me, Mamm." Lydia pressed her hand in reassurance. "It's better to know the truth. But there's not much after that in the journal, and she doesn't mention it again, so I don't know if she was serious or not."

"Surely not. She never gave any hint to me." Mamm shook her head. "Well, she wouldn't, would she? I was married to her husband's brother."

True enough. Lydia had hoped, foolishly, that Mamm might have an answer. "Is there anyone you can think of she might have talked to, if she seriously considered leaving?"

Mamm stared down at the baby, her thoughts clearly far away. Finally she shook her head. "She could not have talked about that to anyone here in the church, I think. If she did confide in anyone, it would be her friend from Ohio. The one whose wedding she was going to when . . . when the accident happened." Mamm stumbled over the words. "They were very close, and I know she wrote to her regularly. I asked her once if it was a round-robin letter, and Diane laughed and said no, that she said things to Faith that she wouldn't want anyone else to read."

"Faith—that was her name?"

"Ja. Her married name is Faith Gottshall. I wrote to her every once in a while afterward, to let her know how you were doing."

"So you have her address?" Hope lifted. If Diane had really intended to leave, surely she would have told her dearest friend.

"Ja, I have it. I'll get it for you." Mamm clasped her hand. "And I will pray that she has the answers you need."

●●●

Lydia knew perfectly well that she couldn't possibly expect an answer from Faith Gottshall for a week or so, but she couldn't help checking the mailbox each day and being disappointed not to find one. She hoped the letter she'd struggled to compose hadn't sounded quite as desperate as she felt.

She wanted the truth from Faith, not comforting lies. Still, there was no denying she longed to know that her parents' marriage had not been a mistake.

Lydia started back up the lane from the road, looking through the mail. The *Budget* had come. She and Adam would both enjoy reading it tonight. Often Adam read it aloud while she did the dishes, making a comfortable end to the day. Maybe he'd feel like doing that tonight.

Or maybe not. Their conversations lately had been as careful as if they were both walking on eggs.

A car pulled up at the end of the lane, sending up a cloud of dust. Lydia turned to see Adam climb out, lifting his arm in thanks as the driver pulled away.

"You got a ride, I see." She waited for him to join her. She'd been a bit upset that morning when she learned he planned to hitchhike clear to Lewisburg to see if the mill was hiring.

"Ja." He caught up with her. "I hardly had to walk at all."

"That's gut." But even as she said the words, she noticed how tired Adam looked. Even if he'd gotten rides there and back, the job search was wearing on him.

Trying to put some enthusiasm into her voice, she said, "How did things go at the mill?"

"No one is hiring." He snapped out the words, his tone sharp. It almost sounded as if his anger were directed at her.

Patience, she reminded herself. "I'm sure things will get better soon. Let's go in and get you a cool drink and something to eat. You must—"

"Enough. I'm not one of the kinder, to be comforted with a treat and a hug."

Lydia pressed her lips together. She would not let them tremble. She would not let herself cry. She kept walking, one foot in front of the other, resisting the urge to run away from the hurt.

Three more steps. Then . . .

"Sorry," Adam muttered. The word didn't sound convincing.

She stole a glance at him. Adam's lips were a thin line above his chestnut beard, and his face might have been carved from stone.

Lydia looked away, staring at the loosestrife that would soon line the lane with purple blossoms. Adam was upset over the job situation. That was all it was. As soon as he found a new job, they would return to normal.

Adam cleared his throat, as if his was as tight as hers. "Where are the boys?"

"I told them to water the strawberry plants. They were looking a little sad after so many days without rain." There, she sounded nearly normal.

Adam shielded his eyes with his hand, staring toward the berry patch. "I don't see them anywhere."

"Ach, where have they gotten to? I told them to water, not play." A glance of movement caught her eye. "There they are, in the orchard. What are they up to?"

"Climbing." Adam quickened his pace. "They shouldn't be climbing that tree. It's not safe."

Lydia trotted to keep up with him. She could see the boys now. Daniel sat on a low branch of the tree she thought of as her mother's. But David—what was David doing up so high?

"David!" Adam shouted. "Get down at once."

Fear seized Lydia by the throat. David could be hurt. He was too little—

The crack seemed to reverberate through the air, setting up echoes as David and the branch crashed toward the ground.

Adam ran. Lydia ran, prayers forming with every step. Daniel was crying, crouched by his brother, but David—was David crying? *Please, Lord . . .*

Adam reached them first, with her a step behind. Lydia dropped to her knees next to David. For an instant he just looked dazed, and then he started to cry, his sobs mingling with Daniel's.

"Daniel, stop the crying," Adam ordered. "It's David who is hurt. We must tend to him."

Daniel sniffed, a little sob escaping him. "Is he dead?"

"Ach, what a way to talk." Lydia ran her hands lightly over her son's body, searching for blood or swelling or indication of pain. "He couldn't cry so loud if he was dead, could he?"

Daniel's giggle was nervous, but her manner seemed to ease his terror.

Adam knelt on David's other side, patting him gently. "Hush, David, hush. Mammi is taking gut care of you. You don't need to cry."

"David, tell Mammi where it hurts," she ordered, trying to conceal the fact that her heart was beating so that it felt it would leap from her chest.

"My head," David said, punctuating the words with a sob. "And my elbow." He lifted the offending joint, rubbing it with his other hand.

Lydia checked the elbow. Scraped and bleeding, but he was moving it normally, so it couldn't be too bad. "What about your neck? Does it hurt?"

David tried to shake his head and stopped, puckering up with tears. "Just my head. My head hurts, Mammi. It needs ice."

She managed to smile at that comment. He couldn't have too much wrong with him if he was diagnosing himself. She ran her fingers through his silky hair again. No cuts, but a lump was forming on top.

"Ja, I think ice is the right treatment." She helped him sit up. "Are you dizzy?"

"No. It just hurts."

"It's my fault," Daniel said suddenly, his voice choking. "I shouldn't have let him climb the tree. I told him he couldn't, and that just made him want to."

"And I should have cut the tree down when I saw it was cracked," Adam said.

His gaze seemed to accuse her. Lydia had kept him from touching the tree, and now David was paying the price. Her heart was sore from the pummeling it was taking.

"We can all find some reason to blame ourselves," Adam went on. "But it was David who climbed, and David whose head will hurt for doing something so foolish." He lifted the boy gently to his feet.

"Komm." Lydia took David's hand, not looking at Adam. "We will thank God that He gives little boys hard heads, ja?"

She led him to the house, not looking back. She didn't want to think about the fact that Adam had been right. It was time for her mother's tree to come down.

Adam and Daniel walked a little behind them, and she could hear the murmur of their voices, but not what they were saying. She was already sitting in the rocker with David on her lap, a cold compress on his head, when Adam and David came in.

"Daniel and I have a plan," Adam said. "He will help me, and we will cut out the bad branches. We'll save the tree if we can. Ja, Daniel?"

Daniel nodded, wiping a tear away and depositing a streak of dirt on his cheek.

Lydia's eyes met Adam's, and she didn't know which concern to voice first. "If you must take the tree down, then you must." She felt as if she had pronounced a death sentence. "But don't you think Daniel is too young for such work?"

"I won't let him get hurt." Adam's face was frosty, as if he was chiding her for doubting him. "Daniel needs to help to make him feel better, ain't so?"

She could only nod. He was right, of course. In some ways, Adam understood their sons better than she did.

She cradled David against her. How seldom she got to hold him this way anymore. Her boys were growing up, and she feared she and Adam were growing apart. Panic flickered in her heart. How were they going to find their way together?

Chapter Eighteen

Despite Chloe's effort to arrive at the restaurant first, Brad Maitland was already seated at his usual table. She threaded her way among tables empty in mid-afternoon, following the manager who insisted on escorting her. Well, why wouldn't he? Brad was one of his best customers, a creature of habit who found a French restaurant he liked and never saw any reason to try something new.

Brad stood at her approach. He hadn't betrayed surprise when she'd called, asking him to meet her, and his narrow, well-bred face showed nothing as vulgar as curiosity now.

"This is such a pleasure, Chloe." He seated her, deflecting the manager's hovering with a gesture. "I'm glad you called."

"I hope I didn't take you away from anything important." Driven as she was to find out what Brad knew about her mother, she hadn't even considered what appointments he might have had to rearrange in order to meet her.

"Not a problem." Behind his glasses, his eyes were assessing her. Some men might take an invitation at face value, but Brad always seemed to be analyzing her motives.

Her thoughts flickered briefly to Seth, who

seemed far more likely to plunge into action than to sit back and analyze.

A server appeared, and Brad consulted with him over the menu and wine list. Chloe waited impatiently, ordering the first thing that came to mind.

Finally they were alone, and Brad turned his attention back to her. "Much as I enjoy having lunch with you, I have the impression there's more to your invitation than the pleasure of my company."

True enough. Chloe hesitated, trying to frame the right words, mindful that Nora didn't want him to know that she'd talked about him. "I hoped you might be able to tell me why my mother left Philadelphia."

Brad's listening face was too well-trained to show surprise. "What makes you think I was in her confidence?"

"You were around the same age. The families have been close forever. Surely you must have been friends, but you've never spoken to me about my mother." Chloe couldn't help the trace of hurt that showed in her voice. Brad might be as dull as Kendra insisted, but at least she'd always thought he was on her side.

He glanced down, seeming to shield his eyes. "You've never asked me about her."

"That doesn't mean I didn't wonder. As a psychiatrist, you must have known I would." It

338

was also the same excuse her grandmother had used for not telling her about her sisters.

"I suppose I did." He met her gaze. "Your grandmother made it very clear that she didn't want me to discuss Diane with you, and I tried to respect her wishes."

"I can understand that when I was a child. But I'm all grown up now, and I'd appreciate a little honesty between us."

"Of course. I wouldn't try to hide anything from you, Chloe."

That was just what he'd done, but she'd let it pass if he'd speak openly now. She stared at him, waiting.

"We were about eighteen, I suppose, when I realized I wanted more than friendship from Diane," he said. "Unfortunately she didn't feel the same way about me." His eyes were softer than she'd ever seen them. "She made it clear she only wanted friendship from me, and she said she needed a friend."

"What was Diane like then?" Chloe tried to picture her mother at eighteen and failed. All she had were studio photos that showed a Main Line debutante, not the real person.

"She'd had a few minor scrapes with the law at that point. Drinking and driving, mainly. Your grandmother had her on a tight rein. Maybe too tight."

"She was unhappy?" Was that why she'd left,

because her parents were too strict? If so, why run to a sect that was far more restrictive?

"Not unhappy, exactly." Brad seemed to be searching for the right words. "She was impatient. Wanting to find something she felt was missing in her life."

Perhaps Diane had found that missing something in Amish beliefs. Or in the person of Eli Weaver.

The server appeared with a laden tray and began putting dishes in front of them. Chloe eyed the tomato basil soup with relief. At least she'd ordered something she could get down her tight throat.

"Did my mother actually talk about her feelings with you?" Maybe there hadn't been anyone else she could confide in.

"A little." He smiled at an image in his mind, it seemed. "I remember one day when I was walking home and Diane's car pulled up to the curb. She told me to get in and wouldn't take no for an answer. She was in such a rush I didn't even think to ask where we were going until we were already on the Schuylkill Expressway."

"What did she say?" Chloe discovered she had no trouble picturing a teenaged Brad—he'd have had the same fine, slicked-back hair, thin face, and glasses.

"Escaping." He blinked, as if he'd teared up. "She said we were escaping. We drove clear down to the shore. No one was there—it was November. Diane ran out onto the beach as if it were summer. She grabbed my hand and made me run with her." He stopped, blinking rapidly.

Chloe could picture the scene so clearly in her mind, but she couldn't get at the emotions. What had Diane wanted?

"What did she want? To be free?"

"Not exactly." Brad seemed to come back from a long distance. "She wanted to be . . . well, *real* was the word she used. She said, 'This is what's real. The earth, the wind, the water. Not all the useless things my mother collects to fill up her life.' "

He fell silent, looking as if he'd exhausted himself. "Your mother left a few days later. I didn't hear anything from her, but I felt quite sure she'd gone looking for something she felt was real."

And she'd apparently found it with the Amish, of all the unlikely places. Chloe had wanted to know why Diane left her home and family and became Amish. She'd found out all she could at this end of her mother's life. If she really wanted to learn more, she'd have to go to the Amish part of the story.

Once Seth had made up his mind, he didn't lose any time. Since letters and phone calls and jars of apple butter hadn't brought Chloe back to

Pleasant Valley, he had come to Philadelphia to do it in person.

Seth drove down a narrow tree-lined street, peering at the numbers on the gracious old homes on either side. This neighborhood had escaped the tendency of the city to gobble up its surroundings, maybe because the people who'd chosen to live here a hundred years ago or so had had enough influence to prevent it.

Caught as he was between Lydia's fears that her mother had planned to leave the Amish and Chloe's unanswered questions about why she'd become Amish, he'd begun to feel like a volleyball being pummeled by both sides. The two of them, unlikely as it seemed, were sisters. The only way for them to begin to resolve their concerns was to do it face-to-face.

He'd tried the museum first, assuming Chloe would still be at work, only to learn that she wasn't there. The guard, perhaps recognizing him from his unceremonious exit on his previous visit, had stonewalled any questions about Chloe.

Fortunately another of the museum's staff had been passing and overheard. She'd looked at him with a lively question sparkling in her dark eyes, identified him before he could identify himself, and told him that Chloe had taken the afternoon off and should be home by now. She'd done everything but take him by the hand to lead him to the house. Bemused, he'd followed her directions, wondering how he'd acquired a friend on the museum staff.

The street was so quiet it was hard to believe people actually lived here. There was the number. Hoping he wasn't about to get a parking ticket for daring to disturb the purity of the area, he drew his car to the curb and got out.

Now the question was whether he'd get in the front door. He imagined Margaret Wentworth guarded by an elite squad of men in dress suits and sunglasses. But the person who came in answer to his ring of the bell was a gray-haired elderly female in an old-fashioned housedress —certainly not Margaret herself.

"Good afternoon. I'm Seth Miller, calling to see Chloe—"

She grabbed his arm and yanked him inside, shushing him at the same time. With a swift move, she propelled him through the hallway toward a swinging door.

"Who is it, Nora?" Another elderly female, by the sounds of it, and a rather commanding voice.

"No one, Mrs. Wentworth. Just someone asking directions." She pushed him on through the swinging door and into the kitchen.

He looked at her questioningly when she released her grasp.

"Sorry. No sense in having a fuss if we can avoid it." She darted a glance toward the ceiling, presumably toward her employer. "You stay here. I'll get Chloe." She scurried up a set of enclosed stairs that must be the means for servants to access the upper floors.

He leaned against a kitchen counter. How did he come to have so many allies among people he'd never met? It was obvious that the housekeeper, like the woman at the museum, had not only heard about him but also sympathized with his desire to get the sisters together.

Footsteps came down the stairs again, Chloe hurrying, the housekeeper a few steps behind her.

"Seth, I wasn't expecting you." Chloe's face was warm with welcome. "Did you have another business trip to the city?"

"Not business, just you and Lydia. You have to come back to Pleasant Valley." Well, maybe he didn't need to be quite that blunt. He didn't want to put her back up.

"Sorry," he said quickly. "I didn't mean to sound so demanding. But neither you nor Lydia can go on this way. She's longing to see you, and the answers you're looking for are in Pleasant Valley."

"That's nonsense." The authoritative voice cut through the kitchen, sending all of them swiveling toward the door. The woman who stood there obviously wished she could incinerate Seth with the stare she directed at him. "My granddaughter has neither the need nor the desire to return to that godforsaken place. Or to see the people who are to blame for her mother's death."

"Lydia isn't to blame for Diane's accident. She's Chloe's sister, and Chloe has every right to see her." The rest of them might be terrified of this woman, but Seth wasn't. He'd be happy to engage in battle.

"I have no intention of arguing with you, young man. I don't know what you hope to gain by this charade, but it won't work. Now get out of my house before I call the police."

"Your orders didn't prevent your daughter from leaving. Are you trying to drive Chloe away as well?"

"Stop it." Chloe sounded every bit as authoritative as her grandmother. "I'm capable of making my own decisions."

"Tell him, Chloe. Tell him that you have no intention of going back there." Mrs. Wentworth leaned on the ebony cane she held, bending the considerable force of her will on her granddaughter.

Eyes wide, Chloe looked back at her. Seth felt her slipping away.

"I'm sorry, Gran." Her voice was soft, but it admitted no room for argument. "I have to go back to Pleasant Valley. I have to find out if my mother found what she was looking for there."

"I won't allow it." But the woman's iron will was weakening.

"You're tired, Gran." Chloe's face was gentle as she touched her grandmother's arm. "Let Nora take you upstairs to have a little rest before dinner."

"That's right." Galvanized, the housekeeper hurried to take the woman's arm and steer her away. "I'll make you a nice cup of tea."

Seth let out a long breath. He'd accomplished what he came here to do, but he had a feeling it might not have been necessary. Chloe had already made her decision.

"I'm sorry . . ." he began.

She shook her head. "I'll walk you to your car. Then I'll have to see to my grandmother."

He understood. Family was family, even when they were downright unlikeable.

They went together back through the marble-floored hall to the imposing front door. The rooms on either side of the hall were decorated in a stiff, formal manner, reminding him of nothing so much as a funeral home.

They reached the car without speaking. He looked into her face and saw the afternoon sun gilding her skin. "I'm sorry if I made things more difficult for you."

"It wouldn't have made a difference. She'd still have reacted that way when she learned I planned to go back."

He studied her face, seeing a new determination there and wondering what had caused it.

"You said you wanted to see if your mother had found what she was looking for. What do you think it was?"

"Real life. That's what Diane was searching for, according to someone who talked to her shortly before she left. Did she succeed?"

He thought of Lydia's discovery. But that was hers to share or not, as she saw fit.

"I don't know. I hope you find out."

And I hope no one ends up getting hurt any worse.

According to her GPS, Chloe was only a few miles from Lydia and Adam's farm. She should feel relieved. She didn't. Nervous, uncertain, wondering if she'd made a mistake . . . those better described her mood.

Why had she committed herself to staying until Monday? What if she found it too strange? What if . . .

That was ridiculous. Her mother had been brought up the same way she had, and Diane had adapted to the Amish way of life. Chloe could certainly stand it for two nights.

She intended to give this visit a fair shot. It was the only way she could think of to understand what had drawn Diane to become Amish.

The anonymous female voice of the GPS announced that the turn was just ahead. A moment later she saw the mailbox Seth had told her to watch for. With a little flicker of anticipation, she turned in at the gravel lane.

Several cows watched her incuriously from a pasture on one side of the lane. On the other side stretched a field that looked as if it had been freshly plowed, not that she knew much about it. There was the house, a simple white frame two-story, and stretching off to the left was the orchard. Behind the house she spotted a barn and several other outbuildings whose use she had to guess at. She hoped one of them wasn't an outhouse. That would be carrying roughing it a little too far for her.

As she neared the house she saw people on the back porch, so she stopped there, rather than at the front. Lydia was already coming to meet her, smiling widely, her face lit with pleasure. For better or worse, she was here.

Chloe slid out and rounded the car. Before she could speak, Lydia had enveloped her in a hug. Chloe hadn't intended to greet her this way, but Lydia's pleasure was so obvious, her grip so warm, it seemed the most natural thing in the world to return her hug.

"I am wonderful glad you are here at last." On her own turf, Lydia was relaxed and smiling, the constraint she'd showed at the restaurant gone. "I've been longing for this day. We all have." She gestured toward the people grouped behind her.

Chloe hadn't expected a welcome party. Adam

348

stood a couple of steps away, still rather severe-looking, but he managed a nod.

"You are wilkom to our home, Chloe."

"Thank you." She smiled. She could be pleasant, for Lydia's sake, even though he seemed to find it a struggle.

Lydia drew an older couple forward. "Chloe, you must meet my mamm and daad. Your aunt Anna and onkel Joseph, ja?"

The woman wore a dark dress and apron that would have seemed drab if not for the smile that lifted her lips and made her blue eyes sparkle. The man had a beard, like Adam, only longer and grayer. His lean face was crinkled with smile lines, conveying an image of strength softened by kindness.

She held out her hand and then wondered whether a handshake was acceptable. But he took her hand in both of his.

"Your father was my older brother," he said, eyes twinkling. "Chust in case you're having trouble sorting out the family."

"Onkel Joseph," she said. Somehow the words didn't sound as strange as she'd have expected. She'd never had an uncle before other than Brad, her courtesy uncle. "Did . . . Did you and our father look alike?"

"Ach, ja," Aunt Anna said. "They were like enough to be twins, folks always said, though Eli was three years older." Without waiting for an invitation, Aunt Anna gave her a swift hug.

So her father would have looked like this, if he'd lived. Black pants, suspenders crossing still-broad shoulders, straw hat perched squarely on graying hair. And an overall sense that here was someone who knew his place in the world and was content. Maybe that was what had drawn Diane to Eli.

"Our three boys wanted to bring their families to meet you, but we thought this was enough for today," Anna said. "They'd be your cousins, though Lydia has always considered them brothers."

Chloe nodded, relieved that she didn't need to meet any more previously unknown relatives today. This was confusing enough. She glanced at Lydia and asked the question on her mind. "Did you know you were adopted? When you were young, I mean?"

Lydia nodded, but it was Anna who answered. She was obviously the chatty one in the family.

"Ja, we explained to her from the time she could understand. She didn't remember anything, you see, so she had to start all over again at five." Anna's lips trembled with remembered sorrow.

"That must have been difficult for you." Chloe tried to imagine what it would be like to have an injured five-year-old suddenly become your responsibility.

"Hard, ja. But God gave us such wonderful

happiness, too." She gave Lydia a loving look, making Chloe's heart twist.

A small figure emerged from behind Lydia. "Is it our turn yet, Mammi?" he asked in a stage whisper.

Lydia smiled. "Ja, David, it's your turn." She drew a slightly taller version of the child from behind her husband and pushed them both forward. "Daniel, David, tell your aunt Chloe you are happy to meet her."

The older boy stepped forward at once. "I am happy to meet you, Aunt Chloe. I'm Daniel. I'm eight."

Chloe held out her hand, and he shook it gravely. "It's very nice to meet you, Daniel." Her throat grew tight at the feel of that small hand in hers. The two boys were very much alike with their fine blond hair cut bowl-shape, their even features, their huge blue eyes.

"I'm David." The young boy seemed to take his cue from his brother, pushing forward. "It's nice to meet you," he echoed. He looked up at her with a sudden, mischievous grin that set him apart from his brother's more serious expression.

"I'm glad to see both of you at last. I never had nephews before."

"We had aunts," David said.

"But not Englisch aunts," Daniel added.

Did he consider that a good thing or a bad thing? She wasn't sure.

"I brought something for each of the boys." She sent a glance toward Lydia. "I hope that's all right." Maybe she should have checked first, but there hadn't been time.

"Ja, that's fine," Lydia said.

Chloe returned to the car and reached in the backseat to pull out the baseball and bat. The sporting goods store clerk had assured her that they were the right size for the boys' ages.

Their eyes seemed to grow even rounder as she presented the gifts. "For us?" Daniel said. He looked toward his parents.

Lydia nodded, smiling. Adam . . . She sensed something negative coming from Adam for an instant, and then it was gone, and he was nodding as well.

Permission granted, the boys seized the presents. David began ripping the packaging from the ball, but Daniel paused. "Denke, Aunt Chloe. It was wonderful kind of you." He elbowed his brother.

"Denke, Aunt Chloe," David responded. "Look, it's just the kind I wanted."

"Why don't you go try them out," Lydia suggested. "We must not keep Aunt Chloe standing outside. Where is your bag? I'll show you your bedroom."

Chloe pulled the small overnight case from the trunk. The men melted away after the boys, and she followed the two women into the house.

The back door led through a small mudroom

into the kitchen. Chloe glanced around, relieved to find that for the most part it looked like any other kitchen. Plain wooden cabinets covered one wall, and what looked similar to a camping light hung over a long wooden table. There were pots of growing plants on the sunny windowsills, and a comfortable-looking rocker stood next to the stove. It was an ordinary gas stove, she was relieved to see.

"Something smells wonderful," she said, inhaling a rich aroma.

"Lydia is making chicken potpie for our supper," Aunt Anna said. "She makes a wonderful-gut chicken potpie."

"Mamm made the fruit pies for dessert," Lydia said, seeming eager to share the credit. She nodded toward three lightly browned pies waiting on the countertop.

"They're beautiful. I know it takes an expert hand to make pastry that light."

Anna flushed a little, ducking her head as if avoiding the praise. "It's nothing."

"Here is the dining room," Lydia said, leading the way through to the front of the house. "But we usually eat in the kitchen. I do my sewing in here, because the room is so light, and the boys do their schoolwork at the table."

A yellow-lined tablet lay open on the table. Someone, presumably David, had been practicing his letters.

"The living room." Lydia gestured as she led the way up the stairs. "In the back of the house is the laundry and the pantry, and up here we have four bedrooms and the bathroom."

No outhouse, then, thank goodness.

"This will be your room. Ours is across, and the boys' there. The other room . . ." Lydia hesitated. "Ach, we had hoped to fill them all up with kinder, but it hasn't happened."

The sorrow in her face was clear, and Chloe wasn't sure if she should speak or not. Surely their strict rules didn't prohibit the use of modern medicine. "Do you . . . That is, have you spoken to a doctor about it?"

"Ja, I went to Sarah first, our midwife, and she sent me to a specialist for some tests. At the big clinic over in Fisherdale. The doctors could find nothing wrong, so I must accept that it will happen when God wills."

Anna was nodding in agreement. Apparently that acceptance was part of being Amish. Chloe wasn't sure she could manage it. And how would her mother have done, in similar circumstances?

"Ach, what am I thinking, keeping you standing here with your suitcase?" Lydia seemed to make an effort to shake off her obvious sadness. She led the way into the closest bedroom. "Here is your room when you are with us."

The bedroom was plain and simple, as she'd expect of an Amish home, but the double bed was covered with a postage stamp quilt worked in a lovely double wedding ring design. Chloe went to it immediately, touching the nearly invisible stitches.

"This is amazing needlework. I can't begin to guess the time it must take to do a quilt like this one."

Her aunt Anna flushed with pleasure but ducked her head as if to avoid the praise. "It is something I love to do, is all. Keeps my hands busy in the winter, especially. I mind your mother wanted to learn to quilt, and I tried to teach her."

Chloe had to smile at the way that was phrased. "Was she impossible with a needle, like me?"

"She was better at other things," Anna said tactfully. "But she did make a nine-patch crib quilt for each of you girls when she was expecting you."

Lydia nodded. "You gave me mine when Daniel was on the way."

Chloe felt a bit lost. Lydia had at least been brought up knowing about their mother in a natural way.

"I still have yours," Anna said, reaching out hesitantly to touch Chloe's arm. "I will bring it to you tomorrow, if you want."

"I'd like that." Chloe's throat tightened, and she made an effort to swallow. Was she destined to be blindsided with emotion the entire time she was here?

"The bathroom is right next door to you," Lydia said. "And don't worry about how much hot water you use. We have plenty."

The news about the bathroom was a relief on several counts. "Okay, thanks." She set her small suitcase on the straight wooden chair in the corner.

"Now, would you like to rest after your trip, or would you like to see the rest of the place before supper?" Lydia asked.

"I'm not tired. Why don't you show me around?" This was her opportunity to ask questions about the life her mother had led in this place, and she wasn't going to waste it. Maybe here she would find the answers she needed.

Chapter Nineteen

Lydia led the way through the house, from the smallest bedroom, where Aunt Anna said Chloe had slept as a baby, to the basement, clean, bare, and empty.

Chloe glanced around. "Do the boys play in here on rainy days?"

"Sometimes, ja. Mostly we use this when it is our turn to host worship service."

"It's a gut space for worship," Anna said. "In Eli and Diane's time, the washer was down here, also the storage for canned goods. Eli didn't want Diane going up and down the stairs so much, especially when she was expecting, so he built the laundry room and pantry upstairs."

It was a little fact about the father whose face and personality had long eluded her. He had been protective of his wife, it seemed. And having seen Joseph, she could begin to imagine his appearance.

"Komm, we'll walk around outside while the sun is still warm." They went upstairs, but Aunt Anna stopped in the kitchen.

"You two go on and look around. I'll chust start mixing the dumplings. It will be suppertime before you know it."

Lydia nodded, and the two of them went back out onto the porch. "She is giving us a chance to be alone together, I think. We haven't really had that before, ain't so?"

Chloe nodded, not having figured out the correct response to the phrase the Amish often seemed to add, turning a sentence into a question.

"You have cows and horses?" That was probably a stupid question, since she could see both animals from where they were standing.

"Ja, just two cows for milk and now a couple of calves we're raising for market. The two horses are used mostly with the buggy and wagon. Daad has a team of draft horses he uses with the plow, and we can borrow them when we need them."

"And that's the orchard you told me about in your letter."

"Ja." They walked toward the trees. Daniel and David, spotting them, came running to join them. The boys fell into step with them, and David's hand slid into Chloe's.

Chloe's heart warmed. Here was one person who accepted her, it seemed.

"Some of the fruit trees were here when our mother and father moved here. Others they added." Lydia waved to a section of what were obviously smaller trees. "Adam and I planted the cherry trees."

It was quiet and shady under the trees, and the very air seemed filled with the scent of growing things. Peaceful. Maybe that peace was part of what Diane had cherished here. Chloe could certainly understand that lure.

"There's something I want to show you." Lydia took her hand as naturally as David had and led her to the center of the orchard. "This was the tree I told you about. Both Mamm and our neighbor, Seth's mother, remembered seeing Diane telling us stories here. They each said how much Diane loved this tree." She tilted her face back to look up into its branches.

Chloe did the same. What had their mother seen in this old, gnarled apple tree that had made her love it? True, the stillness was intense here, the sense of distance from the busy world so real you could almost imagine you were in another time. Another world. Maybe that was it.

"I fell from way up there," David said, pointing to the scar of a broken branch, pale against the weathered bark.

"I hope you didn't get hurt." Chloe looked from the child's face to Lydia's, questioning. "That seems awfully high for him to climb."

"Ja, they both know it was wrong." Lydia gave the boys a severe look that didn't quite mask the devotion in her eyes. "He had some bumps and scrapes, that was certain-sure. And he won't do something so ferhoodled again."

"I won't, Mammi." David studied his toes.

"The tree is old and badly cracked in places," Lydia said. "Adam trimmed it to try and save it. I would not want to see it come down."

"No." Chloe put her hand on the rough bark. It was warm under her palm, almost like a living creature. Perhaps her mother had done the same. It was as if she were touching her mother's hand through the years. "I wouldn't, either."

Lydia found she was breathing a little easier when supper was over. It seemed to her that Chloe stiffened up a little when Adam and Daad were there. But once everyone had eaten probably more than their fill of chicken potpie, mashed potatoes, rhubarb sauce, bread and butter pickles, dried corn pudding, and Mamm's pies, the men had departed for the chairs on the front porch, the boys headed out to do their evening chores, and the women were left alone in the kitchen.

"Let me dry," Chloe said, snatching the tea towel before Mamm could reach it.

"You should relax. You're our guest." Lydia set an armful of plates in the hot soapy water.

Chloe's smile held an edge of determination. "If I'm family, then I get to help. I might not be much of a cook, but I can certainly dry dishes."

"I will put away then," Mamm said, settling it. "Chloe won't know yet where things go, ain't so?"

Giving in, Lydia put the first hot rinsed plates in the drainer. "You are family, that's certain-sure. I just thought you might be tired from the trip."

"Not at all." Chloe glanced out the window over the sink, apparently watching the boys shooing the chickens in for the night. "I guess boys don't do the dishes."

Lydia felt sure her surprise was showing in her face. "Why should they? They have other chores. If I had a daughter . . ." The pause was, she hoped, not noticeable. ". . . she would help in the house."

Chloe shrugged. "One of my friends has three children, and she insists the boys learn to do dishes and laundry as well as their sister. I suppose she feels that when they're on their own, they'll need to know how."

Lydia had told herself she should be ready for questions about the difference between Amish life and the world's ways, but she hadn't expected this one. "Adam and the boys would do what they must if they had to, but why would they need to?"

Chloe set a plate on the counter. "What if you were sick? Or had some other problem?"

That was easy enough to answer. "In times of trouble, I could count on Mamm, or my sisters-in-law, or any of the church sisters. They would be here without being asked to help out."

It seemed so obvious to her, but it clearly wasn't to Chloe. Something about her mutinous look reminded Lydia of David. Surely they weren't going to argue over something as foolish as washing dishes, were they?

"I have such happy memories of washing dishes with my sisters," Mamm said, her voice soothing. "And with your mamm, too. We enjoyed getting the men and boys out of the way so we could talk of women things." Her smile was gentle. "I mind we were washing dishes when she told me you were on the way, Chloe. Susanna was toddling around the kitchen, walking from chair to chair, and Lydia was helping me dry. Funny, how bright a memory can be after so many years. Diane looked so happy and peaceful."

Chloe's hands had stilled on the dish she was drying, and Lydia had to blink away tears.

"Thank you," Chloe said softly. "I'm glad you told me."

"Ja." Lydia could understand why Mamm hadn't

told her that story before, but those years of secrecy had been harmful to both of them. What difference might it have made if she'd grown up knowing about Susanna and Chloe? She wasn't sure.

Unfortunately, there was another story about their mother she'd have to share, and it must be soon. She had to show Chloe the contents of the toy dower chest.

The opportunity didn't come until later in the evening. Or at least, that's what Lydia told herself. Maybe she'd just been putting it off as long as possible.

She stood outside Chloe's bedroom door, the box cradled against her like a boppli. Chloe had just come up, so surely she wouldn't be in bed yet. She tapped on the door.

"Chloe? May I come in?"

Chloe swung the door open. She'd slid her feet into a pair of fuzzy slippers, but otherwise she was still dressed. "Sure, come in." She glanced at the dower chest.

"I wanted to show you this sometime when we didn't have the boys trying to get your attention."

Daniel and David had warmed up to their new aunt, introducing her to the farm board game that was their current favorite. Chloe had played with every sign of enjoyment, though it probably wasn't her idea of the best way to spend an evening.

"I loved playing with them." Chloe sat on the bed, curling one leg under her. "What do you have there?"

Lydia sat down and put the box between them. It was only right that Chloe should know. There'd been enough secrets. But still, she found herself longing for a reason not to show her sister the journal.

"This box is what we would call a dower chest. A toy one," she added. "For a little girl to keep her treasures in. Our daad made it for me when I was small."

Chloe traced the lines of the box with her fingertips. "I know what dower chests are. We have some very old ones in the museum's collection. This is beautiful work. I didn't know he was a craftsman."

Lydia smiled. "I don't know that he would have called himself by that word. It was just something he did on the side." Like Adam's clocks.

"You're lucky to have it after all these years," Chloe said.

"I've actually only had it for a short time." Lydia drew in a breath, wishing this were easier. "Mamm had used it to put some private things of our mother's in. To save for us."

"I see." There was a question in Chloe's eyes, but at least she didn't voice it. She was no doubt wondering how someone like Mamm had come to be drawn into such a difficult secret.

"There is something that should belong to you."
Lydia lifted the lid. "This Bible must have been
hers when she was a girl. It's in Englisch, so I
want you to have it."

Chloe took it gently, handling the Bible as if it
were made of glass. "Are you sure? Your mamm
probably saved these things for you."

"Ach, no, she agreed with me about the Bible. It
is yours." Lydia put her hand over her sister's on
the Bible, and it seemed to her that a wordless
wave of love flowed between them.

That seemed to make the rest of what she must
say even harder.

She cleared her throat. "There is not much
more. A pressed violet, maybe something that
reminded her of our father." She showed her,
marveling at the fragile memento of a long-ago
love, still here when the lovers were gone.

Chloe brushed away a tear. "They didn't have
much time together."

"No." What else was there to say? "And then
there's this." Lydia took out the journal and
handed it to Chloe.

She opened it, maybe not knowing at first what
it was. Then her face cleared. "A journal. Diane
kept a journal of her life here?"

"Ja. I have read through much of it. She didn't
write every day. Maybe just when she had something she wanted to express or remember."

Chloe nodded, her eyes on the book as she

turned the pages. "I never even hoped to find something like this—something that would bring her alive to me."

"Ja, that is how I felt." Lydia took a breath. "But there is something that I found upsetting. I think it is only right that you should see it."

Chloe's eyes were wide, questioning.

Lydia nodded to the book. "Toward the back. I put a slip of paper in it."

She wanted to say more. To explain that it was only one paragraph out of a whole life; to protest that it could have been a whim born of a bad day. But she held her tongue.

Chloe found the page and read. She looked up at last. "But this—this sounds as if she wasn't as happy as everyone has been saying. If she was thinking about going home again . . ."

"It might have been just a passing thought. I could find no other reference to such a thing in the whole book. Only that one time."

"She may not have felt she could write about it other times, even if she felt it." Chloe's voice had an edge.

"Ja, that's true." Be calm, Lydia cautioned herself. "She might have thought it was disloyal to her husband to write it down, even in her private journal."

"She sounds unhappy." Chloe tapped the page.

"Only there," Lydia protested. "Read the whole

thing. You'll see. There are many places where she talks about how happy she is."

Chloe nodded, but Lydia could see she wasn't convinced.

Sorrow closed around Lydia's heart. She and Chloe had begun to act like sisters. To feel like sisters. Was this revelation about their mother going to spoil their relationship when it had barely begun?

Seth followed his mamm and sister toward the picnic tables in Lydia and Adam's backyard Sunday afternoon. Lydia's whole family was invited to meet Chloe, and she'd included the Miller family as well, either because they were the closest neighbors or possibly so Chloe would have another Englischer there.

Seth had a feeling Chloe might need a little support about now. She'd spent twenty-four hours with her new Amish family, which had to be an emotional strain. And now she was undoubtedly the center of attention for a whole crowd of Amish.

Well, now she'd have him, though he wasn't sure how much difference that would make to her.

He spotted Chloe helping Lydia spread a cloth over a picnic table. Lydia's brothers' wives were similarly occupied, and they all seemed to be talking at once. Chloe looked okay, if a little reserved.

He was headed toward her when Lydia's brother Andrew clapped a hand on his shoulder.

"Seth, wilkom. How about helping me set up the volleyball net?" Andy's grin didn't harbor any of the suspicion with which some of the Amish still looked at him. Maybe the Leit were getting used to having him around.

"So I can beat you, Andy?" he asked, grinning.

"You wish," Andy answered with a slang expression left over from his rumspringa. He had been just starting his running-around time when Seth was getting serious about leaving for good.

"Lead me to it," he said, allowing himself to be led off. There'd be some point when he could get an unobtrusive word with Chloe and find out how her visit was really going.

"So, Lydia says we have you to thank for finding her sister Chloe." Andy handed him one pole and began unrolling the net.

"She'd have found her anyway," he said, walking backward to extend the net. The support ropes and pegs dangled, nearly tripping him up. "I just shortened the process."

He wasn't entirely sure he wanted to claim credit for finding Chloe. But then, if things ended badly between Lydia and her sister, he was bound to feel guilty in any event.

"She seems nice," Andy volunteered between thuds as he hammered the pegs into the soft ground. "A little shy, maybe."

"Wouldn't you be shy if you found yourself with a whole new family?" Seth handed him the next peg.

"Ja, I guess. But we're nice, ain't so?" Andy gave the final peg a whack. "There we are. I'll get the ball out for the young ones."

Left to himself, Seth drifted back toward the table. Lydia's kin seemed ready to accept Chloe, despite her being Englisch. Maybe they were a bit more open than Adam was, since Chloe was actually their blood relative, just like Lydia.

Chloe was talking to his mamm, now, leaning forward a little and smiling. Mamm would have said something kind at once about Chloe's mother. That was her way.

Then Jessie was butting into the conversation, probably resenting the fact that Mamm was paying attention to this newcomer. Unfortunately that was *her* way. He hastened his steps, reaching Chloe just as Mamm steered Jessie away.

"I hope my sister didn't say anything she shouldn't have," he said, not bothering to disguise his anxiety.

"Not exactly." Chloe's expression held a question she probably wouldn't want to ask outright.

"Jessie's having treatment for some emotional problems, complicated by the fact that she's apparently bipolar." He shrugged, annoyed by the necessity of telling his family problems to Chloe.

"The doctors throw around a lot of fancy terms, but I'm sometimes not sure they really understand it any better than we do."

"That's . . . difficult." Chloe reached out as if to touch him in sympathy and then drew her hand back. "Is that why you're staying here?"

"Part of the reason. I have to have a base of operations someplace, even though I can tele-commute. This isn't as convenient as being in Chicago, where the company is headquartered, but my mother needs the support. I don't see that changing anytime soon." He wasn't sure why it seemed important to let her know what his priorities were.

"Your mother is very sweet. She was telling me how happy my mother was here. In fact, that's what everyone says." She gave him an accusing look. "I might believe it if not for that entry in her journal. Why didn't you tell me about it?"

He should have seen that coming, but he hadn't. "I don't think Lydia really meant for me to know. It spilled out because she was upset. I'm sure she felt it was her place to tell you, not mine."

"I suppose so." But Chloe didn't sound as if that made it any easier.

"As I understand it, that was the only time your mother even hinted at unhappiness in the entire journal. Isn't it possible it was just a momentary feeling, quickly forgotten?"

"I'd like to think so." She looked at the

surroundings, not at him. "I'd like to believe she found what she was looking for here."

"The reality you said she was searching for?" he asked, keeping his voice down as a couple of the children ran past them.

Chloe looked back at him, her gaze suddenly intense. "She wanted to have a life that was real. I just wish I understood what that meant to her."

It wasn't his place to supply Chloe with answers, but of all the people here, he was the only one who might understand the feeling.

"I think I get that, in some small way," he said slowly. "When I left, I was looking for . . . I don't know, adventure, maybe. Excitement. Something more complex and challenging. And my life out in the world has been all of that. But living close to nature, close to family, united in purpose and beliefs . . . those things are important, too. Is it more real to grow a crop than to design a computer program? Maybe. At least the crop is something you can touch and taste."

Chloe's gaze was focused on him now. "You sound as if you want to come back for good."

"Not exactly." He struggled for the answers he was still formulating. "I don't think I could be satisfied being Amish again. But I'm beginning to appreciate what I gave up."

Chloe nodded, as if that made sense to her. He wasn't sure it did to him.

"I can understand why you love it here." She

waved her hand at the scene. The land stretched out to the distant ridge, green and fruitful. "It's beautiful."

"It is. The life is peaceful, but it's not easy."

"I've seen that already." She frowned at the men, who'd started a game of volleyball while the women scurried back and forth, taking care of the meal. "Is it always like this?" She asked the question abruptly, a tiny frown line between her brows.

"Like what?" He wasn't sure what she meant.

"Men doing one thing; women another." The frown deepened. "Lydia seems to be constantly busy, working every minute since I got here. It looks to me as if the men rule the roost."

She was seeing a patriarchal society in which the men made all the rules, and he wasn't sure he could explain the tenets of Amish life in a few words.

"The Amish believe in the Biblical principle that the man is the head of the family as Christ is the head of the church. That doesn't mean he sits back like some Oriental potentate being waited on."

"Doesn't it?" She sounded troubled.

"No, it doesn't. It means, in practice, that husband and wife each have their own sphere of influence. Most Amish husbands wouldn't make any major decisions without coming to an agreement with their wives." He was getting a little bothered now, even though he understood how Amish life must look to a modern, independent woman. "If you were here studying Amish customs for your museum, you'd probably bring a less biased eye to the subject."

"I guess I would, but it's different when we're talking about my mother and my sisters, not some sociological study."

Seth took a breath and hoped for the right words. "All I'm saying is that you can't judge Lydia's life by the world's standards. You owe it to her to respect her beliefs."

Chloe still looked unconvinced, but before he could say anything else, someone rang the bell that was mounted on the back porch. Everyone began surging toward the tables.

Chloe was swept away by Lydia, and he watched her go with a sense of foreboding.

Chapter Twenty

Relieved that the May evening had stayed mild and dry, Lydia walked over to join Mamm and Chloe where they sat watching the volleyball game after supper. Seth had run his mother and sister home and then come back, and the sisters-in-law were making noises about collecting their young ones and heading home.

"The men act like they're boys again when they start a game," Mamm observed. "Your daad will be grumbling about sore muscles tomorrow, I think."

"They're having fun, anyway," Lydia said, glancing at Chloe. Had she been having fun? Well, probably not fun, exactly.

But this visit had gone better than it might have. There had been those tense moments when she'd had to show Chloe their mother's journal, but afterward they'd been comfortable again.

Chloe hadn't turned her head in response to their comments. In profile, she looked rather like Susanna, except that her face bore a more guarded look than Susanna's gentle expression.

Lydia suppressed a sigh. She still wasn't sure what Chloe thought about their mother's apparent regrets. Probably it was too much to hope that Chloe would open up about her feelings this soon.

She sent a pleading look toward her mamm, longing for some other conversation to fill the silence that seemed to have grown between them.

"I heard Adam did a few days' work with Joseph Beiler at the machine shop," Mamm said, probably saying the first thing that popped into her mind. "It went well, ain't so?"

Lydia nodded. "Ja, I think it was gut. Usually Samuel and Joseph can handle the work themselves, but they'd gotten behind with the concern over Joseph and Myra's new baby."

Chloe turned her head, as if taking an interest,

encouraging Lydia. "Joseph and Myra Beiler are part of our church district," she explained. "They have two little girls, one with Down's syndrome. Such a sweet child. Myra always says God gives His special children an extra measure of sweetness. And now they have a healthy baby boy."

"You said that Adam worked for him for several days?" Chloe's eyebrows lifted. "What about his regular job?"

Lydia wasn't sure she appreciated the edge in Chloe's voice. "He had been working at a travel trailer business in a nearby town, but they had to lay off most of the workforce because orders were down."

Chloe sent a frowning look toward Adam, who was spiking the ball toward Seth's feet. "Why isn't he doing something to find a new job?"

"He is." Lydia's heart sank. For some reason, Chloe and Adam seemed destined to see the worst in each other. "He has applied many places, but jobs are hard to find these days."

"Maybe if he had more than an eighth-grade education it wouldn't be so difficult." Chloe's words were sharp, and for an instant Lydia was shocked into silence.

"That is not our way," Mamm said gently. "Eight years of schooling is enough for the lives our kinder will lead."

Chloe's lips pressed together, and Lydia had a

sense she was holding back the words she wanted to say.

"Is this about Adam?" Lydia asked, her voice soft. "Or are you thinking about our mother?"

Chloe made an impatient gesture. "I'm not arguing about your right to live the way you want. But Diane was raised to attend college, to achieve things, and to have a good life."

Be careful. Don't make her angry. But even as Lydia thought the warning, she knew she couldn't let that pass without an objection.

"People don't always agree about what is a good life," she said. "The Amish believe in humility, not pride. In cooperation, not competition. Those values come from the Bible."

Mamm nodded in agreement, but Chloe was already shaking her head.

"That attitude is just not practical in the modern world."

"And that is the very reason we live apart from the modern world," Lydia said. "Our world is different."

"It seems to me it's a world where men give all the orders and women do all the work. Look at Adam." Chloe flung out her hand, her cheeks flushed.

"What about me?" Adam's words fell into the conversation like a heavy weight thudding to the earth.

Chloe spun to face him, obviously no more

375

aware than Lydia that the game had ended. Lydia could only be grateful that Daniel and David were helping their aunts and uncles get the little cousins into the wagons, so they weren't near enough to hear the sharp words.

"You're not taking care of your family." Chloe shot out of her chair, ignoring a calming gesture from Seth, who stood behind Adam. "I've seen how hard Lydia works, and you don't even have a job. I suppose you're an example of the Amish way of life."

For a moment the silence seemed to sizzle like bacon on a hot pan. Chloe's face was flushed and passionate, while Adam's was pale and set.

Pain clutched Lydia's heart. It was suddenly very clear to her what she must do, and it was an action that would undoubtedly cost her the tenuous relationship she'd started with her sister.

"You are wrong, Chloe," she said, keeping her voice calm with an effort that strained her throat. "Marriage isn't about one person taking care of the other. Marriage is about both people taking care of each other. Maybe, when you marry, you will understand what I'm saying. But I won't allow you to speak to my husband that way."

Lydia heard a surprised, indrawn breath from someone, but she didn't turn her head. She stared at the little sister she'd longed so much to meet.

Chloe's gaze didn't waver. "You wanted me to come and see the Amish way of life. So I did.

And now I understand why our mother wanted to leave."

Chloe zipped her suitcase closed and took a last look around the room the next morning. She didn't suppose she'd be seeing it again.

A strained silence had existed since that unpleasant exchange the previous evening, broken only by a few very polite words. Chloe had lain awake despite the comfort of the bed, going over and over the situation without finding a resolution.

She shouldn't have spoken as she had—she had to admit that, at least. She'd violated a number of rules of polite conduct by speaking so plainly when she was a guest in someone's home.

But it was the truth, wasn't it? She'd said what needed to be said. If her mother had had the chance to leave when she'd wanted to, Lydia and Susanna would have normal lives now.

Chloe's heart twisted painfully. Her mother would still be alive. There would be happy memories of a lifetime spent together instead of an empty place inside her where a mother's love was supposed to be.

Chloe picked up the case and headed down-stairs. She'd say her good-byes, and this difficult interruption in her life would be over.

Lydia was in the kitchen, standing at the sink. She turned at the sound of Chloe's approach, drying her hands on a dish towel. "Adam has left to walk the boys to school already. I'm sorry I couldn't keep them until you came down."

"That's all right. We said our good-byes last night." She'd hugged each of the children, feeling their small, sturdy bodies against her, and wished she could believe she'd see them again. "I . . . should get on the road."

Lydia bowed her head for a moment. "Ja, I understand. I will walk out with you."

They reached the car in silence, and Chloe stowed her bag in the backseat, then opened the driver's side door. Her heart urged her to say something to mend the breach between them, but there was nothing she could say and mean that would accomplish that task.

"Thank you for your hospitality, Lydia." She stood facing her sister for a moment.

Lydia nodded, her face somber. She reached out tentatively, as if not sure her touch would be welcome. Throat tight, Chloe gave her a quick hug and stepped back, turning to slide into the car.

Lydia put her hand on the door as Chloe started to close it. "I am sorry, Chloe," she said. "Sorry that you did not find what you were looking for."

There was nothing else to be said. Chloe closed the door and pulled away, blinking at the tears that stung her eyes.

Go back where you belong, she told herself firmly. *There's no other way.*

She'd nearly reached the end of the lane when she saw him. Seth was leaning against the fence post, looking as if he'd been there for some time. At her approach, he stepped out into the lane.

Suppressing the urge to drive right past him, she stopped and touched the button that would roll down her window. "I suppose you're waiting for me."

Seth placed his forearm against the doorframe and bent his head, apparently to study her face. Whatever he saw didn't seem to make him very happy, not that it mattered to her.

"So you're just going to give up on your relationship with your sister, is that it?"

Her temper flared. "I tried to do what you wanted."

"Not hard enough," he shot back. "You were unjust to Adam. He's a hard worker, none harder. And he's devoted to his family."

"I don't see it that way. Maybe you just think that situation is normal because you were raised that way. You were wrong to get me involved to begin with." She was probably being unfair to him, but unshed tears were pressing against her eyes, and her temples were throbbing.

He stiffened. "It's not wrong for the Amish to live the way they believe God tells them to."

"I doubt very much that my mother was looking for God's will when she joined them."

Seth's face hardened. "Is this about Lydia and

Adam, or is it about your mother? You're letting your feelings about losing her blind you to the quality of Amish life."

Those words hit too close to home, and all Chloe wanted to do was hit back. "You're a fine one to talk. You're trying to have it both ways— waffling between two worlds. What's wrong, Seth? Can't you decide where you belong?"

He flinched at her words, and she instantly regretted them. She was hitting out blindly, trying to ease her own pain. That wasn't fair.

"You know, I figured out from the beginning that your grandmother was prejudiced and unforgiving." Seth looked at her with distaste. "I just hadn't realized she'd done such a good job of passing those qualities on to you." He stepped back, indicating the road with a sweep of his arm. "Maybe you'd better hurry back to where you belong."

"I will." She tramped on the gas and surged out onto the road.

Adam had thought life would return to normal once Chloe had gone home. He'd been wrong. For the few days since Chloe's departure, Lydia's sorrow had been obvious, all the more painful because she tried so hard to hide it.

Adam opened the mailbox and was surprised to find it contained something in addition to the usual copy of the *Budget* newspaper. The plain white envelope was addressed to Lydia, and the postmark was Ohio. He took a breath. This must be the answer to the letter Lydia had written to her mother's close friend out there.

Was this a good thing or not? It could go either way, depending upon what the woman had to say. But at least it might distract Lydia from her grief. He certainly hadn't been able to do so.

When he'd heard her defending him to her sister, he'd thought that things between them were back to normal. But the cost of her speaking had been her relationship with Chloe, and maybe that cost was too high to bear.

Heading back up the lane toward the house, Adam said a silent prayer that the letter would contain good news. In any case, it would be God's will, but was it wrong to hope that in this, God's will was also his longing? The Lord certainly must know that he and Lydia needed something to mend the chasm between them.

A cool breeze swept across the field, bending the grasses. Clouds massed along the western ridge, a sure sign that a storm was coming. A distant rumble of thunder hastened his steps. He'd take the letter to Lydia first, but then he'd best get the animals in and see where the boys were.

Adam took the back steps in a long stride and reached the kitchen. Lydia looked up from the cookie dough she was dropping onto a baking sheet, and his heart hurt at the obvious effort she made to smile in greeting.

"Gut, you're home. I was afraid it might be another long day." There was an unspoken question in her eyes.

"I stopped by the mill, and Caleb Brand was there picking up some wood for a cabinet he's building. He asked me to work a few days for him next week. He and Will have been getting some big orders from a store in Lewisburg, and they could use extra help."

"That is gut news." Her smile warmed to something a little more natural. "Caleb liked the work you did on the clock, ain't so?"

He nodded, trying not to feel pride at the memory. "Ja, he was pleased. He said maybe I should put up some cards around town for clock repair. There's nobody else in Pleasant Valley who does that work."

"Caleb has a clever head for business. It seems like a gut idea, ja?" She looked at him with caution in her face, making him think that he'd been a bit prickly over his job hunting.

"I told him I would talk to you about it." He nodded toward the window. "There's a storm coming down the valley, so I need to get the animals in. But you'll want to see this first." He handed her the envelope. "It looks like a reply to your letter."

Lydia took it, staring down at the envelope with

her eyes wide, almost scared-looking. She sank into the nearest chair. "I never really expected to get an answer so soon, even though I'd been hoping for it every day."

"Aren't you going to open it?" He should be there when she did, in case she needed support.

Lydia nodded, ripping the envelope open. She pulled out several sheets of paper. "It's from my mother's friend. 'I was happy to hear from you, Lydia. I often wondered what happened to dear Diane's kinder, and now I know.'" She glanced up at him. "She sounds like a nice person."

"She does," he agreed, not that he would have expected anything else.

Lydia read her way rapidly down the sheet. "She tells a bit about her family, and asks about Susanna and Chloe. And then she says, 'I was troubled by the question you asked about whether your mamm wanted to leave the church. I think the best answer is in your own mamm's words, so I enclose the last letter she wrote to me.'"

Lydia fumbled with the sheets of paper, and Adam discovered that his heart seemed to be thudding in his ears. He wanted, so much, for this to be an answer that would make his Lydia happy again.

"Here it is." Lydia's voice shook a little. "It looks as if my mother wrote to her in anticipation of seeing her on their trip. Adam, it's almost like hearing her voice. She says, 'I'm so excited to see you again. Eli was afraid the trip might be too much for me with the baby only a year old, but I persuaded him we'd all enjoy it, and I really want you to meet our three precious girls. When I had that postnatal depression after little Chloe was born, I felt as if I were at the bottom of a deep, dark well. But thanks to Eli's love and patience, the help of the family here, and a good doctor, I'm back to normal. I've never been so contented in my life, and I pray my daughters will know the happiness I've found."

Lydia's voice choked on the final words, and he realized she was weeping.

He put his hand on her shoulder, his worry escalating. "I thought you would be happy to have your worries resolved."

"I am." Her lips trembled on a smile through her tears. "It is just so . . . so touching to hear her happiness and know that a few weeks later she would be gone." Lydia straightened, wiping her tears with the back of her hands. "But she and her Eli were together, ja?"

"Ja." Adam's fingers smoothed gently, patting her shoulder. He should mention Chloe, he knew. He should say something to show that he didn't bear Chloe any ill will, despite what had happened.

He cleared his throat. "You will send the letter to Chloe, ain't so?"

To his surprise, she hesitated. "I don't know."

She smoothed the pages out on the table, her touch gentle. "I don't know if I want to part with it."

He frowned, not sure he understood what she was thinking. "You could send a copy. I just meant that you'd want Chloe to see it. Maybe it would make it easier for her to accept what her mother did."

"Maybe." Lydia sounded doubtful. "I thought I understood what Chloe wanted when she came here, but I fear I was wrong. Maybe, instead of wanting to see how her mother lived, she really hoped to prove that her mother wanted to leave."

He digested that, thinking it might well be true. "Even so, she maybe has a right to know what you found out."

Lydia didn't answer, which in his experience meant she didn't agree with him. Should he press the point? It seemed they had changed places in regard to her sister.

Before he could decide, a blast of wind sent a small branch flying against the window, where it clung for a moment before blowing on. A clap of thunder, closer now, punctuated it.

Adam spun and headed for the door. "Where are the boys?"

"In the barn." Lydia came hurrying after him. "I'll get them."

The heavens opened when Lydia was halfway to the barn, and by the time she plunged through the open door, she was soaked. She should have taken time to grab a jacket on her way out, but her thoughts had been on the boys.

They stood well away from the door, their eyes wide in the flash of the lightning. Daniel held on to David, as if to prevent him from rushing out into the storm.

"Ach, you are safe and dry, and I'm all wet." She held out her arms, and they rushed to her. David buried his face in her skirt.

"I'm sorry, Mammi. We should have come in sooner. By the time we saw how dark it was getting, I thought it was too late," Daniel said, taking responsibility.

"You did exactly the right thing." She cupped Daniel's face in her hand, raising her voice to speak above the pounding of the rain on the barn roof. "We're as safe here as in the house. We'll just wait until the storm passes, ja?"

They both nodded, and David was reassured enough by her calm words to release his grip on her skirt. "Where's Daadi?" he said, worry wrinkling his forehead.

"It's all right. He's getting the animals. You stay back from the door while I check and see if he needs help."

One step out the door was enough to drench her again. She spotted Adam coming, leading the two buggy horses by the halter. They danced and skittered with every lightning flash.

The cows, far more sensible, plodded quickly toward the barn. They would come in with or without help, she expected.

"Boys, open the stall doors for the horses. I'll help Daadi."

She was so wet a little more couldn't matter. She sloshed toward Adam, not heeding the jerk of his head telling her to stay put.

"You didn't need to—" he began.

"I was already soaked." She grasped Gray's halter, letting Adam deal with the more fractious Callie. "Komm, foolish beasts. The cows will be there before you."

Gray, finally getting the message, began to trot, and Callie followed suit. Clinging on to the halter, Lydia let the horse tow her along, the wind whipping Gray's mane in her face. The rain pelted down so hard she could barely see a yard in front of her, and the lightning was so close there was barely a discernible pause between the flash and the peal of thunder. She glanced at Adam, running beside the other horse.

He grinned, his face suddenly boyish despite his beard. And her heart seemed to turn over the way it used to when she saw him coming.

"You look wetter than the animals, Lydia Beachy," he said, chuckling a little.

"Not as wet as you," she responded, relieved to find something to relax and laugh about.

A loud clap of thunder seemed to rattle the

barn roof, chasing them the rest of the way inside. Through the open doors she could see the rain blowing in sideways sheets.

The boys stood, each one by a stall door, holding it open. Gray bolted for her stall. Lydia pulled her hand free of the halter, and David slammed the stall door and latched it.

"Gut work, Mammi," he said, making her laugh.

"Wet work," she said. Adam and Daniel had the other mare in the stall already. The cows, not needing to be told, lined up by the stanchions as if ready to be milked.

"Not yet," Adam said, patting the nearest flank. "Daniel, scoot up and toss down some hay to keep them busy."

"Ja, Daadi." Daniel scrambled up the ladder, and Lydia bit her lip to keep from telling him to be careful. His expression told her he was happy to be helping, and she shouldn't spoil it.

Working together, the four of them got the animals settled. *This is how it should be,* she thought. *This is right, no matter what Chloe might think about how backward we are.*

The thought brought its own pain. She'd placed so much hope on Chloe's visit to the farm, she knew. Too much, maybe. Chloe certainly had different expectations than she had.

Lydia glanced at Adam, his hand on David's shoulder, explaining something to him about the feed. Distracting him, most likely, from the storm that raged outside.

She'd been more than surprised when Adam, of all people, had suggested that Chloe should read her mother's letter. She had expected that Adam would be only too pleased to see the last of her Englisch sister. He was thinking of her, Lydia knew, trying to mend what was broken.

But she didn't think it could be mended. It was too late for her and Chloe. One day she'd be able to tell Susanna, at least.

Until then, she had her mother's words to comfort her, and the memories others had shared.

The storm really was right on top of them now, the thunder and lightning almost continuous. She went to stand next to Adam and the boys, who were looking out the open door. He glanced at her and then put his arm around her waist. They held the boys close as the wind and rain battered the barn like an animal trying to get in.

Another loud clap rattled the barn and had David burying his face in her skirt again. "Mammi . . ." His voice caught on a sob.

"It's all right." She rubbed his back, trying to comfort him. "The storm will soon move on down the valley. We'll see the sun again before it sets, I guess."

Continuous flashes of lightning flared as she looked out the door toward the orchard. The worst of the storm seemed to be right over them now, and the trees bent before the wind.

There was a crack, a sizzle in the air, and a spark flared up from the big tree in the middle of the orchard. Her mother's tree. It seemed to shudder, like a person struck a terrible blow. Lydia covered her mouth to hold back a cry as the tree fell, shattered, to the ground.

Chapter Twenty-one

Much later, Lydia stood in the orchard with Adam, her throat so tight she couldn't speak. She had refused to come out and look at the tree until after the boys were in bed, not wanting them to see how upset she was.

They'd seemed to understand, though. They'd scurried quietly through their bedtime routine, and their hugs had been extra tight.

"I'm sorry," Adam said at last, his gesture indicating the scattered branches. The trunk was split and charred all the way to the ground, and the fresh green leaves had already begun to wither.

"The tree was old." She fought to get the words out. "You and Daadi warned me. But I didn't expect this ending." The tears spilled over, despite her best efforts, and her breath caught on a sob.

"Ach, Lydia, I would do anything not to see

you cry." Adam put his arms around her, his own voice ravaged by hurt.

She pressed her face against his chest. The shirt he'd put on after their dunking in the storm smelled of spring and sunshine.

"I can't help weeping." She tried to wipe away the tears, but they just kept coming. "I have lost my sister and the thing that reminded me most of my mother. It hurts."

Adam's arms went painfully taut. "It is my fault."

She drew back, surprise chasing the tears away. "What are you talking about? You could not stop the storm or keep Chloe from leaving."

"Not the storm. But Chloe—that is my fault." His face was so tense that the skin seemed drawn tightly against the bones, and his mouth trembled. Adam, who was always so strong.

"Adam, don't. Don't look that way. Ja, you might have been a little more friendly to Chloe, but that isn't why she left."

"I don't have a job. Chloe was right. I promised to take care of you and the boys, and I've failed."

A spasm of fear went through her at the pain and grief in his face. She'd never seen him look that way. She had to fix this, or it would destroy them.

She thought of all the times she'd said something about how strong he was and how she knew he'd take care of them. Her whole body shuddered. Had she been destroying him by her careless words?

"Adam, listen to me." She grasped his arm, as unyielding as concrete under her fingers. "I meant what I said to Chloe. Marriage isn't about one person taking care of the other. It's about each one taking care of them both."

His expression didn't change. It seemed he didn't even hear her, and her panic grew.

"My mamm says marriage is like two horses in harness, pulling together, going the same way."

That seemed to get through to him. "Your daad said something like that to me once, too. But—"

"I know sometimes I say that I know you'll take care of us." The words seemed bitter on her tongue now that she knew what harm they could do. "But that doesn't have anything to do with a job. I mean that you'll always love us and be here for us." The doubt in his face made her frantic, and she shook his arm, as if that would make him understand her. "I'm glad you're not traveling away to work every day. We would rather have you here."

"Do you think I wouldn't rather be here?" His mouth twisted with hurt. "But we need the money."

"Not that much. Adam, think. Between the jobs you pick up right here in Pleasant Valley and the orchard, we can do all right. We don't need that much to live plain, ja?"

She tried to smile, and it seemed to her that his expression was questioning now, rather than grief-stricken. "My Lydia." He took her hands in his. "You should have everything you want."

She knew the answer to that one. "All I want is you and the kinder. That's enough for me."

He studied her face, as if he had to make sure she really meant it. Then, apparently satisfied, he drew her into his arms.

They stood there, holding each other, and Lydia thought she could feel the gap between them narrowing and narrowing until it disappeared. They were going to be all right.

Adam slipped quietly from the bed before the first light edged over the eastern horizon. He gathered his clothes and then stood for a moment, looking down at Lydia.

Sleep had smoothed away the tiny worry lines that formed when she thought of her sister. They had been close last night—closer than he thought they had ever been—but there was still a shadow between them.

Chloe. He would never feel right about Chloe unless he at least made an effort to mend things between Lydia and her sister. He might not succeed, but he had to try.

He tiptoed out of the room, easing the door closed so that it didn't make a sound, and went downstairs barefoot, carrying his clothes and shoes. He had lain awake for much of the night, watching Lydia sleeping beside him, and trying to figure out how to accomplish the impossible.

There was only one answer that he could see. He would have to go to Philadelphia and try to get Chloe back for Lydia.

The very thought of it made him feel cold inside. He'd never been farther from home than Harrisburg, and that only once. He'd felt so lost there, and finding his brother in such a terrible condition had only made it worse. And now he proposed to make his way clear across the state to a city that would make Harrisburg look like a small town. His stomach roiled.

He would feel better when he'd eaten something, he told himself. Dressing quickly, he grabbed some bread, cheese, and milk for a hurried meal while he tried to compose a note to leave for Lydia.

He soon realized it was impossible to put what he was feeling into words, so he kept it brief, saying he'd try to see Chloe and hoped to be back tonight. No need to remind her of the milking—she'd deal with it. Taking the letter Lydia had received and Seth's cell phone number, he went out into the thin light of early dawn.

Wet grass brushed against his pant legs as he walked to the phone shanty. He'd tried to figure out another way of doing this, but he couldn't. He didn't have enough time to set up a trip with an Englisch driver, but Seth would surely take him to Mifflinburg or Lewisburg, where he could, he thought, get a bus to Philadelphia.

Seth picked up on the third ring, his voice blurred with sleep. "What's wrong? My mother?"

"No, no, nothing like that," Adam answered quickly. He should have realized that Seth would assume the call meant an emergency.

"Adam?" Seth's voice sharpened.

"Ja. I am sorry to wake you." He wasn't eager to ask Seth for a favor, but he would, for Lydia's sake. "I need a ride to someplace where I can get a bus to Philadelphia. Will you drive me?" Seth would understand that he couldn't take a buggy that far.

"You're going to see Chloe? Why?" Rustling noises seemed to say that Seth was getting out of bed.

Adam hesitated, but there was no point in kidding himself. Seth already knew too much about their family business.

"I have something that might change Chloe's mind. Lydia is so sad and upset . . ." He let that trail off, his voice thickening.

"I'll be there in half an hour," Seth said, and clicked off.

Adam stared at the receiver for a moment before hanging up. It was done, and he wouldn't turn back now. He patted the cash he'd stowed next to his skin and set off down the lane. He didn't want Seth driving up to the house and waking anyone.

The air was crisp and fresh after last night's storm. Night creatures were beginning to go to ground as the birds started to chatter, and the moon was a pale silver disc in the lightening sky. He reached the end of the lane and settled himself against the fence post to wait.

It had to be less than half an hour later when Seth's car pulled up. Adam slid into the passenger seat.

"Denke, Seth. I think Lewisburg maybe would be best for getting a bus, ja?"

"No need for that," Seth said. He pulled out, heading back down the road toward town. "I'll take you to Philadelphia."

Adam couldn't help tensing. The truth was that he didn't want to be beholden to Seth. "I don't want to take up your whole day. I'll go by bus."

"That really would take all day," Seth said, smiling slightly. "Look, I'm involved in this already, so you might as well let me take you this next step. Besides, I know how to find Chloe, whether she's at work or at home."

There was much in what Seth said, but still . . . Adam knew why he was reluctant to accept Seth's help, and it didn't reflect very well on him, he suspected.

Seth slowed as they entered the outskirts of Pleasant Valley. The village still seemed to sleep, but there was a light in the kitchen window of the bakery, which must mean Paula Schatz was already at work.

"I'm not under the bann, you know," Seth said, sounding irritated.

"I know." If Adam was going to make Chloe feel accepted, he could make a start with Seth. "If you are willing to take me, I'm grateful."

The tension in the car seemed to ease. "Good." Seth moved his hands on the steering wheel and took the turn that would lead them to the interstate highway. "I saw you had some damage from yesterday's storm."

"Ja. Just the one big tree down. Could have been worse, I guess." Still, his heart ached at the thought of Lydia's loss.

All the more reason why he had to make things right with Chloe.

Seth took interstates all the way to the city, making Adam's stomach churn each time a truck roared past them. Still, Seth said it was faster that way. He made one stop for gas and coffee, and then they were on their way again.

It was late morning when they reached the city. Seth wove his way expertly through the congested streets, ignoring the din that seemed to pound on Adam's skull.

After what seemed an endless onslaught of cars, trucks, people, and noise, Seth turned into a quieter area, and in a few minutes he pulled into the parking lot behind an imposing building.

"This is where Chloe works?" he asked. "Maybe she won't like being interrupted."

Seth drew into a parking space and turned off the ignition. "Let's face it, she won't be exactly happy to see either of us anywhere. But trust me, this is better than taking on the grandmother. You'd be lucky to get a word out before she'd be calling the police."

Adam got out, frowning at Seth's comment. "The woman doesn't like the Amish, I know. But surely she wants her granddaughter to hear the truth."

"I doubt it." Seth's face was bleak for a moment, and Adam wasn't sure what he was thinking. "As far as I can tell, she blames the Amish for taking her daughter away, maybe even for Diane's death. She'd do anything in her power to keep Chloe and Lydia apart." Seth jerked a nod in the direction of the brick building. "Let's go."

They joined several people heading up the sidewalk. Adam caught more than a few curious glances and saw people nudging each other at the sight of him. In Pleasant Valley, being Plain didn't cause comment. Here, people looked at him as if he were something on display in the museum.

It didn't matter. If they wanted to gawk, let them. He was here for Lydia and Chloe, no one else.

• • •

Chloe realized she'd been reading the same page of a report on the latest fund-raising efforts of the museum for at least fifteen minutes. It might as well be written in Greek for all the information she was retaining.

She shoved it aside impatiently and rubbed the tension at the back of her neck. That tight throb, which had begun over the weekend, was threatening to become permanent.

Her grandmother, of course, had been delighted to see Chloe come back to Philadelphia disenchanted with her experience among the Amish. Her "I told you so" refrain had become harder and harder to take. Chloe had found herself biting back a defense of Lydia and her family a dozen times, at least.

Chloe knew perfectly well what was at the bottom of that instinct. She'd had plenty of time to think on the long trip back to Philadelphia, and she'd begun to realize she'd been unfair. She'd been thrown off-balance by reading Diane's journal, and she'd reacted by letting the prejudices she'd grown up with come to the fore. If Lydia hadn't shown her the journal entry, what might her reaction have been to her visit?

The knot in her neck was tight enough to hold back a bulldozer. Lydia had been right to show her, of course, but that had colored all her responses. She'd berated Adam, but she feared her anger had really been toward her father, Eli Weaver. If . . .

Enough. She leaned back in her chair, staring at the ceiling for inspiration. What was she going to do now? That was the important question. Cut Lydia out of her life the way her grandmother had cut Diane out, because she didn't approve of the way she lived?

A tap on the door interrupted that futile line of questioning, and the door opened before she could respond. Seth. And Adam. For an instant she was speechless.

She stood slowly, fingers pressed on the desktop. Maybe she wasn't entirely surprised to see Seth again. Somehow she'd had the feeling that he wouldn't disappear from her life so easily.

But Adam—of all the people who might have come looking for her, Adam Beachy was the last she'd expect. Lydia had implied that he never traveled far away from Pleasant Valley. For him to come all the way to Philadelphia to see her . . . well, it had to be a measure of his love for Lydia, and she was impressed whether she wanted to be or not. Her small, cluttered office felt crowded with the two large men in it.

She found her voice. "What are you doing here?"

"Adam has something he wants to say to you." Seth nudged Adam.

Adam swept off his straw hat and stood,

turning it in big, work-roughened hands. "Lydia is hurting at the way you left," he said. "If I was the cause of trouble between you, I have come to tell you I'm sorry."

Chloe hadn't expected it, and she wasn't ready for an apology. She shook her head. "I don't—" She stopped. "I don't think it was your fault. It just wasn't working out. I just . . . I couldn't accept . . ."

She wasn't usually this inarticulate. What was wrong with her? She took a deep breath, preparing to start again, but Adam beat her to it.

"I know. You feel as if your mother was led into an unhappy life by Eli. Or maybe by the Amish. You didn't like seeing your sister living that same life."

That was the most Adam had ever said to her. She'd had him pegged as stern, unforgiving, and maybe not too bright, but he'd certainly just cut to the heart of her difficulty.

"Can you blame me?" She met his gaze, surprised to see such understanding there. "When I read what our mother had written, I could see that she was trapped in a life she didn't want. And now Lydia is doing the same."

"Lydia isn't trapped," Seth said, looking as if he couldn't be silent any longer. "Lydia chose her life and her husband. She's happy with what she has."

"I know she is." Little though she wanted to

admit it, Chloe knew his words were true. "But if our mother had lived long enough to leave, Lydia would have a completely different life."

Adam winced, and she realized she'd been speaking of a Lydia who would never have loved him.

"This came yesterday for Lydia." Adam held an envelope out to her, his arm stiff. "It's the answer from your mother's friend out in Ohio. I thought Lydia should send it to you, but she feared it was too late."

Chloe found she was staring at the envelope as if it were a snake. She wasn't sure she wanted to know anything else about her mother. Everything she learned seemed to bring someone grief.

"Adam came clear from Pleasant Valley to bring it to you," Seth said, leaning toward her as if willing her to listen to him. "Please don't back away from the truth now. Read it."

She took the envelope, turning away from them to open it.

Not one letter, she found. Two. Quickly she scanned the answer Lydia had received from Diane's friend. Then, her throat tight, she unfolded the letter Diane had written.

Halfway down the page, and the print was swimming in front of her tear-filled eyes. Her mother had written this, and a month later she'd been gone. She hadn't known, of course, how short a time she had. Still, she'd been happy.

Content. The letter was that of a mature woman who'd gone through a great deal and emerged stronger and happier at the end.

Chloe folded the letter gently and slipped it back into the envelope. She'd wanted to know if her mother found what she'd been looking for. Now, at last, she had the answer.

Lydia paced across the living room and back again, trying not to look out the windows. It was full dark now, and Adam was still not back. What had possessed him to go off that way? What if something had happened to him in the city? He wasn't used to a place like that—how would he even find Chloe?

She glanced at the clock he'd made for her, ticking steadily, unperturbed by her worries. She ought to get some sleep. She'd have to be up early.

Sound reasoning, but she knew perfectly well she wouldn't go to sleep in that bed alone, wondering where Adam was. If she was going to be awake anyway, she may as well stay down here.

Lydia forced herself to sit down in the rocker. She picked up a pair of David's pants from the mending basket, trying to decide if the rip in the knee could be fixed.

She smoothed the fabric in her hands, picturing him running full-tilt during recess and rending the fabric. The grass stain around the tear seemed to confirm that guess. She reached for the thread and stopped abruptly, mending forgotten.

That was a car turning in the lane, wasn't it? Headlights reflected from the windows as she hurried to look. A car—no, two cars, pulling up to the back door.

She ran for the door, heart thumping painfully against her ribs. If something had happened to Adam—

She bolted out onto the porch in time to see Adam climb out of Seth's car, giving Seth a smile and a wave. But that wasn't all. Chloe got out of the second car, stretching a little as if she was tired from the drive.

Lydia went to meet them, her thoughts spinning out of control. What on earth . . . ?

"You don't mind that I came back, do you, Lydia?" Chloe looked a little uncertain, and she glanced at Adam, of all people, as if for support.

"Chloe read the letter," Adam said. "She wants to try again."

Lydia opened her arms to her sister, her throat choked with tears. "I'm so glad," she murmured. "So glad you came back."

Her heart was full as she held her little sister in her arms. She looked at Adam over Chloe's shoulder. "You did this, ja?"

He shrugged, smiling. "Let's go inside. Chloe is maybe tired and hungry."

"Ja, for sure."

Chloe shook her head. "Just tired. But very glad

to be here. Thanks to Adam." She glanced at him, smiled, and walked into the house.

Lydia reached out to touch Adam's sleeve, needing to be sure he was really there. "I was so worried about you. I couldn't believe you would go all the way to Philadelphia for Chloe."

"For you," Adam said softly. He drew her against him. "I know you said you had all that you wanted, but I know, too, that you need your sister." He dropped a kiss on her temple. "Amish, Englisch, Chloe is still family. Things had to be made right between you. That was my job."

Lydia looked up at him, her heart full. Thanks to Adam, her hope had been fulfilled. "I love you, Adam Beachy."

"I love you, Lydia Beachy." He snuggled her close against him. "Komm. Let's go in and make your sister comfortable."

They walked into their home. Once, it had been filled with her parents' love, Lydia thought. Now it was filled with hers and Adam's.

Epilogue

The apple trees were full of small green apples, promising a good harvest. Lydia walked arm-in-arm with her sister back toward the yard. Another picnic was in full swing, but this time there would be no quarrel to mar the pleasure.

"I love coming here," Chloe said. "It's so peace-ful."

The boys came running to her across the grass. "Aunt Chloe, schnell. Play catch with us," Daniel said, tugging at her hand.

"Ja, let's play," David said, clutching the other hand and attempting to pull her.

Chloe grabbed them both for a quick hug. "All right, in a minute. But you go find the foam ball and bat I brought, so your little cousins can play, too."

"I'll get it." Daniel raced off, with David following as always.

"What were you saying about peaceful?" Lydia asked, teasing.

"I love being an aunt," Chloe said, her eyes lit with affection as she watched the boys. "I always wanted a big family, and now I have it." She clasped Lydia's hand. "Thank you for finding me."

Lydia squeezed her fingers. "Thank you for coming back. It has only been a month since we met, but it feels like a lifetime."

She hesitated, knowing she should ask but not wanting to make Chloe unhappy. "Are things any better with your grandmother?"

Chloe shrugged. "Not really. She's not com-plaining as much about my visits here, though, so that's an improvement."

"I'm sorry." Lydia truly was. After all, the

woman was her grandmother, too, and she regretted that she'd never get to know her.

"I know. I wish she could unbend a little, but I don't think she will. She doesn't seem to care that she has two other granddaughters."

Lydia suspected she'd never understand what drove the woman. "Speaking of Susanna, did I mention that I saw her again last week? I took in another clock for her shop."

Susanna had succeeded in selling the first clock for what seemed an astonishing amount of money. Adam's business with clocks seemed to grow every day.

"How is she? Any news about her mother?" Chloe asked the obvious question. It wasn't that she didn't care about Susanna's adoptive mother. Of course she did, for Susanna's sake, at least.

"There seems to be nothing new. At least I'm getting to know Susanna through the clocks. I pray that will make it easier for her to accept us when the time comes to tell her."

Chloe nodded, but her gaze seemed directed toward something of interest in the backyard. Lydia smiled. Chloe was watching Seth, who was playing horseshoes with her brothers.

"You've been seeing a bit of Seth, ja?" she asked.

"Once in a while, when he's in the city." Her tone was carefully neutral.

"He likes you." Lydia pointed out the obvious. "Maybe . . ."

"Don't start matchmaking," Chloe said quickly.

"Why not? I just want to see you happy. And Seth is a fine man."

"He is." Chloe's expression softened. "But I think he's still struggling to figure out where he belongs. And I'm not so sure of that myself."

"I see." Lydia tried to repress a chuckle. "Maybe," she said, "you could both figure that out together, ain't so?"

Color came up in Chloe's cheeks. "Don't matchmake," she said again, and then smiled at the sight of a flock of small children running toward her, with Daniel and David in the lead carrying the ball and bat.

"It looks as if I'm wanted," she said. "We'll talk again later."

Lydia was standing and watching the ensuing game when Adam came up behind her. She was not at all surprised that Seth had found some reason to stop playing horseshoes and join Chloe in playing with the children.

Adam slid his arm around her unobtrusively. "Did you tell her?" he whispered in her ear.

"Not yet." She smiled, capturing his hand with hers and moving it to her abdomen, which was no longer as flat as it once was. "I want to hug the information to ourselves for just a little bit longer."

"Your maam will guess, if she hasn't already," Adam said.

"I'm sure. She said something to me just this afternoon about how happy I'm looking. I wouldn't be a bit surprised if she went home and started putting together the pieces for a baby quilt."

"It will be gut to have another little one." Adam rested his cheek against her hair, an unusual gesture for him when there were people around. "Maybe, this time, I'll get to make a dollhouse."

"Maybe," she said, sure he knew that a baby girl was her secret hope. "Boy or girl, a new baby will bring us so much happiness."

He nodded, and she could feel the movement, just as she could feel the beating of his heart and hear the sound of his breath. She had been so blessed.

Only one small flaw remained in her life. Susanna. But one day they'd be able to tell her. Until then, Lydia would cling to the hope that they would be a complete family again.

RECIPES
Apple Walnut Cake

This recipe has been an autumn favorite of my family's for as long as I can remember. It's a good keeper, as it stays moist for days.

4 cups pared, chopped apples
2 cups sugar
2 eggs
½ cup vegetable oil
2 teaspoons vanilla
2 cups flour
2 teaspoons baking soda
2 teaspoons cinnamon
1 teaspoon salt
1 cup chopped walnuts

Preheat oven to 350°F.

Combine the apples and sugar in a bowl and set aside. Beat the eggs in the oil and vanilla in a large bowl. In a third bowl, sift together the flour, baking soda, cinnamon, and salt. Stir the flour mixture and the apple mixture alternately into the oil and vanilla. Add the walnuts and stir. Pour the batter into a 13 x 9-inch pan sprayed with cooking spray.

Bake for one hour. Good served warm with whipped cream or ice cream.

Apple Dumplings

A big hit at the county fair!

6 baking apples
⅔ cup milk
1 large egg
2½ cups sifted flour
2½ teaspoons baking powder
dash of salt
½ cup sugar mixed with 1 tablespoon cinnamon
6 teaspoons butter

Preheat oven to 425°F.

Peel, core, and cut the apples into quarters.

Mix the milk and egg together in a bowl. Gradually stir in the flour, baking powder, and salt. Stir until the mixture forms a soft dough. Turn out onto a floured board and knead lightly a few times. Roll out the dough with a floured rolling pin into a 24 x 16-inch oblong and cut it into six 8-inch squares. Divide the apple pieces among the squares. Sprinkle the apples with the cinnamon-sugar mixture, reserving about a tablespoon for later, and dot each with a teaspoon of butter. Bring the corners of the dough up to enclose the apples and pinch to seal. Place the dumplings in a large baking pan, not touching.

Bake at 425° for 10 minutes, then lower the heat to 350° and continue baking for another 40 minutes. Remove from the oven and sprinkle the tops with the rest of the cinnamon-sugar mixture. Serve warm with cream, whipped cream, or ice cream.

Homemade Chunky Applesauce

We enjoy applesauce made fresh and served warm, so there's usually a bag or basket of McIntosh apples on my countertop year-round.

8 tart apples, such as McIntosh
water
dash of salt
1 cup sugar
1 tablespoon cinnamon

Peel and core the apples. Cut into eighths. Place in a pan and add water just to cover. Add salt. Bring to a boil, cover, and turn down to low to simmer for about 10 minutes. Remove the lid, stir, and add the sugar. Continue to cook slowly, stirring, until the apples begin to fall apart into sauce but some pieces are still whole. Remove from heat and add cinnamon. Taste and adjust the sugar and cinnamon as needed. Serve warm or chill in the refrigerator.

Dear Reader,

Lydia's Hope represents a new challenge for me, as it's the first time I've attempted a "series within a series," as well as the first time I've written an Amish book from the viewpoints of four important characters. I know that challenges help us grow, and I sincerely hope this story has urged me forward as a writer.

Lydia's story is linked very closely with the next book, *Susanna's Dream*, which will follow the continuing tale of the three lost sisters and their efforts to create a bond after so many years apart. I hope you'll be eager to find out what the future holds for all three women.

I believe the bond between sisters is a very special one. No one else knows you as well as your sister, and no one else understands what it was like growing up in your family. A sister is a precious gift, and I've been blessed with a dear sister as well as with four delightful sisters-in-law who are as close as sisters. Writing about sisters gave me an opportunity to express the appreciation I feel every day for their place in my life.

I would love to hear your thoughts on my book. If you'd care to write to me, I'd be happy to reply with a signed bookmark or bookplate and my brochure of Pennsylvania Dutch recipes. You can find me on the Web at www.martaperry.com and on Facebook at facebook.com/MartaPerryBooks, e-mail me at marta@martaperry.com, or write to me in care of Berkley Publicity Department, Penguin Group (USA) Inc., 375 Hudson Street, New York, NY 10014.

Blessings,
Marta Perry

Center Point Large Print
600 Brooks Road / PO Box 1
Thorndike ME 04986-0001 USA

(207) 568-3717

US & Canada:
1 800 929-9108
www.centerpointlargeprint.com